Having been treated for breast cancer aged forty, Ann attended her local college to study for A-levels in order to occupy her mind.

On receiving her exam results, her tutor arranged an appointment for her at the nearest university and she went on to study for a BA (Hons) in History with experience of writing, graduating at the age of forty-nine.

During research for her degree, Ann stumbled across a newspaper article from the 19th century which is the germ of her story. She survived a serious stroke aged sixty-two and was determined to write the story that had been evolving in her mind.

This book is dedicated to my husband and family who have been so patient with me while I was flitting back and forth from the 21st to the 19th century.

Ann Lynn Gillott

IRISH FEVER

AUSTIN MACAULEY PUBLISHERS™

LONDON • CAMBRIDGE • NEW YORK • SHARJAH

ISBN 9781528934923 (Paperback)
ISBN 9781528934930 (Hardback)
ISBN 9781528968072 (ePub e-book)

www.austinmacauley.com

First Published (2020)
Austin Macauley Publishers Ltd
25 Canada Square
Canary Wharf
London
E14 5LQ

My thanks to Claire Hamill, the lyrics of *Underneath My Irish Blanket* are so perfect for my book.

Preface

In the mid-19th century, the Irish were escaping famine and poor living conditions in their own country and migrating.

America and Australia were favourite destinations, but many also came over to Britain, taking advantage of the sixpenny concessionary boat fare sponsored by the government. They would have chiefly landed in Liverpool where many stayed. Some moved on to find work in 'Cottonopolis' – in the cotton mills of Manchester and the surrounding towns.

As with all the industrial towns in Britain, living conditions in Manchester were dirty and overcrowded, with row upon row of jerry-built houses built back to back in mazes of streets. Every yard, every gap between buildings was built into closes of houses which shared a communal privy (an outdoor toilet without plumbing which 'night-soil' men emptied at night). Very often, the communal water pump was situated next to the privy, inviting the inevitable water-borne diseases of typhoid, dysentery and even cholera.

The centre of Manchester has been described as 'an open sewer, underneath a permanent pall of smoke'. The picture was similar in the neighbouring town of Stockport.

Social relationships between the English Protestants and Irish Catholics were inflamed by reports in the local press and even in London newspapers naming the areas in Manchester particularly affected by the diseases and highlighting the high numbers of immigrants of Irish nationality living there (80,000 in the 1851 census).

The letters and articles in the Press even went so far as to call the prevalent diseases 'Irish Fever'.

It is against this background that Oonagh Kennedy, a young Irish girl is living in Stockport with her partner Seamus O'Neil.

Restrictions against 'Dissenters' (Christian people not of the official Anglican faith) had been relaxed, although Roman Catholic priests were not yet allowed to appear in public in their clerical robes.

The Establishment were alarmed by the revolutions in Europe and were concerned that any public gathering could develop into riot leading to revolution. The militia were therefore on 'standby' ready for any such disturbance (as with the massacre dubbed Peterloo, when the cavalry charged a peaceful demonstration of up to 80,000 people, including families, taking part in a peaceful demonstration demanding Parliamentary reform at St Peter's Fields, Manchester).

The characters and most of the action in this story are fictional but are based on fact.

Chapter One
Lancashire Hotpot

Oonagh could hear the horse's hooves on the cobbles outside and she made for the front parlour window squeezing between the six iron beds, their straw-filled mattresses covered in grey and black ticking, and a blanket on each bed that Oonagh was sure used to be cream at some time in the past. She made a peephole in the window glass with the sleeve of her dress. The coalman was lifting the flap of the coal chute that opened into Mrs Watson's cellar; he slammed it against the brick wall. The Watsons lived in the flat above Mrs Watson's gown shop where ladies came in their carriages to be measured for their fine silk and lace gowns.

The house where Oonagh and the others lived was crammed into the yard at the side of the shop along with four more small houses, built right up to the side-wall of the shop, no windows, no doors at the rear. Oonagh quietly slipped through the front door of her house.

The coal wagon was painted red with green lettering across the side 'Cephas Linney, High Class Coal Merchant, Heaton Mersey'. Mr Linney was at the back of his wagon, he turned his broad back to a sack of coal and with arms stretched above his head, he grasped two corners of the top of the sack and tilted the hundredweight of coal in the sack against the leather waistcoat on his back.

Moving to the cellar chute, he bent forward and tipped the coal over his head and down the chute. A cloud of coal dust rose around his head and a couple of shiny black coals fell onto the cobbles. Mr Linney turned to grab another sack of coal and Oonagh quickly darted forward. She snatched the stray coals from the road, and hid them in her apron, then moved stealthily to the front of the wagon and feigned an interest in the horse, stroking its muzzle and murmuring, "I've a friend for you back home, my pa's horse Barney would love you."

The cellar flap banged shut and Mr Linney took off his cap, wiping the perspiration from his face with the lining. Black dust lined the furrows of his brow and his eyes shone white from his blackened face. He folded the hessian sacks, threw them onto the back of the wagon and climbed up onto the wooden bench that was his driving seat. "Gi'up, Dolly," and he shook the reins. Dolly ambled forward, up the steep cobbled road that was signed 'Underbank' high on the wall above the Watsons' shop. Every so often, the wagon wobbled on the cobbles and a couple more coals tumbled out of the bags at the rear.

Oonagh followed closely behind, grabbing the coals and stowing them away in her grey fustian apron, folding the cloth over them, until she could carry no more.

As she slipped back into the house, her cousin, Michael Mahon, was cutting a chunk of bread from the loaf on the table and spreading it with dripping from a brown dish.

"There's no tea in the pot, Oonagh?" he said.

"No, Michael, there was no coal for the range," replied Oonagh. "But there will be soon," and Oonagh tipped her trophy out of her apron onto the hearth. "You had better run now, Michael, or you will lose your job at the mill and you'll be sweeping the workhouse floors instead."

Michael swigged the last dregs of ale, left from the night before, from the jug on the table, kissed his cousin and ran out of the door.

Oonagh grabbed the tin bucket and went out of the door to the top of the yard. She filled the bucket with water from the pump next to the privy that the five houses in Watsons' yard shared, and struggled back indoors. She tipped some water into the enamel basin in the sink and washed her hands and face with the block of hard green soap, rubbing her cheeks until they were pink, on the linen towel her ma had stuffed into her trunk at the last minute that morning when O'Neil the carter had given her a ride to meet the ship that brought her to England. Her pa had pressed the sixpence fare into her hand. He didn't kiss her, just ruffled her flaxen hair with his calloused hand, as he had always done.

Oonagh stroked her belly then wiped a tear from her eyes. It was hard to believe that her brother, Flynn, just four years old, would be an uncle soon.

Someone was banging on the front door. Oonagh hurried to answer it, there was a tall man standing on the step with a tangle of greasy, dark, curly hair.

"Order of the Guardians, the Irish Fever is back, you have to paint all your inside walls with limewash, missus," and he thrust a bucket full of white liquid towards her.

"Here, they even give you a brush. There have been ten in a house up your yard that had to go into the Union Infirmary. And while you're at it, get someone to clean the yard back there, it's in a filthy state."

"There's five houses that use that privy, not just us," retorted Oonagh and she pressed her right hand on her belly as she felt the little one stretching its feet against her ribs, "I cannot do it myself." "All of them are in the Workhouse Infirmary, including the kids," he said and glanced at her belly.

Oonagh slammed the brush and the bucket of lime wash down. "You have to wait until the men come from work."

"How many live in this house?" asked the man from the Guardians.

"There are ten of us," said Oonagh. "And we pay good money to the landlord, Mr Watson, ten shillings every week."

"You're lucky, there's fifty in No. 14 Wesley Street, all Irish," smirked the man with the dirty hair, "everyone is in the Infirmary from No. 16 next door to them," and the man returned to the hand cart in front of Watsons' shop. Oonagh grabbed her black shawl and dragged it around her head and shoulders.

Then with her basket over her arm, she marched to the steep stone steps that led to the marketplace. Halfway up, she stopped, set down the basket and with both hands, pressed her fingers into the small of her back. Picking up her basket, she struggled on up into the marketplace. The weather was becoming warmer as the stallholders were setting up for the Friday market, the busiest day of the week. The greengrocer was carefully piling the carrots into a neat stack, he was engrossed with arranging the carrots – big carrots at the bottom and the little ones up on the top.

But it was not the vegetables on the stall that Oonagh was interested in. She looked under the trestle table for any strays. Yes, there was a carrot and a turnip and a battered onion lying on the street. She dropped her shawl over them carelessly and as she stooped to pick it up, she scooped up the vegetables and pushed them into her basket, concealed in the shawl. Red-faced, she headed for the butcher's shop at the head of the market, past the Protestant Church and the public house, where men were standing around outside with tankards of ale in their hands.

Some lads whistled as she hurried by, and Oonagh's cheeks flamed.

Inside Mr Delaney's shop, there was quite a crowd and Oonagh hung back near the door, her head down, shuffling her boots about in the sawdust, making little mounds then scattering them again. Mr Delaney caught her eye and winked. Oonagh blushed. "Come for some scraps, have you?" said Mr Delaney. The other customers turned and Oonagh smiled at the butcher. Reaching under the counter he produced some bones with meat still clinging to them. He wrapped them in newspaper.

"And I'll give you a cow heel for good measure," he said, "you need some nourishment with a little one on the way." The other customers nodded in agreement.

"Ee, I remember when I was having our Stanley," said an old lady with a blue knitted beret on top of her sparse white hair, "I was mad on Mr Delaney's black puddings, just plain boiled with mustard on, and it can't have done our Stan any harm, he was a right whopper, 9lb 12oz, but I couldn't face a black pudding now." "A little of what you fancy, girl," said a woman with a brown wrap around pinny, who had slipped away from her vegetable stall before the butcher was too busy.

"Thank you, sir," Oonagh smiled as she put the parcel on top of her shawl in the basket and hurried out of the door. She walked on past the stalls selling knitted socks, cotton lengths in bright colours and hanks of wool in every shade, until she reached the big old hotel painted black and white. Carriages were collecting the gentlefolk who had dined there that day.

Oonagh hurried on, now and then stumbling on the cobbles as the soles of her boots peeled back at the toe. Would they have enough money for the cobbler this week? What would she wear while they were mended? Oh to be running barefoot in the green fields back home.

As soon as she was safely back in the house, she tipped the meat scraps onto the table with the vegetables and smoothed the newspaper out, ready to be twisted into kindling for the fire. The date at the top was 15 June 1852.

The headline read 'Irish Fever Back' and then gave details of streets in Stockport which were affected by the fever. Oonagh blessed Father Murphy who had taught her to read back home.

The paper went on to declare that "Districts of Manchester and district occupied by the lower orders, chiefly Irish (of which there are 80,000 in the town) have been in an unsettled state and the Roman Catholic Bishop had appealed to his flocks to preserve the peace". Then the newspaper concluded by declaring that the Roman Catholics should not trifle with the law in a Protestant country.

Frowning, Oonagh rolled the paper tightly into a baton and twisted it around her hand. Picking up the poker she jabbed it into the dead coals in the range's firebox and riddled it hard.

"Well, I don't want to be here in your dirty town," she muttered between clenched teeth. "I want to be back in Ireland's beautiful green fields before that stinking potato blight arrived."

The ash fell down between the bars into the ash-pan leaving cinders in the firebox. Oonagh carried outside the ash-tray and emptied the soft pinky ash into the ash pit in the yard. Then, back in the kitchen, she pushed the empty ash-pan under the firebox. The newspaper twist she placed on top of the cinders with a few pieces of kindling from the coal bucket on the hearth. She balanced on top a couple of pieces of Mr Linney's coal, and striking a match from the box on the mantle shelf, she lit the paper. The kindling caught hold and in no time the coals were alight. She added more coal and fastened tight the door to the fire box, sliding open the flue to start the fire roaring.

She washed her hands in the water in an enamel bowl in the scullery and took down a big copper pan from a nail on the wall above the range. She dropped the scraps and bones that Mr Delaney had given her into the pan, then peeled and chopped the vegetables and added them with the prized cow heel, a good teaspoonful of salt and a handful of barley, Oonagh covered it all with fresh water from the bucket and lifted it onto the hotplate on the range.

Chapter Two
Whitewashing over the Cracks

Oonagh sighed and held onto the table as she lowered herself down onto a kitchen stool, she yawned, arched her back and massaged the tops of her hips with her knuckles. The bucket of limewash was there in the lobby and Oonagh dragged herself to her feet. Mr Watson would be 'round for the rent that evening, he might be expecting the job to have been done.

She dipped the wide brush into the bucket and started painting the caustic liquid onto the walls of the lobby. By the time Michael arrived home, she had nearly finished painting the lobby. He took the brush from her.

"Here, you shouldn't be doing this, let me take over, you have a lie down. Something smells good, what are you cooking?" said Michael, starting to paint the walls of the parlour as Oonagh went to cool her burning hands in the water in the enamel bowl. When she went wearily back into the parlour, Michael had stashed the straw-filled mattresses against one wall and was limewashing around the window wall.

"Ouch, this lime burns," said Michael.

"I suppose it has to, if it is to stop the fever," said Oonagh. "Do you know they call it the Irish Fever?"

"Just sit," said Michael, "until I finish this wall, and then I'll lay the mattresses back on the beds." The bells of St Mary's church struck seven.

"Seamus should be home by now, the others will not finish work until eight o'clock tonight," and Oonagh peered through the window. Sure enough, striding down the road came Seamus O'Neil, hands in pockets and steel-toed boots clicking on the cobbles. Oonagh opened the door and Seamus took her face in his hands.

"I've something for you, my lass, we've been bagging potatoes in the barn at the farm," he said and produced a potato from each pocket. They were still covered in black Cheshire soil.

Oonagh lifted them to her face and savoured the smell of the earth. "Oh, Seamus, no smell of rotting fish, they are beautiful, thank you," she said, "and just the thing for my hotpot, come and see."

"I don't need to see it, I can smell it," said Seamus, "and what's all this Michael is doing?"

"We have to paint the whole house Seamus, they say it's we Irish who have brought the fever," Oonagh told him.

"Rubbish," said Seamus. "The fever is typhoid. One of the farm hands at Leather's farm was telling me, there's a doctor at the Ardwick Infirmary who says it's overcrowding and the water that's the problem, what with the water pumps being right next to the privies. There's a big enquiry into it. Is there any chance we could have a cup of tea, lass?"

Oonagh picked up the water bucket again and moved towards the door.

Seamus took the bucket from her and filled it at the pump in the yard. Oonagh filled the kettle and put the water to boil on the circular hot plate on the range. She washed the two potatoes in fresh water. Leaving the skin on, she chopped the potatoes and dropped them into her hot pot. It was smelling good. She took a spoon and tasted the gravy, it was sticky from the marrow in the cow heel, yes that would feed them all well that evening.

"It's tasty, Seamus," she called. "About an hour now I would say. Just in time for others coming home. Seamus, have you got our two shillings for the rent? And Michael, we need your shilling."

"Great," said Michael. "That leaves me 2s 9d after a full week's work. How much do you get paid, Seamus?"

"11s 4d," was the reply, "or 9s 4d after I pay our rent for this lodging house and I work ten hours most days, in all weathers at the farm. If you would like me to, I will ask if Mr Leather is taking on any more farm labourers, it's almost July now, they will be bringing in the hay and it will be harvest soon but you will have to be up with the lark, you mustn't let me down. If we both get a better wage, we could maybe rent a house between us. With the baby coming soon, we will need something better than this."

"When you've finished organising my life for me, come and take a turn with this limewashing!" shouted Michael, and he threw the paintbrush at Seamus, splashing the limewash on Seamus's trousers.

"You'd still be on the streets and standing in that cellar for a penny a night, if we hadn't taken you in and sent you for a labouring job at the mill!" yelled Seamus.

The water boiled and the kettle whistled. Oonagh made a pot of tea, put plenty of sugar in three cups, shared the remains of the milk in the milk jug between them, stirred the tea, strained it into the cups, stirred them well and passed a cup to each of the men. "Quiet now, you two, that's the last of the tea, it's a shilling a quarter at Seymour's grocers," said Oonagh. "And if either of you catch the milkman in the morning, buy a jug of milk, will you? I'll wash the jug ready, he comes around about four thirty, I'll leave tuppence on the table. "Yes, Seamus is right, it's about time you paid towards the food, Michael," and Oonagh took the last two pennies from the tin on the mantle shelf and put them on the table. "The others will have to put a couple of bobs in the tin every week to pay for food. It cost me (or actually Seamus) one shilling and eleven pence farthing for tea, sugar and milk that's only lasted for two days," said Oonagh. She stirred her hot pot, the potatoes were cooked now. The other lodgers started to arrive back home, Patrick and Thomas Finnegan arrived together, they were both carders at the Portwood Mill where Michael was a labourer, Rose Murphy and Fanny O'Connell worked in the hat factory. Sean Hagerty and Owen Brennan came straight from their work at the rag merchant's yard. The last to arrive home was Concepta Finney who had the grand job of a chambermaid at the Station Hotel. Oonagh was waiting for each of them, to collect their shilling rent, and she rattled the housekeeping tin at each of them for their contributions. When Mr Watson knocked on the door at eight o'clock, she had the ten shiny shillings ready for him. He said very little, just took the money from Oonagh, counted the coins then tipped his hat, "I'll wish you goodnight."

Oonagh laid the table for ten. She held each bone from the pan in a cloth and scraped as much meat off as she could, then shared the hotpot between ten bowls. "I think this is more like soup," she said, "still we can share the last of the loaf to fill it out." The ten lodgers hungrily tucked into Oonagh's Lancashire soup.

"Are we all going to the Nelson for a jug of ale tonight?" asked Pat Finnegan, "Tom will bring his fiddle, won't you Thomas?"

"We have to be ready for trouble tonight," Seamus was solemn.

"I stopped at the church as I walked home. I saw Father Kelly for confession." Oonagh raised her eyebrows at Seamus. "Well, those potatoes in my pockets were stolen, Oonagh," he explained. "The Father had been to the police superintendent, Mr Sadler, this afternoon to tell him about our procession tomorrow afternoon. The police chief told him there had been a Royal Proclamation last week. Catholic Priests are not allowed to wear their clerical robes in public and there are to be no banners or catholic religious symbols in public." "So the beautiful silk banner our parishioners have made and embroidered for the new church has to stay in the church – it's a shame, the little ones keep in line holding the ribbons from the banner," said Michael.

Seamus continued, "Father Kelly told the police that we all intend it to be peaceful. It won't be the Catholics who stir up trouble, and he reminded him that St Mary's had their Protestant procession at Whitsun. The girls are getting ready in Chapel Street at the old chapel and he would like you to help there, Oonagh, if you will. The men and boys will start from the new church. Luckily, I'm only wanted at the farm for a half day tomorrow. I'll be able to help Father Kelly with organising the boys from the Sunday school. How about everyone else? I expect you will be working in the morning, so I suggest you join the procession en route."

Seamus changed his lime splattered trousers while the friends used the remaining hot water from the kettle, and one by one, had what Oonagh's mum would have called 'a cat lick', using the block of green household soap at the sink in the scullery. Finally rubbing their teeth with salt on a finger, then with shining faces a little sore from the strong soap, they left the house. The six men walked together, and the four girls followed. The girls giggled at how the men walked with what they called 'an Irish swagger', hands in pockets. The group walked up the road, and dodging the carts and carriages, across the main road to the Nelson Inn.

Chapter Three
The Meeting of the Waters

The snug at the Nelson was empty, save for old Mrs Flaherty, who, every week without fail, arranged the altar flowers at St Philip's Church. She was enjoying a tankard of brown ale sitting on a stool at the bar, chatting to Mr Costello, the landlord. Mrs Flaherty was wearing a brown wool coat and a worn, brown head-scarf over her wispy grey hair, despite the warm evening.

Seamus helped Oonagh to the bench by the window before ordering brown ale for the ten friends. The landlord took down ten tankards from the shelf above the bar and filled them up. Seamus carried them over to the table in front of the bench, where the other girls had joined Oonagh. The men downed their ale and wiped their salty lips on the back of their shirt cuffs almost in unison. "That was good," and they slammed their tankards down.

Tom strode over to the bar, "Fill them up please landlord," and he passed over the empty tankards to Mr Costello.

"Let's hear 'The Meeting of the Waters' Oonagh," called Michael and his cousin flung back her flaxen hair with the back of her hand as she made her way over to the bar and with her back against the bar she began to sing in her gentle lilting Irish brogue; Tom Finnegan picked up his violin and accompanied her.

"There is not in the wide world a valley so sweet
As the vale in whose bosom the bright waters meet
Oh the last rays of feeling and life must depart
'Ere the bloom of that valley shall fade from my heart.

Yet it was not that Nature had shed o'er the scene
Her purest of crystal and brightest of green
'Twas not her soft magic of streamlet or hill
Oh no – it was something more exquisite still
Oh no – it was something more exquisite still.

'Twas that friends, the belov'd of my bosom, were near,
Who made every dear scene of enchantment more dear,
And who felt how the best charms of Nature improve,
When we see them reflected from looks that we love."

Oonagh wiped a tear from her eyes as she continued with the last verse of the song:

"Sweet vale of Avoca! How calm could I rest
In thy bosom of shade, with the friends I love best,
Where the storms that we feel in this cold world should cease,
And our hearts, like thy waters, be mingled in peace."

The friends cheered and Mrs Flaherty took out her handkerchief and gave her nose a good blow, before going outside for a breath of fresh air. Oonagh sat beside Seamus and took his arm as Concepta jumped up and called across to Tom, "Underneath my Irish Blanket." Tom laughed and nodded, and Rose and Fanny joined Concepta, lifting and swinging their striped grey and brown fustian skirts to reveal their pretty ankles. Tom played the Irish jig on his fiddle and the girls sang as they danced, while the men laughed and drank more ale.

"Come under my Irish blanket,
Kick your boots off, rest your bones,
I have made a loaf for breakfast,
You can make yourself at home.
Come under my Irish blanket,
You have whiskey I have wine,
But by far the greatest pleasure is the treasure in my mind.
Under my Irish blanket you will find your history
Everything you need to know; is in the cleft behind my knee
Underneath my Irish blanket battles were fought, wars were won
Essays written schoolboys smitten,
People died and people born."

Oonagh took Seamus' hand and laid it on her belly, "Can you feel our baby kicking, I think she's dancing a jig?"

"I think you'll be finding it's a boy, I want to call him Sean, Sean O'Neil, it's a grand old Irish name," said Seamus, "I've spoken to Father Kelly and he'll wed us early next month." He took both her hands in his strong hands and kissed her fingers one by one.

The girls continued:

"Kiss my wrists, kiss my lips, kiss my ankles
So that I know I've been kissed!
Tell a story, sing a song,
Write a letter – so that we can better get along.

Come under my Irish blanket, feed your curiosity
You have hands fair fit for working – you can let them work on me!

Come under my Irish blanket while the moon is rising high
I have seen you stripped and sweaty, seen you giving me the eye.
Underneath my Irish blanket, I have music of the best
I'll soon have your feet a-tapping, you must dance before you rest.
Underneath my Irish blanket Christopher Columbus came
Took a look and wrote a book and said he'd soon be back again.

Kiss my neck, kiss my knee
Kiss the part that in the dark just you can see.
Play your fiddle, bang your drum
You can watch me while I dance the devil 'round the room!

If you won't come 'neath my blanket, drink my tea nor stoke my fire
Don't you worry, Monday morning I'll be courting Mick Maguire."

Mrs Flaherty came bustling back into the pub, distressed. "There are some wicked men out there with a stuffed effigy of His Holiness Pope Pius and they were laughing that they are going to set fire to it," she burst out to Tom and Michael who were at the bar, waiting for Mr Costello to refill the tankards. Three young Englishmen now strode into the bar. The first man was tall with red hair, he wore brown breeches, knee-length boots of fine leather and a look of sheer arrogance. His white frilled shirt and maroon cravat were topped by a green tweed jacket with leather patches at the elbow, Tom immediately gave his fiddle to Mr Costello and whispered to Michael, "Here's trouble."

"Do carry on playing, my man," said the redhead as he pushed aside Michael and Tom at the bar, "And carry on dancing you girls, we all enjoy a sight of pretty ankles." "Go carefully," murmured Seamus to the others.

Michael turned to the redhead, "You should wait your turn, it's me the landlord is serving." "This is an English pub for Englishmen," snapped the redhead. "The name says it all – Nelson, the greatest admiral of all time – and an Englishman; not the place for you pestilence-riddled Irishmen."

Michael took a swing at the redhead and Mr Costello shouted, "There'll be no brawling in my pub, get yourselves outside."

The three Englishmen and the six Irishmen moved to the door. "Now you stay in here lass, don't dare move," said Seamus to Oonagh, "I'll be back for you when it's safe, and the same for you other three lasses, don't come outside until I say." With that, he headed out of the door.

Outside there was a crowd of English youths and, as Mrs Flaherty had said, they had taken a black cleric's gown and stuffed it with straw like a Guy Fawkes, mounted it on a broom handle and topped with a mask on which they had written 'Pope Pius 9'. The redhead struck a match and set it to the straw sticking out of the cleric's gown. The effigy blazed and fire soon engulfed the whole of His Holiness – to the cheers of the Englishmen, their numbers increasing at an alarming rate. It seemed that ruffians from miles around were converging on the usually peaceful town that Friday evening.

Michael made a swing at the man holding the burning effigy, but two more English youths held him back, shoving him to the ground yelling, "Filthy Irish Catholics, get back to Ireland with your filthy diseases." Michael staggered and fell to the ground, hitting his head on the cobbles and one of the Englishmen kicked him viciously in the head with his heavy boots.

Seamus lifted Michael to his feet. "Let's get you home, lad," said Seamus, as he grasped Michael under the arms and around his back taking Michael's weight on his broad shoulders.

With Michael's feet dragging on the ground, Seamus half carried, half walked him home to Watsons' Court. As he later testified, once home, he laid Michael on his iron bedstead, took off Michael's boots and covered him with the dingy cream blanket. "I'll be back with Oonagh and the girls," he called as he ran from the house.

Back at the Nelson pub, Mrs Flaherty cracked open the front door to try to hear what was happening. "We'll burn that Papist chapel down and the Papist with it," she heard a ruffian shout.

Mrs Flaherty quickly shut the door and reported to the girls. "They're going to burn down St Philip's Church and the presbytery. I have to warn Father Kelly," she said as she tightened her brown headscarf. Then she left by the back door. Up the back streets that she knew so well, the little lady ran, sniffing into her handkerchief and praying as she ran. She managed to reach the presbytery before the gang of ruffians, who had taken the main road and were too busy bragging to each other about what they were going to do.

Frantic knocking on the front door broke Father Kelly off from his dinner of steak and kidney pie with new potatoes and spring cabbage that his housekeeper had prepared from him before she went home. "You've got to get away, Father," Mrs Flaherty was hanging onto the door frame wheezing, when he opened the door. "They're coming to burn the church," she panted.

"Who?" the Father asked, before, "Now you get yourself off home, have you far to go?"

"No, I'm only two streets away, but you get out, Father, there's at least a dozen ruffians and they're growing into a mob," and Mrs Flaherty set off again as if she were clockwork and had been wound fully before being set down.

"God be with you," called Father Kelly.

"And His angels guard over you, Father," was the prayer over Mrs Flaherty's shoulder.

Father Kelly ran two stairs at a time, up both flights into the attic room then stood on a chair and heaved himself through the skylight on the roof. He remembered with alarm that the church was still unlocked after the evening's Mass. His flock had spent three hundred years worshipping in secrecy. Who was he to lock their church and prevent them from their worship now? From his vantage point behind the chimney, he could see the mob as they turned the corner, reached the church and wrenched open the west door. First they grabbed the prayer books and the hymnbooks, throwing them into the churchyard. The church furniture was next. The beautiful stained-glass east window, given by a devout businessman from a nearby village, was smashed with the chair legs which had been broken from the bishop's seats, amid laughter and cheering from the mob. The altar, the gallery, the rood screen; nothing escaped destruction, and once in the churchyard they were set alight by the thugs. Father Kelly could only wring his hands and watch, helpless and heartbroken, from the roof of the presbytery.

Leaving Michael in bed at the house, Seamus ran back to the Nelson and burst into the snug to find the girls huddled together weeping and afraid. The four Irish men were at the bar while the landlord's wife dabbed the cuts to their heads and knuckles. They quickly told Seamus what was happening up at the church, and cautioning them once again to stay in the pub, Seamus ran through the familiar backstreets that were his route to and from his work on the farm. He arrived at the church moments after the militia who had been on standby for riot ever since the fateful Peterloo. The mob were in the churchyard with the charred remains of the church furniture at their feet and were being read the Riot Act by the police Superintendent Mr Sadler, who was with about fifty special constables from the many he had sworn in ready for Saturday's parade. The mob broke up and sidled off quite freely, while Seamus banged on the presbytery door.

A white-faced Father Kelly opened the door as the rector of St Mary's Church of England rushed up the path quite breathless, red-faced and clutching a bottle of brandy. "I had a feeling you might need a glass of this, Father Kelly. As God is my witness, none of those ruffians was from my congregation, they are from out of town," he tried to assure his fellow clergyman.

There was nothing more that Seamus could do that night. He told the priest that he and the others would help to clear the church and churchyard as soon as they were able, but that he needed to help the girls back to the safety of the house.

"God bless you, Seamus O'Neil," said the priest, and the vicar nodded.

Chapter Four
'Ere the Bloom of That Valley Shall Fade from My Heart

Seamus ran back to the Nelson only to find that the four men had left and the girls were alone.

"They went off muttering something about revenge for our church," said Oonagh. "I think they were heading for the Protestant school on Petersgate."

Seamus replied, "They will only make things worse, hitting back just plays into the hands of these bullies," and he urged the girls to come back to the house with him. He walked as quickly as Oonagh was able, with his arm around her and his eyes scanning around all the way. When they arrived at Watsons' Court, Mrs Watson herself was leaning out of an open window of her flat, her hair twisted into pipe cleaners to curl her white hair and wearing a white flannel nightgown.

"What on earth is going on?" she shouted to them, "I heard glass smashing and I could see smoke and flames coming from Edgeley way, this used to be a decent neighbourhood until you Irish arrived. You women wandering the streets at night – it's a disgrace."

As she ranted, Tom, Pat, Sean and Owen arrived. Seamus scowled at them and spoke through clenched teeth, "Not a word, get inside."

Inside the house Oonagh rushed into the front parlour, which was serving as bedroom to the six men. Michael was lying on the first bed and Oonagh lit the oil lamp and stooped over him stroking his head and black curls. Then dropping to her knees she screamed his name, bringing Seamus and the others rushing into the room. "He's dying, Seamus, he's dying, oh what am I going to tell his mammy and pa, was he alright when you left him, Seamus?"

"On my life, he was," was the reply, "we have to bring a doctor, his head is so very badly bruised."

The Finnegan brothers rushed out saying they would go to the doctor's house on St Petersgate.

Owen and Sean joined them and all four rushed to Petersgate, hammering on the doctor's front door until a thin weasley man with thinning grey hair and spectacles perched on the end of his nose appeared at a top window. "Off with you!" shouted the doctor, "it was you lot who smashed the Protestant grammar school, I saw you from my window."

Ignoring the pleas of the men, he lowered the sash window shut as a brick smashed through the glass, followed by another and another thrown by Owen.

One by one all the windows at the doctor's home were smashed by the four Irishmen who protested that if the doctor didn't come now, it would be too late to save their friend.

Sean was weeping as he threw more rocks, bricks, anything he could find at the doctor's house. "I thought doctors vowed to save lives," he sobbed as he slammed the missiles at the windows.

"Move!" shouted Owen and the four ran back towards Watsons' Court, as the sound of horse's hooves rang on the cobbles and the militia advanced followed by the same special constables who had been at St Philip's church. The police grabbed the four by their shirt collars and dragged them up to the cells in the courthouse.

Back at Watsons' Court, Oonagh was lying beside her cousin Michael on his bed, stroking his arm and crying into his shoulder. Rose and Concepta finally gently helped her off the bed, "He's gone now, my lovely, you have to think of your baby," said Rose as they led her to the girls' shared bedroom upstairs and taking off her boots, they covered her with a blanket, then sat with her until she finally slept, still whimpering in her sleep.

Saturday was fine and sunny, not a cloud in the sky, Seamus was already up and dressed when Oonagh came down to the kitchen, her eyes red and swollen.

Seamus had remembered to have the jug filled when the milkman passed in his horse and cart. The stove was lit, the water boiling and the brass kettle was whistling. Oonagh went straight to her beloved cousin and found Seamus had covered Michael's face with the blanket. Oonagh pulled the blanket back and kissed Michael's cold, bruised cheek. "Farewell, my darling boy," she whispered and her sobbing started over again.

There was someone banging on the door. Oonagh wiped her eyes and her nose on the sleeve of her white cotton blouse. Seamus opened the door to two police constables and the coroner.

"I'm here to examine the body," said the coroner pushing by with his brown leather bag. Oonagh and Seamus left the front room and sat together at the kitchen table with a cup of tea each, well sugared.

"I had to report to the police superintendent that Michael had died, I told him that he'd been beaten by that red-headed man and the other two thugs had kicked him in the head," said Seamus quietly to Oonagh.

"Your friends who attacked the school and the doctor's house are in the cells," said one of the constables, slouching, hands in pockets, with one foot up against the kitchen wall.

"I must go to work," said Seamus, "they need me on the farm," but the coroner, overhearing, shouted that Seamus had to answer some questions first.

"Who was the last person to see the deceased man alive?" "That was me," said Seamus, "I brought Michael back after he was beaten outside the Nelson pub by some Englishmen. Can I go to work now? They need me on the farm and I don't want to lose my job, I need to work for my wife-to-be and our child," and he took Oonagh's hand in his.

The coroner went back to Michael's bruised body saying to the constables, "Take the man to the courthouse, the dead man in here has a broken skull and that man was the last to see him and was almost certainly responsible for his death."

Oonagh protested to the coroner, "But Michael was my cousin, sir, Seamus helped him to get back home after he was beaten, he would never had hurt Michael, we have looked out for him since he came over to England to escape the famine."

The coroner and the Special Policemen seemed not to hear anything of the pleas of the young couple and the police dragged Seamus off to the courthouse cells. "To await an interview," as the coroner said.

Oonagh followed behind Seamus until the police escorted him roughly up the steps into the police station and disappeared through the big oak doors. Oonagh wandered along to the Marketplace, mechanically putting one foot in front of the other as the soles of her boots flapped on the cobbles.

The baker's shop in the market place was always the first shop to open. The door was open and the warm yeasty smell from inside was somehow comforting. Oonagh stepped inside. The loaves were piled high on the counter and the balm cakes were in a basket on the shelf at the back. Mrs Jenkins was a short chubby lady with dimples on the backs of her square chubby hands. She wore her hair in a bun on top of her head save for a fringe which she had pinned back with a hair grip.

"A large loaf, please, Mrs Jenkins, and a large favour," said Oonagh.

"That's seven pence three farthings," said the bakerwoman and passed a large loaf over the counter.

"I'm sorry, hen, but they keep the price of flour high." Mrs Jenkins was Scottish and had not lost her accent.

"No, I'm sorry, Mrs Jenkins, but please, can I bring the money in on Monday morning, I promise I will," said Oonagh and the lump in Oonagh's throat began to choke her as the warm tears trickled down her cheeks.

Mrs Jenkins came around the counter. "Life has not been without troubles for me," and she put her arms around Oonagh. "I can see you are troubled, hen, won't you tell me about it?"

"My cousin Michael was killed last night, we were children together, he was more like a brother, but the worse thing is my Seamus has been taken to the cells, they say he killed Michael and I know he didn't," Oonagh sobbed in the chubby lady's arms. Mrs Jenkins pulled a handkerchief from her sleeve and gave it to Oonagh. When two more customers came into the shop, Oonagh blew her nose, thanked Mrs Jenkins and headed back to Watsons' Court, calling, "I'll be back first thing on Monday, Mrs Jenkins," as she went through the door.

Back in the house Oonagh put the loaf on the table where she and the girls could help themselves to a chunk for breakfast, spread thickly with the dripping from Mr Delaney's shop. Oonagh loved the golden-brown jelly at the bottom of the dish.

Concepta was the first downstairs, and hurriedly drank the tea Oonagh had made, with some bread. Her work at the Station Hotel started early, lighting the fires, laying the tables for breakfast, then washing and drying the breakfast dishes. She had to then move on to making up the bedrooms. First she had to empty and clean the chamber pots, she was hoping the guests had only peed in them and had gone down to the privy for anything else, now there was a gaslamp in the yard. Concepta then carried on making the beds, tucking in the sheets and blankets neatly and tightly. Not finished there, Concepta had the laundry to sort before it was collected by local washerwomen who took laundry in to do in their own homes. Concepta laid a soiled sheet on the floor of the last bedroom and piled other soiled linen in the middle, tablecloths, pillowcases and linen towels. She then drew up the four corners of the sheet and tied them together. She was just in time, Mrs Woods had arrived with her baby in a perambulator to collect the laundry. Concepta took the soiled linen down to Mrs Woods in the yard. Each item had the name of the hotel written in indelible ink on its edge. Mrs Woods lifted her baby out of the perambulator, Concepta put the linen bundle in, Mrs Woods sat her baby at the opposite end and was on her way.

There were still rugs to beat and the floors to sweep, for Concepta. She could see no end to her duties and she did so much want to be in the procession. She did not want to let Father Kelly down.

Back at the house the coroner had had Michael's body taken away and Oonagh was battling with herself whether to take part in the procession, when the priest arrived on her doorstep. He took Oonagh's arm, "Shall we sit down, my dear girl?" And Oonagh offered to make a pot of tea.

The gentle priest sat on a stool at the table while Oonagh busied herself at the range making the tea. She had stood the jug of milk in water in the sink in the scullery and draped a muslin cloth in the water and over the top of the jug, to keep the milk cool in the warm weather, just as her mother had taught her. She poured milk in each cup mechanically and strained tea from the large brown tea pot then pushed the sugar bowl over to the priest, with a teaspoon.

"It's best to keep busy at times like these, my dear girl, please know I am here to help you in your sad loss," and Father Kelly put his hands on her head as she sat on the stool beside him, he offered up a short prayer for God's guidance in her grief. Oonagh explained how Seamus had been taken to the police station.

"I am sure everything will be well," said the Father, "Seamus is a good man."

"Father, I know that Michael would want us to go ahead with the procession, he felt strongly that we should be proud of our faith," said Oonagh, "I will be up at the old chapel for two o'clock to help get the girls ready."

Chapter Five
The Procession

At two o'clock that afternoon, the girls from St Philip's Sunday school left Chapel Street, Stockport dressed in their long white confirmation dresses. Oonagh had tied white satin ribbon in bows in their hair that had been curled in rags all night so that now it fell in ringlets. The girls chatted excitedly as the men and boys of St Philip's Catholic Church came marching down the road from Edgeley, led by a marching band. Conductors, lay members of the church, marched either side to keep the lines of church members straight and to direct the route. The ladies of the church were wearing their best Sunday clothes and hats. If they did not possess a hat then their heads were covered with a silk scarf and those who could afford them wore lace gloves. Mrs Flaherty was there, wearing her best navy-blue hat with a little net at the front and her favourite rosary beads. She was carrying a little posy of flowers courtesy of the florists who supplied the altar flowers each week. Concepta, Fanny and Rose were just in time to join Oonagh at the front of the girls' Sunday school group.

Father Kelly (true to his word) was not in his cleric's gown but in his navy-blue suit. He carried a plain wooden cross as he walked proudly at the head of his flock, flanked by a police sergeant and a constable, who had been reluctant to march with him at first insisting they were not Catholics themselves. The priest had told them he merely wanted protection from any insulting actions or words, and if that happened he wanted those responsible to be taken into custody. The girls of the Sunday school fell into line at the front, behind their priest, and the procession proceeded peacefully down the main road. Rose, Oonagh Fanny and Concepta marched together, watching over the youngest of the Sunday school girls, behind the priest. The overseer for Cheadle, Edgeley and Brinksway was there to observe, and the families of the town of all faiths, attracted by the band, brought their children to see the parade. They lined the route cheering and waving flags. As a safety precaution, the police superintendent had asked for six soldiers to march about 50 yards in front of the procession 'to clear the way'. Down the main road and into St Petersgate marched the procession, into the scene of such trouble the night before. As the procession turned to the right, little Maureen Gallagher from the Sunday school burst into tears. Oonagh stooped to comfort her and learned that the little one had lost sight of her mummy in the crowds. Oonagh took Maureen's hand and they re-joined the 'big girls'. Maureen's tears subsided as the band struck up again and in the sunny weather the people of Stockport of all Christian faiths were in a holiday mood. The happy procession was heading for the Anglican Church in the Marketplace, but as the head of the procession passed the first side road a group of about a dozen men, whom the parish priest had never seen in the congregation at his church, slid stealthily into the head of the procession. The elderly priest was relieved at first because two of the young men took the heavy cross from him and carried it between them, but the remainder of the men linked arms and stretched in a line across the road. It was the same at the next street, men slipped seamlessly into the church's witness parade. Some of the men were still dressed in the working clothes of harvest labourers and some were even carrying their sickles. Each group linked arms across the road. The soldiers halted in front of the Anglican Church in the Marketplace and waited for the procession to catch up. Oonagh spotted a group of men in front of the pub opposite St Mary's – and one man with a shock of red hair in particular. She heard him say, "There go those Irish whores."

Oonagh ran to the police sergeant and caught his arm. "Those men outside the pub, they are the ones who attacked my cousin last night outside the Nelson Inn," she insisted.

"I don't think so, miss. They are from respectable local families. Young Mr Marsland is a farmer's son," said the sergeant turning away.

Once the procession caught up with the soldiers, assembling in front of Father Kelly and his congregation, there were about five to six hundred Irishmen, linking arms across their lines. The onlooking families had dispersed and hurried their protesting children home. The priest took back the plain wooden cross and, standing facing the procession, with his back to the line of soldiers, he demanded in his strongest voice that anyone who was not a member of his church or St Philip's congregation should leave the scene immediately. As he spoke, Special Constables rushed to the scene. Scuffles broke out in the crowd and two hundred men were taken into custody, chiefly Irish, although the police sergeant arrested three Englishmen and himself escorted them to the cells.

Oonagh, Concepta, Rose and Fanny stayed close together and ushered the Sunday school girls away from all the trouble, across the main road to the old chapel to be collected by their parents. The girls then hurried back home to Watsons' Court.

Chapter Six
The Aftermath

The four, determined not to leave the house that night but realised that they only had the bread and dripping left to eat until Monday.

They sat around the table in the kitchen, drank plenty of tea, tucked into the bread and dripping and talked about home in the old days. Oonagh told the others about growing up with Michael and the games they played in the lush green meadows and woods of the Vale of Avoca. She recounted how Michael always included her in his games with the boys. How he had tied a rope to the branch of a tree that hung over the river. He tied a knot at the bottom of the rope. "You go at the bottom, Oonagh, that's the easiest," and four boys climbed onto the rope above her. It was Oonagh's part to run as fast as she could to the river's edge and swing out over the water.

Oonagh ran, with the boys above her shouting encouragement, and jumped out over the fast-flowing water. They were two thirds across when there was a terrific splitting noise above them and within seconds Oonagh was lying on the riverbed with four laughing boys crushing her. Oonagh's worry was that she was wearing the dress her mother had just made for her, but Michael's worry was for his cousin. She would never forget his panic-stricken face as he waded into the water wearing his Sunday best shoes, calling her name, and dragged her out.

Oonagh had spent the rest of the afternoon in her bloomers and vest, playing hide and seek with the boys, while her dress dried over a branch of the tree. Her mam never knew. "You see, it's just as we thought, you always were a little tease," laughed the girls until Oonagh begged them to stop, as she would need the privy but was too scared to go out into the yard. "Too much tea," Oonagh protested, clutching at herself and rushed to the front door. Smoke billowed down the lobby and into the kitchen. Men were dragging the mattresses out of the lodging house next door. They had already set some alight in the yard. One man (he couldn't have been much older than Oonagh) saw her and shouted, "This is the way we get rid of the Irish Fever – we burn their vermin-riddled beds."

Two men came out of Mrs Clancy's house next door but one, Oonagh recognised one of them as being with the red-headed man from the night before, at the Nelson. They were throwing out Mrs Clancy's furniture, tables, chairs, everything they could move. Mr Clancy had only just come out of the Union Infirmary, Oonagh had spoken to Mrs Clancy in the yard. She was a very houseproud lady and used to polish her front doorstep with a bright red paste that she called 'red raddle'. One of the men came out into the yard carrying Mrs Clancy's pans and threw them over towards the water pumps, shouting insults but little Mrs Clancy rushed out into the yard after him grasping a large flower-decorated chamberpot that she had bought from the market especially for her convalescing husband.

"Here, you've forgotten something," shouted the little lady as she hit the insulting vandal on his head with the pot. "Just be grateful that wasn't full, my lad."

Oonagh quickly shut the front door and asked the other girls to come out to stand guard while they each used the privy in the smoke-filled yard.

On Sunday morning Oonagh was awakened by someone thumping on the front door.

She opened it to an angry Mrs Watson, who had finally loosened her grey wiry hair out of the usual pipe cleaner hair-curlers and it was now balanced on top of her head like a cloud of the wire wool that Oonagh's father used to rub the rust off his farm tools. The landlady leaned forward and her thin sharp nose resembled a falcon's beak as she hissed, "You'll have to leave, I can't put up with all this."

"We have already paid for next week," said Oonagh, "and the rioters last night were Englishmen."

"Makes no difference, you have to go," and Mrs Watson turned her back and moved towards Mrs Clancy's house.

Oonagh sat at the table shaking and the other girls came down to ask what had been said. "Don't worry, lovely, we'll look after you," said Rose.

"No, you have lives of your own to live," said Oonagh, "but thank you, anyway. My Seamus will be home soon and we are getting wed. You lovely girls will all be my bridesmaids, but I will not be going to Mrs Watson for my wedding dress, I would rather wear my flannelette nightie."

That morning the girls helped Mr and Mrs Clancy to put their home back together again. Oonagh remembered the man who brought the limewash had told her that the houses in Wesley Street had been hit by the fever. She guessed the rioters must have headed there last night. The girls went there next and found that these were overcrowded lodging houses just as Watsons' Court. They did as much as they could to help the families there but most of the occupiers were in the Infirmary.

Mrs Clancy was waiting when they returned home, "I am so sorry, but the police came and spoke to Mr Clancy while you were away. He had to tell the superintendent the truth, that he heard shouting from your house at Friday tea time."

"Yes," said Oonagh, "you had to tell the truth, but it was only a little family argument, Mrs Clancy, don't you worry now."

Chapter Seven
Magdalene Homes

Oonagh was on the steps of the police station and courthouse leaning heavily on the handrail, ready for them to open on Monday morning. She asked if she could speak to Mr Sadler, the police superintendent, but he was not available. She spoke instead to the police sergeant who had been at the procession on Saturday. He invited her to sit down and sat opposite her at a table in the office. She repeated what she knew about the man with red hair whom he had identified as 'young Master Marsland'. Her cousin Michael's body would be released for the funeral, the sergeant told her, once the inquest had been held, and if all went well that would be Thursday. She was told she was not allowed to speak to Seamus although she explained her position regarding the lodging house and said that Seamus provided for her. The sergeant told her that regrettably unmarried mothers would not be employed in the district in anything but laundry work. "Young unmarried women in your situation are advised to put themselves at the mercy of the nuns of the Magdalene Homes. There are two on the outskirts of town, there is one in Fallowfield and I believe they are building one in Eccles," he explained. "The homes provide you with food and lodging for up to eighteen months and the nuns take care of you at the birth. The nuns support the home by taking in laundry from the district, and you repay them by working in the laundry. In addition the nuns will find a good home for your baby when the time comes, usually when the child is eighteen months old."

Oonagh stared at the sergeant, "But Seamus and I don't want someone else to give a good home to our baby. That is what we will do, thank you sergeant." Oonagh could feel her throat closing up again as if to choke her and she stood to leave. "Thank you, sir," and she left to make her way to pay her debt to Mrs Jenkins at the bakers, with hot tears brimming in her green eyes.

Oonagh handed a silver sixpence and two copper pennies from the housekeeping tin to Mrs Jenkins who rummaged in her drawer to find her a farthing change. "I am so sorry, Mrs Jenkins," said Oonagh, her voice wavering as she felt the tears come flooding back.

"Here now, hen, don't take on so," said the chubby Scots lady as she helped Oonagh to a seat at the back of the counter. "It will all be sorted soon, one thing for sure they will not keep all those prisoners up there for long, and the trial will have to be soon, the cells are overflowing. It will be too expensive to keep them all. They sent for forty loaves from me, I have just been up there to

31

deliver them. They will have to set a date for trial very soon, then you will know where you stand, you and your Seamus. Can you not go home to your ma and pa just until the bairn comes?"

"No," said Oonagh, "I can't possibly go back home, my pa would never forgive my sin, never, and there is nothing to eat in Ireland. Everyone is leaving for America or Australia or coming here to England – or they will starve to death, the potatoes are rotting in the fields and potatoes are our main food, the bread is too dear for the likes of us." Oonagh's sobs continued.

"Well, I think they would be fine once they saw the baby," said Mrs Jenkins, as Oonagh shook her head and sobbed even more. "My Seamus was going to wed me soon, then we could go home for a visit. Oh, I hope my ma and pa and little Finn have not died of hunger, Mrs Jenkins."

Mrs Jenkins did her best to console Oonagh until customers started to come into the bakers and Oonagh thought it best to leave her friend to her work. As she stood to leave, Mrs Jenkins said quietly, "Call in on your way back home, I'll save a pie for you to take to the courthouse for Seamus."

Oonagh walked on through the marketplace taking care not to trip on the loose soles of her boots that were catching on the cobbled road.

As she passed the butcher's shop, Mr Delaney was taking delivery of carcases of meat that were being delivered from the abattoir by the carter. He was fastening an 's'-shaped hook into the ankles of what looked like a sheep. Oonagh slipped after him into the shop and he hung the carcass from another hook in the ceiling at the back of the counter. He smiled at Oonagh. "Good morning, bright eyes," he said and went back to the cart with another 's'-hook, before carrying in the carcass of another animal.

"Is that one a cow?" said Oonagh. "Well, we would call it beef," said Mr Delaney as he went out for another sheep.

The carter made a comment about the amount of meat sold by Mr Delaney and the butcher replied, "Yes, indeed, working folk eat more than just bread and cheese nowadays. Meat is not just for the tables of the gentry. This is the trade to be in, my business is growing every week." After the carter had left, Mr Delaney turned his attention to Oonagh, "Now what can I oblige you with today, young lady?"

"I would like fourpenn'eth of liver please, sir," said Oonagh and took out a threepenny bit and a copper penny from her pocket. Mr Delaney sliced some lamb liver for her and wrapped it in greaseproof paper first then a sheet of newspaper.

"How did you fare in the riots at weekend?" he asked her. "Were you affected at all?" Oonagh told him everything, about Michael, Seamus, the procession and about Mrs Watson's eviction threat.

"Hmm," said Mr Delaney, as Oonagh stepped back outside and hurried over to the vegetable stall as she felt the first spots of rain on her face.

At the vegetable stall, she showed the stallholder her last two copper pennies and the farthing and asked for an onion and as many potatoes as they would buy. The greengrocer put an onion in and four large potatoes in her basket. "I think my missus would agree you can buy those for tuppence farthing, love," he said.

Oonagh flushed and thanked him before making her way back to Mrs Jenkins for the pie.

Mrs Jenkins had the pie ready for her, it was still warm. "Now you take that up to the courthouse quickly and ask them to give it straight away to Seamus," said Mrs Jenkins.

Oonagh almost skipped through the door but was conscious of the flapping soles of her boot.

At the courthouse the sergeant on duty said that the pie would be given to Seamus O'Neil. "Promise," said Oonagh.

"I promise, miss," said the sergeant with a smile, "but it smells very tempting."

A few minutes after Oonagh had returned to Watsons' Court, Father Kelly arrived on her doorstep. He shook his black umbrella and smoothed back his thinning white hair when Oonagh invited him in. "I've reserved Friday for Michael's funeral," said the kindly priest, "and don't worry yourself about any cost, that will come out of the church funds." Oonagh was thankful to the priest and to his congregation. "Will you be going to the inquest?" said the priest. "The superintendent has confirmed it is on Thursday. To tell the truth, I think the cells are so full the police cannot get on with their usual work."

"Yes," said Oonagh, "I want to be there when they release my Seamus."

"Then I will go with you," replied Father Kelly.

The girls ate well for tea that evening, fried liver and onions with mashed potatoes, cooked by Oonagh. "No tea?" asked Concepta.

"No milk," answered Oonagh, "one of us will have to catch the milk man in the morning, which was usually Seamus's chore."

"We will be able to do that," said Rose and Fanny, "we are going onto a double day shift at the hat factory now they have gas lighting, we are on the early shift for this month. The factory should be able to make more hats, and the boss says that will make everyone better off. I feel quite excited about it."

"It will be interesting to see if that is so," said Oonagh quietly.

Chapter Eight
The Inquest

Thursday was a dismal, drizzly day. Oonagh met Father Kelly on the steps of the courthouse at a quarter past ten, the inquest was to start at half past. They made their way straight through to the public gallery and Oonagh sat at the front beside the priest. Four policemen, with truncheons at the ready, brought the prisoners up from the cells and into the dock.

First into the dock were the Finnegan brothers with Sean and Owen. Oonagh gave them a little wave. The priest cautioned her about bringing attention to herself. When they brought in her Seamus, she felt very close to tears again and he looked at her in that special loving way he had only for her.

Everyone stood when the magistrates entered. Father Kelly pointed out three farmers and a hat manufacturer to Oonagh. The chairman of the magistrates entered, proudly resplendent in his mayor's cloak with his chains of office around his neck. The magistrates sat in a row with the mayor in the centre, behind a long oak table facing the dock.

Standing, the mayor began the proceedings:

"This weekend, this town has been the scene of such great disturbances, such as will not be tolerated by the laws of this country. English Protestants have profaned the sacred name of their faith in endeavouring to prevent men (and indeed women and little children) from worshipping God in the way they think best. Firstly we will consider the events of Friday evening last which resulted in the tragic slaying of the young Irishman known as Michael Mahon. I will call first on Police Superintendent Sadler to take the witness stand."

The superintendent testified that the accused Seamus O'Neil had attended the police station on Saturday morning to report the death of Michael Mahon. The superintendent had requested the coroner to inspect the body with all haste.

The coroner took the stand and told how he had attended to inspect the body at Watsons' Court and in his expert opinion the deceased had been unlawfully slain by severe blows to the head which had broken his skull. The accused in the dock had been the last to see the deceased alive having taken him home from the Nelson public house where they had been drinking ale. Instead of the accused seeking medical aid, by his own admission, he returned to the Nelson public house, leaving Mr Mahon to die...

The mayor addressed the police superintendent:

"I believe you have further evidence from a neighbour of the accused?"

Oonagh looked at the priest.

"Yes, sir," said the superintendent, "Mr Clancy is not able to attend in person having only recently been discharged from the Infirmary. Mr Clancy heard raised voices from the home of the deceased and the accused at Friday teatime and the sound of something or someone being flung against the wall. He spoke to me on Monday morning after the coroner had pronounced Mr Michael Mahon dead from a broken skull," said Mr Sadler.

The Mayor interrupted, "I believe the Landlord of the Nelson public house is also to give evidence. Mr Costello, if you would enter the witness box, please."

Mr Costello told how the Irish had been drinking at his pub on Friday evening. He told about the singing and dancing and how Michael had swung a punch at young Mr Marsland.

Mr Costello told how he had demanded that they take any brawling outside his pub, which they did, but that he was unaware of what happened outside as he was attending to his customers at the bar.

"And now," said the mayor, "we will consider the further events of Friday night when the new Roman Catholic chapel was destroyed and property in St Petersgate was wilfully attacked and the windows smashed."

Superintendent Sadler testified that the Roman Catholic priest, Mr Kelly, had attended the Police station on the Friday morning and given notice of his intention to have a procession that weekend and that he agreed not to carry banners or wear his cleric's gown, in accordance with the law and the Royal Proclamation. "I think that word about the Catholic procession spread around the town, sir."

Mayor, "And was the law adhered to on Saturday?"

Sadler, "Yes, sir, it was, but as a precautionary measure, a number of special constables were sworn in and the militia were on standby."

At this point Mr Sadler was asked to step down and the police sergeant was asked to take the stand again.

"Going back to the Friday evening, Sergeant. What was the atmosphere in the town?" asked the magistrate.

"It was unusually quiet, sir, for a Friday night, there are usually fights between Englishmen and Irishmen, but we can deal with the trouble. Then we were called to a disturbance at the new Catholic chapel. When we arrived the priest had had to climb to safety on the roof of the presbytery and a mob, I can only call it that, sir, had dragged the furniture out of the church, the altar, the screen, along with prayer books and hymn books and they had burned them. The stained-glass east window of the church had been smashed, sir, and I believe a plaster statue of St Mary (although I don't hold with such idolatry myself) had been smashed in the chancel of the church. Mr Sadler himself read the Riot Act and the Militia came to our assistance. The mob escaped but I recognised and apprehended the leaders at the procession the following day."

"It was shortly after this," the sergeant continued, "that we were called to a disturbance on St Petersgate and the Militia followed on our heels. It was there that we apprehended four Irishmen who had smashed the windows of the Protestant School and the doctor's house."

"And are these men in the courtroom, Sergeant?" asked the magistrate.

The police sergeant pointed to the Finnegan brothers, Sean Hegarty and Owen Brennan, "Those were the men, sir."

"And the men, who destroyed the Catholic church Sergeant, are they in the courtroom?"

"No, sir, I believe they are still in the cells. They go by the names of Gerald Marsland, Peter Rowbottom, William Newton and George Parry."

The chairman of the magistrates announced they would be retiring to consider their verdict on Seamus O'Neil, Thomas and Patrick Finnegan, Sean Hegarty and Owen Brennan. The magistrates left the courtroom and Oonagh turned to Father Kelly.

"Seamus is not being given a chance, everyone is against him and he did nothing but care, Father, I can't understand Mr Clancy saying that. It was only a family argument and Michael threw the limewash brush at Seamus, not the other way 'round," she whispered.

The magistrates returned after thirty minutes and by this time Seamus and the other four had been moved to the far left of the dock. The redheaded Gerald Marsland and his three friends had been brought to the dock and were separated from them by the four policemen.

Gerald Marsland shouted out,

"On my honour, that Irishman came at me with a sickle, I just acted in self-defence and pushed him away, I swear I did, sir. I went up to the new Catholic chapel to take a look at it, there had been such a fuss in the papers."

The Mayor insisted, "You are not required to give evidence at this point Mr Marsland, you will be given chance at the Assizes."

At this, one of other magistrates leaned over and spoke to the mayor, but the Chairman shook his head.

Oonagh fumed and the priest patted her hand, "Keep calm, my child."

The magistrates retired to consider their verdict and when they returned just forty-five minutes later, Oonagh took hold of Father Kelly's hand and squeezed it tightly.

"In the case of Mr Thomas Finnegan and Mr Patrick Finnegan along with Mr Sean Hagerty and Owen Brennan, who undeniably wilfully damaged the property of the Protestant School and the Doctor's house on Petersgate. They will all be held in custody, pending trial at Chester July Assizes.

"In the case of Mr Ralph Marsland, Mr William Newton and Mr George Parry, you on the evidence of officers of the law and independent witnesses are accused of entering the said chapel, the property of the Catholic Church, with intent to destroy and deface. Such outrages upon religious houses and individuals will not be tolerated in this country. It is our judgement that you will be held in custody pending sentence at the County's July Assizes.

"Mr Seamus O'Neil, you will be held in custody at Chester Castle pending trial at Chester July Assizes, accused of the unlawful killing of Michael Mahon

"We will now examine the evidence regarding the procession on Saturday afternoon and the trouble that ensued, which is all connected to the disturbances of the weekend last."

Police Sergeant Abrams was called to the stand again. He gave evidence that he went on duty at two o'clock on Saturday afternoon, proceeding to St Philip's Roman Catholic Church, where the priest requested himself and the police constable to walk either side of him. "But I refused, sir, as I am not a Roman Catholic, but the priest explained he wanted protection from trouble, sir, and we walked in line with him on the edge of the procession. It was chiefly good-natured, sir. "

The sergeant went on to describe the procession and how the numbers had grown by the time they reached the Anglican Church.

"It was at this point that scuffles broke out between English and Irish, and my constables and I made a good many arrests."

The magistrates retired once again but returned after little more than ten minutes.

"We are satisfied that the remaining prisoners in custody were provoked by the wanton destruction of their church and that their actions in joining the procession were solely in defence of their Roman Catholic faith, these prisoners are therefore acquitted and are free to go."

Oonagh left the court on the arm of the priest. "I think I should make you some tea, my child," he said as they walked back to Watsons' Court.

Chapter Nine
Desolation

Oonagh grasped the cleric's arm tightly until they reached Watsons' Court and then, once she was inside, she collapsed onto the floor of the lobby. "It's all my fault, if Michael hadn't followed me here, he wouldn't be lying cold at the undertaker. If I hadn't wanted Michael to move in with us, if I hadn't been carrying Seamus' baby."

"If, if, if," said Father Kelly helping her to her feet. Oonagh went into the front parlour and lay on Michael's bed sobbing.

The priest stroked her head. "It's all past now, Oonagh, we can only do as we think best at the time and everything you did was with the best intention. Every baby is a gift from God above, Seamus will want you to take care of your baby. Don't forget it is his baby too and he will be relying on you now to do your very best. He was excited about the baby and he so wanted to marry you, he told me so. Seamus is a good man and you should be proud of him, as he is of you." The priest prayed with his hands on Oonagh's head,

"Heavenly Father, we beseech you to give Oonagh strength to cope with the grief that has beset her life and, if it is thy will, find a solution for Oonagh and her baby. Heavenly Father, give Seamus strength and we pray that justice will prevail. I leave these two children and their baby in your hands Lord, I ask this in Christ's name. Amen."

"Amen," said Oonagh, her eyes tightly shut. "But, Father, I am afraid that I am being selfish because I am worrying so much about myself and not grieving enough for my cousin, or Seamus and the injustice to him, I am such a selfish person, Father Kelly. Why would God help me?" "Because you are a child of God, we are all God's children," said the priest.

Father Kelly went into the kitchen and made her a cup of sweet tea. By the time he came into the front parlour her sobbing had subsided and she splashed water on her face from the half-empty bucket on the scullery floor, then dried her face with her skirt.

"We have to think about Michael's funeral," Father Kelly said gently to Oonagh, "but I think we should contact his ma and pa first. I could get word to your parish priest in Arklow. Is it Father Murphy we should write to? I think he would be the best person to break it to them.

"A nun is going back to Wicklow tomorrow. Sister Bernadette has been helping at the Magdalene home in Manchester, she is coming to visit me this evening on her way up to Liverpool and the boat to Dublin. My housekeeper is cooking dinner for us. I think we should wait to hear what his family say about the funeral."

Oonagh's tears started all over again when the priest said he would write the letter back in his presbytery and asked Oonagh to walk up there about five o'clock that afternoon, so that he could read the letter to her before he sent it to Arklow in the care of Sister Bernadette.

"But Father Kelly, I don't want to go to the Magdalene home, the nuns will take my baby from me," cried Oonagh.

"I think we should wait and see what God has in store for you," said the priest, "I will see you at five o'clock Oonagh, try to have a little rest."

Oonagh did just that, sleeping on Seamus's bed where she could still smell his scent on his blanket.

Concepta woke her at four o'clock, she had bought two pies at Mrs Jenkins bakers' shop. They were still warm. Oonagh and Concepta divided one between them and they ate as Oonagh related what had happened that morning at the magistrate's court.

"So all five of our men have to now be tried at County Court?" said Concepta.

"Yes, but the good news is that arrogant redheaded man and his friends are to be tried too," said Oonagh.

Concepta offered to walk to the presbytery with Oonagh, "You're all washed out," she said. "You will have to take care of yourself now, you've only a month to go."

Father Kelly read the letter out loud to Oonagh and Concepta,

"Dear Father Murphy,

It is with great sorrow that I have to inform you that Mr Michael Mahon of your parish of Arklow (and I believe a former choirboy in your church) has been killed in an altercation on Friday evening last in Stockport, the town in which he had settled since coming to England to escape the famine in Ireland. His parents, to whom I entrust you to impart this sad news, can take some comfort in the knowledge that his passing was swift and that his dear cousin Oonagh was with him in his last moments. Oonagh is beset with grief at the loss of her dear one, and asks me to send them her fondest love.

We are aware that money in Ireland is scarce because of the famine and the Catholic Church here in Stockport is willing to undertake all costs of a funeral for Michael. We propose to hold the memorial service on Wednesday morning next at ten o'clock here at St Philip's, Edgeley. If Mr and Mrs Mahon have any other directives could they please contact us via the Catholic church?"

"Thank you, that is just as I would have wanted to say, Father," said Oonagh.

Then she and Concepta bid goodbye to the priest and left as they saw through the window that sister Bernadette was opening the gate to the presbytery. The nun fixed her eyes on Oonagh's belly as the girls hurried out of the front door, "Good evening, my dear, I trust you are well."

"Yes, I'm fine and dandy thank you, Sister Bernadette," said Oonagh as she slammed the gate behind her.

By the time Oonagh and Concepta reached the house at Watsons' Court, Oonagh was breathless. "The baby is pushing on my bladder, and my belly keeps tightening up."

"I'm sure that's natural," said Concepta as Oonagh rushed up the yard to the privy.

"Mrs Clancy has been busy cleaning," called Oonagh, "that lady is a treasure."

When they entered the house, 'the treasure' was sitting at the kitchen table enjoying a cup of tea with Rose and Fanny.

"I've just been saying, I have heard about Seamus and your other friends and I do hope that what Mr Clancy said to the Police wasn't the reason they have to go to County Court. Only Mr Clancy didn't have the fever, you know, I took him to the Workhouse Infirmary because he was paralysed on one side and the doctor there said he had a thrombosis on his brain (that's a clot of blood you know). Well, he hasn't been the same since and he doesn't think straight. He was a clever man, my Henry, he was a train driver – Stockport to Manchester. He can't go back to work yet until his arm is working again. So it's lucky I've got my three jobs charring or I wouldn't be able to pay our rent. I even char for Mrs Watson in the shop and in her flat upstairs. The trouble is I can't leave my Henry for long, he might fall over and he can't do much for himself. So I thought you might take a room in our house, Oonagh. It's going to be hard for you now the birth is getting near. It would only be to make him tea and light the range fire, nothing too heavy for you. Maybe you could just run a few errands for me. You would have to try not to let the dragon see you, Mrs Watson, or she might ask for more rent. I've got a nice spare rocking chair in my kitchen for you. Can you read? Because Mr Clancy likes someone to read the newspaper to him."

"Yes, I can read, Father Murphy taught me back home in Arklow. And that sounds a very kind offer Mrs Clancy. I will do my very best to help you and Mr Clancy."

"So that's settled then," said Mrs Clancy. "You could start from Monday when the rent here runs out, I'll get back to my Henry now and tell him the news."

Oonagh looked round at the other girls, "That's me sorted out but what are you going to do?"

Concepta said that she could live in at the Station Hotel even though that meant she had to do extra work in the bar at night.

Rose and Fanny said they might have extra hours to work at the hat factory now the factory had gas lights. "But don't you worry about us," said Rose, "we might soon meet the men of our dreams."

All four girls slept soundly that night, but were awake at dawn in time to hear the milkman's call at four-thirty as he stopped his horse and cart at the front of Watsons' Gowns. "Milko!"

Mrs Clancy knocked at the door at seven thirty on her way to work, cleaning at the gents' outfitters. "Would you be so kind as to go for some fish for me today, Oonagh," she said, "I usually go to the fish shop at the head of the market, I want three fresh herrings, tell Peter the fishmonger that it is for me. You will eat with us won't you, my dear?" and she handed Oonagh a little leather purse.

"Yes, thank you, Mrs Clancy. I'm pleased to go for you, and I would love some fish for tea," said Oonagh. With that, Mrs Clancy scurried away to her first cleaning job of the day.

At ten o'clock, Oonagh climbed the steep steps up to the market, pulling on the metal handrail to help herself. The baby was quieter today, not as much kicking, but still she had these strange tightenings across her belly. She paused at the top of the steps and sat beside an elderly man on a bench. He had long matted hair and a grey beard. His coat was torn and dirty and he smelt badly. He was eating stale bread hungrily out of a newspaper wrapping. "It smells around here, doesn't it?" he said shuffling closer to Oonagh on the bench, "I think it's the gas works," and when he laughed, Oonagh saw that most of his teeth were missing and the remaining ones were stained brown. "This is my bed," he cackled, "it's not often I have a pretty girl sitting on my bed."

Oonagh flushed and moved to the edge of the bench then, as she stood up he said, "Ahh, I can see you've been lying on someone else's bed." Oonagh hurried away, her cheeks burning.

She passed the butcher's on the way to the fishmongers and as she passed Mr Delaney called to her, "Now then, bright eyes, where are you rushing off to?"

"A tramp has scared me and I'm going next door to the fish shop," said Oonagh.

"Of course, it's Friday," said Mr Delaney, "that accounts for the long queue next door. I have been watching for you, I have read about Seamus O'Neil in the newspaper. My wife and I have a problem that and we thought you might help us with – and we could help you in turn. Perhaps you would talk to my wife. I will give you the money for the horse tram. Would you go today?"

"I can't go today, I'm sorry, I have promised to help my neighbour, Mrs Clancy, can I go tomorrow?"

"Yes certainly," said Mr Delaney, "call in my shop first and I will give you the tram fare and instructions how to get there."

Oonagh joined the queue at the fishmongers and asked for the three herrings when it was her turn.

"There, tell Mrs Clancy, those are especially for her," said Pete the fishmonger, wrapping the fish in newspaper before putting them in Oonagh's basket.

Oonagh hurried back to the Clancy's house and Mr Clancy told her he was just desperate for a cup of tea. Oonagh made a pot of tea and poured a cup for herself and Mr Clancy then settled herself into the rocking chair to rest while she told him about her encounter with the tramp. "The poor man," said Mr Clancy, "there are many people a lot less fortunate than me," and Oonagh leaned over to stroke his hand, "shall I pour another cup for you, Mr Clancy?"

When Mrs Clancy came home in the late afternoon, she was pleased with the plump herrings that Oonagh had bought. She filleted the main bone out of the fish, rolled the fillets in oatmeal then fried them in butter. With a good chunk of bread each it made a hearty meal.

Oonagh told the Clancys that Mr Delaney had asked her to call round to see his wife. "Well, we can only offer you a room until the dragon, Mrs Watson, finds out my dear, and that wouldn't be long once the baby arrives, so best see what they offer," said Mrs Clancy.

"It may be nothing, or maybe they want me to be the sawdust sprinkler in the butcher's shop," said Oonagh with a smile.

Chapter Ten
Baby George

At nine o'clock prompt on Saturday morning, Oonagh was on the doorstep of Delaney's butcher's shop. Mr Delaney had a sheet of paper in his hand. "This is my home address, now take the horse tram from the Square towards Manchester. You will have to cross to the other side of the road. Do not go up the stairs, they are on the outside of the tram and if it rains, they can be slippery. Go inside and it is threepence fare. Ask the conductor for the new chapel stop at Heaton Chapel. When you get there cross the road from the new church and walk down the road opposite, past a big barn on the corner of the first side road and keep going. My house is painted green with a low green gate. There is a pink rose bush on either side of the gate. I have written the address down for you." Mr Delaney gave Oonagh two threepenny bits, and she made her way to Mersey Square.

There was already a queue at the tram stop. Oonagh waited at the end of the line and asked the man in front of her if the tram would be coming soon. He took a large silver watch from the pocket of his waistcoat and answered, "Two minutes."

When the tram arrived the man took Oonagh's elbow and helped her on board. Oonagh sat on the first vacant seat straightened her straw bonnet and smoothed her skirt down. When the conductor came down the tram, she paid the threepence fare and asked him if he would tell her when they reached the New Chapel. Oonagh looked through the windows as the beautiful big houses along the road became grander and grander. She imagined who might live there and if they caught the horse tram. She decided that only their servants would do that and the master and mistress would have a carriage, but then the tram stopped and a fine gentleman in a top hat and dark suit stepped on board and seated himself across the aisle from Oonagh. "Piccadilly please," he demanded of the conductor, and the conductor took his fare.

It seemed only minutes until the conductor called out, "Heaton Chapel."

Oonagh held onto the rails as she carefully made her way to the platform at the rear of the tram. The horse only stopped for just enough time for her to step down onto the footpath, the waiting passengers climbed aboard, then the conductor rang the bell, the driver flicked his whip and the tram was on its way again. Oonagh was at a crossroads and had to cross to the other side, close to a row of shops.

Oonagh made her way hurriedly down the Chapel Road and past the barn as Mr Delaney had described. Not much further on and she reached the house painted green with two beautiful pink rose bushes either side of a low gate. A short path led to an open porch with a red-tiled roof supported by wooden columns. She climbed the two low steps into the porch and lifted the brass knocker shaped like a lion's head.

Two knocks and the door opened. Mrs Delaney was a middle-aged lady about the same age as Oonagh's mother, but with smooth skin, not a wrinkle flawed her complexion. She had brown wavy hair fastened back into a pleat at the back of her head. She was wearing a long brown woollen skirt and a white blouse with a high frilled collar. Mrs Delaney had rolled up the sleeves of her blouse and her hands were floury. "Baking an apple pie for Mr Delaney," she said, "you must be Oonagh, Edward said you would be calling. Do come in my dear." And she wiped her hands on a linen towel as she led the way to the kitchen at the rear.

Oonagh stepped into the cool hallway. On the floor were beautiful tiles patterned blue and white… She followed Mrs Delaney past a big clock ticking soothingly in the hall. "Come into my kitchen," said Mrs Delaney, opening the big door at the end of the hall. The kitchen had a huge window overlooking the back garden. The room smelled of fresh linen. To Oonagh's right was a range and a smoothing iron was standing on the hotplate. Fixed to the ceiling over the range was a creel with carefully ironed bed sheets folded and draped over it to air. In the far-right hand corner beside the window was a large stone sink with a brass tap. Oonagh watched wide-eyed as Mrs Delaney turned on the tap and washed her hands before drying them and letting down the clothes rack with the waxed rope. She draped the sheet that was lying on the wooden ironing table over the rail of the clothes rack and pulled it back up again, fastening it off on the cleat on the window frame.

There was a big pine table in the middle of the kitchen, it was dusted in flour and a ball of pastry was waiting to be rolled and made into a pie. "Do you mind if I finish making the pie? You sit down my dear on the fireside chair," she said, indicating one of two chairs either side of a fireplace with a shiny maroon tiled hearth, and patterned tiles either side of the grate picturing a young girl carrying sheaves of corn.

Oonagh was grateful to sit down as Mrs Delaney rolled the pastry and lined the base of a white enamel plate that had a bright blue rim. The older lady peeled and cored the apples before slicing them and laying them neatly in the pie dish, sprinkling them with sugar and lemon juice. "These apples are the last ones out of the garden from last autumn, I keep them in the cellar wrapped in newspaper, it is so cool down there, and they are really good keepers," she said to Oonagh. After rolling the lid and sealing the top she brushed the pie with milk and put it into the oven. "Now let us have a nice cup of tea," said Mrs Delaney and she warmed the tea pot with hot water before spooning in the tea leaves. "One, two, and one for the pot," and she poured in boiling water from the kettle. "Would you like a biscuit dear?" she said and took a tin from the cupboard next to the range. She took out two small china plates and two cups and saucers with pretty turquoise flowers painted delicately on them. "There we are," Mrs Delaney said as she passed a cup of tea with a saucer and a plate with two digestive biscuits to Oonagh. "You're still carrying high," she said, "how long have you to go? Look you can balance your saucer and your plate on your bump, I would say you've a good few weeks to go yet."

Oonagh startled when she heard a baby's cry and the tea slopped into her saucer Oonagh drank the tea and poured the contents of her saucer into the pretty china cup. Mrs Delaney frowned.

"That's George, our grandson," said Mrs Delaney, and Oonagh handed her cup, saucer and plate to Mrs Delaney as the baby's cry became insistent.

She leaned forward in her seat. "Where is he?" she asked.

"Follow me," said Mrs Delaney, "I wanted to explain before you met him but I can see you have the instincts of a good mother. This way," and she led the way up four stairs onto a small platform then fourteen more treads up to the top, Oonagh counted to herself, puffing slightly as she held onto the shiny polished handrail.

"I think you're carrying a little girl," said Mrs Delaney turning back from the landing, "your bump is all up front."

"Let's hope it's not too long before I know," said Oonagh, "this baby is tiring me out now."

Baby George was lying in a cot in the front bedroom, he was red in the face and had kicked his sheets to the bottom of the cot. There was a small wooden rocking cradle on the floor. "He's just moved up to the big cot, haven't you George?" said Mrs Delaney.

"May I lift him?" asked Oonagh, then, "My goodness, he needs to have his nappy changed, no wonder he's yelling. Is the water in this jug and bowl on the chest for cleaning him up?" Mrs Delaney nodded and Oonagh set about changing his napkin. She removed the soiled napkin and dropped it into the bucket of water at the end of his cot, then laid a towel from the pile on the chest under his bottom. She poured water from the jug into the bowl and dipped a muslin cloth into the cold water. "This is going to be a bit cold, little fellow," said Oonagh to George, who was kicking his legs happily now he was free of his napkin. Mrs Delaney sat down on a stool to watch the proceedings. "It's a relief for me to have five minutes' rest," she said, "To be honest, it will be a lot better for me if George has a nurse, it's too much for me getting up two or three times in the night."

"That's right dear, thank you," said Mrs Delaney as Oonagh dried George then folded a muslin napkin into a triangle and lifting his legs by the ankles with one hand, slid the triangle beneath his bottom with her other hand. Then she brought two corners together round his waist and the other corner between his legs, fastening all three corners with a safety pin, just the way she had helped her mother with Finn. "There we are, little man, all over," she cooed pulling his nightdress back down. She washed her hands in the china bowl then passed him to his grandmother. There was a pink-velvet nursing chair in the bedroom and Mrs Delaney invited Oonagh to sit on the chair while she remained on the stool.

"George's mother was our daughter Mary. She was not much older than you I would think – twenty-one."

"I am eighteen," said Oonagh.

"Our Mary died not ten days after giving birth," continued Mrs Delaney with tears in her eyes which she dabbed with a handkerchief trimmed with lace that she had pushed up her sleeve, "Oh it was such a joyful time for us all, but Mary started with puerperal fever after the birth, the infection poisoned her blood, and our beautiful girl died, God Bless her soul. We've still not got over it, her father and I. George's daddy Theodore has a very important job in Manchester and he asked us to take George. Well, what could we say? The trouble is baby can't drink cow's milk, it is too rich and makes him sick. The doctor told us to give him goat's milk, Edward buys that from a farmer friend. But the best thing for him is mother's milk. Oonagh, have you ever heard of a 'wet nurse', dear?"

"No, not really," said Oonagh, lying George back into his cot and covering him with his sheet and blanket.

"Well sometimes," continued Mrs Delaney, "a mother makes enough milk to feed her own baby and another one, as long as she is healthy and has enough to eat, it can easily be done. Why, mothers feed twins sure enough."

Oonagh raised her eyebrows and looked directly at Mrs Delaney.

"You will soon be feeding your own baby Oonagh, in the meantime we can give George goat's milk. You could live here and eat proper food, no more scraps of meat but proper chops. Come and see the room you would have." Mrs Delaney took her hand and showed her to the other smaller bedroom at the front of the house. There was a single iron bedstead with a straw mattress but on top of that was a feather mattress. "This was Mary's bed," said Mrs Delaney. There were cool white sheets and clean, cream blankets neatly tucked in. Oonagh pulled back the golden candlewick bedspread, felt the softness of the mattress and feather pillow and sighed.

Mrs Delaney moved towards the stairs and Oonagh reached down again to smooth the clean white sheet on the soft mattress.

"I'll show you the garden," said Mrs Delaney as they made their way downstairs and to the back door. "I'll just get the apple pie out of the oven," she said, and the warm sweet smell of the pie wafted through the house.

Down the two steps to the garden Oonagh followed Mrs Delaney. At the bottom of the garden was a brick shed. "That's the lavatory," said Mrs Delaney.

"Is it for all the houses in the road?" asked Oonagh.

"Gracious no, just for us," said Mrs Delaney, "and the night-soil man comes down this lane at the back to collect the waste while we sleep."

Oonagh looked back at the house and realised it was joined on one side to the house next door. "Yes," said Mrs Delaney, "we have neighbours adjoining us on that side, very nice people they are, Mr Cowan is the manager of the printing works down in Reddish. It's another reason why we need a nurse. I do not want our baby waking the neighbours at night."

"Well, what do you think my dear? Shall we say you will move in next week?"

Oonagh looked once more at the lavatory. "Yes please, but it will only be until my Seamus is free again and I promised to help Mr Clancy for a week. Also I don't know when my milk will be ready."

"Let's not worry about that just now, let's get you healthy," said Mrs Delaney, "So a week today then, Saturday? Oh and I forgot to tell you but we will give you a shilling pocket money every week. I would advise you to save it, there is a Manchester and Salford savings bank at the top of the road near the tram stop. Some savings will come in handy for your little one, as it grows. And Oonagh, please be prepared. Mr Delaney has spoken to lots of customers in the shop who think that Seamus may be found guilty of manslaughter, if that is the case, my dear, he just may be transported, but that is thinking the very worse, I am just preparing you but in the meantime we will care for you. Now be very careful on the horse tram and don't be tempted to go up on the top. The sky is darkening and we may have rain."

Oonagh said her goodbyes to the butcher's wife, promising to see her the next week, passed between the two perfumed rose bushes and made her way back to the top of the road to await the horse-tram back to Stockport. The tram was full but one middle-aged man stood and offered Oonagh his seat. Oonagh blushed as she thanked him, and as she sat down she grasped her left hand with her right hand, covering her bare fingers. Huge spots of rain were bouncing on the warm paving stones when Oonagh stepped off the tram in Stockport, she swiftly made her way to Watsons' Court afraid that the soles of her boots would come completely adrift if they became soaked.

"Now tell us all about it," said Mrs Clancy, as Oonagh sank down into the rocking chair, and she told them about Mrs Delaney's offer.

"Mr Clancy has had a friend round from the railway today and he brought some newspapers with him that had been left on the train. He read some of the Liverpool paper to Henry but there is more for you to read this week, Oonagh, to Mr Clancy. Do you know they are advertising for people to go to Australia, you can earn seven or eight shillings a day there, for doing charring in some of the big houses? But I don't think we can go, not with Henry as he is. The sea passage would be too much for him, although it doesn't take so long now, I think I would be sea sick, but my Henry would soon get a job, they've got railways there now."

"It's good to dream," said Oonagh, "and who knows, once Mr Clancy is well again?"

"Do you like tripe and onions?" said Mrs Clancy, "It's Henry's favourite, isn't that so, Henry? I'll make some mashed potatoes and carrots to go with it."

"Yes," said Oonagh, turning away and clasping her hand to her mouth, "I look forward to trying that, thank you Mrs Clancy, and carrots will be good."

Oonagh managed to eat the tripe and onions by shutting her eyes and swallowing hard, "Mrs Delaney told me I will be having proper chops when I move in with the family, with Mr Delaney being a butcher, not that I'm not grateful for your dinners Mrs Clancy, they have been delicious."

"We are glad things are working out well for you dear," said Mr Clancy, nodding his head.

"I've still got a week here with you to read your newspapers to you," said Oonagh.

"You will have to read the page that says they are needing farmers in Victoria, farmers with experience in dairy and wheat. They need to feed the growing population, so many more people are emigrating, a lot are going from Ireland, it's not just for convicts,"

"Australia is a land of opportunity, so it is," said Mr Clancy.

"We'll talk about it tomorrow then, Mr Clancy," said Oonagh, "Mrs Delaney said they might send my Seamus there, that will help with the food situation in Australia, there isn't much he doesn't know about farming. I think I'll go to bed now, this baby is making me tired, wriggling about so much, and I've had quite a day."

"That's a good sign, Oonagh, that your baby is wriggling, it shows it's healthy," said Mrs Clancy, "Good night now, lass."

The next morning Oonagh awoke to the sound of St Mary's bells calling her congregation to Morning Praise. Mr and Mrs Clancy were already in the kitchen and Mrs Clancy was preparing breakfast. "Would you like a boiled egg, Oonagh?" she asked.

"You have been so kind to me Mrs Clancy, how can I ever repay you?" said Oonagh.

"It's a big help for me, you being with Henry while I go out to work," said Mrs Clancy, "and he is so much happier with you for company, you are like one of our own. We thank God for you. To tell the truth Father Kelly asked us to watch out for you, and talking about Father Kelly, would you like a little walk up to St Philip's for the morning service?"

"Yes, that would be good, I want to speak about the funeral, I hope my aunt and uncle have managed to get word back," said Oonagh, helping herself to a cup of tea.

After breakfast Mr Clooney went into the front parlour while Oonagh had a wash in the sink in the scullery. Then Oonagh put on her best white blouse and her grey fustian skirt (the only skirt she owned). Mrs Clancy had stuffed old newspaper into Oonagh's boots and left them by the range to dry out.

When the three were ready, they set off at a gentle pace for church. Mr Clancy leaning heavily on his stick, Mrs Clancy supporting him on his stroke affected side and both stopping frequently to catch their breath. Mrs Clancy was wearing her best straw bonnet and Oonagh tied a blue headscarf over long strawberry blonde hair out of respect, before she entered the church.

The sidesman handed them a hymn book to share, one of the few books that had been saved from the vandalism. The once beautiful east window was boarded up but a glazier had already started work on a new window. The theme, Mr Clancy whispered to Oonagh, was to be 'The Light of the World'.

Mrs Flaherty's arrangement of lilies on the improvised altar table was a successful attempt to give glory to God using the beautiful gifts of nature that He gave to the world.

After the service the priest invited the Clancys and Oonagh to take tea with him at the presbytery. All three gladly accepted. Father Kelly ushered them into the parlour and indicated for Oonagh to sit in the worn brown leather sofa. Mrs Clancy shook a soft cushion and, gently taking Oonagh's shoulder, pulled her forward, slipping the cushion in the small of Oonagh's back. The priest's housekeeper had prepared some sandwiches and made scones which she brought into the parlour on a wooden tray along with butter and homemade strawberry jam. She laid the food on a small mahogany table on which she had spread a white cloth with lace edges. The housekeeper returned to the kitchen with the tray and returned with cups, saucers and tea plates in the finest china and a large pot of tea. The little party gathered around the table, sitting on the carved mahogany chairs upholstered in maroon and cream striped material. Mrs Clancy took over and poured the tea, Oonagh passed the bowl of sugar cubes around and each person added cubes of sugar to their cup, using the dainty silver sugar tongs. The sandwiches of cold cooked ham were delicious and the scones were still warm. Father Kelly's housekeeper popped in to ask if anyone would like a piece of her homemade Dundee cake.

Henry Clancy's eyes lit up. "What a feast we are being treated to, missus," he said to his wife, and she agreed. "You've got a diamond there, Father, my Henry's not had fruit cake in months, it's like Christmas," and turning to Oonagh, "I buy a Christmas cake from your friend, Mrs Jenkins, on the market, my oven gets much too hot, I can't bake in it, everything burns, and the Watsons charge us all that rent."

"Changing the subject, Father, will we hear in time from my family about the funeral, do you think?" said Oonagh. The priest answered that sister Bernadette was returning on Monday as she was helping to set up another Magdalene home in Eccles. "Sister Bernadette promised to call here with Mr and Mrs Mahon's response. I will call on you at Watsons' Court tomorrow evening, if that is convenient, but I have reserved Wednesday morning in my diary and Mrs Flaherty is arranging for flowers for the coffin. White lilies, I thought my dear." Oonagh nodded as the reality of her loss struck her again.

"Would you like me to take these dishes through to the kitchen, Father?" said Oonagh stacking the dishes onto the tray, "We had better not leave it too late to go home, it looks as if it might rain again and Mr Clancy can't walk very fast through those raindrops."

"Won't be long before I'm back to my old self though," said Henry Clancy with a knowing wink to his wife.

Oonagh took the dishes through to the kitchen. "Just leave them by the sink for Mrs Jamieson in the morning," said Father Kelly.

Oonagh and the Clancys thanked Father Kelly warmly for his hospitality as they left the presbytery and made their way down the path to the front gate. "Bless you, it's good to have some company," said the priest.

"Well, you're always welcome to come for a Sunday roast Father," said Mrs Clancy, "just as soon as Henry is back at work, things have been a little difficult, as I told Oonagh, we couldn't have managed if I hadn't had those cleaning jobs we would have had to go in the workhouse."

"God bless you for taking Oonagh in, you will get your rewards," said Father Kelly.

"Just holding this baby when it is born will be enough reward for me," replied Mrs Clancy, giving Oonagh a hug. The three made slow progress home to Watsons' Court but at least the rain held off.

As they passed in front of Watsons' shop, Mrs Watson was at the window of her flat, peering up and down the street. "We've been rumbled," said Mr Clancy, "so as much as we will miss you, it's lucky you have a new home to go to on Saturday."

Chapter Eleven
It's in the News

All three were not long out of bed that evening, the walk to and from church had been good exercise for them all and it had been a long eventful day.

The following morning, Oonagh awoke to the chime of five from the bells of St Mary's church. She could hear Mrs Clancy down in the kitchen. As Oonagh came down the stairs into the kitchen, Mrs Clancy was coming back in the front door with her husband's chamber pot in her hand. "I've just been to empty this, it's not fair to expect you to," she said.

Oonagh bent to empty the ash pan in the range fire. "Now what do you want me to do today?" she asked.

"Could you buy some lambs' liver from your butcher, please? Seven slices should be enough, Henry will eat three and two each for you and I, will that be enough for you? I have onions and potatoes. Now could you make porridge for Henry's breakfast? Although some say it heats the blood too much."

"I don't think so," said Oonagh, "I'll make it half milk, half water."

"Well, I know Henry is looking forward to you reading to him," said the older lady and leaving the leather purse with Oonagh, Norah Clancy called goodbye to her husband and closed the door behind her.

Oonagh lit the range fire and the porridge was ready for Mr Clancy when he came through to the kitchen. "Cup of tea, Mr Clancy?" said Oonagh, straining the tea into Mr Clancy's outsized china cup.

Then she spooned the porridge into a dish and sprinkled it with sugar. "I would rather have syrup," said Henry. "I couldn't find any, I'll remind your wife," replied Oonagh and scraped the pan out for herself. "Shall we continue with the Liverpool newspaper?"

"No, Pete brought a Derby paper, can you have a read through that to me, there are probably more places I know in there. I used to drive the Buxton to Manchester train."

Oonagh picked up the Derbyshire Courier. "19 July 1851," she began and scanned through the pages. "Oh, there's something about the Pilsley wakes and a grass snake here."

"Pilsley, yes, I know that village," said Henry Clancy, perking up.

"The paper is dated a couple of weeks ago," read Oonagh, "It has been Pilsley wakes and tap-dressing or well-dressing as they have in Tissington. There was a temporary pavilion erected by the innkeeper and dinners were provided at a cost of one shilling per head. A party of bellringers from Mottram attended. They played a total of 42 handbells, and as many inhabitants of Matlock Bath attended."

"Matlock Bath, yes I know Matlock Bath," said Mr Clancy, nodding.

"There was dancing well into the evening," continued Oonagh, "but now comes the interesting bit, a large common grass snake had been caught and apparently killed by the villagers and they had formed the reptile into the Duke's crest."

"That will be the Duke of Devonshire from Chatsworth Hall," interrupted Mr Clancy.

"The villagers formed the reptile into the Duke's crest and placed it in damp clay in an ornamental device composed of flowers and crystals etc., but it turned out the snake was only 'scotched' not killed and when the sun came out it glided off, displacing some of the delicately arranged finery by which it was surrounded." Mr Clancy shook laughing. "Can you just picture that, Oonagh, I expect those inhabitants of Matlock Bath were scared half out of their wits while they were eating their dinner at the tables, to see a snake festooned with flower petals sliding across the ground towards them as they tucked into their roast beef dinner and the bellringers will have been thrown off the tune." Tears rolled down his cheeks with laughing. "Oonagh, you're a tonic, I haven't laughed like that since my stroke. Make another cup of tea, there's a good lass."

Henry Clancy's mirth was contagious, and Oonagh had to excuse herself. "I'll be back in a moment, I need the privy now," she managed to say, wiping her eyes and blowing her nose.

"Yes, we had best have a break, Mr Clancy, because I think we will be upset at this next report," said Oonagh, filling the kettle with fresh water when she returned, topping up the tea pot when it boiled.

She poured them both another cup of tea and resumed reading the paper.

"A serious accident occurred on Monday last to a little girl named Gabbitas, belonging to the Dames infant school, it was caused, it is to be feared, to a great measure by a shameful and reprehensible practice of conductors of vehicles driving into the town at a very improper speed. '*From enquiries we have made,*' the reporter says, '*it appears the little girl in question and others belonging to the schools were amusing themselves on the North Road near the Marketplace, when a vehicle containing three men was seen approaching at a fast rate. The child saw the danger and endeavoured to get out of the way but in her fright, fell down. The horse was upon her in an instant and one of its hooves, falling upon the lower part of the face, crushed the jawbone and broke in the mouth in a shocking manner: and one of the wheels, passing over the neck and shoulders, inflicted severe injuries.*

"'*The little girl was apparently immediately conveyed to the surgery of P. Whitington Esquire who promptly attended to the case and did all that he would admit of,*' but the reporter concludes, Mr Clancy, by writing that: '*we regret to state that the child still lays in a very precarious state*'."

Oonagh sat down and drank the rest of her tea. "Well, that poor wee girl, that is just terrible, do you think those men will go to prison, Mr Clancy? Because, if my Seamus is in prison for doing nothing, and they are free, there is no justice in this country."

"Yes, child, you are right," said Mr Clancy, "but please do not upset yourself, it just isn't good for you or your baby. Is there nothing else a little lighter in the newspaper?"

"There is a case here about a servant of the Midland Railway, who was charged with stealing four gallons of whiskey and four gallons of spruce beer, being taken from Nicholson's distillery to Mr Perkins of Heanor."

"What was the man's name?" asked Henry Clancy.

"John Bailey was his name, do you know him?" asked Oonagh.

"The name sounds familiar, what has happened to him?"

"Committed to the Assizes," answered Oonagh, "will that be in Chester too?"

"No, it will be in Derby," said Henry. "But more importantly, has he saved me a dram?" and he winked at Oonagh. "Don't tell my Norah I said that, will you?"

"I wouldn't dream of it," said Oonagh, "but enough talk of stolen whiskey, I have to buy some liver for tea," and she picked up her shawl and basket, "Now you behave while I'm out, be very careful when you go to the privy, the yard is still wet where Norah had swilled it with disinfectant, I won't be long." And, once more, Oonagh struggled up the steps to the Market place.

The tramp was sitting on the bench again, he was very wet. "Spare a penny, miss," he called to her, but Oonagh clutched Mrs Clancy's purse tightly to her and hurried by.

The vegetable stall was selling stew packs of carrot onion and turnip and the two customers in the butchers asked for stewing meat. It was a hot pot day with this drizzling rain.

"Good morning, bright eyes," said Mr Delaney, "well, you have made a really good impression on my wife. I believe you are moving in on Saturday, it's going to be a big help for her – and for you I hope. What can I get for you this morning?"

Oonagh asked for the lamb's liver and the butcher popped an extra slice in the paper after he had weighed it. "That slice is for the baby," he said, "and here is your tram fare for Saturday." He gave Oonagh a threepenny bit which she put in her pocket, and paid for the liver out of the purse.

Concerned about Mr Clancy, Oonagh didn't dally but made her way straight back to Watsons' Court. "I haven't left this seat," said Henry. "But I'm getting impatient to get back to normal."

"Just relax and rest," said Oonagh, "I will read to you again. Now here is something that will interest you:

"Accident at Kiveton Park Station." Henry Clancy sat up straight in his chair as Oonagh continued.

"On Wednesday morning, an accident happened at Kiveton Park station on the Manchester, Sheffield and Lincolnshire Railway, to the train which leaves Worksop at 6.34 a.m. It happened that the train, on arriving at the station, ran against two coal wagons which had been very improperly left upon the line by the porter, whose duty it was to have placed them on a sideline. We are happy to say that beyond the fright and a shaking of the passengers, and the breakage done to the coal wagons, which are rendered totally unfit for use, no further injury was done.

"The porter has been suspended from duty until a thorough investigation has been made into the matter."

"You see," said Mr Clancy, "that's what happens when they don't train enough drivers. I mean, expecting a porter to move those wagons, it's a skilled job. It's all about profit for the railway company and the shareholders, and now that poor man has been suspended. What will he and his family live on? And they complain the Workhouses are full. What is a working man supposed to do? I mean here's me – I can't even read the newspaper for myself. The only reading I was taught was the Bible at Sunday school taught by the rector. Those kiddies up at Tuxford that you read about, will go to the Dame School, that's provided by the Lady of the Manor. We need a proper education for all children in this country, rich and poor."

"I think I would prefer to read something that cheers you up," said Oonagh, "how about this one: The case of Mr Butler who stole an innkeeper's hat in Long Eaton. He has been committed to the Assizes."

"What sort of hat was it?" said Henry, "A bowler hat, a top hat, a bonnet?"

"It doesn't say," said Oonagh. "It doesn't even say if it fitted Mr Butler, or if the colour suited him."

"Poor reporting," said Henry with a laugh.

"That's more like it," said Oonagh, "I'll get on with peeling the potatoes for Mrs Clancy, you should have a little nap, we've had enough merriment for today."

By the time Norah Clancy came home from work, Oonagh had prepared the vegetables and tidied the kitchen. "Cup of tea, Mrs Clancy?" "Mr Clancy has been fast asleep for a good three hours. I prepared some bread and cheese for him a couple of hours ago but I didn't want to wake him. Here I've put a plate on top, it's in the cupboard, would you like it with a cup of tea now?"

"You did right not to wake him," said Mrs Clancy, "you are a thoughtful girl, Oonagh, so caring and sensible. Now, did you buy the liver for me?"

"Yes," said Oonagh, "and Mr Delaney gave me an extra piece free of charge, for the baby."

Mr Clancy stirred and yawned stretching his unaffected arm and leg while his stroke affected hand tightened into a fist.

"Ooh, have we laughed today, Norah! Oonagh has been a real treat, I was crying laughing, really I was. I think I am ready for a cup of tea now Oonagh. Was I sleeping with my mouth open? I am really dry."

Oonagh made a pot of tea and poured them all a cup. "I've prepared the vegetables, we won't have to be too late eating tea, Father Kelly is calling round remember."

"Would you like me to come with you to the funeral tomorrow, Oonagh? I think it will be too much for Henry but you can't go on your own. There won't be many there, will there? So it isn't as if there is going to be a big wake, just the service and the burial. We can invite the Father back here for a bite to eat, I'll go up to Jenkins first thing and buy some pies and I can leave one for Henry. Is that to your liking?"

Oonagh thanked Mrs Clancy and reminded her that the priest had said the funeral would come out of church funds because of all the help they had given at St Philip's.

"So that settles it," said Mrs Clancy.

Father Kelly arrived at half past seven, "Father Murphy sends his respects, Oonagh," he called before he was even over the threshold, he remembers yourself and Michael well. 'Inseparable' was his description. He called on Mr and Mrs Mahon and they were shocked and upset as would be expected. You were right, they cannot afford to travel over here at the moment, things are not much better over in Ireland, although they can at least get bread now with the repeal of the Corn Laws. But having the money to buy the bread is another thing when all the potato crop has been ruined by the blight. They say they leave it in your hands Oonagh, they know how you loved Michael, and they will come to visit his grave soon. They asked for lilies for the coffin, which Mrs Flaherty was arranging for us with her florist."

"We have just been saying Father, would you like to come here after the committal at the cemetery, there will only be a few of us," said Mrs Clancy.

"Yes, that would be good. Is there anything else you would like to ask me?" replied the priest.

"Just one thing, Father," said Oonagh, "would it be fitting if I sang '*The Meeting of the Waters*' in church for Michael? Just the last two verses. After the service, we go straight to the graveyard, for the burial, and the service is at 10.30? Do the undertakers know that, Father?"

"Yes," said the priest, "I shall send the funeral carriage to collect you both in good time. And I repeat, don't worry about the cost, the church will pay."

After the priest had left, Oonagh said, "Well, I think I'll go up to my bed, are you going to tell your wife about the snake that came back from the dead, Mr Clancy? Goodnight to you both now and God bless." And Oonagh climbed the stairs. The rain was still drizzling down her bedroom window as she blew out her candle and fell asleep.

St Mary's Church bells were chiming six o'clock and the sun was trying hard to break through the clouds when Oonagh first opened her eyes. For a moment she thought it was Michael's funeral today, she just wanted to get it over with now, but the funeral was tomorrow, Wednesday. Oonagh listened as the church bell struck the final chime and she wondered how she would tell the time in the night at the Delaney house. Only four more days to go and she would no longer be living in Watsons' Court.

She heard the familiar *clip clop* of horseshoes on the cobbles. Pulling on her dress then pulling up her stockings and fastening them to her suspenders, she pushed her feet into her worn-out boots and crept downstairs. The kitchen was empty and Oonagh slipped quietly out of the front door. The coal wagon was painted red with green lettering across the side 'Cephas Linney, High Class Coal Merchant, Heaton Mersey'. Mr Linney was at the back of his wagon; he turned his broad back to a sack of coal and with arms stretched above his head, he grasped two corners of the top of the sack and tilted the hundredweight of coal against the leather waistcoat on his back.

Moving to the cellar chute, he bent forward and tipped the coal over his head and down the chute. A cloud of coal dust rose around his head and a couple of shiny black coals fell onto the cobbles. Oonagh darted forward and picked up the two coals and handed them to the coal merchant. "You have dropped these, Mr Linney."

"Thank you, ma'am," he said, and threw the coals down the chute into Mrs Watson's cellar.

Oonagh turned and went back through the Clancys' front door.

As she slipped quietly back into the house, her cousin, Michael, was cutting a chunk of bread from a loaf on the table and spreading it with dripping from the brown dish.

"There's no tea in the pot, Oonagh," he said.

"No, Michael, there was no coal for the range," replied Oonagh. "You had better run now, Michael."

"Who were you speaking to, Oonagh?" said Norah Clancy coming out of the parlour and over to where Oonagh was sitting in the rocking chair.

"It was Michael, but he's gone now," said Oonagh, lifting her tear stained face, and burying it in Norah's ample bosom as the older woman stroked her hair lovingly, "There now, my darlin', you wait till you have that baby in your arms, your baby will make you strong, so very strong. Shall I make you a nice cup of tea?"

Oonagh spent the rest of Tuesday morning searching out stories from the papers to amuse Mr Clancy and they walked together down the street, when the rain passed over and the sun made an appearance.

"It's all strengthening that weak leg," said Oonagh, "you should try to do this every day, but perhaps not on your own, maybe wait until Norah gets home."

"Norah and I are really going to miss you," said Henry squeezing her hand. "There, did you feel that? There's feeling coming into my weak hand. That's with your help, that is."

Oonagh kissed his cheek, "I hope so, Mr Clancy, that I really do."

Chapter Twelve
Sweet Vale of Avoca! How Calm Could I Rest

It was a calm day on Wednesday, cloudy but warm. Mrs Clancy wore her best black coat and a black felt hat that she had bought on the market. Oonagh borrowed Norah's black lace shawl that she tied around her head. The carriage arrived at ten o'clock and Mrs Clancy was still leaving warnings and instructions for her husband, "Help yourself to one of those pies I have bought from Mrs Jenkins. By the way, Oonagh, she let me have them at a good price and she sends her love to you. Now be careful, Henry, if you have to go up the yard. Use your chamber pot, we won't be too long," and she bustled down Watsons' Court to the carriage.

They arrived at church in good time and waited for the hearse at the gate. Father Kelly had certainly not economised for the funeral and the coffin arrived in a carriage pulled by a splendid black horse with a plume on its head. The florist had provided enough white lilies to virtually cover the coffin lid and the perfume filled the air as the undertakers carried Michael's coffin on their shoulders into St Philip's Church and rested it in the chancel.

Mrs Clancy took Oonagh's elbow as they followed the coffin up the aisle. Rose and Fanny, their heads covered with black scarves had managed to take a few hours off from the hat factory to pay their respects to Michael. They were sitting a few rows back from the front of the chancel with Concepta, who was wearing a black hat with a veil that a woman who worked in the kitchens at the Station Hotel had lent her. She too had just slipped out of work for a couple of hours and the other chambermaids were covering for her. Oonagh also spotted Mr and Mrs Costello, the landlord and his wife from the Admiral Nelson public house. Mrs Flaherty was sitting with a few other members of the congregation. Oonagh could feel her belly tightening and then relaxing, and with her free hand she touched her belly beneath her ribs on her right-hand side. She could feel a foot (or was it a knee?). No she could feel the baby's head pressing down between her legs so it must be a foot at the top under her ribs. "Shush now, go back to sleep," she whispered and pressed on the foot, but her baby carried on stretching until Oonagh and Mrs Clancy finally seated themselves on the front pew and baby seemed to fall asleep after all the exercise.

Father Kelly read the first prayer for the service from the prayer book and then led the congregation in singing The Lord's prayer. The priest asked Oonagh if she still would like to sing. Oonagh rose and stepped up the two steps into the chancel. She put one hand on Michael's coffin to steady herself and, with no musical accompaniment from Tom Finnegan this time, she sang the penultimate verse of Thomas Moore's poem. Her tears began as she sang the last line, "When we see them reflected from those that we love." Her head went down as she grasped the coffin with both hands and both Father Kelly and Mrs Clancy stepped forward.

Mrs Clancy took her arm, "Come and sit beside me now my darlin'," and she gave Oonagh the handkerchief that she had tucked into her pocket.

"I will recite the last verse for you now," said Father Kelly gently, but Oonagh shook her head and sang the last verse. "I had to do that for Michael," she whispered as she stepped down to the pew and sat next to Mrs Clancy. Oonagh remained seated while the congregation knelt and the priest prayed for Michael's soul. "Amen," she echoed. Father Kelly spoke of Michael's childhood and incidents that his parents had obviously conveyed via Father Murphy.

Oonagh's belly was still tightening and then relaxing as she walked back down the aisle and was greeted with loving embraces from her three former housemates, who excused themselves as they had to get back to work. Mr and Mrs Costello gave their condolences before asking if she knew when the trial was to be in Chester, as Mr Costello had to give evidence. Oonagh replied that she thought it would be in the next two weeks but didn't know for sure.

The congregation followed Oonagh out of the south door and each in turn took her hand and gave their condolences. Mrs Flaherty confided that she had knitted a lemon matinee coat for the baby and was on with the bootees. "I will only just finish them in time from the look of you," she said, "that little one will be here sooner than you think, it has dropped I'm sure it has, do you want a little girl? Because that's what you will have, it seems to me." And she squeezed Oonagh's hand warmly. "I hope all goes well for you, child, it's soon over hopefully, and all pain is forgotten once you have that baby in your arms. You be careful, my darling." Oonagh smiled at the elderly lady and asked if she was coming to the cemetery, because she was sure she could squash in the carriage with them. Oonagh was helped by the priest and Mrs Clancy into the funeral carriage before they and Mrs Flaherty climbed aboard and the carriage followed the hearse, with Michael's coffin back onboard, to Stockport cemetery.

As they travelled slowly up the road, women stopped and bowed their heads out of respect, gentlemen removed their hats, holding them in front of their chests until the cortege had passed, small children genuflected and recited, "Touch your head, touch your toes, never go in one of those." At the cemetery the carriages stopped close to the newly dug grave and the funeral directors lifted Michael's coffin out of the hearse while Oonagh and the little group moved to the graveside. Mrs Flaherty held one of Oonagh's arms, but Mrs Clancy had everything under control and holding Oonagh's other arm, she checked every one of Oonagh's footsteps on the damp grass. Mrs Flaherty took one of the lilies from the coffin flowers which the funeral directors had laid at the head of the grave. Handing it to Oonagh she quietly said, "For you to give, my darling'." When the priest had recited the committal prayers, Oonagh kissed the flower and tossed it onto her beloved cousin's coffin followed by a handful of dirt, and with her head bowed, she quietly said her own private prayer for Michael.

"Will you be requiring the carriage to take you back home?" said the funeral director to the priest.

"Yes, I should think so, with the young lady heavy with child," said Father Kelly.

The little group climbed aboard once more and the carriage took them back to Watsons' Court.

Mr Clancy had laid the table with his wife's finest cloth and china.

"I hope you've been careful, Henry, but well done," said Norah as she warmed the pies. "Now then, would everyone like a slice of meat pie?" And she handed round the plates with a generous slice of meat pie on each. Oonagh was surprisingly hungry and very tired as she rocked back and forth on her chair in time with the tightenings of her belly and the kicking of her baby. The rocking seemed to calm the baby down and Oonagh yawned as her heavy eyelids began to droop.

Twenty minutes later, Mrs Clancy gently roused Oonagh, patting her on the cheek, "Oonagh, Father Kelly and Mrs Flaherty are leaving now."

Oonagh tried hard to open her eyes, "What? Who is leaving?" she mumbled, her mouth was dry and the tightenings across her belly had been replaced by a strong pain at the base between her legs. "Ooh, Mrs Clancy, I think I am in labour." Mrs Clancy stroked her forehead, "Keep calm, my pet, you may just need the privy, come on I'll take you. Henry, can you manage to make our girl a cup of tea?"

The priest and Mrs Flaherty said their farewells as Norah Clancy helped Oonagh up the yard.

"I think it will be best if we get you to Mrs Delaney's," said Norah as they came back in, "she seems to have everything ready for you and baby, once you have had this cup of tea, I will take you up there."

"Oh no, there is no need to trouble yourself," said Oonagh, but Mrs Clancy was insistent.

"It's no trouble pet, I can't let you go on that tram alone, and I want her to know what a diamond she will be getting."

Oonagh drank her tea while Mrs Clancy gathered together the few items of clothing that Oonagh possessed, folding them into her basket.

Leaning heavily on Mrs Clancy, Oonagh crossed the square with her to the horse tram stop on the main road. There was already a queue of some ten people travelling home from work but Oonagh and Mrs Clancy managed to board the first tram that came and there were two seats vacant near the entrance. "The pains are coming stronger and stronger, Mrs Clancy," said Oonagh.

"Keep taking really deep breaths and try to relax. Don't tense yourself," said the older lady.

"Mrs Clancy, have you had any babies?" asked Oonagh.

"No, not me personally," said Norah, "but I have five sisters who have, and I was with them all when they delivered their babies."

Past the fine houses along the main road went the horse tram, then suddenly came to a halt. Mrs Clancy stood up to see what the hold-up was. "Oh no, they are mending the tram lines! But don't panic, I think they are packing up for the day, yes I'm right," and the horse began to amble on again.

"Heaton Chapel," called the conductor and Mrs Clancy took Oonagh's arm and helped her to her feet. As they left the tram and started to cross the road, Oonagh confided to Mrs Clancy, "Oh, dear, I fear I have wet my bloomers, my legs are wet."

"Don't you worry, my pet, it's your waters that have broken, have we far to go down this road?"

"Not too far, past this barn on the corner and about six houses after that. The house with the green door and gate. Oh and Mrs Clancy, I have a threepenny piece in my pocket for the tram fare that Mr Delaney gave me."

"Now don't you bother your head about that, it was my treat," said Norah Clancy, "Is this the house?" And she bustled up the path between the sweet-smelling roses and knocked urgently on the door.

Mrs Delaney opened the door immediately. She had been sweeping the stair carpet with a hand brush. "Oonagh! I thought we agreed Saturday, but this is a lovely surprise, and this lady is, I presume, Mrs Clancy?"

"Yes, I am," said Norah, helping Oonagh into the house, "and Oonagh is in labour, straight upstairs then?"

"I think that would be best, yes," said Mrs Delaney, "Are you sure it isn't a false alarm?"

"No," said Norah Clancy. "I've helped enough babies into this world to know, and anyway her waters have broken."

"Well, I'd better run 'round to Nelstrop Road to fetch the midwife then," and Mrs Delaney pulled on her coat from the peg on the wall near the front door, grabbed her hat from the hat stand and rushed out pulling the door shut behind her.

Oonagh showed Mrs Clancy where her room was.

"Ooh look here, Oonagh, she's laid out a beautiful nightdress for you," said Norah, "let me help you into it, darlin'."

"It will have been Maria's nightdress," said Oonagh, "remember I told you, their daughter who died after having George. Ooh I'm feeling I want to push down."

"Well don't just now," said Norah, "let's wait for the midwife if you can, can we get you on the bed? Look, Mrs Delaney has even put a rubber sheet on the mattress and towels on top, let's get this nightdress over your head." And Mrs Clancy helped Oonagh on to the comfortable bed just as Mrs Delaney called from downstairs, "It's alright now; I've got Sarah Land with me now."

And Mrs Delaney rushed up the stairs with the midwife close behind. "Oh good, you found the nightdress I put out for you."

"I want to push the baby out now," said Oonagh.

"Let me see now," said Mrs Land. "Put your knees up and let them relax like this," and she widened Oonagh's legs, "Yes your waters have broken alright and I can see the top of your baby's head, a mop of black hair it has, go on then, love...push next time you feel that contraction, push hard right down into your bottom."

George started to cry and Oonagh said, "You see to George, Mrs Delaney, I'll be fine." Mrs Delaney left the other two women to help Oonagh and went to warm some goat's milk for her grandson. "You'll soon be having real mummy's milk," she whispered in his ear; when she returned to lift him from the cot and then pressed the teat of his bottle to his lips. "Now that will be better, won't it, my precious boy."

Oonagh was shouting in the other room. "I don't want to frighten baby George," she said to Mrs Clancy.

"You are doing so well, my darlin'," said Norah, rubbing Oonagh's leg that was closest to her, "you're doing so well, isn't she, Mrs Land?"

"Yes, she is," said Sarah Land, "another big push for me now, Oonagh. There we are, your baby's head is out." And Mrs Land concentrated on easing the shoulders out. "Now we are nearly there, some big pushes now and we'll see what is what."

Oonagh grasped hold of Mrs Clancy, and Mrs Clancy lifted Oonagh's head and shoulders and held her close. "Another almighty push and there we are," said Sarah Land, "there, you have a beautiful daughter! Congratulations grandmother!"

"Oh no!" said Mrs Clancy, "Though I wish I was."

Mrs Land cut the cord and tied it off at baby's tummy with a strong yarn. The baby had still not cried to let the first breaths into her lungs. Mrs Land held her by the ankles and gave her a sharp slap on the bottom. The baby girl let out a yell and Mrs Clancy and Mrs Land looked at each other and smiled. Mrs Delaney came into the room now with a bowl of warm water. "Little George has fallen asleep again," she said, "you were so quick, thank heavens, Oonagh, and so restrained, I was much noisier when I had my Maria, I screamed the house down."

The midwife bathed the baby in the warm water and wrapped her in a small cotton sheet once she had dried her on a towel.

"She is so beautiful, isn't she?" said Oonagh, "And she looks so much like my Seamus."

"And such a mop of black hair," said Mrs Delaney, "didn't you have terrible heartburn, my dear?"

"Not with my cooking," said Mrs Clancy.

Mrs Land produced a pair of brass scales from her bag, made baby's sheet into a sling and hung the sling from a hook on the scales. "Six pound eight ounces," she declared.

"Now, you can put baby to your breast as soon as you like, it will encourage your milk to come through, but don't worry, it will take a day or two, eat well and drink plenty," and the midwife looked round at Oonagh's two mums, Mrs Delaney and Mrs Clancy.

Mrs Delaney nodded and said, "Yes, Sarah, I'll take good care of her, will you be coming 'round tomorrow?" "Yes," said the midwife, "I'll pop round to see how mother is."

Mrs Land went downstairs with the baby's bath water and returned with the empty bowl to put the afterbirth into once she had delivered it. "There now, my lovelies, I'll have to leave you now, shall I leave this in your kitchen for you to dispose of, Mrs Delaney?"

"Yes, thank you for everything, drop the bill round and my husband will pay."

"It will be half a crown for the delivery and a florin for any more visits," said Mrs Land, "I have had all my training, you know."

As Mrs Land stepped into the hall, Mr Delaney was coming through the front door. "Congratulations, Grandpa, you have a beautiful baby granddaughter, six and a half pounds – ideal weight for a girl – and she has the loveliest blue eyes I have ever seen!"

"Thank you," said Mr Delaney, "that is wonderful news."

"Kathleen," he called upstairs, "I expect you would like a cup of tea!"

"Lovely, yes," replied Mrs Delaney, "make that three, we have a visitor, Mrs Clancy, and I think Oonagh will be ready for a hot drink, is that not right, Oonagh? But if you wait a moment, dear, I will come down and make it myself, you have been working all day."

Mrs Clancy and Mrs Delaney both kissed Oonagh and went towards the door. "I won't be staying long now, my dear," said Mrs Clancy, blowing the baby a last kiss. "I must get home and cook Henry's tea, and, of course, tell him your good news, but I will come to see you as soon as I can and I expect Henry will want to see you and the baby for himself."

"Thank you, Mrs Clancy, you have been so good to me," said Oonagh lying back on her feather pillow with her baby girl still in her arms. Mrs Delaney crept into George's bedroom and carried the crib back in for Oonagh's little one. "There are two blankets here for the baby and a couple of nightdresses that George has grown too large for."

She went downstairs to the kitchen but returned very soon with a cup of tea and a digestive biscuit for Oonagh. "Well, that was all of a rush, one minute I was sweeping the stair carpet, the next, a baby arrives into this world. What a wonderful surprise, and I am so happy all has gone well for you," and she hugged Oonagh again and kissed her on the cheek. "Could you eat something nice for your tea? Mr Delaney has brought some spring lamb chops home with him. We could have carrots, mash and cabbage with that, but not too much cabbage, we have to keep the wind off your milk."

Oonagh nodded, "Yes, that sounds lovely."

Mrs Delaney went back downstairs and set to work cooking tea, while Mr Delaney sat in the armchair in the kitchen and she told him all about the birth. "Mrs Clancy thinks the world of Oonagh, I think we have struck gold there, Edward."

Mr Delaney took Oonagh's meal upstairs so that he could take a peek at the new little life that his household had been blessed with.

"What a head of hair," he said when he saw the crown of fine black hair covering the baby girl's head, "I could do with a bit of that myself!" He stroked Oonagh's head then kissed her forehead. "You've done well there, bright eyes." But Oonagh was already tucking into her lamb chops.

Mr Delaney left to join his wife downstairs for tea, leaving Oonagh to finish her meal, just as George woke complaining of hunger.

"Come on now, Grandpa's little sunshine." Oonagh heard him say, and Mr Delaney carried George downstairs for his wife to tend to.

When Mrs Delaney popped into Oonagh's room to take the tray away in the early evening, Oonagh had fallen into a contented sleep.

"I've brought you a drink of milk and a chamber pot, dear," said Mrs Delaney, "Have you thought of a name for baby yet?"

"Yes," said Oonagh, "She shall be Kathleen after you and after my ma, we will call her Kitty."

"Well, I'm honoured, that I am," said Mrs Delaney, "wait till I tell Edward!" And she bustled off downstairs to tell her husband the good news. She was back after five minutes, "Oonagh, would you like me to give Kitty a drink of cool boiled water? And then you can put her to your breast." And gathering up Kitty in her arms, she kissed her tiny head and hurried off downstairs with her prize.

"Look who I've got, Edward, isn't she beautiful?" Oonagh could hear her boasting. And she lay back on her pillows and thanked God for the kindness everyone was showing her.

The sun was still shining through the curtains in her room as she drifted off to sleep, dreaming of Seamus and the day they met on the deck of the boat coming over from Dublin to Liverpool. He stood beside her as she leaned against the rail with the wind blowing through her thick strawberry blonde hair. "Have you been to England before?" he had asked, and Oonagh had replied she had never left Arklow, because she was only seventeen. "Don't worry," said Seamus, "I will look after you."

"When will Kitty meet her daddy?" Oonagh whispered into the night as she drifted back into a deep sleep.

Mrs Delaney did not waken her as she replaced Kitty in her cradle and she and her husband went to their bed. All was quiet, but not for long.

Chapter Thirteen
The Milk Siblings

George was awake and demanding attention at three o'clock in the morning. Oonagh could barely open her eyes but struggled into his room and started to change his napkin as Mrs Delaney came into the room carrying a bottle of warm milk.

"I wonder what age he will drop this early morning feed?" she asked Oonagh, but Oonagh did not answer at once, but considered as she changed George's napkin.

"My brother Finn slept with my mother and she breast-fed him until he was two and a half years old," she said.

"We won't be having that," she said, "Mrs Delaney, he will have to learn." Oonagh poured some water from the jug into the bowl in George's room and washed her hands, just as Kitty awoke to let them all know she was in need of attention too. Oonagh brought her into the room and had another napkin to change.

"Look, Kitty, meet George," she said, and George grinned a toothless smile at his new friend.

"I should try Kitty at your breast, that first milk you produce is very rich and good for the baby," said Mrs Delaney.

"I don't know how you know all this," said Oonagh.

"Why it's passed down the ages, mother to daughter," said Mrs Delaney. "There's no way like the old ways."

Seating herself on the feeding chair, Oonagh unbuttoned her nightdress and put Kitty to her breast.

"Like this," said Kathleen Delaney, "hold your whole outer circle and the nipple between your first and second finger and put it into her mouth, so that her gums clamp onto the outside circle. Now then, has she latched on?" Oonagh nodded as the little gums closed and Kitty began to suck strongly.

"It's working," said Oonagh, "I can do it."

"Of course you can, it's the most natural thing in the world," said Mrs Delaney smiling.

"Would you like me to go down and get you a drink, dear? Feeding baby can make you quite thirsty." But when she walked into the kitchen, Edward was already there and the water was boiling.

"It's like old times, isn't it, Kathleen? Do you remember when Maria was a baby and I used to make tea for you in the night?"

"Oh, Edward, isn't this wonderful," said his wife with tears in her eyes, "we have a new baby in the house again, better than that, we have two, and a new daughter to care for." And she wrapped her arms around his neck. The water boiled and Edward kissed his wife then poured the boiling water onto the tea leaves in the china pot. Mrs Delaney put a biscuit on Oonagh's saucer before carrying her tea up to the bedroom and her husband followed with two cups one for himself and one for his wife. "I have to leave early in the morning, the weekend's meat is being delivered at eight," and the Delaneys went back to bed to try to have a few more hours' sleep.

George was sound asleep when Oonagh carried Kitty back to her cradle and climbed back into her soft, cool bed.

It was seven o'clock when Oonagh opened her eyes again, she heard the chimes of the clock in the hall. She checked the cradle to make sure it had not been a dream. Kitty was still asleep with her thumb in her mouth. Oonagh bent and stroked her fine, silky black hair, and Kitty stretched and yawned, her little pink lips resembled a perfect rosebud and Oonagh felt an overwhelming urge to kiss her.

"Yes, I remember you doing that all the time you were in my belly, pressing your feet against my ribs and stretching," Oonagh whispered to her.

There was a hesitant knock on her door and Mrs Delaney said, "May I come in?" Then she came in anyway with yet another cup of tea.

Oonagh thanked her and Mrs Delaney put the cup and saucer on the little table next to her bed. "Kitty has slept well for her first night, but girls are usually easier to rear than boys, bless them, boys always demand attention and it carries on when they are adults." She laughed and as if on cue, George started to yell.

Mrs Delaney left the room to feed her grandson and Oonagh lifted Kitty to feed her. The midwife had been correct, Oonagh's milk was coming in and there was enough to satisfy baby Kitty, her cheeks were red and round like the north wind in Oonagh's picture book back home in Arklow, and the milk trickled out of her little pink lips.

"I think you've had plenty now, my girl," and Oonagh gently took her baby off her breast and carried her into George's room, where the jug and basin were, to change her napkin. "Good morning, Master George," she said to the baby boy sucking furiously on the teat of his bottle of goat's milk.

"I have been thinking, Oonagh," said Mrs Delaney, "would you like to have a nice bath this morning, it will make you more comfortable I'm sure."

"That sounds good, thank you, Mrs Delaney," said Oonagh and once the two babies had settled back to sleep, Mrs Delaney went downstairs to prepare the bath for Oonagh telling the young mother, come down in about ten minutes, "I will warm the water on the range."

Ten minutes later, Oonagh went down to the kitchen where Mrs Delaney had filled a tin bath with warm water. The curtains were still drawn close but there was an oil lamp burning on the table.

65

"I will just add one more pan full of hot water," said Mrs Delaney, "I've put a couple of generous handfuls of salt in the water, it's the finest thing if you have any tears down below. Now there is no need to worry no one will come in, you slip your nightdress off." She held out a towel as a screen at the side of the bath and as Oonagh stepped into the warm water. Mrs Delaney took her arm to steady her.

"Would you like me to wash your hair?" said Mrs Delaney, filling the kettle with cold water at the sink again.

"It's grand not having to go down the yard for water," said Oonagh and she slid her head beneath the soothing warm water. As she looked upwards, she could see a dark blue dress with a white lace collar was hanging neatly over the clothes rack, newly pressed underwear and a pair of blue stockings were hanging beside it. Mrs Delaney followed her gaze, "Yes, I suppose you have guessed, those were my Maria's clothes, I couldn't bring myself to give them to the rag merchant in exchange for a donkey stone for the front step, and it is lucky I didn't. She was about the same size as you, I think." Kathleen Delaney produced a large bar of coal tar soap from the shelf behind the curtain surrounding the base of the stone sink. She rubbed it into Oonagh's thick hair, "Keep your eyes closed," she said, "or the suds will smart."

Oonagh rubbed the soap all over her body while Kathleen Delaney rinsed her hair with fresh water from a jug, the water warmed from the hot water in the pan on the range. Oonagh rested back against the curved back of the bath until she was rinsed of the suds.

"We had a tin bath at Watsons' Court," she said, "but it was difficult having to bring buckets full of water from the pump up the yard into the scullery, then heat the water on the range and it was so much trouble that we had to take turns to use the bath water, Seamus was always last after working on the farm, and I didn't get a bath too often. The other three girls were always in before me. I have been a regular customer at the public baths on Petersgate."

"We can make this a regular bath day if you would like to, every Thursday morning when Edward has gone to work, then he will tip the water out for me when he comes home and put the bath back in the cellar for me," and Mrs Delaney and helped Oonagh to get out of the bath and dry herself. "Would you like to try these clothes on?" She gave Oonagh a muslin napkin to fold and use in her bloomers to absorb the blood she was losing after the birth.

Oonagh pulled on the clothes, first her liberty bodice with rubber suspenders for her stockings, there were rubber buttons down the front of the bodice that would enable her to feed the baby. Then she pulled on her bloomers and the blue dress which also had buttons down the front.

"Yes I was right, my Maria was just your size," said Mrs Delaney, "I will buy new clothes for you as you need them, but these will be sufficient for a start. Now, you are a proper nursemaid, in those clothes, and try on these stout shoes, I am sure they will fit your feet." Oonagh was grateful, especially for the shoes, her boots would not survive another day. She looked at herself in the mirror in the hall and smiled at her reflection.

"Would you like me to plait your hair for you?" said Mrs Delaney.

"Come back into the kitchen and sit on the chair, I used to do this for my Maria and it will be much tidier for you while you are tending to the babies."

Oonagh did as she was bid and found it pleasant to have some attention and to have her long hair brushed and styled into a single thick plait by the older woman.

"I will wash your own clothes for you but I fear they were spoiled yesterday," said Mrs Delaney, "and now you had best get back up to your bed. Mrs Land will chastise you if she finds you downstairs. You should rest in your bed for at least a week."

Oonagh climbed the stairs back to her soft bed, Mrs Delaney had laid out a clean nightdress for her and, after she had removed her nursemaid clothes and laid them on the chair, Oonagh thankfully sank back against the pillows.

Mrs Delaney was soon back upstairs to Oongah bringing her warm milk and tea bread with butter and damson jam. "I have to keep you well, you must eat and drink plenty when you are feeding, and I think in a couple of days you can try to feed George, we will ask Sarah Land when she comes," she said. "Edward is bringing us some nice gammon for tea, I will make some parsley sauce, and would you like Manchester tart for pudding?"

"That sounds good," said Oonagh, "but I have never tasted Manchester tart. How very lucky I am, Mrs Delaney, I am sure I will like it."

Sarah Land, the midwife, called that afternoon and congratulated Mrs Delaney for thinking of the salt bath. "I think you should take one salt bath every other day, that would be advisable for the first week," she directed.

When Mrs Delaney pressed her about how soon Oonagh could begin feeding both babies, Mrs Land suggested waiting until the weekend was over before putting George to Oonagh's breast.

67

Chapter Fourteen
Sentenced

"In the meantime, good food and plenty to drink for mother."

Kathleen Delaney continued feeding Oonagh good food and plenty of it, and Oonagh rested in her room until the following Wednesday, when Mrs Delaney allowed her to sit in the chair in the kitchen after her salt bath. That morning, Mrs Delaney drew back the curtains and the sunshine streamed into the kitchen while Oonagh drank her warm milk and ate bread and jam for breakfast, as usual. First, Kathleen brought baby Kitty down for Oonagh to feed and then when her namesake was satisfied and sleepy, Kathleen carried her grandson down to Oonagh to feed. George was so much hungrier than Kitty but Oonagh seemed to be producing enough milk for him too.

"It's a miracle, Mrs Delaney, I am making enough milk for both babies." Baby George looked up into Oonagh's face and put his chubby little hand onto her breast. Oonagh lifted his hand with her forefinger and kissed the dimples on his knuckles. "You darling little boy," she said quietly, "you must be missing your mummy, but I will try to be a mummy to you," and she carefully placed his hand back onto her breast.

"More to drink?" said Mrs Delaney, "Could you drink a tankard of stout?"

"I think I just about could," said Oonagh. "But I'm not used to drinking ale in the morning."

"It is very good for your milk," said Mrs Delaney, "just look at George's rosy cheeks, he has loved that feed, haven't you, my precious?" And she lifted George high and kissed his cheeks, but George cried and stretched his arms out to Oonagh.

"I'll take him up and settle him, if you wish," said Oonagh.

"No," said Mrs Delaney, "I shall take him for a walk to the greengrocer's shop in the perambulator. Will you wash and dry the dishes while I am gone, please."

That afternoon, Father Kelly visited. "Mrs Clancy told me your wonderful news," he said and laid his hands on Kitty's head as he closed his eyes in prayer.

"Father," said Oonagh, "I want to ask you about Kitty's christening."

"I am afraid, Oonagh, that baby cannot be christened until you have been churched," said the priest.

"When can I be churched?" asked Oonagh.

"I am so sorry my child, but I cannot have a churching service for you because you and Seamus are not married. Speaking of Seamus," he continued, "the Superintendent of Police has told me that Seamus and your other friends, will be tried at Chester Assizes a week this Friday. I know you will not be able to travel that far, so soon after baby's birth. I suggest that I travel to Chester by train. I will let Seamus have your news and I will report to you the verdicts. Would you like to write a letter and I will deliver it to Seamus for you?"

"But Father Kelly," and Oonagh was close to tears, "you know that we were to be married before our baby was born."

"Yes I know that," said the priest, "but I cannot go against the teachings of the Catholic Church."

Oonagh asked Mrs Delaney for some paper and a pen and sat alone at the kitchen table to write a letter to Seamus, while Mrs Delaney sat with the priest and listened for either of the babies wakening.

"My dearest Seamus," wrote Oonagh

"Our baby arrived safely last Wednesday afternoon. A little girl, and I have named her Kathleen. I hope you are agreeable to that name.

She has your colouring, very dark hair and her eyes are the bluest blue. I know you will fall in love with her as I have. My love, every time I look at her, I am reminded of you, she is so delightful.

I fear so very much that you will be sent to Australia, but if so, try not to fear, Mr Clancy assured me it is a land of great opportunity especially for the young and strong. He tells me that they are in need of good farmers to help feed the growing population, and Seamus, there is none stronger and more knowledgeable than you. I have made enquiries about joining you but alas, it is not possible as we were not married in time. I so wish it had been different for us but I must be thankful that the Clancys and the Delaneys have been so kind to me. I am nursemaid to the butcher's grandson, George, who is a dear motherless child.

Father Kelly will answer any questions you may have about our situation.

I pray that you may rightfully be found innocent by the jury in Chester and we can be together once more. I will love you forever, my darling Seamus and I pray that you will soon be able to hold me in your arms again,

Your true love, Oonagh."

Oonagh folded the letter and slid it into the envelope that Mrs Delaney had left for her, Father Kelly came into the kitchen to collect the letter and bid Oonagh farewell, promising to call after he returned from Chester Assizes.

When Mrs Delaney came into the kitchen, after Father Kelly had left, Oonagh was inconsolable. "There now my darling girl," said Mrs Delaney, "it's the baby blues, now how can we cheer you?"

When Oonagh told Mrs Delaney about the impasse over Kitty's christening, Mrs Delaney suggested that she herself spoke to the rector of St

Thomas' Anglican Church. She walked up to the church that afternoon, but the response was the same. "Now don't you fret, Oonagh," she said, "I will speak to the Minister at the Wesleyan church at Heaton Moor."

Mrs Delaney spoke to the Wesleyan Minister, and the following Tuesday morning at ten o'clock, Oonagh and Mrs Delaney walked with George and Kitty in the perambulator up to the chapel in Heaton Moor for Oonagh's churching.

"I prefer to treat this service as a thanksgiving," said Mr Adams, the Minister, a powerful man with a balding head and dark brown eyes.

He placed his strong hands on Oonagh's bowed head as he prayed quite simply:

"We thank you Lord, for the safe deliverance and preservation from the great dangers of childbirth of Oonagh Kennedy and her daughter Kathleen O'Neil, amen."

"Amen," echoed Oonagh and Mrs Delaney.

Mr Adams stepped up to the pulpit and read from a huge Bible: "I am reading from the book of Isaiah chapter 43:

'*Bless the Lord, O my soul and forget not all his benefits,*
Who forgets all our iniquities,
Who heals all our diseases.
He restores my soul,
I' will give thanks to Thee O Lord,
for Thou wast angry with me,
Thy anger turned away
and Thou didst comfort me.
Hold me up, that I may be safe.'"
"And," he concluded, "Verse 25.
'*I am He who blots out your transgressions for my own sake, and I will not remember your sins.*'"

Oonagh lifted her head and looked directly at the bright colours beaming down onto her as the remains of the morning sun shone through the east window onto her head as she knelt at the altar.

"Amen," she repeated, and Kitty started to complain when George, lying at the head of the perambulator, started to kick her in her tummy as she lay at the bottom end.

"We usually dedicate the babies in chapel on Sunday when we can introduce them into the family of the church," said the Minister.

"I am so thankful to you for the service this morning, and I do not want to seem ungrateful, but I have been a Roman Catholic all my life. My baby's father and my intended is a Catholic – I would like to have my child baptised into the Catholic Church," said Oonagh.

"I understand, child," said Mr Adams, "but the doors of the chapel are always open to you and if you ever need help, remember I am here for you."

70

"Thank you, sir," said Oonagh, not quite knowing how to address the Minister.

On the way back home Mrs Delaney pointed out a pleasant house with a colourful border of snapdragons along the front wall and a large white three bar gate. "This is the home of George's other grandmother, his father's mother, Margaret. It would be good for George if you visited one afternoon. George should keep in contact with his other family. I will write to her."

When they reached home, Oonagh was tired after her first walk out since before Kitty was born and both babies were ready for their feeds.

She had fed both babies and taken them up to their rooms when Mr and Mrs Clancy arrived and knocked at the front door. Mrs Clancy had brought a cake from Mrs Jenkins shop. "Mrs Jenkins was so happy to hear Oonagh's news," she said, "and she asked if she would call in with the baby one day if you go to the market."

Mrs Delaney had shown the Clancys into the front parlour. "Please take a seat, Norah, Henry," said Mrs Delaney and called upstairs to Oonagh that the couple had arrived.

Oonagh had not been into the parlour before. There was a strong smell of lavender floor polish from the wooden parquet flooring on the perimeter of the room. In the centre of the room there was a large carpet square in rich shades of red, blue and black thickly woven into a Turkish pattern. The sofa and two fireside chairs were in jade green jacquard, matching the heavy green velvet curtains which were tied back with gold coloured plaited rope at each side of the bay window.

"Hello, I have been churched now, in the chapel, so I can have Kathleen christened," were Oonagh's first words when she entered the room.

"Mrs Flaherty brought round this little gift for baby for me to deliver." Smiling as she thought of the dear lady, Oonagh unwrapped the lemon matinee jacket and bootees. They were the only clothes so far that had not been passed down from George. Henry Clancy was entranced by Kitty and his wife put the baby carefully into his right arm for him to cuddle. "Support her head, Henry," she fussed, until Mr Clancy said petulantly, "It's obvious you want to hold her Norah, take her if you wish."

"I am so sorry, my dear child, that you had to approach a Minister of another denomination, but we are all Christians, we worship the same God, so all is well. Yes, I'm sure Father Kelly will baptise Kathleen into the Catholic Church and I suggest as soon as possible. I hear the Father is going to Chester Assizes on Friday," he said, making faces at Kitty and trying to make her smile.

"That's only wind, Henry, she's too young to be smiling properly," said Norah.

Mrs Delaney carried in a tray with tea and biscuits. Mrs Jenkins' cake was on her finest china plate, and the four had a slice of fruitcake and a cup of tea each. "The cake makes less crumbs than the digestive biscuits," said Mrs

Delaney, dabbing the corners of her mouth with a white linen table napkin which was embroidered in the corner with blue forget me nots.

Henry Clancy brought Oonagh up to date with the repairs to the church. "The east window has been completed, Oonagh, and it looks so beautiful, as good, if not better, than the previous one, the man who designed it is very talented."

"It depicts *'the Light of the World'* you say," said Oonagh and Henry confirmed this. "I know His light was shining on me when I knelt at the altar in the Chapel," said Oonagh, her cheeks flushed.

"You have all been so kind to me, Mr and Mrs Clancy, and you and your husband, Mrs Delaney. I have been wondering. Would you be my Kathleen's godparents?"

"We would be honoured," said Mr Clancy immediately.

"And so would we," answered Kathleen Delaney. "So that's arranged," said Oonagh. "I just need a date now from Father Kelly."

Father Kelly was solemn when he called round the following Tuesday after the trial at the Chester Assizes.

"Well, I won't repeat the judge's summing up, Oonagh, it was much the same as you witnessed at the magistrates' court, but I can tell you that the Englishmen were each sentenced to ten months hard labour for incitement to riot and criminal damage. Your four friends were each sentenced to six months hard labour for criminal damage and I am so sorry it is as we feared and the jury found Seamus guilty of the manslaughter of Michael Mahon and has been sentenced to seven years transportation to Australia. It seemed for a time he might be found guilty of murder as a couple gave evidence that they saw Seamus hit Michael with a poker as Michael was trying to get to his feet. However, the jury were not convinced by their evidence and I am suspicious of their evidence, as they did not come forward at the inquest."

"But," said the priest, "the judge made a very important statement for the Catholic Church. He said that the Queen was advised to say the Roman Catholics should have confidence that the government would not interfere with them in the exercise of their religious service. While they keep within the law, the Roman Catholics should be as much respected as the rights of Protestants themselves. But they should be aware that where two or three gathered together and a riot occurred, then the law must undoubtedly punish."

"I think," said Father Kelly, "that is a big step forward for our Church."

Oonagh jumped up and shouted, "No, that cannot be, that is not justice, he never harmed a hair on Michael's head. He only ever showed him kindness. No, it cannot be, Father Kelly, tell me it isn't so. But did you give him my letter? Does he know about Kitty? When will he go?"

Both the priest and Mrs Delaney put their arms around her and begged her to calm herself. "Sit down, Oonagh, don't fret so, Seamus sends his love, he is very brave, he says he will make a success of this and send for you, please keep calm for his and Kathleen's sake and for your own health," urged Father Kelly.

Once Oonagh was a little calmer, the priest took his leave promising to visit in a week to make arrangements for Kitty's christening. Mrs Delaney and Oonagh sat quietly together for a while and shared a pot of tea, Oonagh sobbing a little now and then as they talked about everything, about Oonagh's life in Arklow, about Michael, her mother and her father. Mrs Delaney sniffed into her handkerchief as she told Oonagh about Mary and the sad events following the birth of George, "And the saddest thing is," she said, "her husband, Theo, is going to marry another girl and my Mary has not been in her grave three months. But that is men, they are not as strong as women, I do maintain." The two women moved into the parlour, where they sat side by side on the sofa and comforted each other until the babies awoke and demanded their attention.

While Mrs Delaney cooked their tea, Oonagh took a kettle of warm water upstairs to wash the babies and put on their nightdresses, then she sat down in the feeding chair to feed first Kitty and then George.

When Mrs Delaney came into the children's bedroom to tell Oonagh that the meal was on the table, Oonagh was gently rocking Kitty's cradle with one hand and stroking George's forehead with the other hand. She was softly singing 'The meeting of the waters' as the little ones reluctantly closed their eyes, then opened them again to make sure Oonagh was still there. As Oonagh crept out of the room, Mrs Delaney asked her in a whisper what the song was. Oonagh replied in a whisper.

"Sure, it's about the Vale of Avoca in County Wicklow, the most beautiful place on earth, my home town of Arklow is there, and further up the coast is Wicklow. There are two rivers flowing down from the mountains, that meet in the vale, one mighty and one minor river, they meet then flow together into the sea. I must take Kitty there soon."

That evening, as Mr and Mrs Delaney sat together on the sofa, Mr Delaney enjoying a small glass of port, Mrs Delaney asked Oonagh to sing 'The meeting of the Waters' for them. As Oonagh sang the tears trickled down her cheeks. "Shush now, dear," said Mrs Delaney, stroking Oonagh's head, "Everything will turn out well and Seamus will be successful and safe you just see, he is a resourceful and capable man. That is the sort of man they need in that young country." Mr Delaney went into the kitchen and made them all hot cocoa to take to bed, "I think this will help you sleep," he said to Oonagh.

Chapter Fifteen
Grandma Margaret

The following Wednesday, Mrs Delaney told Oonagh at breakfast, "Grandma Margaret is visiting us this afternoon around three o'clock, her maid has just delivered a note, I will make some scones and please dress George in something special, perhaps that new sailor suit I bought him from Stockport."

At three o'clock prompt, by the chimes of the hall clock, there was loud rap on the front door knocker and Oonagh opened the door to a tall lady with steel grey hair, wearing a mahogany brown fur stole and a cream linen costume with a long straight skirt to her mid-calf and a high collar on the jacket.

"Good afternoon, ma'am," said Oonagh, as the lady stepped past her and into the hall.

"And you are?" asked the lady.

"Oonagh, the nursemaid," was Oonagh's reply.

"Oh yes, Kathleen said she had employed someone, and about time too, George should not be drinking goat's milk. Take my stole will you, there's a good girl."

Oonagh helped Grandma Margaret to remove her fur wrap, there were six tiny animal tails sewn onto each end of the stole, which was lined with brown taffeta. The wrap and its owner smelled strongly of mothballs and lavender water. Grandma Margaret pulled off her brown lace gloves finger by finger, placed them carefully on the hallstand and then removed an enormous silver and pearl hatpin from her brown trilby hat. Lifting the short veil, she took off her hat, stuck the pin carefully through the buckram and laid the hat beside her gloves on the hall stand.

"Good afternoon, Margaret," said Mrs Delaney coming into the hall, "be a dear, will you, Oonagh, and lay Miss Foster's stole on my bed."

Oonagh gingerly took the fur upstairs (Mrs Delaney told her later that the stole was mink).

"It is such a warm day," said Grandma Margaret, fanning her face with her hand.

There were patches of perspiration staining the cloth of her jacket beneath her armpits.

"You surely haven't walked?" said Mrs Delaney.

"No," said Margaret, "of course not, I instructed Mr Slater to collect me in his cab, I could not face travelling on the Reddish omnibus, it gets so crowded and people of all types take a ride, pushing and gossiping. Mr Slater is collecting me at half past four."

"Do come into the parlour, it's much cooler in here," said Mrs Delaney, and she directed Grandma Margaret into the parlour, the sun had moved over the ridge of the roof now and the room was shaded.

Oonagh went out into the garden to bring George and Kitty indoors. They had taken their naps outside, in the shade of the apple tree, one at each end of the perambulator.

"Oh, Georgie, you have grown I swear," said Grandma Margaret when Oonagh carried him into the parlour. "Oonagh's milk must be good for you. Is she eating good food, Kathleen? I do want my grandson to have the best start in life."

Mrs Delaney smiled at Oonagh, "Oh yes, Margaret, I think you can see by Oonagh's good complexion."

"Talking of food," said Mrs Delaney, "I have baked some scones. May I offer you a cup of tea, Margaret?" Mrs Delaney went into the kitchen, leaving Oonagh with Grandma Margaret and the babies. Margaret opened her bag and produced a bone teething ring with two silver bells tied to it by a blue satin ribbon.

"There you are young man, a special gift from your granny," she said, putting the toy into George's hand. George promptly began to chew the ribbon.

Mrs Delaney returned carrying a large wooden tray, filled with scones, butter and jam, three cups and saucers and tea plates from her best china set, a pot of tea, tiny cubes of sugar in a china bowl and a small jug of milk She rested the tray on the sideboard. The women enjoyed their afternoon tea, while Margaret revealed that her son, George's father, was soon to re-marry. "His fiancée is the daughter of a wealthy timber merchant, she is a delightful girl, but far too young to take on the responsibility of a ready-made family, besides, she would like a child or children of her own very soon, she has confided to me and I know that Georgie is so well cared for here. But do remember, if there is any advice or assistance you need from myself, do ask me. You know, I was a nurse to the youngest child of a successful tailor on Piccadilly Manchester, when I first moved to the town from Cheshire. I was employed in their household as a housemaid, until I came to be expecting my first child Elizabeth." Grandma Margaret looked at Kitty.

"And your husband, Oonagh? Does he live in Manchester?"

"No, ma'am," said Oonagh blushing and looking away. "My husband is overseas, there is just Kitty and myself, until he returns for us."

"I see," said Miss Foster, "well, I would ask you for my stole, Oonagh, as Mr Slater will be here before too long."

Oonagh climbed the stairs to bring Grandma Margaret's stole. Then, as Mrs Delaney showed her to the front door, Margaret Foster turned to Oonagh.

"Now, do bring George to see me very soon, my house is in walking distance, not too far away for strong young legs."

"Yes, ma'am," said Oonagh with a slight curtsey.

Once outside, the waiting Mr Slater assisted Margaret into his small carriage, then climbed aboard onto the driver's seat, flicked his whip on the pony's rump. His pony trotted up the road and quickly out of sight.

The weather was still warm for September and the following Wednesday afternoon Oonagh dressed the two children in their Sunday clothes and pushed them in the perambulator to Margaret Foster's house. George insisted on standing at the front of the perambulator, holding onto the hood like a Roman centurion in his chariot. Grandma Delaney had bought a leather harness for him because Oonagh was so afraid he would tumble out. George rocked the perambulator and Kitty squealed with delight, banging her hands on her thighs and dribbling foamy bubbles down her cute little chin.

"You are just encouraging him, Kitty," scolded Oonagh, but they created great amusement for passers-by on the way to Miss Foster's house.

Maria the maid answered the door to Oonagh's knock when they reached Grandma Margaret's.

"The missus is in the back garden," said Maria, "come through the side gate."

"I am so glad you came," said Margaret pushing her immaculately coiffured hair off her face, with the back of her hand and dropping into her basket the last faded yellow rose that she had clipped from the rose bushes in the circular rose bed which had been cut into the centre of the lawn.

"Maria, fetch a rug for the children to play on the lawn."

"Lay the children down on the rug, it strengthens their muscles when they roll and crawl," she said to Oonagh, "but I am not sure whether it is wise to allow George to stand in the perambulator, he will become bandy."

"He doesn't give me much choice," said Oonagh, "George is very wilful and very strong, watch him." Crouching down on the woollen rug that Maria had laid on the lawn, Oonagh offered George her forefingers and he raised himself to his feet on his bonny little legs. Meanwhile, Kitty rolled over and over to grasp a daisy which she put straight into her mouth, slavering on her fist. She was so dainty against her playmate and milk sibling.

"They have the same milk and yet George is nearly twice the size of my Kathleen," said Oonagh.

"Yes, he is a fine boy like his father," said Miss Foster, beaming, "but in my day we didn't even let the babies sit until they were at least nine months old, it can weaken their bones," she said.

"I don't have much choice with George, he stands in his cot and pulls himself up on the furniture at home, he is such a strong little fellow," said Oonagh.

"We must take both children to the infirmary in Stockport to have a vaccination to prevent them from catching the smallpox," said Miss Foster.

"Oh I'm not sure that I want Kitty to have the pox put into her," said Oonagh. "I am afraid for her."

"It's quite safe," replied Margaret Foster promptly, "Even the queen herself, God bless her, has allowed one of her children to be vaccinated."

"I'm still not sure though, what if it makes them get the smallpox?" said Oonagh.

"You haven't any choice, Oonagh, I am afraid, it is the law that all children under three years of age are vaccinated. I shall instruct Mr Slater to take us in his cab on Friday afternoon at two o'clock, the vaccinations are every Friday afternoon with the Poor Law doctor at the Workhouse Infirmary."

At two o'clock that Friday, Oonagh and the children were ready when Miss Foster called to collect them in Mr Slater's cab. At the Infirmary there were five or six mothers with their children in the waiting room, Miss Foster and Oonagh sat beside a young woman who had a little girl aged about three years sitting on her lap. The little girl had hot red cheeks, a runny nose and was coughing with a strange gulping cough. "That sounds like whooping cough to me," said Grandma Margaret, "you should take her to breathe in the fumes of a pitch boiler. They are laying rail track up to Disley from Stockport and they will be spreading tar on the sleepers. Some folk say you should let a frog breathe into her mouth, or that you should take her for a ride on a donkey, but I think the fumes from the boiling pitch work best."

It was not many minutes until Oonagh, carrying Kitty, while Margaret struggled with her sturdy grandson, went in to see the doctor. They passed a young mother who was leaving, comforting her baby son. "Oh dear, does it hurt?" asked Oonagh, holding Kitty tightly.

"Do come in ladies, I have plenty of children to vaccinate today," called the doctor, holding the door wide open. Oonagh and Margaret walked timidly inside. Pulling up Kitty's right sleeve, the doctor quickly scratched her little arm with a sharp knife and then smeared some liquid from a bottle under her skin with a flat wooden stick. Kitty looked into her mother's eyes.

"I am sorry baby, but this is to stop you being very, very ill," said Oonagh, kissing Kitty's forehead.

"Yes," said the doctor, "smallpox can leave them with so many defects; if they don't lose their life from it, it can ruin their life. It can leave children blind or deaf and it disfigures them badly. Vaccination is the way to banish that dreadful smallpox from this country, and one day from the whole world."

"Are you as brave as your sister, young man?" the doctor said to George as he repeated the process. George screamed and tried to struggle out of his grandmother's arms. Oonagh passed Kitty to Margaret and took George herself.

"I told you he was strong," she said as they thanked the doctor. The doctor waved away Miss Foster's hand as she took out her purse.

"No, ma'am, the vaccination is free, by order of the government," he said as he noted their details into a book.

The two women hurried quickly outside to Mr Slater's cab. He was waiting patiently outside the Workhouse, watching life go by.

Once back at the Delaney's house, Oonagh asked Miss Foster if she would like to come in for some refreshment, but Margaret declined as she said,

"Theodore and his fiancée, Jeanetta, are coming to my home this evening to discuss their wedding plans."

"They have been so very brave, Mrs Delaney," called Oonagh from the hall, "could you take George from me while I retrieve Kitty from Miss Foster?"

Mrs Delaney hurried into the hall and took George,

"You poor little soldier, did that naughty doctor hurt you?" she said, kissing away the tears from George's hot wet cheeks. Oonagh rushed outside and took Kitty from Grandma Margaret just in time as Kitty had her little fingers twisted into Margaret's veil and was tugging the navy-blue pill-box hat from Margaret's head. Grandma Margaret's usually perfect hair was dishevelled and her hat was over one eye.

"So sorry," said Oonagh, stifling a laugh. "Shall we call to see you next Wednesday, Miss Foster?"

Grandma Margaret nodded and attempted to restore her dignity, as Oonagh moved with Kitty towards the house. Mr Sadler flicked his whip and the cab was soon away up the road.

The following Wednesday, Oonagh walked the now familiar road to Margaret Foster's home. The weather was becoming cooler and Oonagh was grateful once again for the late Mary Delaney's clothes when Mrs Delaney helped her into a long dark blue coat that had been her daughter's.

As usual, Oonagh crossed the road at the junction to deposit her weekly shilling in the savings bank. "We will soon have enough money to visit your grandparents in Arklow," she said to Kitty when she came out again with her little blue bank book. "What a surprise they will have when they see you, Miss Kitty!" and Oonagh pulled a face at Kitty, then rubbed her nose against her daughter's tiny nose. Kitty squealed with delight and grabbed at her mother's hair, tangling her little fingers in the golden – red locks.

Maria the maid helped Oonagh to lift the perambulator up the steps into the hallway and the maid smilingly carried Master George into the front parlour where Margaret was seated on an armchair with a crocheted woollen rug on her knees. "It is becoming quite cold," she said to Oonagh. "Maria, take my visitor's coat, or she will not feel the benefit when she goes home." Oonagh smiled at Maria and put Kitty down on the rug to roll and crawl with George, while Maria took Oonagh's coat and then, under instructions from Miss Foster, Maria went into the kitchen to bring tea and cake.

"Miss Foster," said Oonagh, "Forgive me for asking, but how do you know so much about the children's illnesses?"

"Well, you don't rear five children as I have done without learning a good deal," said Margaret.

"Five?" said Oonagh. "I know Theo is your son – but five children? Does your husband, George's grandfather, live here with you?"

"No," said Miss Foster, "that was not meant to be. The children's father is a Polish nobleman." She lowered her voice, "He owns a successful carpet and textile business in Manchester, he has always taken care of us, we want for nothing."

She motioned for the conversation to cease as Maria entered the room with tea and cake on a tray.

"And your husband, Oonagh, has he returned from abroad?" Grandma Margaret continued.

"No, I am afraid not, Miss Foster," said Oonagh, and she once again felt hot tears brimming in her eyes. They quickly developed into sobs when Margaret Foster put her arm around her shoulder, "Sit yourself down my dear, and Maria will serve the tea."

Maria brought some spoons and pans into the parlour to occupy the two children as Kitty was attempting to put her fingers into George's eyes.

"Now, tell me about Kitty's father," demanded Miss Foster, and Oonagh found herself pouring out the whole story.

"Right now, Mr Delaney has calculated that the ship Seamus is sailing in should be nearing the Cape of Good Hope. Mr Delaney used to be a merchant seaman. The ships he sailed on brought spices into Hull, ginger from The Orient, cinnamon, nutmeg, cloves and cinnamon, cloves and mace from the West Indies. And he brought tea from Ceylon and India."

"Tell me how you met Seamus," said Grandma Margaret.

"I was on the deck of the boat from Dublin into Liverpool," said Oonagh, "I was so afraid. Everything was new to me, I had never travelled outside of Arklow before. My pa and ma encouraged me to leave, our neighbours were dying of hunger. Potatoes, the main food of working people, were rotting in the fields. Rotting with a disease called the blight. The blight could spread across a field full of healthy potatoes within a week, the leaves just withered and died and the potatoes rotted in the ground. The stench from the rotting plants was dreadful. The starving people were emigrating in droves, they were fighting to get onto the ships to America and Australia, but my pa did not have the money for my fare to America. The government made arrangements for Irish to come to England on the boat for sixpence.

"My pa had a brother in Liverpool and he told me to make my way to uncle's house. I wanted to take Finn but Finn wouldn't leave Ma. I was on the deck of the ship holding onto the rail, if truth is known, I felt very queasy. Then, suddenly, Seamus was there, black wavy hair and the bluest of eyes, just like my Kitty, his arms were strong, the sleeves of his striped shirt were rolled back above his elbows and the hairs on his arms were thick and glossy black.

"'Are you quite well?' he asked me, and I told him I had never left home before. He told me then he would help me to find work – and he did. He had worked in the farms near Stockport every summer for a few years. He knew exactly where to go, and I always felt safe when his strong arms were around me. Miss Foster, I tell you the truth, Seamus did not harm my cousin Michael, as was alleged. It was not in Seamus' nature, he cared about other folk too much, and he is a good man."

"I am sure you will soon be together again, have faith," said Margaret, handing Oonagh a lace trimmed handkerchief. T\here was a quiver in her voice.

"Tell me about your Polish nobleman," encouraged Oonagh.

Margaret went to the parlour door to listen for Maria.

Once she could hear Maria upstairs busying herself sweeping the floors, Grandma Margaret closed the parlour door firmly and lifted George onto her knee, kissing each dimple on the back of his plump hands.

"Marcus sailed to England from Hamburg with his sister, Fanny. They were escaping Poland because after the wars in Europe against Emperor Napoleon, Poland was divided between Russia and Prussia at the Congress of Vienna. The Polish culture and their language were being deliberately eradicated. Fanny was a music professor at the University but her job was replaced by Prussians, who spoke only German. Marcus was an agent in textiles and decided to come to England to live and work, bringing Fanny with him. I was a maid as I have told you, to a tailor in Manchester, on Piccadilly.

"Marcus came to dinner at the tailor's home to discuss the sale of tweed fabric from woollen mills in Yorkshire. The mill owners had appointed Marcus as their agent. While I served dinner, Marcus watched me constantly and our eyes met over and over again. Oh, he was so handsome, tall and regal, he had fair hair that flopped over his steely blue eyes, and a fine moustache. When I saw him to the door, after he had finished his business with Mr Hargreaves, he pulled me outside onto the doorstep and he kissed me full on the lips. Oh, I'll always remember the intoxicating mix of brandy and cigars on his breath. I had never been kissed like that before, I was a young girl from a little village in the countryside, just turned nineteen.

"The following day was Sunday and Marcus asked permission from the Master to take me for a carriage ride after church. I don't think I need to tell you more, I named my first child Elizabeth, after my sister, Elizabeth Martha, who died of consumption back in Cheshire when she was sixteen.

"The mistress was happy to keep me on as a wet nurse to feed her baby, because better class women do not care to feed their own babies. I know it is quite different for you, Oonagh, because George has lost his dear mother. When my employment with the family came to an end, Marcus provided us with a home and he has always taken responsibility for me and the children financially. Theodore was my second child, he has the same fair hair as his father, two of our children have flaxen hair as I had. Together we had another son and two more daughters.

"Marcus now has a successful business on Back Piccadilly and a beautiful villa in Withington. Theodore is employed as an agent by his father but spends most of his working day in the showroom."

"And Marcus's sister, the music professor?" persisted Oonagh, "What happened to her?"

"Frances is a music tutor at a private school in London," said Grandma Margaret, "she has been most successful."

"Now do not repeat to the Delaneys what we have discussed," cautioned Miss Foster as Oonagh tucked the children back into the perambulator, "It is an entirely private matter."

"No, Miss Foster, of course not," said Oonagh and she bumped the perambulator down the front steps. It was beginning to drizzle and the skies were heavy with rain as she quickened her step on the way back home.

She sang the lullaby '*the meeting of the waters*' to the children that evening, as always, gently rocking Kitty's cradle with one hand and smoothing George's brow with the other. "I feel so sad for your Grandmother Margaret, she has been deceived, and yet she still seems to love that man," she whispered as George's heavy eyelids closed.

Chapter Sixteen
Australia Bound

The first letter from Seamus to Oonagh arrived five months after the trial. It was the day after Kitty's first attempt to crawl. Oonagh declared that Kitty had been frustrated watching playmate George scrambling round the room and getting into mischief. With almighty strength, Kitty rolled onto her tummy, then, lying flat, reared herself up onto her shoulders and pushed, then pushed again. She succeeded in propelling herself – backwards – onto the polished parquet flooring. Once she was there, it was simple to move on the polished wooden floor around the carpet. She slid easily now, right under the sideboard and she screamed "a da da da da".

"Oh bless her," said Oonagh, pulling her to safety, "she is calling for her daddy, I must write to tell Seamus, he will be so delighted."

"I'm so sorry, dear," said Mrs Delaney, "I don't want to disappoint you, Oonagh, but it is the easiest sound for babies to make, still no harm in telling Seamus she called for him."

When the letter from Seamus arrived the following midmorning, Oonagh said to Kitty, who was chewing on a crust of bread and butter, "There, Kitty, your daddy must have heard you call for him, how strange." Kitty blew bubbles in reply, while Oonagh gulped a hot drink herself.

Mrs Delaney had been outside pegging out the washing which she had just passed through the mangle to squeeze out the surplus water.

The mangle was an ingenious device, it was situated underneath a small scrubbed wooden tabletop, roughly two feet by four feet. Mrs Delaney turned the table top over and the green wrought iron mangle with its wooden handle and rubber rollers appeared from beneath, ready for work. She washed the clothes (in this case Mr Delaney's dark blue butcher's overalls) in a metal, barrel-shaped dolly tub, agitating the garments with a posser on a long handle. She used a washboard for stubborn stains, rubbing the soap on the stain then rubbing the clothes against the washboard's ribbed surface. The soap was a block of yellow 'Sunlight' soap which she grated into the hot water that she had boiled in the kettle on the range. Once she was satisfied with the wash, Mrs Delaney passed the soapy clothes through the mangle and then rinsed them in cold water in the sink, transferring the wet laundry at each stage in a large tin bath with handles each side. It was the same bath that Oonagh used to bathe the children in.

The laundry took Mrs Delaney most of Monday and she was always relieved if it was a windy day and the laundry could be pegged out to dry on the washing line in the back garden, pushing the line up high with a wooden prop, so that the wind caught the laundry sending the white sheets billowing.

"I will help you when I have fed the children and they are taking a nap," said Oonagh.

"Thank you," said Mrs Delaney, "heaven knows how I would have coped with George on laundry day, but aren't you going to read your letter?"

Oonagh opened the envelope and read aloud, while she took her breakfast.

"My darling girl,

I pray that you and our wee daughter are in good health. You will have without doubt wondered about my fate as it must be five months since I left England. I have asked one of the crew to post this letter for me on his return to England, but it will be five months since you last heard news of me as the sail home to England will of course take the same length of time as the journey to Australia which was sixty-eight days. I believe that the journey in a steam vessel would have been much quicker and more comfortable but the cost of bunkering for the coal as well as water would have been an extreme expense for the government.

There must have been close to two hundred prisoners, manacled below decks on the ship and we were also carrying live animals, including a huge prize bull which was being sent to Australia to improve the stock.

Some of the convicts were seasick crossing the English Channel and one prisoner took his own life with poison not long after we left Portsmouth, but apart from huge seas across the Bay of Biscay, the sail to the Canary Islands was fairly uneventful.

From the Canaries we sailed in favourable winds across to Rio, where we took on sweet water. The food we were given was sparse, we were given bread and water or gruel made with oats and water, which just about kept us alive.

After we left Rio and sailed south-east for the Cape of Good Hope, we hit a most terrible storm. Many of the men were terrified and being already dreadfully weak and ill with the filthy, overcrowded conditions and lack of nourishment, some men died and were buried at sea. One of those men had a wife and five children back in England, he had hoped to make a fortune and return home a hero. My darling Oonagh, the stench in that ship and the screams of the men still fills my nostrils and ears. Every so often, one of the crew would throw a bucket full of seawater down below, through the hatch, to flush some of the vomit away into the bilges.

It was just after the storm that Captain Barclay, looked down the hatch at us. He was with the bo'sun Mr Petty. 'Unshackle the men, bo'sun, twenty at a time,' said the Captain, 'and let them on deck for an hour's fresh air, that stench is unbearable'.

'And don't you fellows betray my trust,' he bellowed at us.

I was directly under the hatch, he looked me straight in the eye,

'You, my man, you look as if you are from farming stock, can you handle cattle?'

'Ay, sir,' said I, 'five years farming in Stockport and before that in Ireland. I tended the cattle from being a boy'.

'Then get yourself on deck and tend to the bull over yonder, before he breaks loose and does himself some damage. Then turn to with the bo'sun, we have had three crew badly injured in that storm, making good the cargo in the hold 'tween decks'.

'Ay, sir,' said I, and once Mr Petty had unshackled me I climbed up on deck and set about re-tethering the prize bull. He was in a pen in the lee of the raised afterdeck. A magnificent creature he was. He will serve the farmer's dairy cattle well. I checked him all over his hide for sores from horsefly bites and ticks. I fed and watered him and calmed him down, wiping him down with fresh water and cleaning his eyes. Believe me, if he had broken free he could have done some serious damage to himself, and anyone who got in his way.

Once on deck, I was at the bo'sun's bidding and I know he was well satisfied with my work doing all manner of jobs on deck. It was wonderful to have the warmth of the sun on my back and the cool wind on my face after all those months in Chester gaol and weeks below decks. When it was time for the convicts to be shackled down below, Mr Petty grasped my arm and said,

'Not you lad, get your head down in the fo'c'sle, but be very mindful that you are on stand-by, and we are keeping a close watch on you'.

Freedom for me, once more my love, I lay that night dreaming of you and holding you tenderly in my arms again, my face buried in your glorious hair.

For the rest of the sail I tended to that bull, worked on deck, learned a lot about sailing and slept soundly in the fo's'cle with the rest of the crew. My rations also improved but tell Mrs Jenkins nothing compares with her meat and potato pie, or with your Lancashire hotpot, my dearest.

After that terrible storm rounding the Cape of Good Hope, the passage across the Southern Ocean was surprisingly favourable for ship, crew and convicts and of course for that magnificent bull which I named Caesar.

When we finally sailed into Port Phillip, I had become accustomed to a life at sea and was beginning to enjoy it.

My first impressions of Australia are most favourable, it truly seems a land of great opportunity for the free settlers, and for the prisoners once their penance is served. There are plenteous fish and whaling and seal hunting in the Bay. There is no escape although some have tried to swim for freedom.

At the end of their term, many of the convicts head for Ballarat in search of gold, or, with a good work record, Governor Collins may offer them a plot of land to farm with the promise they may own it one day if they tend it well.

It is spring now in Gippsland and the fields are green, but not as lush as our meadows back home in the Vale of Avoca, oh how that melody and the memory of your sweet voice, runs through my brain.

The new owner came to collect Caesar in his wagon and was pleased indeed with the care I had taken of his bull. He talked with Captain Barclay *and recommended a free settler, a widow Charlotte Butler, for me to be tied to for my term. Mrs Butler's husband had been killed during an altercation with an aborigine regarding land rights. I am very hopeful to be assigned to this lady for my term, the farm is large and had been in her husband's family for two generations. I am sure I will be able to manage her farm and of course my work will be checked regularly.*

I thank God that Captain Barclay, Mr Petty and the well-being of Caesar, vouched for me.

Be sure to tell our daughter that her daddy is a good man, who does not deserve to be suffering this injustice and be separated from you both.

Tell her I know I would I love her so, just as I love her mammy, with all my heart and soul.

I am, and always will be your love, Seamus.

Seamus added at the end:

You may send letters with the Catholic nuns who have built an orphanage and school close to Gippsland, I am sure Father Kelly would help you."

"Well, what a letter," said Mrs Delaney, "I am certain Mr Delaney would be really interested to hear that, if you would care to read it to him after tea."

Oonagh read the letter to Mr Delaney and slept with the letter under her pillow. That night she was sailing with Seamus in her dreams. Over the next couple of months she read the letter to herself most evenings. Christmas came and went but no further letters arrived from Seamus, despite Oonagh writing letters to him every month, mostly containing news of Kitty's development. She wrote about Kitty learning to crawl and her first teeth. She wrote how fond of Kitty Mr Delaney had become and how she always sat on his knee at the breakfast table on Sunday mornings. How Mr Delaney dipped his bread into his egg yolk and Kitty opened her mouth wide and eagerly sucked the yolk off Mr Delaney's bread until he only had the egg white and a soggy piece of bread left. Then he would lift her high in the air, kiss her forehead and pass her back to her mummy. *"It has become a routine,"* wrote Oonagh, *"but have no fear, I remind Kitty how much she is loved by her daddy, who has been treated so very unjustly."*

Oonagh passed her letters to Seamus to Father Kelly when the priest visited them each month at the Delaney house. The priest passed them on, via the Catholic Church mail, to the nuns who travelled frequently between Ireland and the Catholic school and orphanage in Gippsland, Victoria.

When Oonagh heard nothing from Seamus for months, Father Kelly assured Oonagh that her letters were arriving at the Butlers' farm. "But you know what men are like, Oonagh, about writing letters, it does not come naturally to them. He will be busy on the farm, their seasons are the opposite of ours, they will be coming into autumn and the harvest time in Australia."

"I try to understand, Father," said Oonagh, "but it is hard, I miss him so and I want to be a family."

"Will you not be visiting your parents soon, Oonagh? Father Murphy has been asking after you and your wee girl."

"I am saving hard, Father," said Oonagh, "but the money does not grow very quickly. Although it was cheap to get to England, it will be an expense to go back and I worry that my pa will not welcome me or my Kitty."

"Sure his heart will melt when he sees you and that angel," said the priest.

Oonagh wrote to Seamus after the Christmas celebrations were over:

"My love,

I trust you are well and happy. I send news of our daughter, who is growing fast. It grieves me that you are not seeing her blossom into a beautiful child, so full of fun and smiles. It is of great benefit that she has a constant playmate in George and they delight in each other.

George's father remarried last autumn and he visited Hamburg on business shortly before Christmas. He and his new wife visited the Delaney home to see George on Christmas Eve. George's stepmother was pretty but quite short with mouse-brown hair. She wore a magnificent long fur coat that reached down to her ankles. She said that Theodore had bought it for her in Germany. They had bought a gift each for the children, a porcelain dolly for our daughter Kitty and a tin clockwork monkey for George, the metal monkey crashed together cymbals when we wound it up.

Mr Delaney was home from work in the evening, he had been very busy preparing the Christmas fowls in his shop. Mr Delaney invited Theodore and his wife to take a glass of port wine with us, and Theodore confided to him that the Germans were producing excellent quality woven cloth which he was importing to be made into lady's mantles and gentlemen's overcoats in Stockport and Manchester. 'The Germans are becoming serious competitors in textile manufacturing, particularly woollen cloth,' he told Mr Delaney.

Kitty was taken with her dolly when she opened the gift on Christmas morning, before we went to church. We attended the chapel in Reddish because the trams to Stockport, and our own church, were infrequent on Christmas morning.

I still sing to the children every night 'The meeting of the Waters' and I hope to take Kitty to visit her homeland and grandparents this spring.

Your own true love, Oonagh."

Soon after Christmas, Oonagh resumed her Wednesday visits to Grandma Margaret's house. On the first visit, she told of Theodore's and his wife's visit to the Delaneys on Christmas Eve. Grandma Margaret was interested to hear about the woollen cloth being manufactured in Germany. "Well, if it is such good quality, I think we should have some made into mantles, one for each of us. It would be good for you to have clothes of your own, not passed on from Mary. It will be a little token from me for the care you take of my grandson. What do you say, Oonagh? I think green would best compliment your colouring. And you must have a new green taffeta gown. Green always suited my colouring, emerald green."

Oonagh smiled, "Thank you, Miss Foster."

"So it is agreed then. I shall make arrangements for the cloth and we will visit Mrs Watson the dressmaker in Stockport."

"Mrs Watson? Oh, yes, I know her shop," said Oonagh.

A week later, Grandma Margaret collected Oonagh in Mr Slater's cab. The cab driver stopped outside Watsons' Court, and handed down to Miss Foster the brown paper parcel tied with string, containing two lengths of the fine green woollen cloth from Germany. Miss Foster firmly pushed open the double doors into Mrs Watson's shop. The brass bells over the door rang and summoned Mrs Watson from the sewing room at the rear. "Good afternoon, Miss Foster," simpered Mrs Watson, removing pins from her thin lips lined in red lipstick, her back was stooped from bending over the sewing table.

"How can I be of service to you?"

"And is this your daughter? I think I recognise you, miss? Have I had the honour of making a gown for you in the past?"

"I think not," said Oonagh, moving to Grandma Margaret's side.

Miss Foster explained exactly what she had in mind for herself and for Oonagh,

"Something very special, we have an important engagement to keep."

Mrs Watson measured both ladies, her thin bony fingers clutched the measuring tape as she passed it around Oonagh's waist, then measured from the nape of her neck to her waist then to her ankles, from her underarm to her wrist, then around her hips and chest. She was scratching the measurements all the time onto a sheet of paper. She dipped the pen nib frequently into an inkwell which was set into her desk and whistled through her teeth. "I wish all my ladies were as skinny, nothing worse than having to flatter a portly woman." Oonagh could see Mrs Watson's pink scalp through her sparse grey hair and the dry flakes of white skin which had fallen from her scalp, lying like snowflakes on the shoulders of her black gown.

Once outside, Oonagh asked Grandma Margaret, "Which engagement have we to keep?"

"I thought you mentioned your intention to visit your parents in Ireland, I will not hear of you going in hand me down clothes."

Oonagh could not restrain herself and she hugged Grandma Margaret, right there in the street.

Grandma Margaret put her hand to her mouth, but she was smiling behind her glove.

Two weeks later, Oonagh visited Grandma Margaret as usual on Wednesday afternoon, only to be met by a worried Maria at the door. "It's Miss Foster," she blurted, "she is in the parlour and has instructed me not to enter, but I think I can hear her weeping."

"Bring our usual tea and cake, if you please, Maria," said Oonagh, "but knock on the door and I will take the tray from you, perhaps George and Kitty will lift her spirits."

Oonagh lifted the children from the perambulator in the hall and, with a child in each arm, resting them on her hips, she pushed open the door with her elbow.

"Miss Foster, are you there?" she called, and a tearful Grandma Margaret stretched her arms out for her grandson. "Whatever has happened?" said Oonagh, "Please don't take on so," and putting Kitty down on the carpet she moved to Grandma Margaret and put her arms around her. "Now tell me what has happened, is it one of your children? Has there been an accident?"

"No," said Grandma Margaret, "it's Marcus, he has married a young woman, no older than you. Her name is Harriet, the only child of a Bradford woollen mill owner. I am broken-hearted, Oonagh, did I never mean anything to him?"

"Oh, I'm sure you did, Miss Foster, you are a fine, elegant lady worthy of any man," comforted Oonagh.

"But not fine enough for him," wept Grandma Margaret her head in her hands.

"There must be a reason," said Oonagh, "perhaps it was for business reasons."

"No," said Miss Foster, "I think we both know the reasons, I do not need telling what a fool I have been, Oonagh. Please say nothing more to me about this."

Oonagh insisted Grandma Margaret sat down for a cuddle with George, while Oonagh poured the tea that Maria brought to the parlour door. The two women sang rhymes to the children, 'London Bridge is falling down' and 'The Grand Old Duke of York'. Kitty chuckled merrily as her mother bounced her on her knee and George clapped his hands to the tune, "Whatever happens," said Oonagh, "no one can take away the joy of your grandchild from you, he loves his grandma; it is plain to see."

By the time Oonagh left with the children (a little later than usual), it was dusk, and Grandma Margaret appeared to be more composed and stronger.

Chapter Seventeen
How Calm Could I Rest

On Friday Father Kelly called to see Oonagh, his face was serious despite Kitty putting her arms out to be lifted by him.

"I'm afraid, Oonagh," he began and Oonagh froze.

"Your father has sent word with one of the sisters from the convent that your mother is very ill and he would like you to go home as soon as possible, she is asking for you."

"I think I will go alone," said Oonagh to the priest and Mrs Delaney.

"You are sensible, it would seem your mother is too sick for a little one to be in the house," said Mrs Delaney.

When Oonagh visited Grandma Margaret that week, she told her of her intentions.

"The children must stop here with me. They are familiar with this house and I have Maria here to assist with their care. You are no longer breast-feeding them full time, Oonagh, except for the morning and evening feed, and it will be an ideal time for them both to be weaned. I have a truckle bed for George to sleep in in my room and I will employ Mr Slater to bring the cot from the Delaney's for Kitty. I will send word to Mrs Watson that we will go for the final fitting for your gown and our two mantles on Friday."

Advised by Father Kelly to sail with all haste, Oonagh decided to leave from Liverpool before the week was out. The manager at the savings bank was smiling, "Buying something special, are you, Miss Kennedy?" he said to Oonagh, winking.

Oonagh blushed, "No, Mr Cooper, I need to go home to see my mammy, she is very ill."

"And where is home?" said Mr Cooper, straightening his cravat and raising one eyebrow.

"I was born in Arklow, Ireland, sir," said Oonagh, "as it says on my savings book. I need to withdraw ten shillings, the fare is five shillings return from Liverpool to Dublin, on deck, with the City of Dublin Steampacket Company. I would prefer to reserve a berth for fear of the sea sickness that a sea crossing brings me, but that would be a price of thirteen shillings and sixpence which would take most of my savings."

"You are most prudent, Miss Kennedy. A lady who has an eye on the future," said Mr Cooper raising his eyebrow. "Perhaps you could find a bench on deck that is sheltered. And when you return, I would ask that you would do me the honour of accompanying me to the theatre one evening. I see you most weeks, Miss Kennedy, when you make your regular deposit into the bank, and I have been full of admiration for you.

"I will see you on your return and I wish your mother a speedy return to health."

Oonagh turned and hurried out of the bank, "Thank you, and good day to you sir," she said, blushing.

Oonagh sent word by the Royal Mail to her pa that she would be arriving at noon the following Friday at Dublin Docks.

When she disembarked the ship, Oonagh was grateful to be back on dry land but could still feel the rocking motion of the ship. As she walked unsteadily toward the dock gate she could see O'Neil the carter leaning against his cart, hands in his pockets, his left leg bent and the right leg crossed over his left knee. His bowler hat was on the back of his head, scarcely covering his black curls, he wore his brown leather waistcoat over a blue striped shirt, his shirt sleeves were rolled up to his elbows, revealing the black shiny hairs on his strong arms. His horse was munching slowly on the hay in her nosebag.

"Well, my goodness, is this Miss Oonagh Kennedy of Arklow? Or is it Princess Oonagh from England? Just let me look at you in all your finery, what a beautiful gown, your majesty," said Mr O'Neil. Taking her carpet bag and swinging it onto the cart, he took both of Oonagh's hands in his, holding them down at her sides, whistling as he admired the beautiful long dark green woollen mantle which was just revealing the frill along the bottom of her emerald green gown. "Let me look at you, have you married a duke? Allow me to assist your ladyship aboard my carriage," he said, taking Oonagh's elbow and helping her to climb up onto the driving bench of his cart.

Once she was settled, he climbed up beside her and jerked the reins. "Gee up Rosey!" he called and his pony trundled along the road. "Your daddy asked me to collect you, luckily I had a delivery to make at the docks," he said, "I hear your mammy is very sick, your pa is worried she will not be with us for much longer. Father Murphy is visiting her most days, so he is."

"Ay," said Mr O'Neil, "We'll never see the likes of that priest again, a true man of God.

"I am taking the coast road, Oonagh, I am collecting Mrs O'Neil from Wicklow, she has been visiting our granddaughter Patty. You will remember her mother, Maggie Connors. When Seamus left last year he left us a special gift and we have been supporting her ever since. It has been hard for us what with the blight and the famine and not much business for me. But we couldn't see our own flesh and blood starve. Did you see anything of Seamus while you were in England? Your pa said you were living in Stockport. He heard from Father Murphy."

"Yes I saw Seamus," said Oonagh, "have you had word from him?"

"Yes," said Mr O'Neil, "we had a letter, Father Murphy read it to us. He has taken him off to Australia, and he is doing very well so he is, managing a big farm for a widow woman."

Oonagh flushed and turned her face away.

At the far side of the town, Mrs O'Neil was waiting at the front door of a little grey stone cottage with a grey slate roof and a low front door painted green, she waved as her husband pulled the pony to a stop. Standing on the deep cill of the only window at the front of the cottage was a little girl aged about twelve months, she was banging with the flat of her hands furiously on the window to get the attention of her grandfather, her black curls were bobbing up and down, as she called to him "Pa, Pa, Pa".

She could be Kitty's sister, thought Oonagh, *good heavens, she is Kitty's sister.*

She had to turn away as Mrs O'Neil climbed aboard the cart and Mr O'Neil went inside the cottage to bring Patty outside to meet Oonagh.

"Patty, this is Her Majesty, Oonagh Kennedy."

"Your Majesty, this is Patty Connors or Patty O'Neil as will be."

Oonagh took the child's hand, "Pleased to meet you, young lady."

She turned to the carter's wife, "She resembles Seamus, Mrs O'Neil, she must bring you much joy," but her words caught in her throat until she thought she would choke.

The carter kissed his granddaughter on the forehead and handed her back to her mother, Maggie, who was waiting in the doorway,

"Good afternoon, Oonagh did you have a good journey?" Maggie said, and Oonagh nodded, "Yes, thank you but I am afraid I am prone to sea-sickness Maggie, I would never be a sailor."

Mr O'Neil flicked his whip on the pony and the pony set off at a trot along the coastal road to Arklow. As they approached the stone Bridge of Nineteen Arches the sun was setting over to their right. A glorious red glow, fading to rose pink, filled the sky above the outline of the hills. To their left the waves were breaking on the rocky beach.

The familiar low, white painted cottages with grey slate roofs lined the main street in Arklow, the scene of bitter battles with the English. The oil lamps were lit in the windows of the inn where her daddy took an ale to slake his thirst every evening on his way home.

Each small window twinkled a welcome as the cart approached.

Oonagh was home.

Once they had driven through the town, they turned right towards the hills, along the lane by the river through the lush emerald green meadows of the valley. Mr O'Neil stopped the cart right outside her parents' front door. "Thank you for the ride, Mr O'Neil," said Oonagh as she jumped down and lifted her bag from the back of the cart, "I beg your pardons, I have been quiet but I am quite beside myself about my mammy. Goodnight to you both and God bless you." And she opened the front door calling, "Ma, it's me, it's Oonagh." Two of the four brown hens pecking around the front door tried to hop inside the cottage with her and she had to scoop them away with her arms. "Shoo, now."

Hearing no response from her mother, she hurried up the stairs to her parents' room. Her mother was propped up on the pillows and the light from the window in the roof illuminated her mother's face – pale, yellow-tinged and hollow-cheeked. Her hair, which she had always fastened into a bun, was long, grey, unkempt and spread across the pillow. She was clutching the crucifix of her rosary beads. "So here you are, my lovely. I have been praying you would come, I feared I would never see you again and now you are here, thank the Good Lord." But the effort of speaking caused her coughing and Oonagh saw the blood-stained rags strewn on the floor beside her bed. "Oh Ma, I'm so sorry, I should have come sooner, I didn't know how ill you had become."

And Oonagh moved to kiss her but her mother warned her, "No, Oonagh, the consumption has got me, I don't want you to be ill like this, my precious beauty, burn these rags for me, will you and wash your hands."

Oonagh threw the rags into the fire that was burning in the small bedroom fire grate, poured water from the jug on the chest into the matching china bowl to wash her hands and put another log on the flames. "Can I make you a drink, Mammy? Have you had anything to eat all day?" On the table beside the bed was a cup of water and a plate with the remnants of bread and cheese. "I'll make you soup, Ma, like you used to make for me when I was sick. I'll just go and put my working clothes on. Will I be sleeping in Finn's room? Where is Finn?"

"He comes home after he's milked the cows and turned them back into the fields, they've turned all the small farms over to dairy cattle, our neighbours are gone on the coffin ships to America and Canada, we've had word that thousands died on the crossing. Some ran out of fresh water or the fever killed others. Thousands who survived the crossing in those rotting hulks died of fever while their ships were in quarantine, when they arrived in New York. Our landlord wanted us away too, but your pa was stubborn, he's growing flax now, we daren't risk potatoes for fear of the blight."

Her mother nodded in agreement with herself, and Oonagh crossed the landing to the only other bedroom. She returned quickly, dressed in the blue gown that had been Mary Delaney's. "Here, Mammy, Miss Foster has sent you some oranges, shall I peel one for you?" Oonagh sat on her mother's bed, peeled an orange and fed one segment at a time to her mother. "There, Ma, that will be good for you, you will soon have roses back in your cheeks. I will pop down and prepare some soup to cook on the range and then I will give you a wash and tie up your hair."

"There should be vegetables in the shed and some leftover ham in the food safe in the scullery," said Ma.

"I'll hurry back," said Oonagh and she stroked her mother's hair back off her forehead and plumped up the pillows.

Downstairs Oonagh found the vegetables, peeled and chopped them, scooped them into a large copper pan, adding water to cover and the leftover ham she found in the scullery. It was all left to simmer on the range, "Thankfully, Pa has lit the fire in the range," she called up to her mother.

"That was Finn," called her mother and started to cough again, as Oonagh called, "I'll just boil some water to wash you, then I will come up, Ma, with a cup of tea." Five minutes later, Oonagh climbed the stairs again, first with a cup of tea for each of them and then with a bowl of warm water and a towel over her shoulder, she put the bowl down on the chest beside her mother's bed and went across to Finn's bedroom to fetch a brush and ribbon from her bag. A short time later and her mother had been washed and her hair brushed and tied back. "There, Mammy, you're beginning to look yourself again. I'll see if that soup is fit yet, for the finest mammy in the land."

Back in the kitchen the vegetables were softened. Oonagh ladled some into a bowl and then mashed the vegetables and bits of the ham into a smooth pulp as Mrs Delaney had taught her to do for the children. Oonagh tasted it, "Yes, that is good soup," she said as she sprinkled a little salt into the bowl and then carried it upstairs to her ma. She fed her carefully, just as she did with Kitty, wiping her mother's mouth gently with one of the best linen napkins, woven and embroidered by her grandmother, as Mammy had told Oonagh since she was small.

"Remember when you fed me like this, Mammy?" she said.

"I remember well," said her mother, smiling.

"Ma, I want to tell you before Pa comes home. Ma, I have a baby girl back in England, the prettiest child you have ever seen, and I have christened her Kathleen after you, Mammy. I call her Kitty."

"So you were married and why did you not come home to let Father Murphy perform the marriage service or ask Pa to give you away. Why Oonagh?"

"No, Ma, we were going to be married but something happened to stop us," said Oonagh.

"And who is her father?" said Ma.

"It is Seamus, Seamus O'Neil. He loves me, Ma, and I love him so much. He looked after me when I was all alone," Oonagh wept.

"Oh yes he loves you," said Ma, "and he loves Maggie Connors too, and I daresay another half a dozen girls. Do you know Maggie had his baby little more than a year ago, a little girl I heard?

"Yes, Seamus O'Neil loves when it suits him, he has a silver tongue that man, just like his father. And Oonagh, didn't Seamus O'Neil kill your cousin Michael? It broke your auntie's heart, so it did." Mrs Kennedy began coughing again. Oonagh put the cup of water to her mother's lips. "Take a sip, Mammy."

"No, Seamus is a good man, Mammy, he helped Michael. He took Michael in when Michael was spending every night in a cellar, paying a penny every night just to stand in the cellar to keep warm out of the rain. Seamus rescued him and he found work for him. Seamus worked on the farms and provided for me, Mammy. Some Irish girls of fifteen and sixteen had to take to work in the whorehouse just for a roof over their heads. It was awful Mammy, it was awful."

"Aye, and it was awful for us here too, Oonagh, but not as awful as for those poor wretches who emigrated to America, and Canada," said Ma, "I thank God that we sent you to your uncle Brendan's in Liverpool, but he says you never went to him Oonagh, we didn't know where you were, until Father Murphy told us you were in Stockport," said Ma as she coughed into her rag, her thin body shaking.

"I hear Seamus emigrated to Australia, that is the story his ma and pa tell. They are supporting Maggie Connor's child, so it will be of no benefit asking there for any help. Oonagh I had best tell your daddy myself, I can't pretend he won't be angry with you. We warned you, Oonagh, not to give yourself to a man until he has married you. Men lose all respect for you once you give in to their carnal urges."

"Don't fret so, Ma," said Oonagh, "I tell you Seamus was dealt with unjustly by the judiciary and as soon as his term is served he will send for us. I have met some very good people who look after me. I work as a nursemaid for a butcher and his wife. I have looked after their grandson George who lost his mammy to the childbed fever, and I fed him with my Kitty. He loves me Ma, like I am his own mother, and I have a good home with the Delaneys they are good people."

"Oh, Oonagh, darlin' but that is no life for you, it isn't what we wanted for you, it isn't how we brought you up. You are a good Catholic girl, you know what the Bible teaches. What does your priest say?"

"Mammy, he says that every child is a gift from God," said Oonagh.

Her mother tutted, "Well, I never heard the like. A man of the cloth encouraging young girls into fornication."

"I'm home, Kathleen," came Pa's voice up the stairs.

Oonagh smiled and kissed her ma's forehead, "Mammy, I love you," she said before she went downstairs.

"Mammy is so very weak, Pa," she said, "I've washed her and made her some soup."

Her pa ruffled her hair with his calloused hand, "That's my girl, good to see you looking so healthy. Not so with many of our neighbours, God rest their souls, may they rest in peace."

"Yes, Ma has told me," said Oonagh, "the people responsible for sending those emigrants to sea in ships that were not seaworthy were so evil, making money out of a heartbreaking situation, when all those families wanted was to escape the famine."

"The great hunger weakened your ma and she has been taken over now by consumption. We just have to keep her comfortable now, she will not recover," her pa sighed and sat down at the table with his head in his hands.

Oonagh put her arm around her father's shoulders. "Would you like some of the soup I made for Ma?"

"Yes, please, Oonagh, and I bought some herring in the village," said pa, "you can fry it for us, there's a loaf in the food safe, I'll go to see what mischief your ma has been up to."

Oonagh rolled the herring fillets in oatmeal as Mrs Clancy had done and fried them in butter. By the time they were cooked, Pa was back downstairs.

Oonagh took her mother's meal upstairs and helped her to eat before she ate her own fish back at the kitchen table.

"Oonagh, it's just a matter of time," said Pa, "we can only hope she has little pain before she passes over. She will be more peaceful now she has you back home with us."

Oonagh said, "Oh, Daddy, I'm so sorry but I can only stay for a few days this time, Mammy will explain to you."

Oonagh could hardly believe how tall Finn had grown when he came home carrying a jug of milk still warm from the dairy. He had the same red hair as Oonagh but was so much taller. "Oonagh," he laughed as he swung her round, "I used to think you were tall, now you seem quite little to me. How's Mammy today?"

"Pa is up there with her, I was shocked when I saw her, I had no idea she was so ill, Finn, and Pa says she won't be getting better." Finn nodded.

"What's this your ma is telling me?" shouted Pa, as he ran downstairs two steps at a time.

"Daddy, don't be angry, please don't be angry. I have been so afraid to tell you, but you will love your beautiful granddaughter Kathleen. Please don't upset Mammy, she is so ill. For Mammy's sake Pa," pleaded Oonagh.

"And with that rake Seamus O'Neil. You fool, Oonagh, what have we taught you? You give yourself to the first man who comes along? And now you're left on your own with him sent off to Australia, a convict. Do you think he cares? Does he care about his other girl in Wicklow? Now his ma and pa are paying for that mistake."

"Once you have that baby in your arms, you will become so strong," Mrs Clancy had said.

"Daddy," said Oonagh, "you cannot call Kitty a mistake. You must not call my Kitty a mistake. Father Kelly says every child is a gift from God. You will love her, pa, just as I do. Oh daddy, she is such a joy, with big blue eyes and a headful of curls. Just wait until she wraps her chubby little arms around your neck, you will melt pa. Please daddy, don't turn me away. I have been so afraid to tell you and Ma, I would have come home but I was afraid." Oonagh collapsed into the chair at the kitchen table, her whole body shaking.

Her father took her in his arms as she sobbed, and he stroked her head with his rough hand, "Oonagh, we love you, don't you understand that? I met your mammy when she was only eighteen and I loved her so much that I waited until she was of age, then I married her, Oonagh. I married her, and I provided for her, I worked and I provided for her. When you were born, I looked after her. We stayed here in Ireland because we love the country, Oonagh, and my love for your mammy is the way it should be, Oonagh. It is what God intended and it is we wanted for you, it is what we want for you now but what man will take you on, with someone else's child?"

"But Pa," interrupted Oonagh, "Seamus does love me, he was wrongly accused and transported to Australia. We were to be married, we will be married. He didn't kill Michael, he didn't kill him. He is a good man." She heard her Ma coughing, "I will take to Mammy a warm drink."

When Oonagh took the drink to her mother, Ma was holding her arms out. "Oh my poor lovely, sit beside me here. Has your daddy calmed? It is only because we love you so much, my darling girl. Now tell me about my granddaughter."

Oonagh's mother fell asleep, propped on her pillows while Oonagh told her all about the little girl with black bobbing dark curls, rosy cheeks and a ready chuckle. She told her about the Delaneys, about Watson Court, Miss Foster, and about baby George. Ma was smiling peacefully when Oonagh crept out of the room to allow her father to climb thankfully into bed.

Finn was already in bed when Oonagh crossed the landing to his room.

"So, you have committed one of the worst sins sister and shamed our ma and pa," was all he said before turning his back to her while she undressed to her liberty bodice and petticoat and slipped into bed. It was back to a straw mattress now for Oonagh. Her sleep was fitful, she could hear her mother coughing in the night, and her father murmuring to her before she heard his footsteps on the stairs and the sounds of the kettle boiling on the range. She crept over to her parents' bedroom, her mother was struggling for breath. Oonagh plumped up the pillows and lifted her mother further up the bed, tucking the bedclothes around her shoulders. "There, Ma," she said, stroking her mother's brow, "is Pa making you a drink?" Her mother nodded, and Pa came back into the room with a cup of milky tea. Oonagh held the cup to her mother's lips, and her mother sipped the warm tea until she eventually leaned her head back and shut her eyes. Oonagh kissed her ma's brow again and left her parents to their sleep.

It was scarcely dawn when Oonagh heard her father rise. She dressed and went downstairs. "Father Murphy will be visiting today," said her father, as Oonagh made him tea and cut him a thick slice of bread.

"Have you butter and jam, pa? Yes, it will be good to see Father Murphy."

"There is some cheese here in the food safe for you," she added, "I will buy butter and jam when I walk into town. I don't imagine Mammy hasn't made her usual batch of bramble jelly."

"Finn has to leave at seven, it's not like him to sleep in, but make sure he leaves on time, he'll be relaxed because you are home. I have a lot to do if I am to have any crops to sell in autumn, the sun is shining this morning but the rain will be back any time. I will return at midday. Your Ma was very ill in the night, I fear it will not be long before she is taken from us."

Pa sniffed, and wiped his rough shirt sleeve across his eyes as he closed the door behind him.

Oonagh took a cup of warm tea upstairs to her mother. Ma's eyes were red and her hair was wet. "Oh, Ma, you're drenched. Have you had the night sweats?" said Oonagh, putting another lump of peat on the bedroom fire. "I'll help you drink this then I'll make porridge, Finn brought fresh milk last night."

Oonagh held the cup to her mother's lips until Ma turned her head away. "Enough now, linctus, Oonagh," she gasped. On the chest Oonagh saw the bottle labelled 'Pritchard's linctus'. She removed the cork and sniffed the spices and black treacle that the apothecary in the town had mixed. She poured the thick black liquid into the spoon and held it to Ma's lips. It soothed her mother's cough while Oonagh made porridge in the kitchen, calling up to Finn when the porridge was thickened. She took a bowlful, sprinkled with sugar, up to her mother. "Here Mammy, try to eat this," Oonagh sat on the bed and fed the warm porridge to her mother. "I will wash you and dress you in a clean nightdress," she said. "Father Murphy will be visiting you today." Her mother ate most of the porridge. "There Mammy, that's the way, you'll soon be recovered," said Oonagh and took the empty bowl downstairs where Finn was enjoying his breakfast. Oonagh boiled more water in the kettle and returned to her mother with a bowl of warm water and a towel. She helped her mother onto the commode at the side of the bed, "I can sleep in my underclothes, Mammy, I'll put my nice nightdress on you that Mrs Delaney bought me for a Christmas gift," she said as she combed and tied up her mother's hair. Oonagh stripped the linen sheets off the bed. "I can wash these Mammy and they will be dry in no time at all, the sun is shining today." Oonagh took fresh sheets from the linen press and made up the bed, tucking in the sheets and blankets tightly before helping her mother back into bed. "There, Mammy, you are clean and fresh for Father Murphy's visit."

When the priest called an hour later, Oonagh was washing the sheets in the scullery sink. The priest put his hand on her head and Oonagh felt a warm glow. "God bless you, Oonagh, and give you strength at this difficult time. I have kept in touch with Father Kelly and he tells me that you have a beautiful little daughter. Have you told your parents that they have a grandchild?"

"Yes, Father, God has forgiven my sin and I have been cleansed. His light shone on me in the church. I have told my ma and pa about Kathleen and I am sure they have forgiven me too. Father Kelly says every child is a gift from God."

"Indeed, that is true," said Father Murphy, "I will reassure your mother of that. I will go upstairs now to see her."

Once she had washed and rinsed the linen, Oonagh hung the dripping sheets over the washing line and busied herself with chores while the priest prayed with her mother, eventually he called to Oonagh to come quickly. When Oonagh reached the bedroom, her mother was bringing more blood up with every cough, she was shivering and perspiring at the same time. The priest left the room. "I will give you some time alone with your mammy," he said.

Oonagh dropped to the floor at the side of the bed to her mother's left, "Mammy, how will I live without you? My Kathleen has not met you yet,"

Her mother stroked Oonagh's head, "Don't cry, my lovely, this is the circle of life, you will manage very well, because that is what we have to do. You never knew my mother and yet I can see her in you, in your glorious red hair and in your green eyes. It is the way of the world, we all have a time to be born and a time to leave, don't be afraid, I am not afraid to die my lovely girl. Remember happy times we had together, remember what I taught you and how I loved you. Let me be a rosy sunset to you, a rosy sunset that heralds the next glorious day. Oonagh, pray for me now." Oonagh stayed beside her mother, seated on the floor, her mother's hand resting on her head, and she recited the words of Psalm 23. Oonagh remembered the words that had been taught to her by Father Murphy:

> *"The Lord is my shepherd I shall not want,*
> *He maketh me to lie down in green pastures*
> *He leadeth me beside the still waters, He restoreth my soul,*
> *He leadeth me in the paths of righteousness for his name's sake."*
> Then Oonagh whispered quietly,

> *"Yea though I walk through the valley of the shadow of death I will fear*
> *no evil, for thou art with me, Thy rod and thy staff they comfort me,*
> *Thou preparest a table before me, in the presence of mine enemies,*
> *My cup runneth over. Surely goodness and mercy will follow me all the*
> days of my life, and I will dwell in the house of the Lord forever."

"Amen," whispered Oonagh, and her mother mouthed, "Amen," before Oonagh dampened her dry lips with water from the cup beside the bed.

Oonagh looked into her mother's damp, pale face. Her mother asked in a whisper, "Sing to me, Oonagh, sing '*The Meeting of the Waters*'."

As she had at Michael's funeral, Oonagh started from verse three:

> *" 'Twas that friends, the beloved of my bosom, were near,*
> *Who made every dear scene of enchantment more dear,*
> *And who felt how the best charms of Nature improve,*
> *When we see them reflected from looks that we love.*

> *Oh sweet vale of Avoca*
> *How calm could I rest in thy bosom of shade, with the friends I love*
> *best,*
> *When the storms that we feel in this cold world should cease,*
> *And our hearts, like thy waters, be mingled in peace."*

Her mother's cough developed unto a rattle as she struggled to breathe. Then, closing her eyes, she sighed and it seemed to Oonagh that she had fallen asleep, her hand still resting on Oonagh's head. Oonagh took her mother's hand gently and kissed it. Then wiped her own tears away with her mother's hand, before placing it carefully on top of the bed sheets. "Oh Mammy," she cried, "no, don't leave me yet. How can I live without you? I should have come sooner to take care of you," but there was silence as the lifeblood drained from her mother's cheeks. "Mammy," pleaded Oonagh, "no, don't leave me, I'm sorry, I'm sorry."

The sun was shining through the window in the roof, straight onto Ma's bed as Oonagh called down to Father Murphy. He hurried upstairs to pray for the soul of Kathleen Kennedy, as she lay in the light of a golden sunbeam.

Oonagh stayed beside her mother, holding her hard-working hands with both of hers, until her father returned as the village church bell chimed twelve. "God always takes the good ones when they are still young," said pa as Oonagh took him in her arms and comforted him, "your mammy held on until you came home, he said. For the next few days, Oonagh took over her mother's role in the household, caring for her father and brother. Her mother was to be buried with her own mother and father in the graveyard in the next village. Spaces in the graveyards were scarce, so many villagers had died during the famine.

Mr O'Neil offered his services to carry the casket in his cart, as he had done with so many others. Local families during the famine had no money for the undertaker's hearse and fine black plumed horse.

As was the custom, on the morning of the funeral, Mammy's pink satin-lined casket was left open on the best table in the parlour, Mammy was dressed in her Sunday best gown with her hands laid on the crucifix of her rosary beads which were fastened around her neck.

The casket was to stay open in the parlour all morning, for mourners to pay their respects before the church service. Every curtain in the cottage was tightly drawn. Oonagh rose early and took her cup of tea outside the front door, the sun was just creeping into the sky above the bay. She leaned back against the cold, stone wall. The sun was casting a thick scarlet line on the horizon, as if a giant's thumb had smeared Mammy's blood along the joint between sea and sky.

The clouds were being driven hard down the wind. A line of gnarled and twisted trees on the cliff path opposite the cottage, were crouching, cloaked in misty green lichen and moss, bracing themselves against the wind, like the line of fishermen who, every morning of Oonagh's childhood, would wend their way down from their cottages in the hills to their fishing boats.

In the howl of the wind, Oonagh fancied she could hear the wails of the children of the wretched people in those coffin ships heading to the 'land of opportunity'. The twisted branches of the trees were their mothers' piteous arms flailing to the heavens, imploring for water, as the rotting hulls of their ships were dashed against the raging ocean's merciless waves.

"Mammy," whispered Oonagh, "where are those sunny days of picnics with Cousin Michael under the tree at the meeting of the waters? Mammy, I have so much to talk to you about." Oonagh walked silently into the parlour, her shoulders low, her arms hanging loosely by her side. She kissed her mother's cold forehead and stared hard at her face trying to imprint those beloved features on her mind.

When the time came, the casket lid was fastened down, the pall-bearers carried it outside and lifted it onto O'Neil's cart.

Mr O'Neil stopped at the lychgate of the chapel and Finn, Pa and two cousins carried Ma into the chapel. Oonagh followed, dressed in her fine green dress and coat with a black lace scarf covering her head. She was supported either side by Uncle Patrick and Auntie Bridget Mahon.

As had become the custom in these troubled times during the great famine, each mourner brought a contribution for Ma's wake. The villagers, without exception, had some act of kindness to tell Oonagh about her beloved mammy. "Yes, I am proud of who my mammy was, she was a good woman. There are so many good people here in Ireland, but I have to say that I have been shown kindness in England by many people."

It was just a few days later that Oonagh, concerned about the children, bade farewell to her pa and Finn, promising to visit in the summer with Kitty.

"Daddy," said Oonagh, "will you and Finn not come to England, there is plenty of work on the farms or in the cotton mills."

"There's no one to persuade Francis Kennedy to leave this farm, not the landlord with promises of a new life in a young country nor you Oonagh. This is my farm and my father's before me, this is where I belong. My life is here in my country, on my farm."

"Yes, Daddy," said Oonagh touching his weather-beaten face with her hand, "I'll be back to see you soon."

Cieran O'Neil was taking produce to the docks in Dublin for export to England and he said he was grateful for Oonagh's company on his journey. Oonagh caught the early ferry to Liverpool.

Disembarking from the boat in Liverpool mid-afternoon, Oonagh took the train to Manchester and walked through the city to London Road station for the train to Heaton Chapel. On the approach to the station a girl was sitting at the side of the road selling posies of sweet violets from a basket. Oonagh searched her pockets for a few pence to buy a posy for Mrs Delaney.

"Thank you, missus," said the girl.

It was dusk and it had been a long tiring day. Presuming the children to be tucked up in bed, when the train arrived at Heaton Chapel station Oonagh went straight to the Delaney's. The couple were thrilled to see her and were anxious about her mother. Oonagh explained that her ma had passed away but that she had not stayed any longer with her father for fear the children were pining.

"If anything, it is George who has been distressed," said Mrs Delaney.

"When I visited them, Miss Foster said that she had trouble keeping him in the truckle bed and he had been climbing into her bed in the middle of the night. She no doubt enjoyed it, but he will be back in the cot when he's here."

"Oh dear," said Oonagh, "I will collect the children early in the morning."

It was a relief for Oonagh to lie on her soft feather bed again and the familiar, hypnotic tick-tocking of the hall clock lulled her to sleep. She slept soundly until Mrs Delaney brought her a cup of tea in the morning. "It is eight o'clock, Oonagh," said Mrs Delaney. "I wasn't sure what time you wanted to collect the children," and hugging Oonagh, she said, "Oh I have missed you and the babies so much, and I worried about what was happening about your mother, God rest her soul. I am so happy you are back home safe with us, darling girl." And she kissed Oonagh on the cheek.

"It's good to be home with you," said Oonagh, her arm sleepily around Mrs Delaney's neck. "But I have been thinking, what will I do now that George has been weaned and you no longer need me to be his nurse."

"Well you can just stop that worrying," said Mrs Delaney. "You are part of our family now, Mr Delaney and I have discussed this and you must live with us, you can help with the housework and with George as he grows. We love you Oonagh, you were a gift to us when we lost our beloved Mary, and Oonagh, by the way, a letter has arrived for you, I presume it is from Seamus."

"From Seamus indeed?" said Oonagh, "Well that can wait until later."

An hour later, the two women were walking to Grandma Margaret's house. "I feel quite excited," confided Oonagh.

Miss Foster was still taking breakfast when Oonagh rapped on the front door. "Oh, we are sorry, are we interrupting you, is this an inconvenient time?" said Mrs Delaney as they were shown into the dining room.

"Not at all," said Miss Foster, "Maria bring two more cups and saucers please, our guests may like to take tea. And then bring the children downstairs." Turning to Oonagh, she explained, "They were both still asleep and I thought I would snatch a short time in peace."

Maria attended to the babies while the three women sat around the table taking tea and toast.

Soon Oonagh stood, "Oh I cannot wait a moment more, may I go upstairs to them, Grandma Margaret? "

Kitty, too large for the little cradle, slept now in the cot. She was sitting up watching intently while Maria was changing George's napkin. When she caught sight of her mother she stretched out her arms and squealed. Oonagh lifted her and Kitty immediately began to nuzzle her breast. "Well you haven't forgotten me then," said Oonagh, sitting on the bedroom chair and putting Kitty to her breast. Grandma Margaret and Mrs Delaney came into the room.

"That is remarkable," they said together.

"Yes, I expressed my milk as you both advised, in fact I had no choice when I first arrived in Arklow, my milk was overflowing. My ma instructed me and I expressed in her bedroom. I think it brought us closer in her last couple of days. Kitty you would have loved your grandma so much and she would have loved you too."

When Kitty had drunk her fill, her cheeks were pink and milk dribbled from the sides of her mouth. Oonagh passed her to Maria to be washed and dressed.

When George saw Oonagh, he yelled, "Mamma, mamma."

Oonagh lifted him. "You tug at my heart, little man," she said, "shall we see if you have forgotten?"

She put George to her breast. He had not forgotten.

"They were both taking the bottle, and even drank from the cup, but I did give them goat's milk," said Grandma Margaret.

"I will introduce solid food and allow them to wean when they are ready, as my mammy advised me," said Oonagh firmly. And she glanced at Mrs Delaney who was smiling as her grandson fixed his eyes on Oonagh's face, his plump little hands on either side of her breast. Oonagh looked across at Miss Foster who was tight lipped. "He was weaned while you were away," she said through pursed lips, "you'll have him soft."

"I don't think so," said Oonagh, "you can't love a child too much." And Mrs Delaney winked at her.

Oonagh smiled and Grandma Margaret said, "We must register the children for Saint Thomas church school, time will fly now, they will be five years old and ready for school before we know it."

Oonagh responded immediately, "No. I will be sending Kitty to the Catholic school in Reddish."

"Oh dear," said Kathleen Delaney, "I hope that doesn't upset the children, having to go to different schools."

Grandma Margaret smiled, "They will have to be separated sometime soon, George's father and grandfather will no doubt have plans for his future, he is the male heir to a man of noble birth let us not forget."

Chapter Eighteen
The Truth Will Out

Oonagh read the letter from Seamus in the privacy of her room directly after tea while Mr and Mrs Delaney played with the children.

"My darling girls," Seamus began, *"all is well here in Victoria. All the crops are in and winter approaches. Overall, it has been a wet summer but we have also had some glorious, warm and sunny days.*

"Charlotte is thinking of growing fruit trees on the farm and I am willing to try, although I have no experience in this type of farming. We have ordered some root stock which will have to be planted soon so that they are well established before the spring. The officer from the penal colony calls each week and Charlotte has given a good account of me. Our neighbours and Charlotte's relatives visit frequently too, I suspect it is to check on the safety of Charlotte and her son Jack.

"Jack is a fine young man not yet twelve years old and he is a good help on the farm. Our flock of merino sheep has expanded considerably and Charlotte has been a fast learner with the lambing. She delights in feeding the little orphan lambs when the ewes have twins or triplets and are unable to feed them all. She has also learned to milk our small herd of cattle and tells me she will be happy to teach you when you come to Australia. She really is a wonderful lady and I am sure you will be firm friends,

"After four years and with Charlotte's recommendation to the governor, I should hopefully be allocated a unit of land on which to farm. It would be up to you to request of the Lord Lieutenant of Ireland an assisted passage to Australia, allowing you to be sent out here with Kitty. Charlotte has made enquiries and it may be up to the Governor of the Colony to grant permission for you both to join me here but I remain hopeful that with Charlotte's help and recommendations it will not be too long before we are together.

"I send all my love to you and our dearest Kitty.

"Yours Seamus."

Oonagh read the letter over again. "Charlotte this, Charlotte that," she chanted.

Immediately the children were laid down to sleep, she took paper and pen into the dining room. Mrs Delaney knocked on the door and came quietly in. "Was it bad news in Seamus' letter, my dear?" she asked timidly.

"You could say that," said Oonagh, "but my letter will be worse news for him."

"Seamus," she had written

"I have just returned from nursing and then burying my dear mother in Arklow and I found your letter waiting. I am so happy your sentence is being served working for such an understanding and altogether wonderful woman. When I arrived in Dublin, your father was kindly waiting at the docks, at my father's request, to take me home to my sick mother. On the journey home, we stopped in Wicklow to collect your mother, who had been visiting Maggie Connor's little girl Patty. The child bears a striking resemblance to my own daughter, Kitty, and your parents tell me Patty is your daughter and their granddaughter. Apparently, they have been supporting Maggie and her child for some time now.

Regarding your recommendation, that I should contact the Lord Lieutenant of Ireland once four years of your penal servitude have been completed. I have to tell you that Father Kelly has made enquiries on my behalf and this concession only applies to wives of prisoners. I am curious as to which of us women should be regarded as your wife."

She simply signed *'Oonagh'.* and thumped the blotting paper hard onto her letter.

"Could you check my spellings please?" she asked of Mrs Delaney, her eyes brimming with tears as she thrust Seamus' letter and then her own into the older woman's hands.

"Oh, my poor girl," said Mrs Delaney once she had read the letters, "a cup of tea, I think is called for." She filled the kettle and put it to boil on the stove. Oonagh folded her letter into four and sealed it, ready to pass the letter on to Father Kelly when he visited.

It was almost three months later before Oonagh received a reply from Seamus:

"My darling Oonagh, my first love,

My four years penal servitude have been served, I have had an excellent report from Mrs Butler and from the officer at the penal colony. I have been offered a small unit of land of fifty to sixty acres on which to farm at a token rent each year of ninepence per acre. After five years of satisfactory farming I will be given the freehold. However, I do not have the money to pay the sea passage for yourself and Kitty to join me here yet. The only way I can see to get the money together is to go to the goldfields at Ballarat as so many of the other convicts have done before. I am therefore, heading for the goldfields next week and it may be some time before I can write to you again. Please Oonagh trust me that you are the only girl in this whole world that I want to be my wife.

With my eternal love
Seamus."

Oonagh read the letter over and over again and shook her head at herself in the mirror.

"Do I believe him?" she asked Mrs Delaney later.

Oonagh wrote in reply to Seamus:

"My dearest,
I am so happy for you that you will at last be free from your unjust servitude. The fare for myself to Australia is fourteen guineas and I would imagine that Kitty's fare would be equal even though she will of course share my cabin. I will give the matter my careful thoughts, dearest, but I cannot help but think you will be needing as much gold as you can prospect at Ballarat to earn the money to build a house and buy stock, seeds and farm tools for your farm. I think your first purchase should be a horse and of course you must build a house.

God keep you safe, my love
Oonagh and Kitty."

Oonagh passed the letter to Father Kelly when he called that week.

"You are being very sensible, my child," he said when she explained what she had written, "but you must think of all your futures, you have been strong to come this far and you need to be together. It does sound an exciting life in Australia though, the sisters have been trying to persuade me to take over the ministry in Gippsland. There is a small chapel adjoining the school and orphanage and a dire need for a priest for marriages, christenings and funerals, but I loathe to leave my flock, they are very dear to me."

Oonagh took her role as a teacher to George seriously until the children were ready for their respective church schools.

In the garden at the Delaney's she taught them the colours of the flowers in the garden. When Mr Delaney brought home a dozen tulip bulbs from the market Oonagh took the children into the garden together and they divided them into six each, and then planted them so that they would be in the sight of Grandma Delaney as she worked in the kitchen. They bloomed a brilliant scarlet in late spring.

Together Oonagh and the children gathered conkers from the horse chestnut trees in the park in autumn and counted them into little piles, before breaking open the coverings then Mr Delaney bored holes through them and baked them in the oven. Then he showed the children how to thread strings through them, knotting them at the bottom of the hole. He taught them to play conkers. Both the children had a prize conker by the end of autumn, victorious by the numbers of their opponent's conkers it had smashed.

Oonagh taught them about the seasons, the months of the year and days of the week. They learned to tell the time by the big clock in the hall. Every afternoon Oonagh and the children sat in the parlour with Grandma Delaney and recited nursery rhymes. Kathleen Delaney put dried beans in a cocoa tin and Kitty delighted in shaking the tin while they sang, while George banged on an upturned pan with a wooden spoon. They even performed for Grandma Margaret when she called around. "I expect George's father will arrange for him to take music lessons, he seems to have such natural rhythm," Grandma Margaret said with pursed lips and little finger curled as she sipped her tea from one of Mrs Delaney's best china cups.

Kitty dropped her cocoa tin down on the carpet and hid behind her mother, thumb in mouth, clutching on to Oonagh's apron as she peeped around the folds of her mother's skirt with big eyes.

"And Kitty was very good too," said Grandma Kathleen, "you should hear her sing '*The Meeting of the Waters*'," poor Oonagh has to sing that to the children every evening when they go upstairs to bed.

One Wednesday afternoon, on his regular visit, Father Kelly brought with him an envelope addressed to Miss Kathleen O'Brien. Later, Oonagh and Kitty sat in Oonagh's bedroom and they read it together:

"My sweet wee girl,
Forgive me for not being there when you took your first breath in this world, I am sorry I was not there when first you opened your beautiful blue eyes. Forgive me for not comforting you when you woke startled in the night, for not being there when your first sharp little tooth pierced your pink gums. I am sorry not to be able to lift you into the air or twirl you around in my arms. I am sorry I missed your first hesitant steps and I regret not hearing your ready laugh or seeing your dark curls bob as you run. I dream of showing you the colourful birds here in Australia and the wonderful animals, the like of which you have never seen.
"Forgive me for not being in your young life but remember, I love you no less.

"Your daddy, Seamus O'Neil."

"You must treasure this letter," said Oonagh. "We will find you a special box to keep it in."

Chapter Nineteen
The Beaching of the Mexico

The summer before the children started school was sunny and warm. Oonagh, with Theodore Foster's permission, travelled with both the children over to Arklow to spend time with Kitty's grandfather Francis Kennedy and Uncle Finn. They stayed at Uncle and Aunt Mahon's cottage. The couple delighted in the children's company.

On the Tuesday after they arrived Oonagh and auntie Bridie were sitting on a blanket on the river bank at the meeting of the waters. Oonagh stretched out her legs and hoisted her thick skirt up to her knees.

"I'll let the sun warm my legs," said Oonagh

"We will need to move out of the shade of this big tree then," said her aunt.

"I need to be close to the children," replied her niece.

Kitty and George were intent on throwing twigs into the gentle twinkling waters of the smaller river and delighting as their twigs met the powerful current of the wider river to be carried along and trapped among the rocks of the river bank or swept out into the estuary.

"Mine's the winner," squealed Kitty, "Mine's the winner."

George threw a whole branch in the little river and stomped off down the river bank

"I'm looking for fish anyway," he said, "twigs are boring." The current had carried his branch into rocks at the river side. Then Oonagh's heart sank as she heard George yelling, "Kitty, Kitty." Oonagh jumped to her feet and ran to the river bank. Kitty was sitting on the wet muddy clay of the bank, "I was throwing a twig and I slipped in Mammy, but a kind man lifted me onto the bank," she said as her mother took her arm and pulled her onto the grass. "What man?" said Oonagh, "Did you see a man, George?" George shook his head. "He had black curly hair like me," said Kitty.

Oonagh and Bridget's eyes met. "Michael?" murmured Auntie Bridget.

Oonagh led the children over to the blanket for the simple picnic that she had prepared and the four sat on the blanket eating bread and cheese and drinking mineral water from the glass bottle. "You must be very careful by the river, children," she said, "the current is very strong and can carry you out to sea." "Will it take us to America?" asked George.

"Not really," said Auntie Bridget, "the rivers flow east towards England, but you are not a twig you need to go on a boat or you will drown."

Kitty and George looked at each other alarmed and George put his arms protectively around Kitty, "I won't let you drown Kitty."

"Kitty so reminds me of Michael," Auntie Bridget whispered to Oonagh, "those dark curls and big blue eyes. As soon as you left for England, he wanted to follow you. Was he happy Oonagh, those last few months?" Oonagh told her aunt about Michael's labouring job at the mill and the happy times the friends had together, how all the household had enjoyed their evenings, singing while one of the Finnegan boys played the fiddle.

"Yes, I am sure he was happy, Aunt," Oonagh reassured her aunt and confessed to her that Seamus O'Neil was Kitty's father. "Seamus had asked Michael to live with us once the baby arrived." She recounted all the events of that fateful night and the parade on the following day.

"And will Seamus come back for you, Oonagh? It is a long sea journey for a young woman to take on her own with a small child, you would be very vulnerable," her aunt cautioned.

"I really do not know aunt, I only know that I loved him with all my heart," Oonagh replied. "But Auntie, I have written to him and it is all over between us since the summer Ma died and I discovered that Maggie Connors also had his baby that same summer that Kitty was born. Auntie he told me I was his first love and I would be his last,"

Then, "Hurry, children," she called before her aunt could reply, "the sun has disappeared behind those black clouds, we must run if we are to keep dry." Oonagh and her aunt rolled up the blanket, tying it with string, and hurriedly collected the remains of the picnic into the basket. The children laughed as they ran to the Aunt's cottage, trying to dodge the huge raindrops splashing on the road.

That evening Uncle Patrick brought them all fish suppers home, from the Daly's fish and chip shop in the front parlour of the Daly's home on the main street. White flaky cod with thick crispy batter cooked in delicious beef dripping. "No chips I'm afraid," said Uncle Patrick.

Once the children were asleep in bed, Auntie Bridget confided to Oonagh, "I have been thinking about Maggie Connors and her wee one, and the only way to know the truth is to ask her, Oonagh. She is working at the woollen mill in Arklow, Mr O'Neil put a word of recommendation in for her, the carter takes the mill's consignments of shawls and blankets to the Dublin docks, they sell very well in London at all the best shops."

"I will go tomorrow to see her," said Oonagh, "I really must know the truth, the matter is eating at my heart."

The following morning Oonagh walked down to Arklow with the children. As they approached the woollen mill, Oonagh spotted Maggie Connors sitting alone on a low wall outside the weaving house drinking tea from a white enamelled tin mug. "You run and play on the grass children, and don't go near the water wheel or river," said Oonagh.

"Hello Maggie, have you time for a little chat?" "Just a little while Oonagh, I have had to stamp my card to clock off," said Maggie.

"May I ask you a personal question, Maggie?" Oonagh said, sitting beside Maggie on the wall. Oonagh took hold of Maggie's hand and held it in the folds of her blue serge skirt.

"That depends what it is Oonagh."

"Can you see that your Patty and my Kitty have a resemblance of each other?" began Oonagh, "I do not wish to offend you but I would ask you, is Seamus O'Neil, Patty's father?"

Maggie looked Oonagh straight in her green eyes. "Is he Kitty's father?"

"Yes," said Oonagh.

"No," said Maggie.

"Then why do you let Mr and Mrs O'Neil believe they are her grandparents?"

"Because she brings them joy. They thought Seamus was the father, they were the only ones in the town who didn't judge me when I had no one to support me and my child," said Maggie, "My ma and pa and my wee brothers were on that fateful sailing barque the Mexico. They sailed from Liverpool on 29th October heading for New York, under Captain Winslow. The ship was wrecked off New York on 8th January."

"Oh you poor, poor girl," said Oonagh, "having to face that and your baby on the way, whatever happened?"

Waiting off New York there were many other square-rigged boats, they were all waiting for a pilot. Their lanterns were lit requesting a pilot but the seas were so rough that no pilot managed to get to them. It was unbearably stormy and cold. The captain of the Mexico stood off but a violent gale blew up and they were no longer able to hold to wind. Their ship was blown fifty miles off shore. Six of the crew were badly frost bitten leaving only the captain, the mate and two seamen.

On Monday morning the mate took a cast of lead and told the captain that they had five fathoms beneath them. The captain thought they had enough water beneath them to stand off but the ship was grounded, off Hempstead beach.

For three quarters of an hour the ship bumped and thumped the bottom heavily. The captain ordered all the passengers (there were over one hundred of them) on deck.

Maggie took a handkerchief from her the pocket of her dress, wiped her eyes and blew her nose. Oonagh put her arm around Maggie's shoulders as Maggie continued.

"And Oonagh, men women and children huddled around the captain on deck under frosty blankets, shivering and terrified for their lives. Some of the mothers had five and six wee ones."

Maggie sobbed and Oonagh hugged her close, "There, there, Maggie, were none saved?" "No Oonagh, none were rescued save for the captain and crew. The rescue boat came for them from the shore, but could not, would not, return for the passengers – for my ma and pa and my two wee brothers, because the seas were too rough. They say the screams and wails from those on board could be heard from the shore all that morning."

"How did you learn about the tragedy, Maggie, and how did my Seamus become involved in this?" asked Oonagh gently.

"Why I learned of it from the Dublin newspaper, Oonagh," sobbed Maggie, "I had taken work at the Inn when I was expecting Patty. Many men took liberties with me, but that night, when I had read about the shipwreck, when I realised I had lost all my family, I had no patience with the men. It was then that Seamus came into the inn, he talked to me, he was kind, he was understanding and he challenged the men to leave me to my grief. Oonagh, I must go back to my work soon, the overseer is looking for me." Maggie stood to leave.

"Aye," mused Oonagh. "that is my Seamus, kind and understanding."

"I wish to heaven that he was the father of Patty," said Maggie. "He stayed in my room that night, he had had too much ale and did not want to drive his father's horse and cart in the dark, but he laid on my bed and directly fell asleep. He came to see me for a few nights after that evening, he was willing to let me talk in my grief. He comforted me that my family would have lapsed into unconsciousness quickly in the severe cold, which gave me some comfort. After he left for England, his mother came to see me. Then when Patty arrived and she was the same dark colouring as her son, she assumed Patty was her son's child and she just fell in love with her. I could not bring myself to tell her the truth. Patty for her part loves her adoptive grandparents, she is at their house now while I work. But Oonagh, I must be back to work or I will lose my job. I hope I have helped you." Oonagh kissed Maggie. "Thank you for being truthful with me Maggie, you have helped me a great deal and I wish you and Patty the very best in life."

Chapter Twenty
First Days of School

It rained on the first day that the children went to school. George, dressed in new grey trousers to his knees, a white shirt and a grey and blue Fair Isle pullover that Grandma Margaret had knitted for him, went to the Anglican school, funded by the Anglican parish church, next door to it.

Kitty wore a grey dress covered by a white broderie anglaise pinafore, her hair tied back with a huge white satin ribbon. She and her mother were heading in the opposite direction, to the Catholic school attached to the new Roman Catholic Church.

Grandma Delaney took George and Oonagh walked with Kitty. "Now, remember the teacher will call you Kathleen," Oonagh said to her.

"Goodbye, George," said Kitty at the garden gate, tears welling in her eyes and trickling down her cheeks.

"Be brave, Kitty," said George, his hands in his pockets.

"Good heavens, you'll see each other at dinner time," said Grandma Delaney and they went their separate ways, the rain hammering on the big black umbrellas held by the two women.

It was a good half hour before the women were home again. "I'll put the kettle on," said Mrs Delaney, shaking her umbrella in the porch before standing it in the umbrella stand in the hall.

Oonagh swallowed hard. "I felt as if my heart would break when I left her in that schoolroom. Her coat was soaking wet and all the children had hung their coats over the rail, close to the stove in the middle of the room, some children were so wet that they had even had taken their shoes and woollen stockings off, oh the smell in that schoolroom of damp wool!"

"It was much the same when I left George," said Mrs Delaney, "it seems so sad to split them up, they have always been together."

It seemed as if the morning would never end and Oonagh carried the lump in her throat until it was time for the children to be collected from school.

When Kitty came out of the door signed 'Girls', at the Catholic school at midday, Oonagh was waiting at the big iron gate.

Three or four other mothers were waiting at the railings and their children ran to them. Their mothers fed the children from their breasts through the railings. Oonagh smiled at a young woman in a patterned headscarf who was closest to her.

"We've just slipped out of work at the mill," said the woman, "it is so much better now the children are at school, it was dangerous to take them into work with us, some little ones have been killed, crawling under those big weaving machines."

Oonagh nodded. "How dreadful, that must have been."

She bent to fasten Kitty's coat.

"How very lucky we are Kitty to have Mr and Mrs Delaney," she said as Kitty skipped alongside her, holding her mother's hand.

"I couldn't see out of the windows to look for you, they were too high up, Mammy," Kitty said, "and Mammy, Bernard Dolan says my daddy is a murderer. Is my daddy a murderer, Mammy?"

"No, he is not," said Oonagh, "your daddy is a good kind man, who loves us very much and we will one day all be together. Now tell me about school, what did you do?"

"We had to sit on a long seat, that they call a form, at a long table, the forms are all in a row across the big room and when you get cleverer you go onto the next one. I think I will be moving onto the next form soon because I can count already. The teacher stands at the end of the room and writes with chalk on the big blackboard. We have to chalk too on our little boards with wood around them they are called slates."

"It all sounds like a lot of fun," said Oonagh as they hurried home for dinner.

After dinner the two women helped the children into their coats, "Where are we going?" said George.

"Back to school," said his grandma. "I've already been there," said George, "Do I have to go again?" The two women glanced at each other and couldn't help but smile.

Kitty was correct, it was not long before she was moved onto the next form and then the next, and then she announced one afternoon, "Mammy, I am the new form monitor, for form three. Miss Holden told me today. I have to walk along the form and help all the other scholars (that is what Miss Holden calls the children). Miss Holden writes words and sums on the blackboard and the scholars have to write the letters and the sums on their slates. I have to walk up and down my form and make sure they are doing it right. I am going to get a badge, Mammy."

Oonagh and Grandma and Granddad Delaney were "so very proud", they told Kitty. George hugged her and said, "I am proud of you too, Kitty."

Kitty told Oonagh everything that happened at school. One day, as they walked home at the end of the school day, she announced, "Eleanor Miller's ma has had a baby boy. He was nine pounds. Miss Holden said 'What a whopper,' and Mammy, Billy White had bugs in his bedroom, he said they were in his bed and all up the walls. The men from the corporation are going today to kill them all. Ma what are bugs?"

Oonagh explained to Kitty that it wasn't Billy's fault and the Corporation men would get rid of the insects, "Because they bite and make you have itchy lumps on your skin," but she asked Kitty to promise not to join in if others teased Billy.

"Whenever I ask George what he has been doing at school, he tells me 'nothing' or that 'he has forgotten', Kitty tells you everything," said Mrs Delaney.

"That is girls for you," replied Oonagh laughing, "That is girls for you alright."

Chapter Twenty-One
Ballarat

George and Kitty were approaching their seventh birthdays before the next letter arrived from Seamus:

"My darlings,

I have only recently arrived back at the Butler farm from Ballarat. I was very successful at Ballarat. I now have enough money to send for you both and more than enough left to establish my own farm.

For the present though, I feel a duty to help Charlotte as she has had problems with foxes in my absence. I will repair her hen houses and make them fox proof. I also will renew her fences as the foxes have been killing her lambs. She will employ me as her farm manager, recompensing me in part with livestock for my unit of land which is close enough for me to begin work on while living at the Butler farm.

I fear that there is trouble brewing among the diggers at Ballarat. Victoria has only recently separated from New South Wales, and has its own government. Many of the gold prospectors are educated men and others, like me, are the victims of miscarriages of justice. Despite the growing population at Ballarat, the prospectors have no representation in government. Any gold found is already taxed by government but not long ago, a license charge of £1.10 shillings each month was imposed, this was quickly doubled to £3 and no official method of collection was arranged, leaving it open to corruption.

You may recall Mr Patrick Lalor, the landowner, back home in Queens County. Mr Lalor is a Member of Parliament at Westminster and a campaigner for home rule.

His son, Peter, arrived in Ballarat in 1853 seeking his fortune in the goldfields. Peter quickly became close mates with a Mr Gillies.

Peter Lalor, like his father, is a powerful orator and has been rallying the miners against the corrupt and disorganised collection methods for the license levy. He has formed the Ballarat Reform League.

Tempers were becoming heated and resulted in a murder at the Eureka Hotel. I left Ballarat immediately, as I had no intention of becoming involved in any disturbances, being mindful that I had been granted a unit of land by the governor, and having served only four years of my seven-year sentence.

When I was leaving Ballarat, the prospectors had united under the flag of the Southern Cross with Peter Lalor as their Commander in Chief. I tell you Oonagh, there is more trouble to come.

Charlotte has kindly said that she will sponsor you as her domestic servant, and then you and Kitty will have free passage to join me, as one child under the age of twelve years is allowed. I am hoping to hear from you by return and we can put things in place for your voyage.

I am longing to hold you once more in my arms.

Your true love,
Seamus."

"I'm not too sure I am impressed with the idea of you travelling all that way to be a domestic servant," said Mrs Delaney, when Oonagh read the letter to her. "I know we share the housework here, but this is home for you and Kitty."

"Yes," said Oonagh, "and a very loving, comfortable home it is for us, for sure."

Oonagh sat at the dining table, facing the old apple tree, that had been a part of so much of the children's lives, shading them from the sun as babies and then a sturdy frame for them to play and climb on as they grew. The old tree was weighted full of apples this year, they were only small yet, but they would swell and grow with the rain and sunshine and it would then be time for them to be harvested and stored in the cool cellar.

She wiped her eyes with her lace handkerchief, before she lifted her pen and dipped it into the inkwell:

"My darling Seamus,
Oh how I yearn to be in your arms, my love. This will be the hardest letter I have ever had to write and it is breaking my heart to write it.

I am so happy for you that Mrs Butler has made you her farm manager and that your own unit of land is close enough for you to begin work on it.

Our daughter is doing well at her school and has been recommended by her teacher, Miss Holden, to be a pupil teacher. After a course at teacher training college, there is every possibility she will become a qualified school teacher. This could bring a salary of £90 per year and a house provided, which will secure her future. Mr and Mrs Delaney have said they will pay her fees, but for the moment she will be in training already as a pupil teacher. The teaching profession is so respected in this society and I am very proud of our girl, as I am sure you will be.

My love, it hurts me so to write this. The truth is that when we were together before Kitty was born, my dream was to make a life with you here in England or over in Ireland, either would be wonderful. My only wish was to have a small farm together and a little cottage. I never dreamed of living on the other side of the world.

Since we have been separated, I have been lucky to make many friends who love me. The Delaneys love me and Kitty as their own family, Mr and Mrs Clancy care for our welfare and are always there for us. Father Kelly has always been such a large part of our lives here in Stockport and Kitty adores him. When we are in Arklow, Father Murphy is also supportive of us, as he was when he was my teacher all those years ago. George, God bless him, regards me as his mother and loves Kitty like a brother would love his sister. Even Miss Foster loves us a little, although I don't believe she would ever admit to it.

It would break their hearts, and mine, if we were to leave them. My love, this is where we belong.

My father is alone now, I think Finn will be leaving home soon he is already courting a local girl, Molly Daly, whose parents have a fish and chip shop. Pa will never leave Ireland. If Kitty and I came to Australia, we must harden our hearts never to see him again. He has so enjoyed our visits with George these past few years.

When we sail to Dublin, I am seasick and I cannot face the thought of the discomfort of ten weeks on a ship.

After speaking to Maggie Connors whose family were lost off the coast of America, when their ship was beached in a horrendous storm, I fear to put our daughter through the dangers of the oceans.

I know that you love your new country and are excited by the opportunities. I must say then, darling that you must carry on your life without me, but you are and always will be the love of my life,

Oonagh."

She blotted her letter then placed it carefully on the mantle shelf ready for Father Kelly to pass on for her, sure that the letter would arrive safely, in the care of one of the nuns.

Mrs Clancy called to see them, unannounced, the following week.

"Henry and I would like to buy Kitty's dress for her first communion this summer, as her godparents we would really like that. Mrs Watson has a display of white ready-made organza dresses in her window. Kitty will be about a twenty-six-inch chest I think, will she not?"

Looking across to Mrs Delaney, she said, "That is unless you were thinking…Kathleen?"

"Yes, that is agreeable to me," said Mrs Delaney, "I thought we would buy rosary beads for our goddaughter."

"So that's decided," said Mrs Clancy.

Oonagh told her all the news, about Seamus and Australia. "We have had encouraging news about Kitty too," said Oonagh. "Her teacher is recommending her as a pupil teacher. She is already form three monitor, but she will be given her own small group of scholars and a room off the main hall in which to instruct them." "When she finishes her schooling here aged twelve," she continued, "she will attend a teacher training college in Liverpool, she will be taught history and geography as well as reading, writing and arithmetic. Her teacher says she will make a wonderful teacher, and if she manages to secure a position at country school she could earn £90 per year and have a house provided. It is a good career for a girl, that it is."

"Yes, and Mr Delaney has agreed we will pay her teacher training fees," said Kathleen Delaney.

Mrs Clancy took tea with Oonagh and Kathleen, after they had collected the children from school. "If you search in my bag, Kitty," began Mrs Clancy, but Kitty was already searching in her Godmother's handbag for the usual aniseed balls that Mrs Clancy bought in the market for the children.

"After tea please, Kitty," said Oonagh.

The children ate tea in the kitchen and Mrs Clancy took Oonagh's arm.

"Could I have a quiet word with you please, dear?" "I would never want to come between yourself and Seamus but my Henry has felt so guilty that it may have been his evidence that partly led to Seamus' transportation." "Of course, Mr Clancy, how is he, is he back to work? How rude of me not to ask until now," said Oonagh.

"They will not allow him to drive his beloved trains but he is a guard for now, and much happier to be with his friends," said Mrs Clancy.

"But the thing is Oonagh, he has searched his memory, now that it is a little clearer, and he is absolutely sure that he heard an altercation coming from your house at Watson's Yard on that fateful night."

"Yes," said Oonagh, "that was at tea-time, I was there, Michael threw a limewashing brush at Seamus."

"No, my dear," said Norah Clancey, "Henry says it was much later than that, it was after the riot started. It was past ten o'clock, he had been up the yard to the privy before we went to bed. He heard shouting from your house then he saw Seamus come out slamming the front door and he was shouting as he left but Henry did not catch his words.

"You have been so strong for yourself and Kitty, you have a good life now and you are surrounded by people who love you. I do hope you will forgive me Oonagh for speaking out but Henry has been so concerned about what he heard." Oonagh put her arms around Norah, "Thank you for telling me, but my mind has been made up as to what I must do, and tell Henry not to worry, Seamus is making a good life for himself."

Chapter Twenty-Two
Derbyshire

Grandma Margaret announced at her next visit that George's father and grandfather would like a meeting with the Delaneys. It was agreed they should call round for supper the following Thursday.

"I will come straight to the point," said Theodore. "I, or rather we," he said, indicating his father Marcus and his mother Margaret, "would like George's education to be broader than that which he is receiving at the church school. We propose therefore that he should attend a private school in Derbyshire, as a boarder. The school has a very good reputation and will set him in good stead for the career that we have envisaged for him. He will, of course, be expected to enter the family firm."

Mrs Delaney was shaken and her lips quivered, "but, he is only a boy and has never been away from home, except for the short visits to Ireland with Oonagh and Kitty, and they are as close to him as a mother and a sister. No, he is too young to be sent away."

Mr Delaney put his arm around his wife's shoulders. "No, Kathleen, if it is to benefit our grandson then we must not stand in his way. He will stop here with us during the holidays, won't he?" he asked of Marcus and Theodore.

"Yes," said Grandma Margaret, "it will be good for him to have the company of better class young men, I sometimes think he and Kitty are too close."

She pursed her lips and turned her head away, lowering her eyelids.

Kathleen Delaney excused herself and went into the kitchen to bring a tray of scones and a pot of tea into the parlour. The children were in their night clothes leaning over the bannister. "What do they want, Grandma?" whispered George.

"Nothing for you to worry about," said Grandma Kathleen, sniffing and wiping her tears away with her apron.

"We will have to make it into a big adventure, and be sure to tell George I will collect him anytime if he is homesick," said Granddad Delaney after the others had left. "It really will be good for him, my dear, and he will be breathing good country air. Theodore and Marcus assured me that I may go with them when George is introduced to his headmaster later this month."

That month, Grandma Margaret took George twice into Manchester on the horse tram. "We must buy your school uniform from the school outfitters on

Deansgate," she told him. Kitty was not invited, although George said he wished she had gone, "Because it was boring."

Chapter Twenty-Three
A Recreational Facility for Working Men

"The children seem so solemn about George's boarding school," Mr Delaney said to his wife and Oonagh, on the Sunday evening of George's last weekend at home, before boarding school. "I think we need to do something to lift their spirits. Tomorrow afternoon is the grand opening of Vernon Park. The council have had people working on it for almost a year. I believe it is a wonderful place and a credit to our town. The best thing is, it is a people's park for recreation for the working man and his family. It was just wasteland before and was donated to the Council by Lord Vernon. There is to be a splendid parade with brass bands. The Lord Mayor himself will be there and the Marquis of Westminster.

"I could shut the shop at dinnertime and meet you in the square, we could all go, what do you think? The children will enjoy the parade. Customers have told me that the mills will be shut for the day, it promises to be a fun day."

"That is a wonderful idea, yes I agree, it would direct their minds away from boarding school," said Oonagh, and Kathleen nodded in agreement.

"I suppose we can delay wash day to Tuesday," she said.

Monday dawned bright and sunny, the horse trams down to Stockport were filling fast, but the four reached Mersey Square in plenty of time for the start of the parade at half past twelve. Granddad Delaney was waiting in front of the theatre as promised and he had a bag of treacle toffee and flags for the children to wave. The friendly societies were assembling under their colourful embroidered banners, The Grand Order of Oddfellows, The Order of Foresters and Stockport Lions Club. The Lord Mayor, wearing his splendid regalia and chain of office, was to lead the parade under a banner of the Stockport Corporation Coat of Arms and at the head of all the councillors, dressed in their Sunday best clothes, the men wearing top hats, their wives seemed to be in competition as to who could wear the largest and most colourful adornment of feathers and flowers on their hat.

There were in total about five thousand people in the parade with fourteen brass bands marching in between. The parade started promptly, and as the bands struck up they marched through streets hung with bunting and crammed with cheering, flag waving onlookers. They arrived at the gates of the park at three o'clock. The various societies took up their allotted positions while Mayor William Williamson, along with the Marquis and the Mayoral party took the platform.

The park was on four terraced levels with wide gravelled walkways three yards wide, edged by shrubberies and flower beds and leading to small lakes and basins. The children enjoyed running across the little rustic bridges. Every now and then there were seats and chairs to rest on. One handsome seat bore a brass plaque announcing it had been donated in memory of Frederick Wilkinson by Portwood Mills. The three adults rested on this seat while the children climbed the flight of steps leading up to the next terrace

"There were sixty steps altogether," Kitty announced as she climbed onto Oonagh's knee, "there is a lovely fountain up there at the very top, Mammy, and some statues."

"I don't think I will be climbing those steps just now, and coming down again would be even more painful for my elderly rheumatic legs," said Grandma Delaney, as a man shouting through a megaphone announced that the Stockport Choral Society would now sing *The Old Hundreth Psalm*'.

Following this performance, the Mayor gave a brief address congratulating his fellow townsmen on the provision of the park, which he said would now rival any park in the neighbouring town of Manchester.

The mayor continued by thanking all the builders and gardeners who had been employed, on the completion of such a beautiful recreational facility for the workers of Stockport to enjoy.

"The Mayoral party," he said, "are invited to a grand dinner at the town hall this evening, and the council has donated a bullock, twenty loaves and two barrels of beer for the enjoyment of all the builders and gardeners who had been so enthusiastically involved."

At a signal from the Mayor, the bands struck up and all those assembled stood to attention as they played "God Save the Queen". This was followed by a twenty-one-gun salute, after which the Choral Society gave an inspiring rendition of the '*Hallelujah Chorus*'.

As the last notes floated away, Mr Delaney led the ladies and children to see a grey stone statue, no more than four foot high. It depicted a hawker of sand, cap in hand. Mr Delaney said the man was a well-known, local character and still alive.

"I believe there is a massive bronze statue close to one of the smaller lakes," he said, "it was donated by India Mills, and there is another smaller one of Venus at the bath."

"I think we have seen enough for one day," said his wife, taking her husband's arm, "the children must be tired."

The five wearily caught the tram from Mersey Square and Mrs Delaney said she was afraid it would be bread and jam and a cup of warm milk for tea, when they arrived home.

The children were rosy-cheeked and asleep as soon as their heads lay on their feather pillows that evening.

Chapter Twenty-Four
Boarding School

The following Saturday, Kitty and Oonagh accompanied the Delaneys to the railway station, as the Delaneys and George, (handsome in his blue and maroon blazer, knee length grey trousers and school cap of blue and maroon) boarded the train for Derbyshire.

The train doors were slammed shut, the station master blew his piercing whistle, the stoker shovelled more coal into the firebox, steam puffed from the engine's chimney, the huge wheels slowly started turning and the shiny green locomotive pulled out of the station belching smoke. George waved to Kitty through his open carriage window until the train was way past the end of the platform.

"He will be back home in nine weeks, the time will fly," said Oonagh, hugging a tearful Kitty, "and Grandma Delaney has told me she will take us on the train to meet him one Saturday afternoon very soon, we can take him out for tea in the village where his school is." Kitty continued to wave even as the train chugged out of sight into the distance, grey smoke billowing from the engine.

"Bye-bye, George," she sniffled, and Oonagh took her hand as they hurried down the station approach.

"You can help me prepare tea for Grandma and granddad Delaney for later this afternoon," she said, "and we might bake a cake, you like to do that."

"Yes, but only when George helps me to scrape the mixing bowl," said Kitty.

George's first letter arrived in the middle of his first week. It was brief:

"My dear grandpa and grandma and Oonagh and Kitty,
Our housemaster told us that we must write a letter home.
Everything is pleasant. There are six boys in my dormitory including me, they all seem jolly fellows.
One boy has already had a beating from the master over using foul language. The food is fine but I miss grandma's fried bread.
With fond love,
George."

Kitty wrote a long letter back to George immediately, telling him everything that had been happening at home. About Grandma Margaret's visit the previous week, the important news that Miss Holden her school teacher was to marry a policeman next summer, the nit nurse had been to school but she, Kitty, had not got nits which she was glad about.

"My letter is much longer than George's letter," she told Grandma Delaney.

"That's because you are a chatterbox," said Kathleen, "but I expect George will be pleased to receive it."

"You said time would fly, Mammy," said Kitty on the way home from school at the end of October, "but time is not flying, when will we go to see George at his school?"

"Grandma Delaney has suggested this Saturday, would you like that?" said her mother and Kitty skipped all the way home.

On Saturday afternoon, the two women and Kitty, dressed in their best hats and mantles, set off on the train for Derbyshire. There was just one other person in their carriage, he lifted a large suitcase onto the luggage rack above his seat. Grandma Delaney chatted to him and he told her that he was an agent for Macintoshes. He was travelling to Bakewell to a gentlemen's outfitters, and was hopeful to make a good sale. His wife's family came from just outside Buxton and he had a little boy named Edwin. He gave Mrs Delaney his business card and Oonagh blushed when she saw the name 'James Linney Esquire'.

"Does your family have a coal merchant's business?" she asked.

"Cephas Linney is a cousin of mine," replied James Linney.

"We were customers of his when we lived in town," said Oonagh.

The scenery was beautiful, green rolling hills with flocks of sheep grazing between the dry-stone walls. Now and then, there was a low, grey stone farmhouse with half a dozen cattle grazing close by.

"I expect the farmers have a couple of pigs by the farm house in a sty, and some chickens too," she said to Kitty

"Yes and maybe some ducks, I would like to keep a duck," said Kitty.

The train passed through the Chatsworth estate and the carriage was plunged into darkness as the train entered I a long dark tunnel. Kitty moved closer to her mother and took hold of her hand. Oonagh removed her glove and held Kitty's small hand with her own warm hand.

"The Duke did not want to see the trains and their smoke from his stately home so a long tunnel had to be built to hide the trains," said the Macintosh salesman, "And this is where I get off." As the train pulled out of the tunnel and into the autumn sunshine again he took down his suitcase from the luggage rack, the train pulled into the station, Mr Linney opened the carriage door and turned to wish them a pleasant afternoon, as he stepped down onto the platform.

"And good luck to you, young man," said Mrs Delaney.

Their stop was the next and they were soon walking out of the station into the pretty little village. Walking towards them was George in his school uniform. Kitty ran towards him.

"Don't hug me, Kitty," George said as soon as she was within earshot, "the other boys might see me."

Kitty froze, dropped her shoulders and sighed.

"I'm learning Latin, Kitty," he said.

"Whatever for? Who speaks Latin?" she asked. "Go on then, say something."

"Puer puellam per silvam fugit," said George.

"What does that mean?" said Kitty, legs akimbo and hands on hips.

"The boy chases the girl through the wood," and he ran to tickle her under her arms. Kitty squealed and ran, with George fast on her heels.

George directed them to the tea rooms that he had visited with his father and Grandma Margaret the previous Saturday.

Grandma Delaney ordered tea and cakes. The waitress brought the cakes on a trolley and the children were allowed to choose two each.

"Why are you learning Latin, George?" asked Kitty.

"Oh, that's in case Father wants me to go to University, you have to know Latin," said George, "Or Greek."

"I think your father would like you to start an apprenticeship at your grandfather's firm when you are twelve, George, that is what we were given to understand," said Grandma Delaney, breaking into a cream filled chocolate choux bun with her fork.

Once they had finished their afternoon tea, the waitress cleared away the china and Grandma Delaney paid the bill, leaving a sixpence under the remaining saucer for the waitress's tip.

"They rely on their tips," said Mrs Delaney.

George asked if they would like to walk up to see his school.

"I don't think we will be able to go in, but you can see the sports field and the tennis courts, and my dorm is at the front, you will be able to see the window of my dorm."

The school was a large red brick-built building,

"It just looks like one of the big houses on Wellington Road," said Kitty.

"That's the refectory, that big bow window on the ground floor," George pointed out.

"It isn't as big as I imagined," said Oonagh, "and at least you can look through the windows, Kitty's school windows are too high up aren't they, Kitty?"

"Well I feel a little more at ease now I have seen where you are living," said Grandma Delaney.

Oonagh and Grandma Delaney gave George a hug and Kitty took hold of his hand.

"Goodbye, George," she said, "see you soon, I'll write another letter to you."

"I'll walk back to the station with you," said George still holding onto Kitty's hand.

"It will be Christmas soon, Kitty," said George, "and I will be home again." They boarded the train home and it was his turn to wave until the train chugged into the distance. Kitty hung, waving, out of the window of the carriage until her eyes watered from the smoke and soot of the engine's chimney.

Soon after George arrived home for the Christmas holidays, Oonagh and Grandma Delaney took the children on the tram into Manchester. Oonagh bought them a bag of hot roasted chestnuts each from a man with a barrow in Piccadilly Gardens.

Mrs Delaney took them over to see the wonderful Christmas display in the three huge windows of the department store on the corner of Market Street and Piccadilly.

In the first window was an enormous Christmas tree, dressed with tiny candles in holders and coloured glass baubles, with a beautiful angel doll at the top of the tree.

In the middle window was a traditional nativity scene, the Virgin and baby in the stable. Joseph stood by Mary's side and the shepherds, kneeling in artificial snow, close by.

In the next window the three kings in splendid velvet robes and golden crowns were riding through sand on camels made of wood and paper mache, holding their gifts for the Christ child.

High above the stable, lamps were lit behind silver stars and angels with wide organza wings were suspended on wires as if hovering in the sky. The children stared open mouthed in wonderment at the magical sight and their warm breath clouded the window.

Oonagh and Grandma Delaney led the children into the store and bought Christmas gifts for the family. Oonagh put them quickly into her shopping bag as soon as they had been purchased at the counter and wrapped in brown paper bags by the shop assistant.

Kitty chose a pretty handkerchief with pretty flowers embroidered in the corner for Grandma Delaney and a small bar of lavender scented soap for Grandma Margaret. Oonagh gave her half a crown to pay for her gifts at the glass-fronted counter. The shop assistant slipped a small sheet of blue carbon paper between the first two sheets of her receipt pad and wrote the details of the purchase and the cost of both items, then added the two amounts together, gave Kitty the receipt and pushed her own copy onto a steel spike on a wooden block by the cash drawer, she dropped the half crown into the drawer and gave Kitty two and a half pence change. Kitty's purchases were slipped into white paper bags and the assistant passed them over the counter to Kitty's outstretched arm.

"May I have another half crown, Mummy?" she asked Oonagh, "I would like to buy a gift for someone else."

"I'm afraid not, my dear," said Oonagh, "I had to withdraw money from my savings for this little trip and I would like to visit granddad Kennedy this summer." Grandma Margaret has insisted that George should spend Christmas

Eve at her home and that they should go to Theodore's home for Christmas dinner. "I have asked Mr Slater to take us in his cab."

"It will be pleasant for George to spend some time with his sisters Violetta and Adele, Jeanetta's children, they are five years and three years now," she said.

When the children were told, by Grandma Delaney, Kitty's shoulders dropped and she stomped upstairs to finish the story she was writing.

George followed her, "It isn't my wish, Kitty, and they won't be so much fun as you are, they are babies. I'll be back home for Boxing Day."

It snowed on Boxing Day, George was back home with Oonagh and Kitty.

Mr and Mrs Clancy had been invited for a dinner of cold roast beef with potato and onion salad. Mrs Delaney had made apple pies, as well as her mincemeat pies, using the apples that they had stored in the cellar.

Mrs Clancy had to shake the snow from her mantle as she stood in the porch.

The children were already in the back-garden stamping footprints in the snow.

The snow did not remain. By the time the Clancys left to catch the tram back home, the snow had disappeared apart from a little that was sprinkled here and there on the garden walls.

On the following Sunday, George returned to boarding school. It snowed very heavily, and Granddad Delaney said it was quite deep in Derbyshire.

"George and his school friends were having a snowball fight in the tennis courts, when I left him," he said.

Chapter Twenty-Five
Cricket Whites

On the first Sunday morning that George returned for the Easter holidays from boarding school, he and Kitty were sitting with his grandparents at the breakfast table, tucking into Grandma Delaney's fried bread and eggs. "You make the best fried bread, Grandma," said George, dipping the crispy bread into the bright yellow yolk, "Granddad, I will need cricket whites for next term, shall I mention it to Grandma Margaret?"

"I think that is something we can buy for you, lad," said Edward Delaney, "could you take him to the school outfitters, Kathleen?"

"Yes, we can all go," said Grandma Delaney, "you'd like to come too, would you not, Kitty?"

Kitty nodded and the two children asked to be excused to play catchers outside with a tennis ball. "George, I have a skipping rope," said Kitty, "Grandma cut it from the old washing line."

Grandma produced a used floor polish tin and, having chalked numbers on the garden path with a piece of limestone, they played at hopscotch. At the end of that first day at home, Oonagh said, "Well, you both have rosy cheeks, I have not seen you all day." "Kitty is usually writing in her bedroom," she told George, "if she is not writing letters to you, then it is stories she writes. We are fortunate that our neighbour works at the print works and brings paper home for Kitty."

During the first week of the Easter holidays, Mrs Delaney suggested that they went into Manchester for George's cricket whites. She and Oonagh and the children waited for the tram to Manchester at the top of the road. The children were eager to travel on the open top deck, in the sunshine.

"I do not think I will come up-top, but I will tell the conductor and pay your fares," said Grandma Delaney, as the children excitedly climbed aboard, and up the stairs at the rear of the tram, with Oonagh behind them. As the tram travelled past the huge trees in the gardens and the park, the overhanging branches reached into the tram.

"Take care, those branches do not hit your faces," called Oonagh to the children, "it would be prudent to sit beside me on the left-hand side of the tram." They alighted at Piccadilly and Kitty was the first to read the huge sign on the windows of the department store 'Red Letter Day' she read aloud as they crossed onto Market Street. "We will just have a little peep inside," said

Mrs Delaney taking Oonagh's arm, "I read in the newspaper that they have lady's costumes for sale at seven shillings and eleven pence, Edward said I should treat you if there was one to suit you." Just inside the door of the store was a rail of ladies' linen suits. An assistant was polishing the counter, removing the numerous finger marks from the glass front with a duster.

"Yes madam," she said as she moved towards Oonagh, "would you like to try on one of the linen costumes, or we have more costumes in all-wool serge."

Oonagh looked at Mrs Delaney.

"No, I think the linen. It is coming into summer," said Kathleen. The assistant measured Oonagh with her eyes and Oonagh followed her into a fitting room to try on a cream skirt and fitted jacket with white poplin collar and lapels. Kathleen Delaney called through the door, "So, let me look at you," and Oonagh came out of the fitting room, the skirt of the costume came down to her ankles, with a little pleat at the rear hem and the fitted jacket flattered her slim waistline. "Oh yes, you look lovely, you will need something elegant to wear when we attend cricket matches at George's school. I think a pair of white gloves will complete the outfit and a cream handbag," she nodded at the assistant who produced the accessories from the display behind the glass and laid them on the counter, before ushering Oonagh back into the fitting room to remove the costume.

When Oonagh came out of the fitting room, Mrs Delaney said, "They also have velveteen on sale which has been reduced to one shilling and four pence a yard. I would like to buy some to make cushions for the parlour."

Grandma Delaney went with the assistant to the haberdashery counter, she chose four yards of velveteen in a mustard colour.

The assistant cut the fabric, folded it carefully in tissue paper and wrapped all the purchases in brown paper before tying the parcel with string. Mrs Delaney paid for the purchases while Oonagh took the impatient children outside, into the sunshine.

"Look," said George, "Grandma Margaret is across the road." Miss Foster was coming out of Lyons tea rooms.

"You have good eyes, George, I can only just glimpse your grandma between all the traffic," said Oonagh, "Oh yes, now I see her. She has a white broderie parasol, very pretty."

"Yoo hoo! Miss Foster," she called.

Margaret Foster turned and waved, just as Mrs Delaney came out of the store.

Dodging the carts and carriages, holding high her parasol, Miss Foster arrived at their side.

"Well, what a coincidence, George, my darling boy, Kathleen, Oonagh, how lovely to see you all. I have been to see George's grandfather on business and just popped into Lyons for a cup of tea. Coincidentally I have an errand to run in Spring Gardens, would you like to accompany me, George?"

George edged over to Oonagh and slipped his hand into hers.

"We are going to buy my cricket whites for school, Grandma," said George, blushing. "You should have asked, George, it is for your father and me to buy your school uniform and sportswear," said Grandma Margaret.

"No," said Mrs Delaney, "Edward is insistent, we would like to buy his cricket whites, Edward is a huge cricket fan, he used to play himself."

"Oh well," said Miss Foster, "I will not argue with you if Edward is insistent. He is George's grandfather after all, but let me treat us all to tea and buns afterwards."

"Yes, thank you Margaret, would you care to accompany us to the school outfitters?" said Mrs Delaney

"I will indeed," said Miss Foster, "there are some dual and triple gas chandeliers that I would like to consider in a shop on the corner of Victoria street and Deansgate. I am to have gas piped to my home, it will be so much more convenient than oil lamps. Do you not agree Kathleen?"

"I am sure you are correct, Margaret," said Mrs Delaney, "but my priority is to have an indoor water closet as soon as the sewers have been continued into our district. It will be so much more pleasant than making our way up the garden path on a freezing winter's night."

"Shall we make our way to Spring Gardens? There is a quality grocer there and I have some purchases to make. My elderly neighbour has been quite unwell and I would like to take a jar of beef extract around to his wife so that she might make him some beef tea which will, I am sure, assist his recovery. This Friday George's two sisters are stopping with me overnight while Theodore and Jeanetta attend a ball at the Memorial Hall in Albert Square. I must buy some breakfast chocolate, I usually buy the quarter pound block. It is simply made at the table by adding hot milk to a chunk of chocolate in the cup and stirring vigorously. It is a treat for the girls. Would you like to come over, George, to play with the girls?"

"Thank you, Grandma Margaret," said George, "but Kitty and I were intending to go to Vernon Park," he squeezed Oonagh's hand, looked up at her, and winked, as granddad Delaney would do. "Were we not, Oonagh?"

"Yes," said Oonagh, "they had asked me to pack a picnic. Perhaps another time, Grandma Margaret."

George squeezed Oonagh's hand again. They all walked with Miss Foster to the grocer in Spring Gardens. Mrs Delaney purchased a bottle of coffee essence for Mr Delaney and she also bought some of the quality tea that the grocer was selling. The grocer scooped the tea out of a sack into a blue paper bag, and weighed it on the brass scales, "Half a pound, madam? That will be one shilling and two pence."

Purchases complete, they left Spring Gardens and set off down the back streets, crossing behind St Ann's church along King Street and onto Deansgate. The school outfitters was across the road but the rest of Deansgate down to Market Street was blocked. "Road Closed," Kitty read out loud, "New improved gas lights are being fitted by Bray and Company of Leeds." "I believe there have been attacks on policemen by unruly drinkers when the officers have tried to enforce the licensing laws," said Mrs Delaney. "The street lighting will make law enforcement safer for the police."

"I doubt I would venture into town unaccompanied at night, would you, Kathleen? Drunks and footpads, it just is not safe anymore," said Miss Foster.

"Indeed," said Kathleen Delaney, "but I never have occasion to venture out at night without Mr Delaney. Doubtless the improved lighting will be a deterrent to miscreants."

The group reached the school outfitters shop; there was a display of cricket wear in the double window along with cricket stumps and a mannequin of a boy wearing cricket whites and a school cap, holding a cricket bat at the stumps.

The assistant looked for George's measurements in the card index, then at Grandma Delaney's request, laid a full set of cricket whites on the counter. White linen trousers, white shirt and a white V-necked pullover with George's school colours of blue and maroon in stripes on the welt and the neck, with a flourish, the assistant presented shin pads and put those on top of the clothes along with white socks. "Would sir care to try the trousers on, mother?" he winked at Oonagh. "Young men grow so quickly at this age," he said.

"Yes, George, I think that would be wise," said Oonagh, smiling at the assistant. Oonagh went into the changing room with George, "Yes I think we need the next size," she said, "I cannot get my fingers into the waistband. Too many cream teas, young sir, and your legs are definitely longer." The assistant brought in a larger pair and Oonagh was satisfied they would last George for that cricket season, at least.

Back in the shop, Mrs Delaney paid for the cricket whites and the shin pads, then the assistant parcelled the items in brown paper, tying the parcel with string before passing it to George to carry. Once back outside in the sunshine, they all accompanied Grandma Margaret to view the gas chandeliers at the shop in Victoria Street. "The triple chandeliers with the fluted glass globes are most elegant. I will decide on those for the parlour, dining room and my bedroom," said Grandma Margaret.

"You must be extra careful to turn them off fully," said Grandma Delaney, "I have heard of two children living on John Street, who have died of gas poisoning."

The shop assistant nodded, "Yes indeed." "I will count the number of lights I need and my son Mr Theodore Foster will arrange the installation," said Grandma Margaret, "thank you, young man." Kitty and George were happy to leave the musty shop, knowing the next stop was Lyons Tea Rooms. They followed Grandma Margaret as she led the way to Cross Street, past Sinclair's Oyster Bar and up to Market Street where the gas lighting street installation extended to. They passed a Gentleman's Outfitter and Kitty stopped to look in the window at the red hunting jacket with shining brass buttons, shiny black riding boots and an assortment of horse whips.

"Poor horses," she said.

George said, "Poor fox," but was more interested in the hat display, top hats, bowler hats and flat tweed caps. "I think I will wear a top hat when I go to work."

The waitress in Lyons wore a long grey skirt and a long starched white apron with a bib and straps over the shoulders, crossed at her back then tied back around her waist with a bow at the back. Her hat was stiffly starched, trimmed with lace and clipped into her short mousey hair at both sides with kirby grips. She showed them to a table by the bow window and carried a fifth chair over. "Tea and buns, please Miss," said Grandma Margaret, the waitress nodded and wrote her request on a small notepad along with the table number. George sat down on the chair closest to the window and Grandma Margaret immediately sat beside him. George raised his eyebrows at Kitty and she sat opposite him. Mrs Delaney sat beside her namesake and squeezed her hand. Oonagh sat at the head of the table, where she presided over the teapot once the waitress arrived with a wooden tray and placed china and cutlery on the crisp white tablecloth along with a pot of tea in a large brown teapot. The waitress carefully laid the china around the table. Gleaming white cups and saucers with an elegant turquoise stripe around the rim and the Lyons name on the cups. She excused herself and returned with sugar-sprinkled buns and fruit cake on a mahogany cake stand.

Oonagh poured tea for the children and asked the waitress for extra milk when she returned with the buns. George and Kitty plopped two sugar lumps each into their milky tea. George sneaked a lump into his mouth when Grandma Margaret was looking the other way. Oonagh did not miss it though, she wagged her finger at George and winked. Both children helped themselves to a bun and the ladies all chose fruit cake. Grandma Margaret removed her white lace gloves and cut a small slither of fruit cake from her slice with a small cake knife, placed the morsel elegantly in her mouth and wiped each side of her lips with the white linen napkin. "Delicious," she said once her mouth was empty and she sipped her tea with her forefinger and thumb gripping the handle of her tea cup and her little finger crooked, "Mmm, that was good."

Kitty was wriggling on her seat, shifting her weight from hip to hip. She looked across to her mother with hot cheeks.

"Yes, Miss Wriggles?" said Oonagh, "would you like me to take you to the ladies' conveniences in Piccadilly gardens?"

"Yes please, Mammy," said Kitty. Oonagh took her hand, left the tearooms hurriedly and walked across the road with Kitty, George followed close behind.

"I do wish that child would refrain from calling her mother 'mammy' and refer to her as 'mother'," Miss Foster said to Mrs Delaney.

"Oh, they are back already," said Grandma Delaney getting to her feet.

"The water closets are very clean and smart with taps and basins to wash your hands," said Oonagh, "does anyone else want a top up of tea?" and she filled the tea-pot with more hot water from the hot water jug. "Not for me thank you, there is only so much tea that I can take," said Miss Foster.

"You know me," said Mrs Delaney passing her cup and saucer to Oonagh. The children looked at Oonagh and then Kitty indicated the buns with her twinkling eyes.

"Yes, as far as I am concerned," said Oonagh, "but you should ask Grandma Margaret, it is her treat."

Both the children pounced on the sugar topped buns as soon as Grandma Margaret nodded that she was in agreement. "Now, about Saturday," said Grandma Margaret, "I take it we may join you on the trip to Vernon Park. I will of course come by Mr Slater's cab with your sisters, George, I am afraid I cannot bring myself to travel by horse tram, they can become quite crowded at weekends."

"How will you be returning home today, Margaret?" said Mrs Delaney.

"Oh, I will take a cab," said Miss Foster, "as I say I cannot abide the trams, and why should I? Marcus has his own carriage, he and his wife would never take the tram or omnibus,"

"Yes certainly, we would be delighted if you join us on Saturday," said Oonagh, "would we not, children?" George frowned at Kitty, "Yes, fine" he said. Oonagh turned to Mrs Delaney, "Would you be able to accompany us?"

"Try to stop me," said Mrs Kathleen Delaney, "it will give me the opportunity to return your kindness Margaret, shall we say ten-thirty in the morning at the little tea rooms by the Grand fountain."

The group parted company at Piccadilly Gardens. Miss Foster hailed a horse cab while Oonagh, Mrs Delaney and the children boarded the tram back to Heaton Chapel. They sat all in a row on the long seat, downstairs, at the left-hand side of the tram. When the conductor came to collect the fare, with his black leather money bag over his shoulder and across his body, Kitty asked if she may pay the fare and she was thrilled with the purple tickets that were clipped and, issued, "We can play at trams with these George," she said. "Yes," mumbled George, "but granddad and I are going to practice bowling on the park, so I won't be playing games very much now these holidays."

"That is agreeable to me George," said Kitty, "I want you to be selected for your school cricket team, then I can come to watch your matches."

Chapter Twenty-Six
Hide and Seek

At 10.00 am on the Saturday morning, Oonagh, Mrs Delaney, and the two children passed through the huge wrought iron gates into the park and made their way up to the grand fountain, passing the flower beds which were ablaze with colour. Orange and magenta antirrhinums filled one semi circular bed. "Now, I would never have put those colours together," said Mrs Delaney, "but they look amazing." The children ran to the steps leading up to the next level and raced each other to the top. "I've won, I've won!" shouted Kitty when she reached the side of the lake with the glorious fountain and the statue of Venus at bath. Oonagh and Grandma Kathleen made their way slowly up the steps. Oonagh took the older woman's arm to assist her, while Grandma Kathleen pulled heavily on the handrail. "I get a little breathless these days and my knees are not what they were," said Grandma Delaney.

"Let us find a seat at the window of the tea rooms," said Oonagh, "we can keep alert for Grandma Margaret." The other lady soon arrived, struggling a little up the steps, pulling on the handrail. Halfway up, she paused to catch her breath and look around her. Oonagh and Mrs Delaney waved, but Miss Foster did not appear to see them, instead she took a lace-trimmed handkerchief from her handbag and wiped her upper lip and brow. She caught sight of the other women and waved her handkerchief. Violetta and Adele trudged up the steps. They were dressed in long organza dresses, Violetta in pale blue and Adele in peach. They both wore straw boaters, trimmed with huge bows tied at the back. Violetta trod on Adele's foot. Adele screamed to her grandmother and pulled Violetta's hair. Grandma Margaret wagged her finger at them both and Violetta began to cry. Then they saw George and screamed, "Georgie, Georgie!" running to him and pulling on the sleeves of his coat. "Pick me up, Georgie, twirl me round," begged Adele. George raised his eyebrows to Kitty. "We are playing at hide and seek," he said to his younger half-sisters. "Oh, can we play? Can we play?" said Violetta. Grandma Margaret turned to George, "Take care of your sisters, George," she said and continued to the tea rooms to join Oonagh and Mrs Delaney. "You girls hide and I will count to one hundred," said George, putting his hands over his eyes, "one, two, three."

"Quickly now, hide," said Kitty, "Can't we hide with you?" begged Violetta.

"No, you must find your own hiding place, it's more fun," said Kitty. "See there are lots of places to hide, behind shrubs, behind seats. Lots of places," said Kitty as she ran up the steps, and made herself as thin as Grandma Delaney's clothes prop and stood on the plinth of the statue of Venus, holding firmly around Venus's waist. Violetta followed her and hid behind a big rhododendron bush which was resplendent in glorious deep red blooms, "Violetta," said Kitty in a stage whisper, "don't stand on those anemones, the blue flowers, the parkie will be angry."

"I can stand where I want," said Violetta, "my daddy says his rates are very expensive and his rates have paid for this park for the workers." "Shush," said Kitty, "George will find us."

Adele had run the other way and hid behind the Portwood Mills bench at the bottom of the steps. "Coming," called George, ignoring little Adele hiding behind the seat.

Violetta saw the park keeper walking up towards them, picking up pieces of litter. She tip-toed across to the statue and tried to step onto the plinth.

"There isn't room for two of us," whispered Kitty, but Violetta pushed her foot against Kitty, treading on Kitty's foot. "Move over," she said.

"There's no room," said Kitty, "one of us will fall in the lake. You go back behind the red flower bush," Violetta managed to get both feet onto the plinth but knocked the brim of her straw boater against the statue of Venus. She screamed as her boater fell into the lake and floated gently away, rapidly filled by the water from the fountain. Violetta leaned out, holding onto the leg of the statue with one hand. "Leave it, Violetta," cautioned George, who had run up the steps, alerted by the screams.

He was too late.

Violetta fell into the lake which was fortunately only waist deep to the five-year-old. She struggled to her feet and waded to the side of the lake into George's outstretched arms. George helped her out. Then she ran, her mouth, wide open in a silent scream, her long blue organza dress was now streaked a muddy brown and was clinging, soaking and bedraggled to her body, her ringlets were gone (so much for bearing the discomfort of curling rags in her hair the night before) and her long wet hair stuck to her face. "I'm telling," she managed to gulp out, before resuming her silent scream and running to the tea rooms and Grandma Margaret. Kitty ran and collected Adele from behind the park seat, "Come along, Adele, we will go to Grandma Margaret in the tea room."

Violetta had arrived in the tea-rooms well before George and by the time Kitty and Adele arrived, she had calmed a little and her silent screams had become sobs as she turned between each sob to look into Grandma Margaret's eyes.

"She did it," she said, pointing at Kitty, "she knocked my hat off and made me fall in the water, Georgie saved me."

"Young lady, that was an unforgivable, nasty thing to do to a younger child," said Grandma Margaret. "What do you have to say for yourself? And George, I asked you to take care of your sisters, your father will hear of this."

134

"I was on the statue first," said Kitty, head bowed and moving beside her mother.

Adele, thumb in mouth took her sister's hand and scowled at Kitty. "I'm sure Kitty would not have done that on purpose, Margaret," said Mrs Delaney. "No, she lost her footing," said Kitty, "I thought of that hiding place, there was not enough room for two at the bottom of the statue, I told her to go back to her own hiding place."

"But you told me the parkie would get me," sobbed Violetta.

"I think Mr Slater will be waiting to take us home, it is a quarter to twelve," said Miss Foster glancing at the clock on the wall of the tea rooms, "Let me take you home, Violetta, and into some warm clothes."

Violetta continued to sob and was now clinging to George's arm. "Come home with us, Georgie," she pleaded between sobs, looking up at her half-brother with big red eyes and a very snotty nose. "I can't, I'm sorry," said George, "I am practising bowling on the field with granddad Delaney, every night now, until I go back to school."

"Come along now, girls," "said Miss Foster, tutting at Kitty while ushering the girls out of the tea rooms.

"Thank you for your hospitality, Kathleen, I'm just sorry it all had to end this way," and she fixed Kitty with a steely glare. Kitty blushed fiercely and hid behind Oonagh's skirt. "Yes, I am so sorry Violetta fell into the lake," said Mrs Delaney, we must just be grateful the water is not deeper or it could have been a real tragedy. As it is, it is only a wet dress and bruised dignity. Goodbye Violetta, goodbye Adele."

Oonagh, Kitty and George repeated together, "Goodbye Violetta, goodbye Adele, and goodbye Grandma Margaret."

"Now then you two, would you like some ginger beer?" said Oonagh, as soon as Miss Foster had left. She caught the waitress's eye. "And raspberry buns?"

Oonagh turned to Kitty, Kitty was crying, plump tears plopping down her hot, red cheeks. "I didn't push her in Mammy, honestly, she was trying to squash onto the bottom of the statue with me."

"No, I don't believe for one moment that you did, Kitty but I know one thing, you must never step onto the statues again, they are a work of art, and as such they deserve your respect. Remember that." George and Kitty sat together and drank their ginger beer out of tall glasses. After they had finished their raspberry jam buns, Mrs Delaney paid the waitress and they all walked to the tram stop. There was no sign of Mr Slater's cab, "They will be home by now," said Grandma Kathleen.

"I am sorry about my sisters, Kitty," said George, "We will not tell them if we go again."

That evening, after tea, granddad Delaney took George to practise his bowling on the open land, at the top of the road, while Kitty washed the dishes and her mother dried them. It was dusk before Granddad and George came home. George was excited to tell Grandma Kathleen and Oonagh that Granddad thought he would make the school eleven definitely."

"Up to bed with you now," said Oonagh, "Kitty was asleep long ago."

"I was amazed at how quickly George took to spinning the ball and how far it moved, he has some real power in his wrist," said Edward Delaney to his wife.

For the rest of the holiday, Kitty was persuaded by George to play cricket every fine day. Granddad Delaney bought a cricket bat for him as an 'early birthday present'.

Kitty never quite learned to bowl overarm, "But it is still good practice for my batting," said George. When the day came for George to return to his school, Kitty confided to her mother, "I can go back to skipping now Mammy, I think I will call 'round at Annie Clark's house and see if she can come out to play."

Chapter Twenty-Seven
The Sport of English Gentlemen

It was only two weeks into the summer term that the Delaneys received a letter from George, announcing proudly that he had been selected for the school cricket team and that they had a match against Bakewell school the following Saturday afternoon. "We mustn't miss that," said Edward, "I feel confident to leave Herbert, my assistant, in charge for the Saturday afternoon. The boy is learning fast and I will give him a nice piece of silverside for his mother in extra payment."

Oonagh, Kitty, and Grandma Delaney met Mr Delaney at the train station on Saturday at twelve, noon and they took the train together to Bakewell. As soon as George saw them, he hurried over to greet them, looking quite a young man in his cricket whites and his fair hair oiled and combed back in a quiff. "I think you have grown a good few inches," said Oonagh, then stepping back she looked him up and down, "I hope your trousers are still long enough." Then striding over, came Mr Shepherd, his sportsmaster, "Now then, young Foster, are you going to introduce me?"

"Yes, sir," said George, "my grandparents, sir," and he indicated Edward and Kathleen Delaney. "Pleased to meet you sir, I am Edward Delaney and this is my wife, Kathleen," said granddad Delaney, shaking Mr Shepherd's hand vigorously. "And I believe it is you that we have to thank for George's bowling skills," said Mr Shepherd, "I am a cricketer myself. He is coming on a treat, a fine strong bowler, and with that left-handed spin of his he is a remarkable force to reckon with at such a young age."

"Well, I have played a little myself in my younger days, wonderful game, and good for a lad's character building," said Granddad.

The handsome sportsmaster turned to Oonagh who was looking elegant, her red hair curled and shining in the sunshine and wearing the cream linen costume that Mrs Delaney had bought for her in Manchester. "And you, I take it are George's mother, delighted to meet you Mrs Foster." Bowing, he took Oonagh's right hand and kissed it. Oonagh blushed a little as George explained, "Well no, I mean yes, kind of, and this is Kitty, my kind of sister and my best friend, who helped me practise my batting," and George put his arm around Kitty's shoulders. Kitty blushed and she told her mother on the way home, she wanted to hug George right there but was worried his pals might see. Bakewell had erected a marquee for refreshments and Mr Shepherd insisted on escorting Oonagh to take a glass of lemonade before the match began and then showed her to a seat on a bench in front of the cricket pavilion as the match commenced. Grandma and Granddad joined her with Kitty.

The home team captain won the toss and decided to take the field. George and his room-mate Pollitt opened the bowling for the visitors. George took the wickets of both their opening batsmen and trapped their fourth man lbw. George also helped Pollitt shine, by taking two magnificent catches. The home side were dismissed for 56. As a middle-order batsman George kept his team's innings ticking along and saw them pass the target of 56. At six-thirty, stumps were drawn and as the visiting team's batsmen came off the field to rapturous applause from the pavilion, granddad Delaney positively glowed with pride as he patted his grandson's back, his smile was from ear to ear.

Mrs Delaney, Oonagh and Kitty stood in line to hug George and congratulate him on a splendid display.

The sportsmaster came across to say farewell and that he hoped to see the family again very soon. Oonagh blushed as he took her hand again, "It was so delightful to meet you, George's 'sort of mother', and you Miss Kitty," and he ruffled Kitty's dark curls.

On the way home on the train, Mr Delaney promised them all fish and chips from the shop next to the station, to celebrate George's success.

They all sat on the long seat outside the chip shop and ate their fish and chips, sprinkled liberally with salt and malt vinegar, out of newspaper wrappings. "It is the perfect ending to a perfect day," said Mr Delaney, hugging his wife to him and giving her a salty, infrequent public kiss. "I could do with a nice cup of tea," said Mrs Delaney as they walked down to the tram stop. As soon as they walked through the front door of home, Oonagh hurried Kitty up to bed and she heard Mr Delaney fill the kettle in the kitchen.

Chapter Twenty-Eight
Dr Gould FRCS

When Oonagh returned from walking to school with Kitty on the Monday following the cricket match, she was alarmed to find that Mrs Delaney was still in her bed. The older lady had usually stripped the bedding and was well on with the washing by this time on Mondays. "Shall I bring you a nice cup of tea and some toast?" said Oonagh

"Just some tea please, love," said Mrs Delaney. "I really don't fancy anything to eat, I think I have a temperature and my feet are hurting dreadfully."

"I really think you should eat a little something," said Oonagh, "maybe I could tempt you with a baked egg custard, I'll put it in the oven immediately and perhaps you will eat a little at dinnertime."

Oonagh felt Mrs Delaney's forehead, "Yes you are hot, put your tongue out, yes it is quite furry. Would you like me to ask the doctor to call?"

Mrs Delaney was more concerned that Oonagh started on the laundry. "Just wash the bottom sheets and put the top sheet to the bottom," she said, "then you won't have as much to do, I am concerned you are having to manage alone."

"Don't worry about that," said Oonagh, "I have much more time now that Kitty walks home alone. I like to walk to school with her to make sure she is safe and it gives us time to talk together. Now you rest there and I will bring you a nice cup of tea. Perhaps you are overtired. We were out in the fresh air all afternoon on Saturday. Do you think you caught a chill?"

"Well I must admit I was quite uncomfortable sitting on those seats in front of the pavilion and it was breezy even though the sun shone. I will see what Edward thinks when he comes home. There is a new doctor he says on Tiviot Dale."

While the water boiled for the tea, Kitty mixed the eggs and milk, added sugar and poured the mixture into a buttered dish, she grated nutmeg on the top and placed the dish in a bain-marie before putting it into the oven. "There now, maybe that will tempt you, dear lady," she said aloud and carried a cup of tea to Mrs Delaney, "Now it's my turn to take care of you," she said, kissing Mrs Delaney's cheek.

Mr Delaney brought lamb chops home for their tea, Oonagh had already prepared the vegetables and soon prepared the meal. "Mrs Delaney has not been well today and I advised her to rest in bed," she told Edward as the vegetables simmered and the chops sizzled in the frying pan on the range. "Yes, she complained of acute pain in her joints, particularly her hands and feet, yesterday," said Mr Delaney. "I just thought she was stiff from sitting so long at the cricket match."

"I think she should eat her tea upstairs," said Oonagh, "there is no point in her struggling on those stairs," and Oonagh laid a pretty embroidered cloth on the wooden tray that Mrs Delaney kept in the tall kitchen cupboard.

Mr Delaney took the meal up to his wife, "Kitty and yourself must start yours, don't let them get cold," he called over his shoulder. When he joined them at the table though, Oonagh brought all three meals out of the warm oven, "Kitty must learn her manners grandfather Delaney," she said, and grandfather Delaney winked at Kitty. On Tuesday morning, as Mr Delaney drank hot tea from his special large china cup and munched on his thick slice of toast spread with home-made blackberry and apple jam, he told Oonagh, "I will send Herbert to Dr Gould with a note. I will request that the doctor calls around some time today." "Is she no better today?" said Oonagh, stirring sugar into the cup of tea that she had made for Kathleen.

"She was in a lot of pain with her feet in the night," said Edward, "she says she cannot sleep for the pains shooting down into her toes. I offered to rub them for her but she could not bear for me to touch them. I came downstairs and filled the stone bed warmer with hot water. I wrapped it in a towel and she put her feet on it. It gave her some relief, but I think my cuddles and attention helped her most."

Oonagh carried the hot drink up to Grandma and woke Kitty, "Time to get ready for school my little one."

Kitty, still in her flannelette nightdress, came first into Mrs Delaney's room to give her adoptive grandmother a hug. "I hope you are better soon," she said and Kathleen stroked Kitty's dark curly hair and kissed her forehead. "Thank you, I feel so much better for that hug," she said, "now do as your mammy says and wash and dress for school, and don't forget to clean your teeth after breakfast."

Kitty's toothbrush was beside the sink in the corner of the kitchen. Her mother had bought a little flat tin containing a pink block of paste. After her breakfast, Kitty rubbed her wet toothbrush head on the paste and then brushed her teeth vigorously. "Miss Holden told us all at school that we must clean our teeth after every meal, but some of the children don't have a toothbrush," said Kitty through foamy pink lips. "Perhaps the council will provide them as the government is encouraging better dental care," said her mother, "now you hurry along, I have to be back here, the doctor will be coming to see Grandma Delaney."

At eleven thirty, there was an urgent rapping on the brass knocker. Oonagh was laying the fire in the front parlour, in preparation for Kathleen's recovery. She wiped her hands on her cotton pinny as she hurried to the front door. She opened the door to a tall young man carrying a black doctor's bag in his left hand and wearing a top hat, a navy-blue suit, crisp white shirt and a navy-blue bow tie. He removed his hat with his right hand and introduced himself with a little bow, "Dr William Gould FRCS." "Oh yes, doctor, do come in," said Oonagh, taking his hat and hanging it on the hat stand. "I am presuming you have come to examine Mrs Delaney, this way doctor." Oonagh indicated for the doctor to follow her up the stairs. Once in the bedroom, the doctor introduced himself to Mrs Delaney, then looking across to Oonagh he said, "I'm sure you would not wish your maid to remain."

"Oh no, Oonagh is not my maid," said Mrs Delaney, "she is my second daughter, sent to me by God above, I would like her to stay."

Oonagh sat by the window which overlooked the back garden. She stood up and opened the sash window a little, "I'll let some fresh air in," she said, "it is a lovely day today."

The doctor felt Mrs Delaney's forehead, "Well, you don't have a high temperature now, my dear lady."

"No doctor, but I had a high temperature yesterday," said Mrs Delaney, "and fierce pain in my feet and hands. I felt really unwell and I don't have any appetite, although I did eat the lamb chops you cooked last night, Oonagh, thank you. She has been looking after me well doctor, God bless her."

The doctor asked his patient to cough as he listened to her chest through a trumpet shaped instrument. "And do you have pain anywhere else beside your feet and hands?" "Yes, doctor, all the joints in my body are painful, my knees, my hips, my neck and I have developed lumps on my elbows," Mrs Delaney explained, showing the doctor her arms.

The doctor sat on the chair bedside the bed, "I think what you are suffering from, and I emphasise suffering, is rheumatic arthritis. The ideal situation would be for you to live in a warmer climate. If that is not possible, then a visit to take the waters and bathe in the spa baths in a town such as Buxton or Harrogate may be beneficial.

"Now your diet, Mrs Delaney. Keep sugar to a minimum. Plenty of white fish and mutton. Fresh vegetables but limit your potatoes, Cod liver oil may help, a dessertspoonful every day first thing in the morning. Keep yourself warm, gentle exercise must be taken and keep your bowels regular. Alcohol is totally forbidden, but I do not imagine you partake of mother's ruin."

The doctor turned to Oonagh, "I stress that this is only be taken when the pain is totally unbearable, but if that occurs and I stress that this is only then, Opium may be taken, you can buy it from the apothecary, that or laudanum. Now I will leave this tincture of belladonna and opium which must be applied gently and sparingly to the affected joints when the pain is acute." The doctor opened his bag and put a small black glass bottle with a cork stopper onto the bedside cupboard. "Do not allow children to touch this tincture," he cautioned and closing his bag, he stood. "I will deliver my account to your husband's shop, a fine butcher he is, first quality meat." "Thank you, doctor," said Mrs Delaney, settling back on her pillows. Oonagh showed the doctor to the front door and handed him his top hat which he replaced on his fair head. His horse cab was waiting for him and he climbed inside to continue to his next house call.

After the doctor had left, Oonagh lit the fire in the front parlour, dusted the furniture, swept the carpet and polished the parquet floor in the room ready for Mrs Delaney.

Then she carried a bowl of warm water upstairs and helped Kathleen to wash and dress. As she walked backwards in front of her dear friend down the stairs, she warned, "Hold firmly onto the handrail and go slowly, there, we are safely down. Now come and sit in the front parlour, the fire is lit. I will just slip upstairs and fetch a shawl for your legs. Once Kathleen was comfortable, Oonagh made a cup of tea and brought the rest of the egg custard to her in a glass dish. "Here you are, this is nice and cold, it has been on the slab in the cellar, I know you enjoyed the other half yesterday." Mrs Delaney ate all the remaining baked egg custard. "I feel so much better now I am dressed," she was saying as there was a loud knocking on the front door. Oonagh jumped up to answer and Mrs Delaney could hear a man's voice and then the door being closed again and the bolt slid into place. "Who was that, Oonagh?" she called and Oonagh replied, "oh, only the postman with a letter for me."

Oonagh did not return to the parlour, and Mrs Delaney presumed that she was continuing with the household chores. When Oonagh had not returned after the clock in the hall had struck four, Mrs Delaney went into the kitchen to look for her only to find Oonagh sitting weeping on the arm chair. "Whatever is the matter my dear?" said Mrs Delaney and Oonagh handed her the letter that she was holding, now crumpled and wet with tears. The letter had been written on Easter Monday in Victoria, Australia and had taken ten weeks to arrive at their home.

"My darling Oonagh and Kitty, Charlotte has urged me to write to you to convey our latest news. Although you will always be most welcome to join me here in this wonderful country, for legal reasons that I will explain, Charlotte and I are to be married. The wedding will take place with all haste, Charlotte is not a well lady and the doctor fears that she will not see Christmas this year. I think I told you that I feared there would be more trouble at Ballarat. Charlotte's son Jack, like many young men, went up to Ballarat dreaming of making a fortune to purchase his own farm. Unfortunately, he was drawn into the pitched battle at the Eureka Stockade between Imperial Troops, under Captain Thomas, and the protesting miners who had united under the flag of the Southern Cross with Peter Lalor as their Commander. Forty of the miners were killed and a large number were wounded, among them was Jack. I travelled to Ballarat to bring him home to Charlotte but I am sad to tell you he lost his left leg to gangrene. He has adapted well to his wooden leg and still rides and can perform many of the chores around the farm, but he can by no means totally manage the farm alone. Charlotte obviously wishes to leave the farm to him entirely, but her late husband's brothers, hearing of Charlotte's illness, are laying claim to a share of the farm. When she and I are married

then the farm will automatically pass to me and she trusts me to take care of Jack's interests. My allocated land adjoins her farm and I have not yet built a homestead but we are in need of that land to expand our flock of merino sheep as their wool is much in demand for the textile market being less coarse than some of your European fleeces.

My loves, you will always be welcome here. Both Charlotte and I would be so happy if you were to join us, the house is large and there is plenty of room for all the family, to be truthful, I would be grateful for your help.

Kitty, I will always be your loving daddy.
Oonagh, although I am very fond of Charlotte, remember you are my first and last love, in my heart you will always be my wife.
With my eternal love Seamus."

Mrs Delaney held Oonagh in her arms, "There now my love, it is probably for the best, you did not want to travel all that way and leave your father, and what would granddad and I do without our girls?"

By the time Kitty arrived home from school, Oonagh was calm and was preparing the vegetables for tea. Grandma listened to Kitty read her school book. "Very well read, Kitty, lots of expression, and there were some difficult words, your teacher must be very pleased with you."

"Yes, Grandma," said Kitty, "and I am very pleased with the slow readers, they are trying very hard in my little classroom and I enjoy being a teacher."

Edward had brought four steaks of cod for tea. "You could not have bought anything better, on doctor's orders," said Oonagh and Mrs Delaney explained what the doctor had said.

"He certainly lost no time presenting his account," her husband said, "the doctor's wife brought the invoice into the shop later this afternoon. I, of course paid her, but she paid a considerable amount back to me to settle this month's account for their household."

We will have to see what we can do about a visit up to Buxton, my love, I believe there is a splendid hotel there, it would be good for both of us and we could arrange to meet George perhaps. Yes, we will see what we can do," and granddad Delaney winked at Kitty.

Chapter Twenty-Nine
Buxton Spa

It was a month later that George wrote to say his school would be playing cricket against the Buxton Cricket Club, junior cricket team on the last Saturday of June. Edward Delaney wrote a letter immediately to the Imperial hotel to reserve two rooms for that weekend.

"Would you come with us, Oonagh, and take care of Grandma during the day, I am sure that sitting outside all day watching the match is not good for your health Kathleen," he said.

"You can sit with me, Kitty, and watch George play."

Early on the Saturday morning, the little family caught the train to Buxton. Oonagh carried her carpet bag with a change of clothing for herself and Kitty. Granddad Edward complained, "What have you packed into this trunk Kathleen?" as he carried their large trunk up the station approach. Fortunately, a porter with a hand barrow spotted him and took the trunk from him. The porter lifted it into their carriage when the Buxton train stopped at the platform. Granddad pressed a sixpenny piece into the porter's hand.

"Thank you, my man." "They rely on tips," he confided to Oonagh.

At Buxton station, Granddad hailed a carriage to take them up to the hotel. Lined up at the foot of the cream polished marble steps were uniformed hotel porters dressed in royal blue blazers with brass buttons and wearing top hats, one stepped forward and lifted down Granddad's trunk and Oonagh's carpet bag, then disappeared into the huge reception. Granddad took Grandma Kathleen's arm while she held firmly onto the polished brass rail with the other hand. Together, they slowly climbed the gleaming steps. Then she held her husband's arm for support as they crossed the thick blue carpet patterned with a heaven of silver stars. Straight ahead was the reception desk where Granddad spoke to a tall man with black hair, oiled and swept back. He was sporting a huge moustache waxed and curled upwards at the ends. He allocated adjoining rooms to the little family. Oonagh took hold of Kitty's hand and followed the Delaneys slowly up the magnificent central staircase to their rooms.

"Oh, am I glad to sit down," said Grandma Delaney, as she sank into the blue velvet armchair in the first bedroom.

Granddad gave the porter a tip and asked for a tray of tea and biscuits to be brought to their room, "Enough for four please."

Oonagh and Kitty investigated their adjoining room while they waited.

"It is just like a palace," said Kitty as she stretched out on the bed nearest the window, "but Mammy, where is the privy? Is it at the bottom of the garden?"

"No," said her mother, "it is somewhere along the landing I think, I noticed a sign." Together they investigated.

As they left, the room the maid was arriving with a tray of tea, she directed them along the corridor to a room with a shining brass plate on the door. "Bathroom, read Kitty, she opened the door and gasped. There was a white bath with polished brass taps and a water closet with a blue patterned porcelain bowl. Above the water closet was a black tank with a steel chain hanging from a lever system with a black rubber pull handle at the end. Oonagh pulled the chain and the water closet flushed with water. Kitty had to try the equipment out and was sitting on the polished mahogany seat with her bloomers around her ankles when Grandma Kathleen came into the bathroom. "Now, this is what we need at home," said Grandma Kathleen, as Kitty washed her hands at the basin that was shaped like a shell. "There is even scented soap and a towel here. I think this is how the queen lives," said Kitty. "I expect she does," said her mother, "now let me brush your hair, the cricket match will start at two o'clock and you can watch with Granddad while I take Grandma to the spa baths. Turning to Grandma she said, "Did you remember to bring your dressing gown for the spa baths? We will leave you now to freshen up." Oonagh and Kitty returned to the Delaney's room and Oonagh poured tea for them all. "I was thinking I would ask Mr Shepherd, George's sports master, to eat with us later," said granddad, "do you have any objections? He will be good company for me and I know he has taken a shine to you, Oonagh. Added to that, it will be convenient in that he can accompany George back to the school, the rest of the team will have left."

Oonagh nodded, "I have no objections whatsoever."

Just as soon as Kitty had her hair brushed and plaited, Granddad left with her for the cricket club. Mr Shepherd hurried over to greet them. "Oh, no Miss Kennedy today?" he said. "No, she is assisting my wife who has not enjoyed good health since last we saw you," said Edward.

George ran to them and hugged Kitty and his grandfather.

"Now just play as you did last time and you will succeed famously," said Granddad shaking his grandson's hand. "And, we would be honoured if you could join us in the hotel restaurant after the match, Mr Shepherd. You would be good company for me, with our shared love of the game."

"The honour will be all mine," said Mr Shepherd, "it will give me the chance to renew my acquaintance with Miss Kennedy."

"Shall we say seven thirty in the restaurant then?" said Edward as he took Kitty's hand and they walked over to take a seat in front of the stand. The commissionaire at the reception desk hailed a cab for Oonagh and Mrs Delaney. The cab driver took them to the spa baths. Oonagh accompanied Grandma Kathleen into the steam bath, both ladies clad in their underclothes.

The attendant gave Kathleen a glass containing the special mineral rich water from St Ann's well.

"What does it taste like?" asked Oonagh, "It tastes like it smells," said Grandma, "rather like bad eggs, I think they say it is sulphur. Still if it does me good I'm willing to try anything." She drank the whole glass and handed the glass to the attendant who directed them into the spa bath. Oonagh had wrapped Kathleen warmly in a dressing gown and asked the attendant for one for herself, "Although I will not be partaking of the spa bath, thank you."

She accompanied Kathleen into the spa bathroom, helped her into the bath and sat beside her while Kathleen relaxed in the warm waters, sleepily cooing. "Yes, this is definitely what we need at home, I can feel this doing my poor aching bones the world of good." It was all too short, though, after fifteen minutes the attendant brought the bag containing their change of clothes into the room and they were ushered to separate changing cubicles.

When they emerged, Kathleen was glowing, "I feel so dreamy and relaxed," she murmured and held onto Oonagh's arm as they stepped out into the sunshine. Oonagh hailed a cab to drive them back to the hotel, "We must keep you warm," she said, wrapping the fine cream wool shawl around Grandma's shoulders, "perhaps you may have a little nap before tea, I wonder how George's match is progressing, I don't think it would have been wise for you to sit outside to watch, we don't want you to catch a cold."

Once back in the room, Grandma Kathleen coiled her hair into curls around her finger and clipped each curl in place then lay on her bed for a nap, while Oonagh went back to her own room to prepare herself for the meal. Oonagh was wearing the emerald green dress that Grandma Margaret had bought for her. She had been complimented many times on how well it flattered her, particularly the colour, which accentuated her green eyes. By the time Kitty came bursting excitedly into the room holding George's hand, Oonagh was ready, "Mammy, George caught two of their players out and scored twenty-one runs."

"Well done George, so did your team win, George?" said Oonagh, hugging him.

"No we lost," said George, hanging his head and kicking the floor with the toe of his shiny brown shoes.

"No matter," said Oonagh, "you played well, that is all you can ask of yourself, congratulations young man," and she kissed the top of his hot moist head, "I expect you are both hungry."

"I'll say we are," said George, his arm around Kitty, one leg crossed over the top of the other.

"George!" scolded Oonagh, "you are scuffing your splendid polished shoes, stand up straight." George released his arm from around Kitty and stood soldier-like to attention. Kitty slipped her arm through his. Oonagh pinched her cheeks and with her forefinger spread a little rouge on her cheekbones then with the same rouge shaped her lips into cupid bows. The family was already seated at the table when Mr Shepherd joined them, he slapped George on the back, "Splendid game again, young Foster," he said, "Good evening my dear ladies, you are looking particularly delightful this evening," and he took the seat beside George opposite Oonagh and Kitty. Mrs Delaney was positively glowing as the young sportsmaster lifted her hand and kissed it. She smiled at Oonagh. "The men will have hearty appetites after breathing the fresh Derbyshire air all afternoon." Mr Delaney's mind was on business, as with his knife he spread a little mustard onto each mouthful of his entrecote steak. "I wonder who supplies their beef, it is first class quality, almost as good as I sell, but I'm afraid I don't sell so much this cut of beef, only very occasionally to my best customers." "Such as Doctor Gould," he said aside to his wife, giving her his special wink. When their meals were finished and the waiter had cleared the table, Mr Shepherd asked Oonagh if she would like to accompany him across to the winter gardens where a band was playing in the pavilion. "Can we come too? "Kitty quickly asked.

"Oh, but I thought you and George would like a dish of ice cream and strawberries each," said granddad Delaney, as Oonagh stood. "I shall not be long out of bed, so I will say goodbye to you now, George, and thank you for returning him safely back to school Mr Shepherd, it is very kind of you."

"No, it is for me to thank yourself and your husband for a delicious meal and your delightful company," said Mr Shepherd with a little bow. Grandma Delaney took George's face in her hands and kissed him, "We will see you soon George, be good and work hard." Oonagh and Mr Shepherd walked down the drive of the hotel and crossed the road as carriages were arriving, carrying people to the open-air concert and light festival, Mr Shepherd took Oonagh's gloved right hand with his right hand and placed it firmly in the crook of his left arm. As they entered the winter gardens, he did not release his grip, "May I say Miss Kennedy, that you look lovely this evening."

"Thank you, Mr Shepherd, you may address me as Oonagh."

"And my Christian name is Henry," said Mr Shepherd. Every tree, every shrub, in the garden was twinkling in the twilight with small lights fastened along their branches

"It is so very pretty," said Oonagh, as the band struck up. "There are some famous members of the Royal Vienna Opera appearing tonight," said Henry, as a little head with a mop of dark curls appeared between their shins and Kitty turned her face upwards so that her big blue eyes met Henry's big blue eyes. "And how did you enjoy your dessert, little minx?" he said as he whisked her up and lifted her high above his head. "Careful!" cautioned Oonagh, "she has just eaten a big meal and a large bowl of ice cream."

Too late! Kitty's meal came back over Henry Shepherd.

"I am so very sorry," said Oonagh. You had best come back to the hotel, perhaps Granddad has a shirt you could wear while I try to clean your jacket and trousers, I was just about to say I am one of a pair, now you know the worst implications at first hand. Kitty, where is Granddad, surely you are not alone."

"No," said Kitty, "George and Granddad have gone in to listen to the concert, I could see you in the garden and Granddad said I could come straight over to you while he watched me."

Once in the hotel, Oonagh begged a clean shirt for Henry from Grandma. A maid was sent to the room to take Henry's suit away to sponge clean. Oonagh sat on the blue velvet couch in their bedroom while Henry used the bathroom down the corridor. "Mammy," said Kitty, "Are you going to marry Mr Shepherd?"

"I really don't know," said Oonagh, "Why do you ask?" "Because I thought Daddy was your husband," said Kitty, "he won't like you to marry someone else."

" These are grown up things, Kitty, and nothing for you to worry about, I will not do anything to upset you, anyway Henry has not asked me, yet," said her mother and gave her a hug as Henry knocked on the door and entered the room dressed in one of Granddad's shirts, with a towel around his waist. By the time Granddad returned with George, the maid had returned with Henry's suit which she had managed to clean, although the unpleasant smell stayed with the sportsmaster and George all the way back to school on the train.

Chapter Thirty
A Romantic Postcard

The following Friday, the postman delivered a postcard to the Delaney house, addressed to Miss Oonagh Kennedy. On the front was a pretty watercolour painting of a posy of violets, and on the reverse was a handwritten poem:

The fountains mingle with the river
And the rivers with the ocean
The winds of heaven mix forever
With a sweet emotion
Nothing in the world is single
All things by a law divine
In one another's being mingle
Why not I with thine?
See the mountains kiss high heaven
And the waves clasp one another
No sister-flower would be forgiven
If it disdained its brother
And the sunlight clasps the earth
And the moonbeams kiss the sea
What are all these kissings worth
If thou kiss not me?

Percy Bysshe Shelley

"Oh, it is all so romantic," said Kathleen Delaney when Oonagh showed her the post card, "Mr Shepherd is so very charming and good looking. Did you see how he kissed my hand at Buxton? And he is so athletic. Oonagh you are so lucky to have such an eligible suitor. I will wager he asks you to marry him, but the most important thing is he is so fond of George and Kitty, how calm he was when she was sick all over him. I think we should invite him to the house for the day. What do you say Oonagh? It will soon be the summer holidays from school. Where does he live? Is he still living with his parents?"

"I really don't know, Kathleen, I did not have the chance to ask him, before Kitty came between us, but yes, I would like him to visit. Should I write to him at the school?"

Oonagh wrapped her arms around Kathleen Delaney and put her head on Kathleen's shoulder. "I know I should be happy but why do I feel so very sad? I just keep seeing Seamus's face."

Kathleen stroked Oonagh's head, "My lovely girl, you have to turn the page now and start another chapter in your life, so much has happened and you have made your decision, you are a wonderful mother to Kitty and yes, to my grandson too, but you must have a life yourself, Seamus has made his choice. You must think what is best for you." Kathleen brushed Oonagh's hair back from her tear-stained face, "Now, you write a letter to that young man." Kathleen opened the top drawer of the dresser, took out the best writing paper, pen and ink pot and put them on the kitchen table. Oonagh sat at the table and wrote a letter to Henry Shepherd, thanking him for his card and inviting him to spend the day with the family during the first week of the summer vacation, "As I am not aware of your home address and not sure how far you will have to travel, I leave it for you to suggest a date that is convenient to yourself," she wrote.

Mr Delaney promised to send the letter for her to the school first thing the following morning from the main Stockport post office. "I will ask Herbert to take it, he will be pleased to have a break from scattering sawdust."

Henry Shepherd suggested that he should visit on the first Tuesday of the first week of the summer vacation. His home, he explained, was in Nottingham, so he could travel by train. He stayed with his parents during the school vacations. His father, he wrote, was a manager at one of the collieries.

Mrs Delaney suggested that she would cook lamb for tea and Mr Delaney boned and rolled a shoulder of lamb and brought it home from the shop on Monday evening. "I will make a nice onion sauce, mashed potatoes and cabbage," Grandma Kathleen announced at breakfast.

George and Kitty screwed their noses up at the mention of cabbage.

"Cabbage is good for you, it makes you strong," said Oonagh. On the Tuesday, it was midday before Henry arrived. The children were eagerly waiting at the bay window in the front parlour.

"I love this room," said Kitty to George, "it always smells of lavender polish." When the young sportsmaster arrived in a cream linen suit with a white shirt and swinging a black rolled umbrella with a cane handle, Kitty screamed, "He's here Mammy, he's here." Oonagh calmly left the kitchen where she had been preparing the vegetables (this task Mrs Delaney found difficult now with arthritic hands). Oonagh waited until Henry knocked on the front door with the brass lion knocker, before she answered the door.

"Do be calm, Kitty," she said, as Kitty and George joined her at the door, pushing their way 'round her legs. "Do come in Henry," said Oonagh, ushering the children over to the cloak stand.

"It is a glorious day," said Henry, "but one can never be too sure with English weather," and he stood his umbrella in the umbrella stand. Oonagh's cheeks were pink as she invited him into the parlour. "Children, go into the garden, I am sure there is plenty for you to do in the fresh air."

"Perhaps we should all sit in the garden," said Henry. Oonagh closed the parlour door behind her back and they all proceeded out of the rear door and into the garden. Mr Delaney had made a rustic bench under the apple tree. Henry sat on the bench and immediately George and Kitty sat either side of him. Oonagh went back inside the kitchen to make a jug of lemonade and carried it outside on a tray, with glasses for them all. She rested it on a little table that had previously been in the parlour but had been damaged with a hot teapot.

"George and Kitty would like a game of cricket, is there somewhere we could go?" said Henry. "Yes, I suppose we could play on the waste ground, up near the main road," said Oonagh, ", but each time we see you your clothes are spoiled." From the cellar, George collected the wickets and bails that granddad Delaney had made for him, and the cricket bat and ball that were his early birthday gift from Granddad. All that afternoon, Oonagh played cricket on the waste ground with Henry and the children. At teatime, they all made their way back home, Oonagh was carrying the wickets, bails and bat, she was red-cheeked and her hair, which she had so carefully curled then tied up at the back of her head, were loose and damp around her face. Henry's fair hair was brushed back from his forehead, he still looked as cool and handsome as when he had arrived. The children were holding one of his hands each.

Granddad Delaney spotted them as he alighted from the tram and quickened his pace to catch up with them. He and Henry immediately fell into conversation about cricket. Oonagh trailed behind the group. Arriving back at the house, Oonagh went into the kitchen to wash and Kathleen brushed her hair and helped her to pin it back up. The children and Henry washed at the kitchen sink together, Kitty laughed as Henry pretended the soap was too slippery to hold, until Kathleen interrupted the revelry and invited everyone into the dining room. They all quickly rinsed and dried their hands and took their seats at the dining room table. Grandma Kathleen served the roast lamb meal and Mr Delaney served a bottle of wine which he took from the sideboard cupboard and served in fine crystal glasses, a wedding gift from his parents.

After the meal, Oonagh carried the dishes into the kitchen, while Grandma Delaney took the children upstairs to see them into bed. "If you behave, I will tell you a story," she promised. "Now say thank you to Mr Shepherd and good night."

Kitty raised her face for a kiss, Henry obliged to her delight, and George stood to attention and shook his teacher's hand. They both thanked him politely and wished him a pleasant journey home on the train. "Well done, I am proud of you both, now up to bed," said Oonagh.

"You and Henry go into the parlour and I will bring you a cup of tea directly the children are in bed," said Kathleen. In the parlour, Oonagh sat on the couch, leaving Mr Delaney's chair free, and Henry sat beside her. "I thought we would never be alone," said Henry, "Oonagh, the London

Shakespeare Company have a production next week at the Theatre Royal. If I may have the pleasure of your company, I will buy tickets."

Oonagh said she had never studied Shakespeare and had never in fact been to the theatre.

"I will be delighted to accompany you Henry," she said as their eyes met briefly. On the following Monday evening, Henry called for Oonagh in a cab, the children knocked on the window and waved as he helped Oonagh into the carriage. Once she was seated inside, Henry gave her a little posy of sweet violets which she pinned to her new blue velvet gown. The Shakespeare production was 'The Merchant of Venice'. They claimed their seats on the front row of the balcony with fifteen minutes to go until curtain rises.

"I taught this play to the upper school last term," said Henry, "and we actually put on a production for the lower school, but Alfred Butcher somehow did not make an ideal Portia. Were you aware that I teach English Literature as well as sports, Oonagh?"

Oonagh smiled, "I realised that you were familiar with Literature from the charming Shelley poem that you sent to me. For myself, I love Literature and poetry. In particular I love that most famous poem by our own Irish poet Thomas Moore 'The Meeting of the Waters', it has been set to music and I sing it to the children every night. It has become a ritual and even now they are almost nine years of age they cannot settle without it."

"Oonagh, I meant every word of Shelley's poem," said Henry, taking Oonagh's hands in his, "at night, I dream of kissing your lips and caressing your glorious hair." Henry leaned towards her and kissed her gently on her lips, while stroking her hair. Throughout the play, Henry's knee was touching Oonagh's and she could still feel the warmth of his lips on hers and the warmth seemed to be spreading through her whole body. On the way home in the cab he had hailed, Henry took Oonagh's hands again. "Oonagh, it seems so soon to tell you but I am in love with you, I can think of nothing but you. Oonagh you are the most lovely woman and all that I dream of. I am asking you to be my wife, please tell me I am not dreaming in vain. A position has been advertised in the newspaper for an English Literature teacher, with an enthusiasm for sport, at the Grammar School. The school will provide a small house close by with this position, I am giving it my consideration to apply. George told me that he will be leaving the boarding school when he is ten years old to be apprenticed at his grandfather's company. The Grammar School has an excellent reputation and a good cricket team, I am sure he would benefit from spending his final year there."

The cab passed through Longsight and then as they passed the farm opposite the biscuit factory, Henry kissed her again as the driver turned the horse left towards the Delaney house, and Oonagh returned his kiss. "This has all happened so quickly Henry," said Oonagh, "I will need some time to consider and I would like you to meet my father in Ireland, it is still customary, I believe, to ask his permission."

"Of course," said Henry, "and for my part, I would like my parents to meet you, I am sure they will fall in love with you and with Kitty."

As the carriage stopped at the front of the Delaney's house, Oonagh could see there was a chink of light through the heavy curtains in the parlour.

Kathleen Delaney opened the door as the horse cab drove off and Oonagh stepped smiling into the hall. Unpinning the sweet violets from her gown she gave them to Mrs Delaney, "I will put these in a little vase for you, they are so pretty, did you have a wonderful evening? Has Mr Shepherd engaged you?" Kathleen said without taking a breath. "I think we should go into the parlour," said Oonagh as she spotted two little faces peering between the spindles of the stairs. "You two children go back to bed. It is almost eleven o'clock."

Oonagh and Mrs Delaney sat together on the couch in the parlour.

"I have been reading the Derbyshire newspaper by the light of the lantern, there is the most awful case in court of a chimney sweep who beat his young apprentice almost to death. The poor boy was rescued by a lady passing in her carriage. It has upset me so," said Kathleen, "I will leave the newspaper for you to read tomorrow."

"I think I will go up to bed now if you will excuse me," said Oonagh, "I will tell you all about the play in the morning, but for now, goodnight." And she kissed Kathleen on the cheek before climbing the stairs to her room.

As soon as Oonagh had taken off her blue velvet gown and slipped into her nightdress, she took the bundle of letters tied in ribbon out of the box on top of the bedroom tallboy. She held the bundle to her chest as the soft feather mattress and pillow enveloped her, and then held the letters to her lips and whispered, "Your bed was hard metal, the mattress made of straw; they burned it in the street, they called us Irish swine, they said we brought the fever, Irish fever." She kissed the bundle of letters. "You will always be my wife," you said, "I cannot wait until I hold you in my arms," you said; but you are holding Charlotte in your arms at night. Charlotte this, Charlotte that, holding Charlotte with your strong arms your shirt sleeves rolled up to the elbows and the black hair shining on your forearms. Bowler hat on the back of your head of black curls, "He's just like his father," said mammy, "he loves the girl he's with, Mr O'Neill is Patty's granddaddy." The scent of Henry's shaving cream lingers on my cheeks, his cheeks were smooth and soft, and his fair hair fell over his violet blue eyes, his lips were full and soft on my lips. Your skin was hot and flushed with the weather, the black stubble rough on my skin. Your black curls were strong between my fingers. You kissed each of my fingers that night you told me that we would be married within the month. *"Kiss my wrist, kiss my lips, kiss my ankles so that I know that I've been kissed,"* Oonagh sang softly to herself:

"Come underneath my Irish blanket with your full soft lips and smooth cheeks, smelling sweetly of shaving soap, lie here with me on my feather bed."

"Seamus, hold me in your arms tell me I am yours." Her tears fell onto the bundle of letters and the ink smeared in her fingers. Kathleen knocked gently,

"Oonagh,", she whispered, "I've brought you a nice cup of tea, are you awake?"

Kathleen sat on the bed beside Oonagh, "Whatever has happened, my dear?" she said.

"He kissed me," said Oonagh, "and he wants to marry me, what shall I do?"

Kathleen Delaney put her arms around Oonagh, "I think you should be measured for you wedding dress, my love. Congratulations, I will wake Edward up to tell him the wonderful news that our girl is to be wed to a fine handsome gentleman, with good prospects."

"Please, Kathleen, I have to think about it. I mean, you are not getting any younger and your health is not good. I want to take care of you. You have done so much for me, and there is Kitty to think of, yes she is fond of Henry but she only knows Seamus as her daddy and she thinks I am his wife. It is all too much for her to understand. My responsibility is to my child, my innocent child. I belong to Seamus, he was my first love. It would not be proper for me to marry Henry while I still love Seamus so, and my innocence was taken by him."

"Oonagh, my love, Henry cannot fail to realise that another man had taken you, but he accepts Kitty and seems to be truly fond of her, I am convinced it will be well. As for Edward and myself, we want you to have a life and be happy. We will find a maid to live in and help with my care. That must not prevent you from having your own life. We love you Oonagh, as we loved our own daughter. Now try to sleep and we will talk more in the morning." Kathleen covered Oonagh with the bedclothes and tucked them in, then stroked her head, "Now goodnight and know that you are loved."

The following morning, Oonagh told the children at breakfast that they would be going to Ireland to see grandfather Kennedy. Very soon.

"And surprise, surprise. Mr Shepherd will be coming with us, but we will of course have to ask your father first, George. I don't think there will be any objections as you have been there several times before. He and Jeanetta usually holiday on the east coast with your sisters and Jeanetta's parents at the beginning of July, we will walk to Grandma Margaret's house this morning. Where is the Derbyshire newspaper that you wanted me to read, Grandma Kathleen?"

Oonagh and the two children walked to Grandma Margaret's house that morning. While George and Kitty were playing with a ball on the back lawn, Oonagh told Margaret the news about Henry's proposal.

"If Henry is offered the position then he will be provided with a house close to the school. If George attends the Grammar school for the final year, prior to his apprenticeship at the textile company, then he could live with us, he would not need to board, and he would be happy to be with Kitty." Miss Foster turned her back in silence for a few minutes then turned with lips pursed and eyes partly closed. "What makes you think my grandson should live with you and this school teacher? You must not lose sight of the fact, Oonagh, that you are not George's mother. No, he is perfectly happy at the Derbyshire boarding school and that is where he will be staying until he joins his grandfather's firm."

"I am hoping it will be convenient for George to spend a week in Ireland with us as he has for several years. Would you please ask his father on my behalf?" said Oonagh. "I will do that gladly," said Miss Foster, "it is definitely more convenient that George does not travel to Scarborough with Theodore and Jeanetta and their family."

It was a fine day and the sea was calm on the Monday of the third week of July. Oonagh and the children sat with Henry Shepherd on the deck of the steamship, forward of the funnel. "I usually suffer from sickness when sailing," Oonagh admitted to Henry, "but the steamships are quicker and more stable." "Your granddaddy is so eager to see you children," she said to George and Kitty, "and uncle Patrick and auntie Bridget. You will be sleeping at their house." "I really do not wish to be an inconvenience," said Henry, "there must surely be an inn where I could stay."

"No, I insist," said Oonagh, "I think Daddy would like to get to know you."

Once they had become used to the motion of the boat the children went to the rails to watch the white foaming wake of the boat as she cut through the waves, Henry unbuckled the straps of his leather case and took out a new book, 'The Water Babies' written by Charles Kingsley. He said, "I thought I could read this book to the children this week, it has just been published and I believe it will be very interesting to them. It is about a poor young boy who is apprenticed to a chimney sweep, Mr Grimes, who beats him unmercifully and makes him climb inside the chimneys to brush the soot out of them." "That is what happened to the little boy that I read about in the newspaper," said Oonagh to Henry. "The little apprentice was beaten by his master and fell into the river. He would have died for sure had it not been for a lady who was passing in her carriage. He was rescued by her carriage driver and taken to a doctor, he fortunately lived. An older boy who also worked for the chimney sweep gave evidence in court and the chimney sweep was sent to jail."

"What happened to the little boy?" said Kitty, who had returned to eavesdrop on her mother's conversation

"I am afraid it does not reveal that in the newspaper, but you will discover what happens to the little boy in Mr Kingsley's book. It seems that Kitty is interested already, Mr Shepherd."

"I can hardly wait until bedtime," said Kitty, moving closer to Henry Shepherd. "I am persuaded," said Henry and he opened the book at the first page. "We shall commence, you sit on the other side of me, George." For the rest of the crossing Henry read to the children. Kitty listened intently, her head inclined to the right, looking up at Henry, sniffing occasionally in the salty air and wiping her nose on her handkerchief. Her mother would have to admit she enjoyed the story, although Henry's words were blown away at times as she pulled her shawl around her head to protect herself from the salty spray, the sea was rougher than it had ever been before, when Oonagh had sailed with the children on their summer visit to grandfather Kennedy.

Chapter Thirty-One
The Water Babies

Immediately Oonagh's feet were on the dock, her queasiness disappeared although she felt the ground was moving beneath her feet.

"That feeling will soon pass," she told the children.

Henry Shepherd carried her carpet bag along with his tan leather case. George carried the two small bags with spare clothes for himself and Kitty. It had begun to rain quite heavily and Oonagh was relieved to see O'Neil the carter at the dock gates, shrouded head to ankle in a black oilskin cape, his familiar bowler hat pushed to the back of his head.

"Mr O'Neil," called Kitty, and she ran into his open arms. "I am so happy to see you, I have missed you," she cried as she planted a kiss on his wet ruddy cheek.

"This child has the Blarney in her," said the carter to Oonagh.

The carter helped the two children into the back of the cart. They sat on their cases and Mr O'Neil covered them with a sheet of tarpaulin. He moved to take the luggage from Henry but Henry resisted.

"Oh, I rather thought we would take the stage," Henry said.

"You've missed the midday mail coach and you will be waiting another four hours for the next one, it will be a long four hours in the tavern. Best to get you all home, Oonagh's daddy will be waiting," said Mr O'Neil, taking Oonagh's arm and helping her up onto the driver's seat.

"I must tell Seamus you have a young man, he asks after you in his letters to his mammy and me," confided the carter.

Turning his attention to Henry, he took their bags and tucked them under the tarpaulin next to the children. He took his spare oilskin from the cart and passed it to Oonagh. "Here you are, you can share this with your young man, pull it over your heads. This squall has set in now, will you take a look at those dark clouds."

Henry obediently climbed aboard beside Oonagh and they covered their heads with the oilskin.

"Your daddy asked me to take you directly to your Aunt Bridget's cottage," said Cieran.

Rosie the Welsh mountain pony trotted steadily most of the way to Avoca, stopping only once to drink water from the bucket that the carter carried in the cart. There was little chance to have a conversation with the carter as the heavy rain beat against their smarting faces.

They arrived at Bridget's cottage and Henry reached into his pocket to pay Mr O'Neil.

"Oh no," said Cieran wiping his face with his red handkerchief, "Mr Kennedy has paid me already."

Aunt Bridget was waiting at the door. "Come along in, the kettle is boiling, pleased to meet you, Mr Shepherd, my brother has told me about you," she chatted as she hugged her niece and the children and held out her hand to Henry, who took her hand and kissed it bringing a flush to Aunt Bridie's cheeks. Cieran O'Neil passed the bags inside the door as Bridie instructed. "Now, George, we thought you and Mr Shepherd could stay here with Uncle Patrick and myself."

"Kitty, you and mummy can sleep at your granddaddy's, Uncle Finn is stopping at the Doyles'. Yes, Oonagh, there is to be another wedding in the family this summer, is that not exciting? It does not seem a week has gone by since I was bouncing Finn on my knee, such a bonnie wee lad he was. Mr O'Neil, have you time for a cup of tea before you take Oonagh and Kitty to her daddy's? Mr Shepherd, two sugars is it?"

"Please call me Henry," said Henry Shepherd.

"Yes," said Auntie Bridget, "after all we are going to be family, I hear."

Oonagh blushed and Kitty scowled at her.

"Shall we take George's luggage to his room, Kitty you can help me?" she said taking Kitty by the arm and leading her upstairs.

"Now, what was that scowl about, young lady?" said Oonagh to her daughter. "I thought you liked Mr Shepherd?"

"Yes, he is very kind," said Kitty, "but I do not want him to be my daddy. I already have a daddy and he will be sad if you marry someone else." Kitty reached into her coat pocket and produced a crumpled letter, the letter that Seamus had written to her when she had just started at school and could barely read.

"Oh, Kitty, why have you brought that letter with you?" said Oonagh.

"You said I should treasure it, mammy," said Kitty, "so I thought I should keep it by me. It is all that I have of daddy, I do not even know how he looks."

"Oh, Kitty, my sweetheart," said Oonagh, hugging her daughter, "you have so much of your daddy, you have his beautiful black curls and his long dark lashes. You have his caring ways, his love of fun and his interest in the nature all around us. Every time I look at you, I can see your handsome daddy and if you do not wish me to marry Mr Shepherd then I shall not marry him, it can just be you and me until daddy comes back home for us. Now you go back downstairs to George, I will join you soon."

Aunt Bridget came out of her own bedroom across the landing, at the front of the cottage and took hold of Oonagh's arm as Oonagh followed her daughter to the stairs. Pulling her niece back into her bedroom, she asked, "Why do you not tell the wee lass that her daddy has married the widow woman in Australia, my lovely? Do you not think it is wrong to keep up this pretence that Seamus is coming back for you both?"

158

"I cannot, Auntie," said Oonagh, "she is too young to understand and she will think that she has been abandoned by her daddy. To tell the truth, Auntie, I do hope that Seamus will come back for us. I still love him. Of course I am very content with Henry and he will make a splendid husband, but am I wrong to marry him when I still love Seamus?" Oonagh wiped her tears away on her sleeve, "Oh I wish mammy was still here, I do not know what to do."

"There now my lovely, perhaps a week at home will help you decide."

"I believe that children should always be told the truth, they will come to terms with it in their own way," said Auntie Bridget, "but you must do as you see fit, my lovely. Now come back downstairs and drink your tea before it is too cold to drink."

By the time Kitty left with her mother and Mr O'Neil, the rain had cleared and Henry Shepherd was sitting in his mackintosh on the wooden bench by the open door of Auntie Bridget's cottage, his hands were clasped around his second cup of hot tea, admiring the red glow of the sun dropping behind the emerald hills.

The air was chilly and Kitty snuggled close beside Mr O'Neil as he drove her mother and herself to her grandfather's cottage.

"My daddy is in Australia, so he is," said Kitty.

Cieran O'Neil looked at Oonagh and raised his eyebrows.

"Do I know the lucky man, Oonagh?" he said, but Oonagh turned her head away to wave goodbye to Henry Shepherd.

"I think we shall take a picnic to the Meeting of the Waters tomorrow, Kitty, what do you think?" said Oonagh.

"Granddaddy will have some bread and cheese I am sure. Mr Shepherd will like to see our favourite beauty spot, where Sir Thomas Moore wrote his famous poem and we shall sing the poem to Mr Shepherd, shall we?"

Francis Kennedy was waiting at the door when the carter pulled the pony to a stop at his cottage.

"I thought you had lost your way in this awful weather," grand-daddy said, as he lifted his granddaughter down from the cart, hugging her close and stroking her wet dark curls back from her forehead with his calloused hands.

Cieran O'Neil left now, giving his pony a little flick on her rump with his whip, but Rosie knew her own way and eagerly trotted on toward her warm stable and the bag of fresh hay that would be waiting there, beside the O'Neil's cottage.

Francis Kennedy took his daughter in his arms. The familiar warm smell of the fresh sweat of hard work on his shirt mingled with the smell of his pipe tobacco brought the tears that had been welling in her eyes, tumbling down her cheeks. "It seems as if mammy is still here in the house, everything is the same as when I was a little girl." Her father stroked her hair back from her forehead, held her shoulders and stood back to look at his daughter.

"Now it is time to let your mammy go, it is nine years now since she passed on. You are looking well my lass, it is so good to see you. Nothing has changed here, apart from the small herd that I have managed to scrape together. I was lucky to buy two cows that were early in calf, you can see them tomorrow."

"I understand how hard it must be for you, daddy but I would like mammy's advice right now.

"Have you been cooking for us, daddy?" said Oonagh. "I can smell something delicious cooking in the kitchen."

"Indeed I have, I can still hear your mammy's voice, chastising me in the kitchen, but I thank my Maker that she taught me to cook, and Oonagh I knew your mammy well enough to pass on her advice to you, you can confide in me," said her father, taking three plates from the shelf and spooning out the stew from the pan on the range. "I wish we could have afforded meat for your mammy when she was so poorly. There now, eat your fill, and help yourself to some of this crusty loaf. I bought it fresh this morning from the village."

Their bellies were full as mother and daughter curled up together in Finn's bed and they slept soundly and contentedly until the sun shone through the window in the roof and Kitty awoke. "Mammy, we have to wake up, George will be here soon."

Her father was already working in the fields, Oonagh could just about make out his familiar form, pushing a handcart full of silage down to his small herd of dairy cattle. They would soon be grazing on the fresh spring grass.

Oonagh was preparing porridge for breakfast and Kitty was outside feeding the hens when George arrived, he was alone. Kitty was throwing the corn onto the dry dirt at the back door, then jumping back as the hens pecked too close to her feet. Granddad had tied a lettuce on a string to a nail on the shed and the hens fluttered up to peck at it when they had had their fill of the corn. They went back to pecking around her feet, picking up the corn, and the gravel for their craw.

"Why do the hens eat stones, mammy?" Kitty called.

"Because hens do not have teeth, they need the grit to grind their food and to help them make the shells for their eggs."

Kitty stooped to try to peer in a hen's beak and the hen pecked at her nose, sending Kitty screaming into the kitchen.

"We saw granddad Kennedy working in the field," said George, when he appeared at the open door.

"Mr Shepherd stopped to speak to him."

Kitty peeped out from behind her mother's apron.

"They told me to walk on up to the cottage and Mr Shepherd said he would be here shortly.

"Granddad said there are eggs in the foodsafe. He said to hard boil them if you are still intending to take a picnic on our walk, and he said there are apples in the shed."

"Thank you, George," said Oonagh, "Kitty, will you fetch four apples from the shed and put them in my basket please?" and she gently slid four eggs into a pan of hot water on the range.

George held Kitty's hand and they went together to fetch the apples from the shed.

The eggs had boiled for six minutes and Oonagh was running cold water on them when Henry arrived, fresh-faced from the walk. He had pushed his fair hair under a tweed cap, which he removed before entering the cottage, wiping the sweat from his forehead onto the cap's lining.

"It is promising to be a fine day and too warm for my cap and rain coat," he said, pulling off his coat and hanging it on a nail at the back of the door, he flicked back his fair hair from his eyes with the back of his hand.

"I spoke to your father Oonagh dear, I believe you girls have plans for me to walk even further this morning."

Over his blue striped shirt Henry was wearing a sleeveless hand knitted jumper in a multi coloured pattern.

"What a beautiful pullover, I presume your mother knitted that for you. Mrs Delaney is teaching Kitty to knit," said Oonagh. "Yes, I have prepared a picnic for a walk, did Auntie Bridget make breakfast for you, or would you like some porridge?"

George immediately sat at the table, holding a spoon upright and eyeing the jar of honey on the table. "The walk has given me an appetite," he said.

Henry sat on the settle by the range and stretched out his long legs. "I have eaten my fill," he admitted, "your aunt is very hospitable."

It was late in the morning, when they reached Oonagh's favourite picnic spot at the Meeting of the Waters. The grass was still damp from the rain of the previous day. Oonagh spread her mother's picnic blanket under the big old tree by the water's edge. She set the basket on the blanket and sat beside Henry in the warm early summer sun. Henry leaned on one elbow and looked up at Oonagh. "I have spoken to your father Oonagh. He was happy with my prospects and he approved of our marriage."

Oonagh smiled, pushed her hair back from her face, turned her head away and watched the river, "Yes, I was sure daddy would like you."

The smaller river had been tumbling down from the hills all night, gathering before it all the swollen little streams and brooks. Then, gushing and tumbling over the stones, it seemed to be laughing as it nudged into the major river, trying to push it to one side, but the wider, stronger river engulfed the little upstart and together they headed out towards the sea.

Kitty and George grabbed a branch each that the storm had snapped from the tree. Together the children slid down the wet bank to the water's edge. George had spotted a boot that had caught in the stones.

Between them they tried to retrieve the discarded footwear. Kitty managed to force her stick down into the boot and lifted it triumphantly aloft.

"I saw it first," George complained and tried to push his branch into the boot too as Kitty attempted to twist around and land the boot onto the bank but she slipped on the wet clay into the rushing water. "George, no!" she screamed as her black curls were swallowed by the rushing river.

Oonagh and Henry jumped to their feet and rushed to the bank.

George, clutching the boot, was dragging Kitty up the muddy bank. Henry stooped and lifted a very muddy bedraggled Kitty onto the grass. He carried her to the blanket and her mother wrapped the blanket around her.

"Will you two never learn? Your dress is soaking wet," she scolded.

"Mammy, that man was here again, he lifted me out of the water and brought me to the bank," Kitty spluttered when she caught her breath.

"No Kitty, it was Mr Shepherd and George who rescued you between them, you have too much imagination," insisted her mother.

"He was perhaps an angler," said Henry, "Kitty you may wear my jumper if you wish," he said, pulling the jumper over his head.

"How very kind of, Mr Shepherd," said Oonagh to Kitty, "what do you say?"

"Thank you, Mr Shepherd," said Kitty hanging her head as her mother pulled the wet dress off Kitty under cover of the blanket. Oonagh hung the muddy dress over a branch of the tree to dry.

"Perhaps the man was looking for his boot," said George.

Oonagh scoured her eyes along the bank but there was no one in sight.

"He had black hair," said Kitty, "but really mammy I would have been quite safe, I would have turned into a water baby, just like Tom in Mr Shepherd's book, and I would have met all manner of wonderful creatures as I swam out to sea."

"Oh no, Kitty, that is just a story, it was in the imagination of Mr Kingsley who wrote the book. I am afraid you would have drowned, my little dreamer, then what would we have done without you?" said Henry.

"See, I have brought the book with me and we can continue with the next chapter, if you wish," and the two children sat eagerly beside him as Henry continued Charles Kingsley's story.

Oonagh spread the picnic on the blanket and passed the food to the children and Henry, he prised the stopper from the neck of the glass bottle and they passed the bottle between them, the fizzy lemonade tingling on their lips, until the bottle was empty and there were only apple cores and breadcrumbs left on the blanket, Oonagh shook the crumbs onto the grass for the sparrows to eat and the children threw the cores into the shrubs for the blackbird. Kitty urged Henry to read just another chapter of the book while Oonagh laid her head on Henry's lap and drifted off to sleep in the warmth of the sun. When she awoke, George and Kitty were throwing a grubby white tennis ball that Kitty had found in the shed to each other on the grassy lawn between the rivers.

"I have made them promise to keep away from the river bank," said Henry, "Your aunt has invited us all to tea. Your uncle Pat is bringing home fried fish. I am grateful we have a long walk there or I will be too portly to be a sports-master with all this food."

He helped Oonagh to her feet, she rolled up the blanket, laid it across the top of her basket and they set off home. Henry thankfully realised the walk to her aunt's cottage was downhill.

"I walked over to speak to your father this morning," said Auntie Bridget, quietly to her niece while they were buttering the bread together in the scullery, "we both agree that Henry Shepherd is a good match for you, there will not be many men willing to take on another man's child. Francis says Henry is hopeful to be taking a position at the grammar school in September, your wedding will have to be soon. Oonagh you need a good man to take care of you, think about this seriously. Please talk to Kitty about it soon before you lose this man. Believe me lovely girl, this is the advice your mammy would have given you."

"Yes auntie, today has proved to me that he would be a good daddy to my girl – and to George," said Oonagh taking the plates down from the cupboard and putting them in the oven to warm in preparation for the fried fish.

When they had finished tea Oonagh urged Kitty to change back into her dress and give Henry his jumper back. "Your dress is muddy, but it is dry, little dreamer," she said, "we must hurry now, I do not wish to walk those lanes in the dark."

"Of course I will accompany you, I cannot let you walk alone," said Henry to Oonagh's relief as Kitty's eyelids were already closing and the prospect of carrying her daughter home was not attractive to Oonagh.

"The fresh air has been good for you all so it has," said Auntie Bridget, "will you look at your rosy cheeks." And she hugged Kitty, "I do love your visits wee girl, and you George. It takes away some of my hurt, I still miss my Michael so."

"And we love our visits home," said Oonagh, "Don't we, children?" The children nodded wearily.

Henry carried Kitty on his broad shoulders all the way to granddad's cottage and then carried her up the stairs. In the bedroom, her mother struggled to remove Kitty's mud stained dress and stockings before she snuggled under the counterpane and she was soon asleep while her mother sat with Henry in the parlour.

Francis Kennedy was sitting on an old kitchen stool in the backyard enjoying a pipe full of tobacco and breaking the remains of a stale loaf into crumbs for the hens pecking at his feet.

He called to Oonagh when she came into the scullery to make a hot drink for herself and Henry.

"Oonagh, I spoke with Henry Shepherd this morning," he said, "he asked me for your hand in marriage and I agreed, I hope that was right by you. Your aunt and I agree he is the perfect husband for you. His prospects are good, he loves you dearly, he has told me so, and he has loved you since first he saw you, just as it happened to myself with your dear mammy. Oonagh you will not get many more chances like this, not many men want to take on another's child. I only ask you one thing Oonagh; that Father Murphy should be the priest to marry you to Henry. He was so caring with your mother, he married your mother and me, he christened you and Finn and he schooled you both,"

"Daddy, I do not know if that is possible, as Henry is not of the Roman Catholic persuasion. His parents are Wesleyans."

Chapter Thirty-Two
A Good Catholic Boy

"I will not allow my daughter to marry a Wesleyan," insisted Francis Kennedy. Standing up, he laid his pipe down on the stool, shooed the hens into the shed and kicked the door shut securely behind them. "He will have to convert."

Oonagh carried mugs of tea into the parlour for the three of them and her father followed her.

"Now then, young man, my daughter tells me your family are Wesleyans," said Francis.

"Indeed we are, sir," said Henry, "my father is a manager at the mine in a village just north of Nottingham and he is a lay-preacher at the local chapel."

"My daughter," said Francis, "is a Roman Catholic. In my eyes, there is no marriage unless it is to a Roman Catholic, witnessed before God in a Roman Catholic Church and the ceremony is conducted by a priest of the Roman Catholic faith."

"Well," said Henry, standing beside Oonagh, "I struggle to find a solution to this problem sir, I love your daughter and your granddaughter, I want to look after them both and Oonagh wants to marry me." He looked to Oonagh, she linked her arm through his and smiled up at him, "I do."

"I suggest that we speak to Father Murphy in the morning," she said, "Please sit down Daddy and drink your tea." Francis sat on the wooden rocking chair and tipped a good measure of Irish whiskey into his tea from his hip flask, then offered the flask to Henry.

"Thank you, but I will leave soon," said Henry, "your sister will be waiting for me to be home."

Oonagh accompanied him to the door and he held her face in his hands, "Thank you my darling for an enchanting day. Look at the stars above. We both worship the same one God, we can't let the church where we worship Him prevent two people in love from marrying, Oonagh, my darling, my father will marry us in his church if your faith will not allow our union."

Henry pulled her close and kissed her gently.

"And I love you, Henry Shepherd, with all my heart," said Oonagh as Henry pulled on his cap and set off with a long stride, walking down towards the lights of the town and Auntie Bridget's cottage, turning to wave to Oonagh as he reached the turn in the lane. "Good night, Mrs Shepherd," he called.

"Good night my love," she answered and went back inside the cottage and straight up to her bed.

The following morning Oonagh sat Kitty down at the table in the scullery with a mug of tea and bread spread with dripping and brown jelly.

"Now wee girl, you have to know that Mr Shepherd and I will be married. Your daddy in Australia will always be your daddy, but Mr Shepherd loves me and I love Mr Shepherd. I am going to be Mrs Shepherd this summer. Would you like to be my bridesmaid, Kitty?"

Kitty's eyes opened wide, "Will I have a long dress and flowers?"

"You surely will," said her mother.

Later that day, they all walked to the church. As Oonagh and Henry entered the church the air was thick with the aroma of incense mingled with the scent of lavender polish that an elderly lady was using to clean the communion table.

Oonagh dipped her fingers in the piscina and, head bowed, crossed herself with the consecrated water. Father Murphy was preparing for that summer's confirmation class, setting a prayer book on each place along the two wide front pews, in the central nave below the chancel and in front of the rood screen. He laid two books on the front pew of the Lady chapel.

"God bless you my child, it warms my heart to see you," said the old priest.

"How many are in the confirmation class this year Father? I remember attending every Wednesday evening, I used to walk here with cousin, Michael," said Oonagh.

"It is still the same evening, Wednesday, and there are twenty youngsters, along with two adults who are converting from the Church of Ireland," said the priest.

"Father, this is Henry Shepherd, we have come to ask if you will marry us this summer," said Oonagh.

Henry held out his hand and the aging priest took it with his own hand, which was twisted and gnarled with arthritis.

"And are you a good Catholic boy?" asked the priest of Henry.

"Henry is a Wesleyan, from a good Christian family," answered Oonagh. The priest let go of Henry's hand and turned to the elderly cleaner. "There is a clean altar cloth in the vestry Mrs Kearney." Then turning back to Henry he asked.

"Do you want to convert to our faith, my boy? It is a matter of studying the basis of our faith, learning the order of service and its meaning, then confirming your faith before our congregation. There is plenty of room in my class for you, we are only on Week three, I can explain what we have covered so far, I am a good teacher, am I not Oonagh?"

"Thank you, Father Murphy but I have my own faith that I have followed all my life, I have read the Holy Bible and I know that we worship the same God. Father can I ask if you are willing to marry us in the presence of The One True God?" said Henry.

"I am afraid I cannot do that, my boy, for it is written in the Holy Bible, '*Be ye not unequally yoked together with unbelievers*'."

"But I am not an unbeliever," said Henry, "I will meet you in the town Oonagh." He thrust his hands into the pockets of his breeches, turned his back and walked out of the church into the sunshine, where Kitty and George were playing with their marbles on the path.

"We shall walk into town, I would like to meet your Uncle Finn, Kitty, do you know where Doyle's fish shop is?"

Finn was helping at the Doyle's fish and chip shop and the appetite-tempting smell of the hot beef dripping reached Henry before the shop came into view. Henry introduced himself to his future brother-in-law and bought the children a portion of chips each. They were all three sitting on the wall outside the shop enjoying the best chips Henry had ever tasted, when Oonagh joined them.

"I thought we could spend the afternoon on the beach, what do you think children?" she said.

"Henry, Father Murphy suggested we might approach the rector of the Anglican Church to marry us, the rector of the church in the Marketplace seems very pleasant and was very kindly to Father Kelly after the riot."

For the last few days of their visit they played cricket and relaxed on the beach, Henry's fair hair was bleached by the sun, but Oonagh kept her red hair firmly fastened beneath her bonnet in the sunshine.

Before they left for England, Oonagh asked her father if he would come to England to give her away to Henry on her wedding day.

"I dare not leave the farm, Oonagh, the landowner would dearly like to repossess my little farm and it has been in our family for generations, and I am hoping for generations to come. I am looking to Finn to carry on the family name, he is courting a good Catholic girl. No I am sorry my darling girl but I cannot take the risk and I will only give my beloved daughter away to a Roman Catholic man, as much as I respect Mr Shepherd."

"I understand, daddy," was all that Oonagh could find to say as her father stroked her hair back from her forehead, and she kissed his weathered cheek. "We will try to visit again soon, daddy."

They all sat together on the deck for the sail back to England. A boy sat beside Kitty and George with a scruffy brown and white mongrel dog with wiry hair and a string tied around its neck. The dog sniffed at Kitty, then licked her hand and gazed at her with sad brown eyes as she stroked its head.

"Can we have a dog, mammy, when you marry Mr Shepherd?" she asked, winking at George.

"I think we will have to wait and see," said Henry, "I do hope I have been offered the position at the grammar school, Oonagh, there is a house included, and it will be so convenient.

"It has just two bedrooms but you will be able to attend Father Kelly's church again, there are shops close by and you are only a tram ride away from Mrs Delaney."

Chapter Thirty-Three
An Inside Water Closet

Mrs Delaney answered the door excitedly to Oonagh and the children, when they returned home. They had left Henry on the train to continue his journey to Nottingham.

"Come see, Oonagh, come see," she said taking Oonagh's hand and leading her upstairs. The small rear bedroom had been divided into two rooms. The first small narrow room had a splendid water closet with a blue Wedgewood patterned bowl and a polished mahogany seat. Mrs Delaney grasped the black rubber handle on the end of the chain hanging from the lever of the black water filled tank high on the wall, she tugged on the chain and the water flushed around the bowl.

"See Oonagh, see children, no need to walk down the garden path in the dark and the rain, and wait until you see in here," she said opening the door of the larger room with a flourish, "and no more tin baths in front of the fire, children."

On the right-hand side of the room was a splendid white enamelled bath with shiny chrome taps and underneath the window was a hand washbasin in the familiar blue Wedgewood pattern.

"The water is heated from the fire in the parlour and stored in a copper cylinder in a closet on the landing," she said.

"I am astonished that all this work has been finished while we have been away," said Oonagh, "but this will be so much better for your arthritis, Kathleen. Auntie Bridget said to be sure to recommend Epsom salts in your bath water, she and Uncle Patrick send their best regards to you and granddad Delaney."

"Grandma Kathleen," said Kitty, "mummy is going to marry Mr Shepherd and I am going to be a bridesmaid and have a long dress and a posy."

"And," said George, "we are going to have a dog."

"Not here you aren't," said Grandma Kathleen, "your granddad would have something to say about, they are a huge responsibility."

"Never fear Kathleen, we are only thinking about it, it all depends on whether Henry is offered the position at the grammar school. There is a small house included with the position. Henry will be involved with the cricket team and their matches are usually at weekends, he will need to live close to the school."

"When will he hear?" asked Grandma Kathleen.

"He is hoping a letter will be awaiting him at his parents' home," said Oonagh.

Chapter Thirty-Four
A June Wedding

On Monday morning, Oonagh knocked on Father Kelly's door early. He was shaving and came to the door, towel in hand, drying the shaving soap from his shining cheeks.

"Oonagh, what an unexpected pleasure, come in my dear, come in."

He led Oonagh into the room on the right, his dining room.

"Father, a young man, Henry Shepherd has asked me to be his wife, he is a teacher, Father, of Sports and English Literature."

"Is he a good Catholic boy, Oonagh? Which church does he attend? I may know his parish priest."

"Father, he is a good Christian. His father is a Wesleyan Minister in Nottinghamshire. He loves the same God as us Father, he attends church, and he is a good Christian. Please Father, will you marry us? He knows my past and he loves my little girl."

"I cannot go against Rome, Oonagh. He must convert to our faith."

"Father, it would be going against his own faith, the faith he was brought up with and that has made him the good man that he is," insisted Oonagh.

"Oonagh, as much as I would like to join you in Holy Matrimony to this man, my dearest girl, and I am sure you have chosen a good man, I fear the only solution is that you ask the rector of the Anglican church in the Marketplace, he was a good friend to me when our church was vandalised," said the priest, "but promise me, Oonagh, that you will still worship at my church."

"I will speak to him now," said Oonagh, turning to the door. She walked swiftly to the rectory next to the church in the marketplace, and knocked firmly on the brass polished door knocker. The door was answered by a smiling, plump, middle-aged lady wearing a pleated tweed skirt and a pink hand knitted cardigan, her wavy grey hair was clipped back from her bright blue eyes. Oonagh asked if the rector was available regarding a wedding and the lady ushered her into a wood panelled room off the hall.

"I have to ask if the rector will marry me and my fiancé Henry, as I am a Roman Catholic and he is Protestant. A mixed faith marriage is not allowed in my church," said Oonagh

"Oh, a wedding, how lovely, what month were you thinking of?" said the lady, who introduced herself as the wife of the rector.

Oonagh turned as a short, rotund gentleman in shirtsleeves and a grey striped waistcoat with a monocle hanging from a chain in the top pocket entered the room. He was carrying a china cup and saucer, the cup was full of his morning tea. He placed the cup carefully on the green leather top of the mahogany desk and carefully stirred his tea.

"And your fiancé, what faith is he, young lady?"

"He is a Christian, sir, whose father is a Wesleyan Minister."

"Then I would be honoured to join you in Holy Matrimony, shall we look at my diary?"

He opened the top drawer and took out a large red leather-bound book, putting the monocle to his eye he bent over the diary.

"Let me see, June… June 26th is free in the afternoon at two o'clock. Miss erm?"

"Yes," said Oonagh, "yes, oh yes, Kennedy, sir, Oonagh Kennedy."

"Now I would like to meet your young man, can you come one morning this week to see me and we will complete the necessary documents, we will have to read the banns and I would hope you will be in the congregation when your banns are read. Shall we say tomorrow or Wednesday? I could meet you in the church and you can familiarise yourself with our place of worship, it dates back to the 14th century, you know, but only the chancel remains of the ancient structure. Of course, back then, the priest was answerable to Rome, I am advised by my Bishop."

"I shall speak to my fiancé and we shall call to see you tomorrow, will ten o'clock be convenient sir? We are hopeful that Henry will be offered a position at the grammar school and I am eager to hear if he has news, so if you will excuse me."

She offered her hand to the rector and he took it, "Until tomorrow, my dear."

Oonagh left the rector and walked the familiar route through the deserted market to Mr Delaney's shop.

"It's booked for 26th June, Granddad Delaney, will you give me away?"

"Sweet girl, thank you I would be honoured, but will your father not want to give you away?" and Edward kissed her on her forehead.

"No, Daddy does not want to leave Ireland, he says he does not want to leave the farm but I think he does not want to see me marry a Protestant," Oonagh said.

"I am sorry to hear that," said Edward, "but his loss is my lucky gain, sweet girl."

"26th June, Herbert," he said turning to his assistant, "Can I leave the shop in your safe hands?"

His assistant was chopping stewing meat on the wooden table and piling it onto a tray at the back of the shop. "Yes sir, Mr Delaney. I am pleased to hear your good news, Miss Oonagh."

"Thank you kindly Herbert," said Oonagh, "goodbye to you both now, Grandma Kathleen will need a rest from those two little pickles. I had better hurry home."

Oonagh caught the horse tram from Mersey Square to Heaton Chapel. As she walked down the road she could see Henry was waiting for her at the front gate. As soon as he saw her he waved a letter above his head,

"I have been offered the position, Oonagh, my dear, I have been offered the position, the letter came by first post this morning," he called, and Oonagh quickened her step.

"That is just as well, my darling, because I have booked our wedding for 26th June at Stockport Parish Church," she said when she reached him, "the rector would like to see us on Wednesday morning, he has some documents to complete. Have you replied to the offer Henry?"

"I have already replied and posted the letter. We have so much to do. My parents are eager to meet you, my love," said Henry.

"Will they object to me being of the Roman Catholic faith?" asked Oonagh.

"I am an adult, I can judge for myself and I could not have dreamed for a better wife for myself, but I know they will fall in love with you, tender girl," said Henry and he lifted her into the air.

"Mr Judge, the headmaster has given me the key to our new home, I suggest we go tomorrow although the decorators may be there. They are painting all the walls for us. The headmaster has suggested a particularly pleasant route for me to take you there."

"Everything is happening so fast, I feel that I can scarcely breathe. When we are married, I will be able to come back here to help Mrs Delaney, will I not?" said Oonagh dropping her voice to a whisper as they stepped into the hallway.

"Most certainly, my dear, the horse tram is direct," Henry assured her.

"I fear her illness is worsening, she is having difficulty climbing these stairs, and the laundry will shortly be too much for her, I will have to arrange to put it out to the laundry in Longsight, even Edward's overalls, I believe the laundry makes a collection, but it will not come without objections from Kathleen, she is so independent."

Grandma was in the kitchen and Oonagh confirmed with her that the children would stay with her on Wednesday while she and Henry kept their appointment with the Reverend Platt, "I've made us all a nice dinner, it will be ready shortly, please look if you can see the children, they were calling round at Annie Clark's house to play."

Oonagh left Henry chatting with Mrs Delaney and she smiled as she saw him taking the tablecloth and cutlery from her and opening the door to the dining room.

Oonagh crossed the road and ran up the avenue leading to Annie's house. Along the footpath of the avenue there was a queue of girls with their dress hems tucked into their bloomer legs while stretched across the road in front of Annie's house was a length of rope. There was a girl at either side of the road turning the rope. Kitty was in the middle of the road jumping as the rope was turned, her dark curls bobbing as the children chanted, "Salt, mustard, vinegar, pepper, salt, mustard, vinegar, pepper," and the rope was turned faster and faster.

Kitty spotted her mother and chanted, "House to let, apply with in, when I go out, Annie Clark comes in," and she pointed to Annie, who ran over and stood in front of the rope, the little girl gauged the rhythm of the rope then jumped in. The rope turners quickened the pace as they chanted "salt mustard, vinegar, pepper" and little Annie Clark struggled to skip in rhythm, her dress dropped back down out of her bloomer legs and she became entangled in the rope.

"You are out, Annie," called the rope turners. "It is Hannah's turn." And a tall girl with long blond plaits stepped out of the queue. "Yes, Annie Clark, it is my turn."

"But it is Annie's rope, it is her mammy's washing line," called Kitty as Annie ran to her side. "Shall we take your skipping rope to your house, Annie?" Annie nodded close to tears but Kitty marched up to the nearest rope turner, took the end of the rope out of her hands and walking across the road toward the other rope turner wrapped it from her hand to her elbow and then handed the coil of washing line to her friend, "call for me tomorrow, Annie," said Kitty, as Annie ran up her garden path and through the side gate.

"Kitty, dinner is ready, where is George?" said Oonagh.

"He is up the road playing football," said Kitty, pointing to the top of the avenue.

"George, dinner time," Oonagh raised her voice now. The other girls began to wander off in different directions, no doubt their own dinners were ready.

Oonagh called to George again and he ran to her. "George, where is your best jumper?" said Oonagh.

"It is a goalpost, sorry," said George, and he ran to pick up the beautiful Fair Isle jumper that Grandma Kathleen had knitted for him, despite the pain in her arthritic hands.

"Hurry children," urged Grandma Kathleen when the three stepped through the back door, "dinner is ready and you seem to have forgotten that we have a visitor."

Henry was sitting in the fireside chair in the dining room, his long legs crossed.

"The temperature seems to be rising," said Oonagh as she wiped her forehead with a handkerchief and they took their seats around the table as Grandma Kathleen spooned the steak then the vegetables onto the plates.

The children's plates were clean as always when it was Grandma's stewed steak and dumplings for dinner

"Well, it seems I will have no washing up again," said Grandma and the children laughed. Oonagh gathered up the crockery and took it through to the kitchen.

Henry stood, "Thank you for a delicious meal, Mrs Delaney, but I am afraid I must take my leave now, I would like to tell my parents our news." Henry followed Oonagh into the kitchen.

"You must excuse me now, Oonagh, my love, but I will collect you tomorrow and take you to see our new home." Henry grasped Oonagh around the waist and lifted her slightly until she was standing on tiptoes. She lifted her face for a kiss.

"You are like a little bird," he said, "my little bird." He kissed her, "Until tomorrow, my pretty little bird."

Chapter Thirty-Five
A Home of Their Own

By ten o'clock on Tuesday morning, Oonagh and Henry were on the tram travelling along the Buxton Road.

"This is our stop," said Henry just before they reached the bottom of the Davenport Road. He stood and led Oonagh to the front of the tram as the driver brought the horse to a halt. He took Oonagh's hand as they crossed the main road and walked up the lane. Eventually Henry guided her down a tree-lined avenue, the spring fresh leaves were lime green and the branches heavy with blossoms of pink and white. The petals, loosened by the slightest breeze, fluttered down onto the couple.

"It is pink snow," Oonagh laughed. On both sides of the avenue were villas, joined together in pairs. Each individual house had its own front garden, most had flowering shrubs and trees against the low front walls. Some had already planted annual bedding plants along the edge of the path that led from the gate to their front door.

"Is our house one of these Henry," Oonagh asked, squeezing his hand and turning her face to him for another kiss.

"I am afraid not, my love," Henry answered, "but we will be just as happy as the people living on this avenue and, one day, who knows, we may have a house like one of these."

At the top of the avenue were the gates to a small park. In the garden that bordered the park a lilac tree, heavy with purple flowers, lowered its branches over the footpath. Henry pulled a branch down and taking the blooms gently into his hands, he inhaled their sweet perfume, offering them to Oonagh to enjoy with him.

"I tell you, sweet girl, there is not a perfume on the dressing table of the finest lady in this land that would equal the delightful scent of this bloom. Will you carry lilac on our wedding day, especially for me?" "I will, my love," said Oonagh, and Henry opened the black, wrought iron gates into the little park. The birds were flitting busily, gathering nesting material or scratching at the leaves in the undergrowth and pecking in the soil, searching for insects and grubs for their babies in the nests high in the trees. Henry knew most of the names of the birds. "Blackbirds are my favourites, and thrushes, I love their songs," said Oonagh.

"They are the same family," explained Henry.

At the end of the pathway was another pair of wrought iron gates, painted black. Henry pulled the gates open and led Oonagh into another street, lined with terraced houses. "No 38, we are looking for," he said. Oonagh spotted the house first. It was a corner house with a low wall to two sides. There was a door to the front with the number in polished brass, and a door to the side of the house which faced another street.

Henry took the key from his pocket and gave it to Oonagh, it was warm, he had been turning it over and over in his pocket with his left hand while he held Oonagh's hand with his right hand.

"Your new home, my love," he said with a sweep of his arm and bowing low.

"Our new home, a home of our own." She turned the key and they stepped together into the lobby. There was a strong smell of paint, which explained why the windows had been left open.

To the left of the lobby was the door into the front parlour, "Take care," said Henry, "the paint is not quite dry."

There was a small fireplace on the outside wall and a bay window onto the front of the street

"I did not see that," said Oonagh, "there is a rhododendron shrub there in the front by the door. Mr Delaney has one of those, it has purple flowers in June and see, there is room for me to plant more flowers."

They went back into the lobby and a door led into the kitchen which had a large table in the centre covered by a heavy maroon velvet cloth with tassels around the edge. When Oonagh lifted the cloth she revealed wooden drawers under the table top.

"We can store our cutlery in here, Henry," she said.

"The school provides basic furniture," explained Henry and opened the door into the scullery. There was a large stone sink in the corner, a metal washing tub and a mangle. Outside the back door, there were two more doors. One opened into a coal shed and the other was an earth toilet.

"The headmaster said all the schoolmasters' houses will shortly be having indoor water closets installed," Henry reassured Oonagh.

Back into the lobby and up the steep stairs the couple discovered two bedrooms. The larger one was at the rear with two windows overlooking the side road.

"Kitty's room overlooks the front," said Oonagh, "but where will George sleep when he stays?"

"He will be going back to Derbyshire to boarding school, my love, for his final year, and I thought you said Grandma Margaret is insisting he live with her in holidays from school and when his apprenticeship begins. Now we must register Kitty at her new school, but that must be another day. We must hurry to the church now, I have arranged to meet my parents there, they are eager to meet my bride."

Henry locked the front door and, hand in hand, they hurried to the tram stop. Soon they were passing the town hall where they alighted the tram and walked along the side of the splendid building. As they approached the market place, a tall slim lady with fair hair covered with a royal blue patterned head-scarf and waving frantically calling, "Henry, Henry, my dear, we are here, we are here."

She ran to them, arms outstretched, "Oonagh, Oonagh, my dear, Henry was wrong he said you were pretty but my dear you are beautiful and I am so happy to meet you," and, taking Oonagh's face in her hands, she kissed her firmly on both cheeks, then holding her hand in her own she led her over to a man with dark hair, glistening with hair oil and sporting a magnificent handlebar moustache. "Peter, this is our new daughter, the daughter I have always wanted. Oonagh, this is Henry's father, Peter."

Peter took Oonagh's hand and kissed her forehead.

"I am so delighted to meet you finally, my dear, I know you make my son very happy and my Martha and I are so pleased to welcome you into our family."

Oonagh smiled up at Henry and he put his arm around her waist as the rector came out of the front door of the rectory.

"Good morning, Miss Kennedy, and this I presume is your fiancé, Mr Henry Shepherd?"

"Yes," said Oonagh, "and these are his parents, my future parents-in-law."

The rector shook Peter Shepherd by the hand, "A man of the cloth I understand, and very appropriate names, if I might say," the rector smiled, and led them into the church.

"Yes, a fine building, built to the glory of God many hundreds of years ago, there have been such changes in the Christian church over that time," said Peter, "I will come straight to the point, reverend. With the permission of my son and his bride, my wife would like to read a passage from the New Testament during the wedding service, and I would like to make the address. Would you all be in agreement with that?"

Henry and Oonagh nodded and the rector took Peter's hand. "My dear friend, I would be so happy to have that conciliation between our churches. Personally, I like to think there will be a day when the Anglican, the free churches and even the Roman Catholic Church can be reconciled."

Reverend Platt discussed numbers of guests, "I need a number, so that my verger knows how many hymn books to prepare. He will distribute them as the guests take their seats. Bride's family to the left of the chancel and the groom's family to the right. The verger will direct them, no worry for you, Miss Kennedy."

Oonagh explained that Mr and Mrs Delaney were her only family here in England and that she did not think her family would be travelling from Ireland because her father was a farmer.

"That is understandable," said Peter, and the rector nodded in agreement.

"But I have three good friends, whom I have known since I first came to live in Stockport, I must get word to them at the hat factory. They will be surprised that I am to be married. Oh and there are the Clancys, they have been like family to me."

"You see, you have quite a large family here in England, people who love you, and now you have Henry's family too."

"We could walk down to the hat factory on the way home," suggested Oonagh, "I would like to ask my friends if they will make my wedding veil and of course invite them to our wedding."

"My parents have reserved a table for us for dinner at the big hotel," said Henry, "if we have finished here shall we make our way there. Thank you Reverend Platt," and he shook the rector's hand firmly.

"If you would like to arrange flowers in the church on the evening prior to your wedding, Miss Kennedy, I will ensure the south door is open and Reverend Shepherd, if you could let me have a note of the Bible passages you will use, I will arrange for the Bible to have bookmarks."

"Would you and your good lady care to join us for dinner now, Reverend Platt?" said Peter Shepherd and the rector hurried off to collect his wife.

Mrs Platt appeared in minutes from the rectory, smiling broadly and brushing stray hairs from her shoulders. "So kind of you to invite us," she enthused to Henry's parents and the little party made their way down from the church in the marketplace to the big black and white coaching inn. Peter Shepherd and Reverend Platt remained in deep conversation throughout the pleasant meal while the two ladies chatted pleasantly. After dinner Henry and Oonagh walked to the hat factory and Oonagh enquired at the front desk if Rose Murphy and Fanny O'Connell still worked there. "Indeed they do," said the commissionaire, who was resplendent in a red jacket with brass-polished buttons and a black top hat. Oonagh asked if he might pass a note to them. He agreed and she scribbled a note to Rose which she handed to him.

"I will give this to Miss Murphy, when she clocks out later." Oonagh had asked that her friends meet herself and Henry to take tea in the hotel later that afternoon. "The girls will tell Concepta, I am sure," she said to Henry, "we could call and tell the Clancys before we return to the hotel, I must bid your parents farewell, I will not be seeing them before the wedding, I have so much to do."

Mr and Mrs Clancy were in the kitchen, when Henry and Oonagh knocked at their door. They were delighted to see Oonagh and to meet Henry, Mrs Clancy hugged Oonagh and then hugged Henry too. "Are you sure you would not like to have tea with us, it is your favourite, Oonagh, tripe and onions." "What a pity," said Oonagh, "but we have eaten at dinner time."

After Oonagh had invited the Clancys to the wedding, the couple took their leave, explaining that they were meeting Rose and Fanny at the hotel. As they walked hand in hand down to the hotel Oonagh whispered to Henry, "I promise never to cook tripe and onions for your tea."

Mr and Mrs Shepherd were still in the lounge of the hotel, the rector and his wife had left. Oonagh waited in the front lobby until her friends arrived. They had called on Concepta at the Railway Inn and brought her with them.

Henry's mother ordered another pot of tea and, after introductions, they all sat around the table for tea and cakes. Oonagh quietly asked her friends if they would make her veil and they whispered in agreement. Oonagh and friends moved to the adjacent table to discuss the details and it was agreed the veil should be in silk net with Brussels lace.

"The mother of Kitty's friend, Annie Clark, is a dressmaker," said Oonagh, "I shall ask her to make my gown."

"I thought you would ask Mrs Watson," said Concepta and the girls collapsed into giggles.

Mrs Shepherd enquired why the girls were laughing but Oonagh was laughing too much to speak. "You would have to know this lady to understand, I will explain later," said Oonagh putting her hand onto her mother-in-law's gloved hand.

"Oonagh, it is not kind to laugh at other people no matter what they have done in the past," chided Mrs Shepherd.

The three girls promised to come to the Delaney's home the weekend before the wedding for a dress rehearsal and Henry's parents hugged Oonagh before leaving for the railway station for their train to Derby and onwards to Nottingham. Henry kissed his pretty little bird as he helped her aboard the horse tram that took her home and then ran after his parents onto the railway platform.

Oonagh explained all her plans to Mrs Delaney that evening and talked about Henry's request that she carried lilacs.

"I thought I would wear lilac in my hair, do you think it will still be in bloom? Fanny and Rose said that they would come with my veil on the Thursday before the wedding, and they will come on the wedding morning to fashion my coronet from fresh flowers."

"Now that is something I could help with," said Kathleen Delaney, "I will ask the neighbours along the road if they can spare lilacs from their gardens, but I think you should wear and carry the white lilacs. We can decorate the church with the purple lilac from our garden. Now I think you should make haste to ask Mrs Clark about making your gown for you."

Annie's mother was delighted when Oonagh explained that she would like her to make her wedding gown, "But we will have to hurry now to buy the material, that is, unless you would like white satin, I have five yards that I bought for another lady but she was a victim of breach of promise, her groom-to-be has sailed off to the Colonies. If you agree to the satin, I could start work tomorrow. I shall take your measurements now," and she took her tape measure and a notepad from her apron pocket.

When Oonagh arrived home, Mr Delaney was finishing his tea, scraping out the rice pudding dish. "I do so love the skin from around the edges," he said.

The children had long been asleep, having eaten their tea of bread and jam together in the kitchen.

"I have reserved a room at the Victoria Hotel for your wedding breakfast, I told them you would furnish them with the final numbers of guests, and I took the liberty of ordering ham salad for the meal, I supply them with the hams so we can agree a fair price."

"Yes, ham salad will be refreshing, especially if it is a warm day, thank you," said Oonagh.

On the Thursday evening before the wedding, Rose and Fanny sat in the dining room at the Delaneys home and Kitty watched entranced at their speed and dexterity as they worked on Oonagh's veil. They held the silk net in one hand while they wove the silken thread on their fine needles with the other hand, in and out, in and out, like a machine. The edges of the veil they embellished with Brussels lace with the same fine stitching.

"There now," said Rose, laying the veil on the dining table, "that is ready to fasten to the floral coronet."

"Mammy, I think I would like to be a hatter," said Kitty when her mother kissed her goodnight.

"If that is what you would like to be, I am sure there is always employment in Stockport," said Oonagh.

Chapter Thirty-Six
The Wedding

The morning of the wedding dawned bright and sunny. Mrs Delaney gave up her bedroom for Oonagh to dress. "There is a full-length mirror in my room that will assist you in dressing," she said to Oonagh, "I hung your wedding gown in my wardrobe yesterday when Mrs Clarke delivered it, and it is covered with a bed sheet."

Oonagh's girlfriends arrived as Oonagh was enjoying breakfast with the children and Mr Delaney in the kitchen. Grandma Kathleen had left the house with a sharp pair of scissors and was begging sprigs of lilac from the neighbours, "We have plenty of white lilac on our own tree," she said, "I will cut that last of all."

Oonagh bathed then her three friends Rose, Concepta and Fanny (already dressed in the pink dresses they had made for themselves) came upstairs to the Delaney's room carrying the white lilac blossom, florist's wire and buckram.

Oonagh was standing by the tall sash window looking out over the rear garden.

"The apple tree is full of fruit this year, see the fruit has already formed. I remember when Kitty and George were babies, shading them in the perambulator under the apple tree for an afternoon nap."

Fanny and Rose set to work weaving the lilac onto a circle of wire and forming a floral coronet. Concepta helped Oonagh into her underclothing and white stockings.

"This is like the old days when we shared a bedroom," said Concepta, carefully lifting the long satin gown over Oonagh's head. Soft folds of satin gathered the gown under Oonagh's breastbone and tiny pearl buttons fastened the gown down the length of Oonagh's spine. "Your dressmaker has made the most beautiful gown I have ever seen, now don't look in the mirror until we have your veil in place." Oonagh sat on the pink velvet bedroom chair while her friends called to Kitty to come upstairs to be dressed. Granddad Delaney was instructing George in the skill of tying a grey satin tie around the collar of his crisp white shirt. Kathleen Delaney was ready, dressed in a royal blue linen suit and wearing a matching hat made by Rose and Fanny. "I am pinning a rose to my hat," she called from the lobby where she was pinning a lemon rose through the white ribbon that trimmed the crown of her splendid hat.

Kitty was assisted by the friends into her bridesmaid's dress of pale pink, and white lilac pinned to a satin bow for her hair. "There, you look so pretty," said Fanny, and handed her the little posy of purple lilac that she had made.

"George, Kitty," called Grandma Kathleen Delaney, "Mr Slater has arrived, time for us to leave, I will send him back to collect you girls. I will see you at the church Edward and Oonagh." Turning, she hurried upstairs as fast as her arthritic legs would allow and, taking Oonagh's face in both her hands, she kissed her. "You will be a married woman by tea time, my lovely girl. God bless you, you are beautiful."

Oonagh dabbed her eyes with her handkerchief. "Thank you, Kathleen, thank you for everything."

Mrs Slater had tied white ribbons through the horses' mane and white ribbons and bows to the little grey carriage which Mr Slater had polished until he could see his face in the doors. The neighbours were watching from their front gates and waved as the cab carrying Grandma Kathleen and the children set off at a trot down Manchester Road.

As soon as Mr Slater reached the church in the Marketplace, Mrs Delaney helped the children down then sent the cab back to collect the three friends, urging Mr Slater to hurry back as the church was filling up.

Mrs Shepherd, dressed in a powder blue dress and wearing a straw bonnet with flowers sewn around the crown, was seated on the front pew beside Peter Shepherd. The rector was chatting earnestly with them, turning frequently, watching the west door for signs of the bride's arrival.

Oonagh's three friends were waiting in the shade of the porch, keeping Kitty and George calm. George had escorted his Grandma Delaney to the front pew as Oonagh had instructed him. Kitty was constantly sniffing at her posy, which made her sneeze.

"Did you not bring a handkerchief?" asked Rose.

"Yes, it is pinned to my bloomers," said Kitty lifting her dress up, unfastening the safety pin that held her handkerchief, and giving a good blow of her nose. The congregation turned as Kitty was pushing her handkerchief under the elasticated leg of her bloomers.

"Kitty, put your dress down," said Oonagh in a whisper as she and Edward Delaney arrived in the porch. Oonagh's face was covered by the short veil while the long veil flowed behind her, Rose arranged the Brussels lace edging of the long veil around the rear of the bride and whispered to the children, "Do not tread on it, and watch where you are walking."

The rector strode down the south side of the nave and greeted the bride just as the organist started to play *The Arrival of the Queen of Sheba.*

With her arm on Mr Delaney's forearm, Oonagh and Edward walked slowly and elegantly down the central aisle followed by the children and her three friends.

When she reached her groom at the steps of the chancel, Oonagh passed her posy to Fanny and the bridesmaids took their seats on the pew behind Mrs

Delaney. Oonagh pushed back her short veil and smiled at Henry, who was wiping tears from his eyes.

The rector invited the congregation to stand for the first hymn. During the final verse Henry's mother stepped up to the pulpit for the first Gospel reading.

"The first reading is from St Paul's letter to the Corinthians chapter thirteen, verse thirteen:

"*And now abideth, faith, hope and love, but the greatest of these is love.*'

"I would like you all to hold that in your hearts," she said, as she stepped down from the pulpit.

Mrs Shepherd took her seat beside her husband Peter, and the rector invited the congregation to stand for the second hymn, "*Love divine, all loves excelling,*" while Oonagh and Henry knelt at the chancel steps. The rector prayed for God's blessing on the couple and Reverend Shepherd quietly stepped into the pulpit.

"As St Paul says, 'The greatest of these is love'. Friends and family we are gathered here today because of the love of this young couple. No matter what their creed is love has overcome, because 'the greatest of these is love'.

"As St John says: 'Anyone who does not love does not know God, for God is love'.

"This young couple, my son Henry Shepherd and Miss Oonagh Kennedy have loved and known God since childhood. In different churches yes, but they know God, and we are here to witness their promises to each other, before Our Lord God."

Reverend Shepherd looked up as Father Kelly slipped into the pew at the back of the church.

"And now, I will hand you back to Reverend Platt to take Henry and Oonagh's vows, with this final message from the Holy Gospel of St John chapter One:

'*Beloved, let us love one another because love comes from God. Everyone who loves has been born of God and knows God.*'"

Peter Shepherd bent his head and prayed quietly to himself and then stepped down to join his wife on the front pew while the rector, Reverend Platt took over the service. Oonagh and Henry stood to make their vows to each other and George stepped forward with the wedding rings on a grey satin cushion.

Their vows and pledges to each other completed, the couple accompanied the rector into the vestry to sign the marriage register, while the congregation sang the third hymn. Mr and Mrs Shepherd and Mr and Mrs Delaney (in loco parentis) followed after them with the bridesmaids and the children,

The registration document completed, Henry and Oonagh left at the head of the procession from the vestry as the joyous wedding bells rang out over the market place. Father Kelly was the first to step forward and congratulate them as they reached the west door. He then took Peter Shepherd's hand and shook it firmly, "Thank you, my friend."

Mr Delaney invited the Father to join them at the hotel for the wedding breakfast, and Father Kelly was pleased to accept as his housekeeper did not cook for him on Saturdays.

The Oonagh carried the edge of her long veil over her arm as the wedding party made their way through the Saturday market and down to the big hotel. The crowds parted as they passed and applauded, shouting out their good luck messages over the sound of the bells. Reaching the hotel steps, Oonagh threw her wedding bouquet of lilacs over her head and Kitty caught it.

"I'm next," she shouted excitedly.

"But my darling, you are only ten years old," cautioned her mother as Kitty took George's hand. Grandma Margaret closed her eyes, shook her head, tutted and turned her back on Oonagh, Kitty and the rest of the wedding guests as they began to file into the hotel, greeted by a waiter serving sweet sherry.

Mrs Shepherd shook her head in refusal to the waiter and raised her hand, "No thank you, not for me."

Margaret Foster approached Mr and Mrs Delaney in the hotel lobby.

"Of course, George will be returning to boarding school tomorrow until the end of term, his father will collect him in the morning from your house.

"Theodore has spoken to George's headmaster because his examination results in all subjects have been so good, and George has a guaranteed apprenticeship at his grandfather's company, he has dispensation to leave school aged ten, although Mr Gladstone's recommendation is aged twelve.

"My son insists," continued Grandma Margaret, "that George should live with me from now, in preparation for the beginning of his apprenticeship to his grandfather's company in September. You have cared for George so well but I know your health is deteriorating, my dear lady, and your circumstances have changed now that his nurse has married."

Grandma Margaret concluded, "I will collect George's belongings from your house one day next week."

Grandma Kathleen searched the hotel lobby for George and took his hand, "So, my darling boy, you will be commencing work soon after your tenth birthday. Your granddad Delaney and I will miss you so much."

"I will visit you often, Grandma Kathleen," said George, smiling and giving her a wink, "and I will be visiting Kitty, of course, I can travel on the tram almost to their door. Grandma, may we have fried bread and bacon in the morning, before father collects me?"

Mrs Delaney squeezed his hand and kissed his forehead.

Soon after they had finished breakfast the following morning, George was collected by his father. The coachman carried a large trunk into the hall at the Delaney house.

"If you would be good enough to pack George's belongings, my mother will collect them this week," said Theodore and he shook the hands of Mr and Mrs Delaney.

"Goodbye sir, goodbye dear lady and thank you for all you have done for my son."

"I should have said he was my Mary's son as well," confided Kathleen to her husband once George and his father had left.

"We all know that, my love," said Edward Delaney, putting his arm around Kathleen's shoulders, "we all know that."

Three weeks later George had finished his schooling.

The morning after he arrived back at Grandma Margaret's, Mrs Delaney was busy in the kitchen when George burst in through the back door. "Grandma, may we have bacon and eggs and fried bread?" he asked as he hugged her around her waist, laying his head on her chest and pleading up at her with his big blue eyes.

"You have only just arrived in time, I was about to wash the frying pan," said Grandma Kathleen, kissing his forehead, "Kitty and Ma Oonagh are coming over this afternoon, you will be happy to hear."

That afternoon, George and Kitty played cricket in Annie Clarke's avenue. For the next few weeks until September, when George was to begin his apprenticeship, he and Kitty played together as before. They played on the waste ground, in the street or in Grandma Kathleen's back garden. Some days Grandma Margaret insisted he stay at home to play with his two half-sisters.

"They are too young, they cannot play cricket, they cannot bowl overarm," protested George, but remained at home to please his grandmother.

Some days George and Kitty were allowed by Ma Oonagh to take the horse tram to Vernon Park. They took jam sandwiches and a bottle of water.

George began his apprenticeship in September while Kitty had to continue her schooling. Oonagh made enquiries about an apprenticeship for Kitty at Bassendales hat factory in Ardwick. Bassendales exclusively made bowler hats and top hats (which were worn by the elite of the mill workers, the weavers). The weavers even had their own exclusive room 'the snug' in the public houses, Mr Bassendale told Oonagh.

Shortly after Christmas, Kitty started work at the hat factory, "I am only learning and watching," Kitty told her mother, "I have to sweep the floor and keep everything tidy for the journeymen."

George caught the tram that Kitty was travelling on most days from his closest tram stop outside St Thomas' church.

Every Wednesday after work George went to Grandma Kathleen's house for tea, and every Wednesday Kitty and Oonagh met at Grandma Delaney's house to hear about George's progress.

George explained that the customers came into the warehouse to view the carpets, "There are some beautiful designs woven in Turkish or Persian patterns, in wonderful rich colours. The carpets are woven in various widths; up to sixteen foot. They also manufacture a width of just eighteen inches. The narrow one is for the staircase. Oh and there are carpets just a yard wide for the hall. Once the customer has settled on a pattern, we call around to their house and we have to measure where the carpet is to be laid. I had to visit two customers today on Dickenson Road. I went with Archie to measure so that he could show me what I had to do. I had to write the measurements down neatly in a book that grandfather gave me – and make diagrams. Tomorrow we will have to work out the price. The customers will come to the warehouse again and if the price is acceptable they have to go into grandfather's office to pay a deposit, Grandfather's clerk will then order the carpets from the manufacturers. Grandfather says that soon he will take me to these companies, (there are some in Kidderminster) so that I may see the huge looms that the carpets are woven on. However, for now I must learn to sew the tape around the edges of the carpets, once they have been cut to the correct size, to stop them from fraying. I do hope these customers that I visited today, order the carpets, I do so want father and grandfather to think well of me."

The following week George's wish was granted and both the customers from Dickenson Road paid their deposits. Grandfather Marcus was 'very pleased' with George he said, because one customer, Mt Whalley, was a solicitor, but George insisted it was only with Archie's help that he had been successful.

Two weeks later, the carpets arrived from Kidderminster and Archie showed George how to cut the different widths to the correct size for each room and for the staircase.

"We will fit the carpets next week," said George to Grandma Kathleen, "I am so enjoying my work."

Two months later he accompanied Grandfather Marcus by train to Kidderminster.

"Grandfather has travelled all over the world to buy carpets," said George when he made his weekly visit to his Grandma Delaney's, "he has even been to China and Persia to purchase carpets, they are beautiful."

"I will have to persuade granddad to buy one for me for the parlour," said Grandma Kathleen, "I do believe Grandma Margaret has a Chinese rug in her parlour."

"Grandfather Marcus says I remind him of himself when he was young," said George, "he says there are business opportunities all over the globe and one day he may ask me to negotiate with carpet makers abroad."

"That sounds very exciting George," said Grandma Kathleen, "but we will miss you. The journeys will take many months, despite the new steam ships. Granddad Edward says that on the new fast steamships, the passage to New York takes less than two weeks. The cost is fifteen guineas and you can reserve a superior cabin. There are chefs on board and even a doctor."

"I fancy I will take you with me then, Grandma," said George, hugging Grandma Kathleen, "to save me from loneliness, or I may take Kitty with me."

"You will have to see what Ma Oonagh says about that," said his grandma.

George repeated all his news to granddad Edward Delaney when he arrived home rather later than usual.

"The town is busy this evening," said Edward, "one of our parliamentary members, Mr Watkins, is addressing his constituents at The Mechanics Institute. Now tell me all your news, young George."

When George arrived at Grandma Kathleen's house the following week on the Wednesday evening, his fingers were sore from sewing the tape onto the coarse carpet backing. Ma Oonagh bathed his hands with cold water and spread zinc and castor oil cream onto them, before wrapping them with a piece of old sheet.

"We do not have to bind the underlay," he said, "because that is made of felt and does not fray. Every foot along the binding of the carpet we have to sew a brass ring. The rings fasten to the hooks which we knock into the wooden floorboards. Mr Whalley has wooden parquet flooring which will border the carpet square. Their maid polishes it just as Grandma Kathleen does here at home."

"I will not be doing that polishing on my hands and knees for much longer with these rheumatic knees and hands," said Grandma Kathleen.

"I think the time has come for you to have a maid," said Oonagh, "you know I will do as much as I can for you but could Edward not put a note in the shop window?"

It was two weeks later, when Oonagh came to visit that she found a sweet young girl, Bernadette Gallagher, was the new maid.

Bernadette lived in and had been given Oonagh's old bedroom.

"She is an absolute treasure," said Kathleen, "I am so glad you insisted that I have help in the house."

Oonagh smiled that Kathleen had bought a maid's uniform, complete with cap for thirteen years old Bernadette.

"I know that you will be happy here, my dear," said Oonagh to Bernadette, "The Delaneys are kind people."

"Yes, ma'am," said Bernadette.

Chapter Thirty-Seven
After the Ball

It was the December following George and Kitty's seventeenth birthdays, when Grandma Margaret made yet another attempt for her grandson to meet 'an eligible young lady who was more of his class'.

Tickets had been purchased for him to accompany his half-sisters to the Christmas Ball, organised by the Manchester and Salford Chamber of Commerce. It was to be held in rooms adjoining the town hall.

Kitty was spared the hurt of waving George and his sisters farewell. They left by carriage directly from Grandma Margaret's house.

By ten o'clock the following morning, George was knocking on the side door of Ma Oonagh's house.

"Shall we walk to Vernon Park, Kitty, I will treat you to tea and cakes."

Kitty finished her breakfast and pulled on her cream Macintosh and red cloche hat, with matching gloves.

They were sitting in Vernon Park on the bench donated by Portwood Mills, when Kitty asked,

"Well did you meet an eligible young lady of your own class?"

"The only eligible young lady that I could ever want," said George, taking her face in both his hands, "is Miss Kitty O'Neil." And George kissed her on the lips, "There, take that. Kitty, will you marry me? I have spoken to Doctor Gould, we are milk siblings only, we are not blood related."

"George, we are not of full age," said Kitty.

"That is no matter if we have our parent's permission," George assured her, "Ma Oonagh will agree, and if Grandma Margaret does not agree…"

Kitty shook her head and frowned, "Then Grandfather Marcus will. Grandfather Marcus is very fond of you, he says you have a good appetite and I would never go hungry."

George took a royal blue box out of his pocket and opened it, inside was a yellow gold ring, set with two perfect diamonds.

"This was my mother's ring, it was made especially for her. Grandma Kathleen has kept in safely for me in her dresser, ready for when I met the right girl, but if you wish you can choose another at the jewellers. She says we can live with her and granddad Edward until we have our own home. Please say yes, Kitty."

"You have told Grandma Kathleen already, then?" Kitty asked.

"Yes and she is very excited, she says she is over the moon."

"Well, then I must not disappoint her," said Kitty, "after all, who else could I wish to marry?"

George put the ring on Kitty's finger, "Now we can tell Ma Oonagh and Mr Shepherd."

George took Kitty's hand, "I will race you up the steps to the lake."

Chapter Thirty-Eight
Any Just Cause or Impediment

Oonagh was working in the scullery pulling the bed sheets, steaming and dripping, out of the boiler with tongs and transferring them into cold water in the sink before winding them through the mangle. The water from the rollers of the mangle gushed into a tin bath below. Oonagh swilled the water onto the paving stones at the back door where the tomcat from next door left his calling card.

"I have had to change the bed linen early," she explained, "Henry would like me to attend the carol service at the grammar school on Monday, did you enjoy your walk?"

Kitty lifted her left hand and sparkled her diamond ring to her mother.

Oonagh hugged her daughter and George.

"Oh my, my, my, I am amazed. I thought it would happen one day, but not quite yet. You are not of full age, either of you, and George, what will your family say? Henry, come downstairs we have some wonderful news. George will you be stopping for dinner? Which church will you marry in?"

"We have not decided Mammy," said Kitty, "but it was very pleasant at your wedding in the church in the marketplace. What do you think, George?"

"Yes," said George, picking up the newspaper from the table, "I see the Grammar school beat Manchester Grammar School at football, Mr Shepherd, you must have a good team."

"We have," said Henry, "They are my cricket team for the summer term, football gives them exercise over winter."

Grandma Margaret was sitting in the front parlour, when George arrived back at her house that evening.

"Grandma, I have some news for you," he said, "Kitty and I are to be married."

"That you are not," said Grandma Margaret getting to her feet, "you are not of full age for another four years. Is that girl in the family way? Is she claiming it is of your doing?"

"Grandma, we love each other, I do not want to spend my life with anyone else," insisted George.

"We will see what your father and grandfather have to say about this. Her father is a convict, her mother has come from Ireland where her family are nobodies. Your grandfather is of noble birth, his sister is a music professor. You grandfather and father are successful businessmen. You should choose a bride from a family of equal status in life. Please, George, listen to me, have you considered whether this marriage would be incestuous?"

"Grandmother, my mind is made up," said George, "it is not incest. Kitty is not of my blood, I have asked Dr Gould. Now I shall retire for the night. Goodnight, grandmother."

George's half-sisters Violetta and Adele were in the dining room, drinking hot chocolate and munching on toast spread with bramble jelly, when he went down to breakfast the following morning.

"George, your father brought the girls this morning and I have told him of your intentions. He asked me to tell you that your grandfather Marcus is sending you to Australia to negotiate with a new carpet company in Victoria. Your father thinks you should gain more experience before you go, but your grandfather is convinced you are learning the business very quickly on your visits to other manufacturers with him. Your grandfather, Marcus, is too old to undertake the passage now and he has the responsibility of his young wife. As for your father he has responsibilities here, too, in Manchester with the company to take care of. What is more, Jeanetta does not wish to be left alone with the children and the household to care for."

George went into the hall and when he came back into the dining room he was wearing his navy-blue woollen Crombie coat.

"Are you going out, George?" said Grandma Margaret, "I had hoped you would take the girls to the park."

"Goodbye, Grandmother, I must go into work now, I am late already. Do not expect me at teatime I am visiting Grandma Kathleen."

"I expect Mrs Delaney knows of your crazy plans?" said Grandma Margaret as George closed the front door firmly.

"There you are George, my boy," said grandfather Marcus, as George stepped into the warehouse showroom, "I wondered if you would decide to come to work today, Come into my office."

George wiped the dust off his top hat with the sleeve of his Crombie coat, and hurried into his grandfather's office.

"I am sorry grandfather, Grandma Margaret wanted me to..." apologised George.

"No matter, no matter," interrupted Marcus, "We are travelling to Axminster tomorrow, you and I. Be at the London Road station by 8.00 am. I have negotiated a huge contract to supply a new hotel in Manchester and they are asking for plain royal blue carpet. If we give them an attractive quote, there will be more business from them, they are building more hotels in Liverpool and Glasgow."

"Yes, Grandfather," said George, "will that be all for now? There are customers in the showroom."

George left the office to speak to a middle-aged couple who were inspecting the rugs.

"The pile is so thick, but will this rug be too heavy for me to lift over the washing line to give it a good beating in spring?" said the lady, Mrs Jackson.

George noted their name and their address in Ardwick, on the order form. "If you would take this order form into the office, please. The clerk will take the money, issue a receipt and arrange a convenient day for delivery." George bade farewell to Mr and Mrs Jackson, shaking Mr Jackson's hand firmly. "And goodbye to you, dear lady, I hope to see you again soon," he said to Mrs Jackson, giving a short bow.

George introduced himself to a young couple who were examining the Turkish patterned carpets, "We are furnishing our new villa in Didsbury," said the man, who introduced himself as Mr Rose.

"Yes, sir, I could come early next week to measure, I am afraid I am away on business tomorrow," said George, "meanwhile, if you choose a carpet now I will make a note of the manufacturer and pattern number."

George was waiting by the ticket office at the railway station at 7.30 am, when Grandfather Marcus was brought by his coachman. "We have a first-class carriage reserved, close to the restaurant car," said Marcus as he took George's arm and ushered him to their gleaming carriage. George helped his grandfather up the step into the carriage with its sumptuous upholstery in maroon and black.

George took off his top hat and overcoat and laid them tidily on the overhead rack, then took his grandfather's coat and laid it on top of his. Grandfather opened his battered brown leather case and took out a sheath of carbon copies of typewritten papers. He passed them to George. "I thought you could examine these figures while we are travelling. You should be aware of the profit margins we will be discussing. Of course you must be able to negotiate alone when you visit the new manufacturer in Australia."

"Yes, Grandfather," said George, "I thank you for giving me the opportunity to negotiate with this new supplier. Father has told me you wish me to represent the firm at the company in Victoria."

"Yes," said Marcus, "I was only 18 years old when I ventured to Manchester as an agent in textiles, you will be 18 this summer and I paid good money for an excellent education for you as heir to my company. I am too old to travel to Australia now, and I am not in the best of health I have a recurring cough which no linctus can cure."

"Grandfather," said George, when they sat opposite each other at a table with starched white tablecloth in the dining car waiting for their order of beef broth.

"I would like to take Kitty with me to Australia, would that be agreeable to you?"

"Yes, my boy, it can be very lonely when you are on business in a foreign country. When I came to England my sister, Fanny, came with me and when she moved to a public school in London after a few months. I felt very alone, that was when I met your grandmother. Fortunately, I also had an uncle who lived in Manchester but sadly he has passed away. He married a Scottish girl and he never managed to persuade her to return to Poland with him.

"If Kitty will travel with you then you have found an ideal match, especially as she has a good appetite," he winked at George. "Your grandmother would never travel with me. Now, my wife, Clarissa, has accompanied me to Scotland where I hope to open a new showroom, we have been to New York, she even came to China with me. I need a lady with me to take care of my needs, fasten my tie, tell me which shirt to wear, that sort of thing. Yes, my opinion is to take Kitty with you. She has a happy spirit and that would be good for our business, but to be correct, you must marry the young lady first."

"Oh yes, Grandfather, Kitty and I would like to marry soon," said George.

"Do not leave your marriage date too late in the year, I would not want our competitors to be given the sole agency. I have corresponded with the company and they expect you in May."

"I must ask Kitty to hasten the wedding plans," said George, "the problem is convincing Grandma Margaret."

"You have to be strong, boy, leave her to me," said Marcus.

Chapter Thirty-Nine
A Christmas Wedding

"Grandma Margaret, would you agree to a wedding for Kitty and me on Christmas Eve, in the Cathedral?" said George, "Grandfather Marcus suggested it, and he said to tell you that he would buy you a new mink coat in case of cold weather."

Grandma Margaret examined her own reflection in the hall mirror and preened her hair. "I think I shall buy a new hat with a fine blue peacock feather."

"George, may I invite Mr and Mrs Montgomery who live opposite the park? You know who I mean, Mr Montgomery owns the woodyard. He is very successful in business due to all the building at present in Manchester. Mrs Montgomery is the chairwoman of the ladies' society at church, I have intended to apply for membership for many years. Has your grandfather Marcus agreed to pay for your wedding breakfast? I would like a better menu than a ham salad for my grandson." George travelled straight to Ma Oonagh's home the following evening after work, as Oonagh and Kitty had not been at Grandma Delaney's the previous evening. George could hear Kitty's voice raised as he knocked on the front door.

"Ma, at least allow me to ask Daddy if he will give me away at my own wedding, at least give him the opportunity," Kitty was shouting.

"Grandfather Delaney has provided for you and I, your father has not shown any interest in us for years now, but yes, you write to your daddy, I'm sure he loves you just the same, but it is a long journey from Australia and he would have to leave the farm for many months."

"I shall write to daddy immediately and ask father Kelly if the nuns will take my letter to him," said Kitty over her shoulder as she opened the front door to George.

"Your daddy will have to sail soon if he is to be here for Christmas Eve."

George explained his grandfather's plan to persuade Grandma Margaret to agree to the marriage. "If Grandma Margaret agrees, then father is less likely to object, but believe me Kitty I will marry you no matter for them. I have more news, grandfather has asked me to travel to Australia to negotiate with a new carpet manufacturer in Victoria and determine the range of their products that we will offer. Who knows, if your daddy cannot come to the wedding we may go to visit him."

"Can we arrange the wedding for Christmas Eve, Ma Oonagh? Grandfather will meet the wedding breakfast costs."

"I am sure I can make the arrangements, I shall go to the Cathedral tomorrow," said Oonagh.

Kitty wrote to Seamus and left her letter with Father Kelly to pass to the nuns. "You must have your banns read in both parishes, my child," reminded Father Kelly.

On Christmas Eve there was just a fluttering of snow as Kitty left the Delaney's house dressed in a full-skirted, ivory lace wedding dress and a white fur shrug. On her black curls she wore a coronet of sparkling mock diamonds and pearls that Mary Delaney had worn on her wedding day. It was fastened to the silk and Brussels lace veil which she borrowed from her mother.

"No princess could look more beautiful," said Kathleen Delaney as she scooped Kitty's dress into the small carriage which had been loaned by Theodore and Jeanetta.

Edward Delaney climbed in beside his 'adopted' granddaughter.

"This makes bride number three I have given away," he said, "Mr Slater will be along soon to collect yourself and Grandma Margaret, we will meet you at the cathedral, Kathleen."

Saturday shoppers along the road into Manchester stopped to watch the bridal party pass by. Snow blew into the coach driver's eyes and stuck to the carriage roof.

"I am sure Daddy would come if he could," said Kitty, her eyes scanning the crowd outside the west door of the cathedral. Granddad Delaney climbed down out of the carriage and came around to help Kitty. "Yes, but it is a long journey to make, my sweet girl. Do not think badly of him."

"Could that be my daddy?" said Kitty indicating a man dressed in black breeches and gleaming white shirt. He had wavy black, oiled hair and tanned skin.

"No, sweet girl, that is an Italian waiter. There are many Italian immigrants in Manchester, they say you have more chance of being served at the bars in the town, if you can speak Italian. The Italian families have started businesses making ice cream and then selling it by horse and cart around the town and outskirts. Come along now sweet girl, your groom will be waiting." Granddad Delaney took Kitty's arm, helped her down the steps of the carriage and onto the paved square in front of the cathedral. The flagstones now had a light dusting of snow.

"Take care, sweet girl," said Granddad Delaney.

George was waiting at the chancel steps his arms behind his back, his left hand grasping the right sleeve of his grey morning suit. He had placed his grey top hat on the front pew. He smiled at Kitty as she lifted her veil back from her face and mouthed 'Boo' to him.

The service followed the authorised version of the Anglican marriage ceremony. Kitty promised sincerely to obey her husband and to forsake all others. She smiled at George as she spoke her vows strongly and clearly, in the presence of their family and friends. George spoke clearly looking all the time into Kitty's eyes, but shuffled from foot to foot as he made his vows, until Kitty took his hand.

Thirty minutes later, the register was signed and the cathedral bells pealed out.

Kitty and George were married and not even Grandma Margaret could change it. The two carriages ferried first the wedding party, then the guests, to the big hotel by the station in the centre of the town.

The wedding breakfast menu had been chosen by Grandma Margaret.

According to the menu cards on each table, there was to be served roast rib of beef, roast potatoes and vegetables followed by orange jelly then mince pies and coffee with cream. Grandma Margaret had arranged the seating and was herself seated on the top table beside her grandson.

"I have to ensure that the waiters are attentive to our guests," she explained to Grandma Kathleen, who was seated on the table to the right of the top table. "Marcus has paid good money for top class service, and I think roast beef is so much more appropriate for a high-class wedding. Oh, excuse me, yes, Mrs Montgomery yourself and Mr Montgomery have been allocated the table just to the right of the top table, with Mr and Mrs Delaney May I say how utterly splendid you are looking, that is a magnificent fur coat, but you should leave it with the cloakroom attendant, that is where I have left my new mink, it will be quite safe. I am sure, in such a high-class establishment."

Mrs Montgomery returned to the lobby to pass her fur coat over to the cloakroom attendant before returning to the banquet room. She nodded politely to Grandma Margaret.

"Have you considered joining our ladies circle at church, Miss Foster?"

Grandma Margaret glowed.

After the meal was finished and the wedding party were enjoying coffee and mince pies, the speeches began. Granddad Delaney gave a speech that brought tears to Oonagh's eyes.

George's best man Freddie Eastwood spoke for close to an hour and after all the customary acknowledgements he concluded:

"When George joined our school and was selected for the cricket team, our position in the league took a sharp rise. This was primarily due to George's unquestionable skill with willow on leather, but also due to his secret weapon. Every time he hit a good strike, George looked with pride to the boundary where Kitty was leaping up and down cheering.

"Whenever a team made a return visit, their first question was invariably, 'Is Kitty here?'

"If Kitty can be just as supporting as a wife, I can think of no better wife for George. Congratulations, old man and your lovely lady!" and Freddie raised his glass to George and Kitty.

Kitty looked at George and then at her stepfather, Henry Shepherd, who nodded his head in agreement and raised his glass to her.

George whispered in Kitty's ear, "I am so happy he made a long speech, it takes the pressure off me."

George stood to great applause. He thanked everyone for attending and for their gifts, he commented how beautiful his wife looked and how smart all the guests were, then he quickly sat down with a sigh of relief and Kitty took hold of his hand under the table.

George and Kitty returned to the Delaney home for Christmas day and visited Grandma Margaret on Boxing Day.

In January and March Kitty prepared for their trip to Australia. "When we return Grandma Kathleen, we shall search for a house of our own to rent," said George.

"There is no hurry, no hurry at all," said Grandma Kathleen.

They were to sail out of Liverpool, "I have booked a superior cabin on the new super fast clipper-built ship 'The Queen'. The clerk said that the superior accommodation is well known, the ship carries a surgeon and the dining is reported to be first-class. We sail around the Cape of Good Hope. Our first port of call is Cape Town, then onwards, across the Southern Ocean, to Melbourne, where we disembark and the ship continues to Sydney. We sail at the beginning of March."

Oonagh and Henry accompanied George and Kitty to Liverpool for their departure. A steward took their trunks aboard.as George and Kitty made their way up the gangway round to the taffrail at the stern of the ship. George held his arm protectively around his wife's waist as she waved and called to her mother and Henry.

As the ship left the dock to the rousing music of the Liverpool Brass Band, Oonagh continued to wave to her daughter, who was by now clutching her little red cloche hat to her black curls as the sea breeze tugged at the hat and threatened to blow it away into the dock.

"I am afraid for my children," said Oonagh, wiping away her tears, then waving her handkerchief as the ship sailed off the quay. "I cannot help but remember the fate of Maggie Connell's family when they sailed to America."

"My darling, the ship they sailed in was doomed from the beginning, it was not seaworthy and badly in need of repair. The ships were chartered by the landowners to relieve themselves of responsibility for their tenant farmers during the potato famine. Government legislation demanded that the landowners should feed their starving tenants. Some provided soup kitchens but when that hit their pockets too hard, their answer was to encourage their tenants to emigrate. The landlords chartered any available ship in whatever condition. So many were wrecked that they were called 'coffin ships' by the newspapers at the time.

"This ship, 'The Queen' is new and well founded. George and Kitty will be quite comfortable and safe, and the progress of the ship will be reported in the daily newspaper. We will know when they dock in Cape Town and when they reach Melbourne. It is a great adventure for a young couple. There are many free settlers aboard the ship, embarking on a wonderful new life in South Africa or Australia. There are so many opportunities in those countries."

"Oh my," said Oonagh, "I hope and pray they return to me."

Chapter Forty
Gippsland

It was 9 May before Oonagh's fears subsided. Henry brought home the Liverpool paper and, among all the other shipping arrival and departure notices, was the reassuring notice that 'The Queen' cutter had docked in Melbourne, Australia, after a safe and comfortable voyage. Oonagh hugged Henry.

"Oh what a relief that is to me. I must call and tell Granddad Delaney tomorrow when I walk into town." While her mother was reading the arrival notice in Stockport, Kitty was sitting on the balcony of her hotel room in the warm late afternoon sunshine, writing the journal that she had promised her mother she would complete on her trip:

"It was approaching noon when we docked in Melbourne. George had been notified of the address of the hotel where the carpet manufacturer had reserved a guest room for us. The town was in easy reach by carriage of the carpet factory. The porter on the dock carried our trunks to the carriage that took us to the railroad station.

It was comfortable, if a little crowded aboard the train but George arranged a first-class carriage to accommodate ourselves and the bulky trunks. Mammy I should not have brought so many clothes, but Mrs Clark had made so many pretty gowns for me with lengths of printed cotton cloth she had purchased from Stockport market. I do hope there are laundrymaids at this hotel.

As the train progressed, I could see a huge wooden viaduct over a ravine. I was alarmed that it appeared so flimsy and I remarked to George that it was not nearly as sturdy as the magnificent brick-built viaduct that carried the railtrack across the river Mersey in Stockport. George reassured me that it was perfectly safe and that the engineers could only use the materials that were available to them. We traversed the ravine safely and I was much relieved.

When we arrived at our destination town, we took a carriage to this hotel which is very elegant.

There is a beautiful verandah surrounding the ground floor and above the verandah, the balconies to each guest room provide shade and ensure the interior of the hotel is maintained at a cool temperature. The verandah and balconies are edged in fine filigree wrought iron, the railings are painted white and the effect is most tasteful.

The carriage driver carried our trunks into the hotel lobby, George gave him a generous gratuity and requested that he return to drive him to the factory tomorrow. The lobby and the wide staircase of the hotel were covered in thick scarlet carpet. There were two sparkling chandeliers hanging from the ceiling in the lobby and two ceiling fans hummed as they kept the entrance cool. A small library with comfortable armchairs caught my attention. Directly opposite the entrance, a smart young lady, dressed in a dark skirt and white blouse with a dark blue navy bow at the throat was seated behind a mahogany desk. She noted our details and gave George the key to our guest room, I think from her accent that she was from Ireland but I thought it would be rude to ask. Nevertheless, I may ask tomorrow if she has any knowledge of the whereabouts of daddy's farm.

Our room is splendid, the bed has fine white linen, feather pillows and a gold coloured candlewick counterpane. I am convinced we will be very comfortable here. The clerk had arranged for tea and fruit cake to be delivered to our room and I am now seated at a small table on the balcony enjoying my tea. We will shortly go downstairs to the bar where we understand the meals are served. I will first unpack the trunks and decide which garments must be laundered. I may decide to have George's suit pressed in preparation for his visit tomorrow to the carpet factory."

Kitty heard George return from the bathroom along the corridor, closed her red leather-bound journal and stepped back into the bedroom to lay out George's clothes for him to wear that evening. George took her in his arms and kissed her hair. "I love the smell of your shaving soap, George," said Kitty, "you smell like Granddad Delaney." She searched carefully through the trunk for George's lounge suit, pulling out soiled shirts, collars and undergarments. Kitty hung the clean clothes in the ornate walnut wardrobe and laid soiled garments on the bed until she reached the bottom of George's trunk. "We must enquire in the lobby if they have a laundry maid and request that she collects this laundry," she said, as she brushed the shoulders of George's jacket with the clothes brush from the dressing table.

Kitty brushed her own hair, tied it back with ribbon, and they were ready to go down to the bar.

It was close to seven o'clock, by the big oak-cased clock in the lobby, when George and Kitty entered the bar for their meal.

"It is 'table d'hote'," said George, looking at the menu board.

"What does that mean?" said Kitty.

"It is like being at home with Grandma Kathleen," said George, "one menu for everyone. I think it is roast lamb," George whispered.

George helped Kitty into a chair at a scrubbed wooden table and went to the bar. He returned with a tankard of ale for himself and a jug of water for Kitty. The waitress soon arrived with two generous platefuls of food for the couple.

"This is nearly as good as Grandma Kathleen's cooking," said George.

As Kitty enjoyed her meal, she watched a young man who was sitting alone on a high wooden stool at the bar, one foot resting on the stool's stretcher bar while his other leg was stretched straight out beside him.

"George, that young man at the bar must only be the same age as you and yet he appears to have a wooden leg," Kitty said quietly.

"What a tragedy, he must have had an accident," said George as the waitress brought a plate full of food to the man.

On the bar beside the man was a battered accordion. He pushed the instrument further down the bar when another diner walked to the bar, spoke to him, and paid for the young man's tankard to be refilled.

When his plate was empty the man picked up his accordion, turned towards the other diners and began the first few chords of a tune that seemed familiar to the other people in the bar as they joined in the chorus.

The words of the song told the story of the Eureka Stockade and the brave men who died standing up for their rights.

One by one diners went to the bar and bought the singer an ale or dropped a few coins into his upturned hat.

In between songs George and Kitty left the bar, tired from the day's journey and satisfied by the good food.

The maid had collected the soiled linen from their room and had pressed George's lounge suit. It was hanging on the wardrobe door ready for George's visit to the factory the following day.

"My company business should be completed in three or four days, and after the weekend we shall attempt to find your pa," George told Kitty.

"I shall remain at the hotel tomorrow, George," said Kitty, "I shall continue with my journal for mammy and Grandma Kathleen, I also would like to explore the little library in the lobby."

The following morning Kitty helped her husband into his starched white shirt secured his collar with a mother of pearl collar stud, fastened his cuffs with matching cufflinks, then helped him into his best lounge suit before breakfasting with George. His carriage arrived early to take him to the carpet factory just six miles away.

Kitty waved goodbye from the front verandah of the hotel as George climbed into the carriage carrying a tan leather Gladstone case (a gift from Granddad Delaney).

"Good luck, George, I am so proud of you."

Kitty spent the whole of the morning in the shade on the balcony of their guestroom, continuing the journal for Oonagh.

In the afternoon she selected a book of poetry from the bookcase in the lobby and then back to their room to await George's return.

George strode smiling into the hotel lobby as the clock struck five. He climbed the stairs two at a time and hurried into their room. Kitty was reading the poetry book on the balcony. George lifted her to her feet and hugged her.

"I do believe Father and Grandfather Marcus will be very happy with my work, I have negotiated a good price for the supply of carpets, in fact the price is so favourable that I have already made an advance order for a consignment to be shipped to Grandfather Marcus's new warehouse in Glasgow. I have estimated the average quantity for a villa in Manchester. There is so much construction currently in Manchester that demand at such reasonable prices will soon require a repeat order. I was much impressed with the quality of the carpets and the efficiency of the factory, they have most advanced looms. The company are drawing up a contract immediately which I will return in the morning to sign. I am convinced that my father and grandpa will be contented with my decision. Come see the samples, they are beautiful. Help me wash and dress dear Kitty and we will go down for tea, I shall order a bottle of champagne. You have brought me luck, my love."

Kitty wore a lemon cotton gown printed with pink rosebuds, made for her by Mrs Clark. Annie had said, "I think Ma is more excited about your trip than I am." As they entered the bar, Kitty noticed the young man with the accordion sitting once more at the bar. Again, the waitress brought him a plateful of food.

George ordered the champagne to be brought to their table and the couple were toasting George's success when the singer picked up his accordion and turned to the other customers.

"This song is dedicated to the lovely lady who welcomes us all into the hotel and ensures the guests are given the correct keys to their rooms, Miss Maeve Keogh."

He indicated the clerk from the front desk who had ventured into the bar and now sat alone on one of the high stools nearest to the lobby.

As the singer played the first few chords of another song, George said to Kitty, "It is Ma Oonagh's song '*The Meeting of the Waters*', please sing with him, Kitty, for me."

Kitty held back while the young man sang the first verse and then George took her arm and walked with her to the singer's side at the bar

"May my wife join you in this song?"

"Sure she can," said the singer.

Kitty sang as George sat on a bar stool beside her:

"Yet it was not that nature had shed o'er the scene
Her purest of crystal and brightest of green
'Twas not her soft magic of streamlet and hill,
Oh no – it was something more exquisite still.

"'Twas that friends, the belov'd of my bosom, were near,
Who made every dear scene of enchantment more dear,
And who felt how the best charms of Nature improve,
When we see them reflected from looks that we love.

"Sweet vale of Avoca how calm could I rest
In thy bosom of shade, with the friends I love best,
Where the storms that we feel in this cold world should cease,
And our hearts, like thy waters, be mingled in peace."

Kitty brushed tears away and looked along the bar to Maeve Keogh who was weeping too.

The singer took Kitty's hand and introduced himself,

"Jack Butler, thank you, ma'am. My stepfather sang that song to me every night when I was a boy."

"Kitty O'Neil, now Foster, pleased to make your acquaintance, Jack Butler. My mother sang that every night when we were children; to myself and to my husband George, who is almost a son to her."

George, introduced himself and shook Jack's hand.

"Yes," said Jack, "I feel I have known you a long, long time Mrs Foster, your father is, I take it, Seamus O'Neil. Seamus married my mother Charlotte. Butler, he was our farm manager for many years before they married."

"Oh yes, Charlotte," said Kitty, "I remember my mother mentioned Charlotte."

"My mother has passed now," said Jack.

"And my father is he well?" asked Kitty.

"I am afraid he has not enjoyed good health since my mother's passing. He has very dark moods," said Jack, "if you wish, I will collect you in the morning and drive you to the farm," Jack turned to George, "will you accompany us, sir?"

"I am afraid not," said George, "I have business to conduct, the appointment has been made, it is most important that I attend, but the following day would be convenient. Kitty I would prefer to accompany you."

Kitty protested, "But, George, Jack is a relative, I am sure I would be quite safe."

"No, Kitty, we will go together on Friday if Jack would be kind enough to collect us."

The three young people said their goodnights, Jack promising Kitty he would collect them early on Friday. "You will be wondering how I lost my leg, Kitty."

I was injured in the Eureka Stockade rebellion, your father came to Ballarat to rescue me. He was too late to prevent me from taking part in the battle but Seamus took me to the nuns who tended to my wounds. He saved my life, it is sad to see him so troubled now, but he must be lonely now my mother has passed. I am fearful to go home some nights."

The following morning, George left early for the meeting at the factory.

"I should be home at midday Kitty," he said over breakfast, "and we could go to the beach, I shall arrange for the coach driver to I take us."

Kitty continued to write her journal and read her book of poetry.

"I have been reading a book of Mr Wordsworth's poetry," Kitty wrote in her journal, *"he writes of the most beautiful places in Cumberland and Westmorland. You must visit these places mammy. I am sure Mr Shepherd will accompany you on the train on my return.*

This afternoon we are to visit the seaside.

Miss Keogh, the clerk at the hotel, says the beaches are unrivalled, but she says I must remove my boots to walk along the beach and I must take a small towel to brush the sand from my feet. We have not visited the beach since our last visit to granddad Kennedy in Avoca, mammy, although Mr Shepherd promised we would take the train and visit Blackpool on the Lancashire coast one day.

Tomorrow George and I will visit my father, I know I will recognise him from your descriptions, but mammy, did you know that he had married Charlotte Butler? Charlotte's son Jack will collect us in the morning. My tummy feels as if I am on the sea again.

I am so grateful that you gave this journal to me, I feel as if I am speaking to you."

Kitty closed the red leatherbound journal. She heard George calling her name as he entered their guest room.

"Kitty, fish and chips dinner is being served in the bar, the coach driver is joining us, he is waiting in the bar."

When George and Kitty entered the bar, the coach driver had already ordered their dinners and was seated at a scrubbed table with two large tankards of ale and a small glass of sweet sherry awaiting. The waiter swiftly brought three plates of hot fish and chips to them.

Kitty asked, "Is this fish, cod?"

"No, ma'am," said the coach driver, "we call it barramundi hereabouts, the fish is plentiful in the bay."

"I do believe it is tastier than cod," said Kitty, "do we have barramundi in England, George?"

"If we do, it is not on the menu at the station chip shop," said George.

After dinner, the coach driver took them to the nearest beach. He arranged to collect them in three hours. George checked the hour on his silver pocket watch, then replaced it in his waistcoat pocket. Kitty and he sat on the steps leading down to the beach and removed their shoes and stockings, Kitty put them into her basket with the towel.

"I love the feel of the sand between my toes," said Kitty, as she and George walked hand in hand along the long sweeping bay. Kitty held her parasol over her head but the sea breeze was determined to turn it inside out. Kitty relented and rolled it together, letting the breeze tousle her dark curls. "I don't think I could ever be happier than this George, for tomorrow I will see my daddy."

The sky was dark the following morning, dark clouds swept off the sea and blocked the warm sun of the day before.

"Melbourne weather," said Maeve, pulling her shawl around her shoulders, "one day sunshine, and the next day rain like stair-rods."

Kitty had dressed in her long grey serge skirt and white blouse. As they waited in the lobby for Jack Butler to collect them with his cart, George helped her into her macintosh.

"And here, you wear my tweed cap to keep your hair dry," he said, and he pulled the cap onto her curls.

The rain damped the dust of the road out of town but as they drove into the country, the horses' hooves and the cartwheels churned up clouds of beige dust behind them George held a handkerchief to his mouth and Kitty hid her face behind George's shoulder.

Either side of the dirt road, fields of yellow grass stretched for miles. Small herds of grey cattle struggled to graze on the sparse vegetation.

"All this will be transformed into lush green, if this rain continues for long enough," said Jack, raising his voice against the wind.

Every few miles a township was announced by a painted sign held aloft by wooden poles. Each township was the same as the last, a straight row of wooden stores on a raised wooden verandah. Wooden steps led off the dirt road onto the platform. Each township had a baker and a general store. Occasionally the township was supported by a haberdashers or an ironmongers and Kitty noted a familiar red and white striped barber's pole mounted outside one of the wooden shops.

"Not far now," said Jack as they passed through a small township, "you can see our farm in the distance there," and he pointed into the distance while turning the horse onto a long farm track. "I hope Seamus has fed the hens at least. He was in a very dark mood last night. He was wandering in the yard in the black of the night and into the barn. It was the dogs barking, that roused me. I saw Seamus, he was in the barn shouting. I went out thinking there was an intruder. Seamus was shouting 'Michael, Michael Mahon and threatening the shadows with his gun'."

Jack stopped and climbed down off the cart to open the farm gate, climbed back on and drove the cart up to the front of the wooden farmhouse. Two dogs were prowling round the yard and barked at George and Kitty.

"I am nervous of such big dogs," said Kitty, clinging to George. Jack took hold of the dogs and ordered them into their compound, locking the iron gate after them.

"Welcome to Butler's," Jack said, opening the weathered wooden front door. Kitty entered alone.

The door opened into a large room. In the centre was a big wooden table surrounded by chairs. Under the window beside the front door was a pottery sink that had been white but was chipped with age and stained brown. By the fire on the end wall was a wooden rocking chair. An elderly man dressed in dirty brown overalls stumbled into the room through an open door leading from a bedroom. His hair was steel grey and long to his shoulders, it merged with the grey beard flowing down to his chest stained yellow around a pink fleshy mouth. Seeing Kitty he held back his head and poured the last liquor from the whiskey flagon into his mouth, then looking her up and down, threw the flagon at her yelling, "Get out, Michael, get out, leave me alone."

"Seamus, this is Kitty," shouted Jack, getting between Seamus and the couple, "it's your Kitty. I told you she was coming to see you."

"Daddy, it's me, I'm your daughter – yours and Oonagh's," cried Kitty.

"Oonagh? Where's Oonagh?" demanded Seamus, lurching towards them.

Kitty and George backed out through the door. The dogs in their enclosure started to howl.

"Kitty, the only thing that calms him when he's like this is '*The Meeting of the Waters',* sing, Kitty, sing."

Kitty began to sing in a quavering voice. Jack and George joined in for the first two verses.

Seamus swung the door open, "Where's my girl, where's Kitty?" he growled.

"Come in my girl, come in. What are you doing out here in the rain. I thought you were that wretched Michael Mahon. You've got his black curls."

"Yes, Daddy, black curls like you," said Kitty hugging her father.

Her father held her close then, "My girl, my Kitty, where have you been? Where is your Ma?"

"She's back in England, Daddy, just where she was when you left. You know she doesn't like to sail. Daddy, this is George, my husband."

"Yes, George, I heard about you my boy," and Seamus slapped George on the back, "landed on your feet with my girl you have." Seamus took Kitty's hands and held her arms down at her sides, "Just look at you, you are a beauty, but you have not got your mother's glorious red hair, I dreamt of burying my face in her hair, but she will not come to me."

"Shall we go inside, daddy? I think you need a cup of coffee," said Kitty. Jack took George to show him around the farm while Kitty led Seamus back inside and they sat together by the fire, Kitty opposite her father's rocking chair.

The rain rattled on the corrugated tin roof.

"Come closer, I have something to tell you," whispered Seamus. Kitty leaned forward from her chair.

"He has come to kill me, was it you who told him I was here?"

"Who has come back, Daddy?"

"Michael, Michael Mahon, he was in the yard last night, the dogs were howling, they knew it was him," Seamus insisted.

"No, Daddy, he's gone, Michael died," wept Kitty. "He died after the beating he had outside the inn."

"No," whispered Seamus, "he's here, Michael's here, he was in the barn last night. I killed him, Kitty, that night in Stockport and he has come back for me."

"You did not kill him, Daddy, you were blamed unjustly, the English fellows killed him," Kitty wept.

"No, you do not understand, girl, I killed him alright, I killed him. When I carried him back to Watson's yard, I told him Maggie Connors had a baby girl. I told him my ma and pa were supporting her. I asked him if the child could be his. He said that Maggie was a harlot and the child could be any man's in Avoca. I hit him and threw him onto his iron bedstead. His head crashed against the metal, he screamed. I should have fetched the doctor. I killed him Kitty, there was blood coming out of his ears, I should have fetched the doctor, then. The doctor would not come when Sean went for him, it was too late anyway. He has told your Ma, Kitty, Michael has told your mammy, that is why she will not come to me. Make him go away, Kitty."

"Daddy, No! Michael is back home at the Meeting of the Waters, I have seen him. I have seen him there twice, he saved me from drowning in the river, Daddy. I swear I have, I have seen him there myself, Daddy, he is back home."

Kitty concluded her journal before tea as their ship sailed up the English coast on the way back to Liverpool in August.

"My darling Mammy,

How happy I am to be nearly home to you and our family. I am pleased that you insisted that I wrote this journal every day. This way you will be able to share our adventure. And mammy it has been such an adventure. George has negotiated a good contract with the carpet manufacturer, his father and grandfather, will be so proud of his work for the company and I know granddad and Grandma Delaney will be pleased with his attainments.

For my part, mammy, the adventure has convinced me that I would never desire to live so far away from you and our family.

My past has been with you mammy, I know my future is with you too. For every joy in my life I know I want to share with you.

I met my daddy, and I bless you for always giving me a positive picture of him.

I will conclude this journal mammy by saying that we have together been very blessed and I thank God above that you met Henry. I know he loves you to the stars and back. We are blessed to have granddad and Grandma Delaney in our lives, and of course my own darling George. There are so many people who love you and I know that is because you give so much love to others.

George and I will soon be home, ready to face an exciting future with our family.

Kitty"